breakwater bay

Also by Shelley Noble

Stargazey Nights (novella)
Stargazey Point
Holidays at Crescent Cove
Beach Colors

breakwater bay

SHELLEY NOBLE

wm

WILLIAM MORROW
An Imprint of HarperCollins*Publishers*

BREAKWATER BAY. Copyright © 2014 by Shelley Freydont. All rights reserved. Printed in the United States of America. No part of this book may be used or reproduced in any manner whatsoever without written permission except in the case of brief quotations embodied in critical articles and reviews. For information address HarperCollins Publishers 195 Broadway, New York, New York 10007.

HarperCollins books may be purchased for educational, business, or sales promotional use. For information please e-mail the Special Markets Department, at SPsales@harpercollins.com.

FIRST EDITION

Designed by Diahann Sturge

Library of Congress Cataloging-in-Publication Data has been applied for.

ISBN 978-0-06-231914-2

14 15 16 17 18   OV/RRD   10 9 8 7 6 5 4 3 2 1

To my mom,
who taught me to appreciate the moments that take your breath away

Acknowledgments

As always, many thanks to my agent, Kevan Lyon, and my editor, Tessa Woodward, for nurturing both book and author and for their insights and guidance, and to the talented William Morrow team.

Thanks to my home team, Irene Peterson, Pearl Wolf, Gail Freeman, Charity Scordato, Lois Winston, and to my friends and colleagues at Liberty States Fiction Writers, who offer a place for exchanging ideas and expertise as well as encouragement and vision.

To my online team, Women's Fiction Writers Association, many of whom I have never met in person, but consider friends.

And a thousand thanks to the people of Newport, who love their town and are caretakers of their history and have always happily answered my questions or sent me to someone who knew the answer.

And to Newport itself. I fall in love again every time I visit.

Prologue

Alden wasn't supposed to take the dinghy out today. That's the last thing his dad said when he left for work that morning. "Don't go on the water. There's a bad storm brewing."

He'd only meant to be out long enough to catch something for dinner, but the storm had come in too fast. Now the water boiled black around him. Already he could hardly tell the difference between the black clouds overhead and the black rocks of the breakwater. Knives of rain slashed at his eyes and slapped his windbreaker against his skin. The shore looked so far away. He knew where the tide would pull him before he got there.

He was scared. His dad would kill him if he wrecked the dinghy. A huge wave crashed over the boat, throwing him to the floor. One oar was snatched from his hand and he barely managed to grab it before it slipped from the lock. And he forgot all about what punishment he would get and prayed he could stay alive to receive it.

He pulled himself onto the bench and started rowing as hard as he could.

And then he saw her. A dark form. Standing on the rocks. At first he thought she must be a witch conjured from the storm.

He tried to wipe his eyes on his sleeve, but he couldn't let go of the oars.

She waved her hands and began to scramble down the rocks. And then she slipped and disappeared.

He stopped trying to save himself and let the breakwater draw the boat in. He knew just when to stick out the oar to keep from crashing. Held on with all his strength. The dinghy crunched as it hit, and he flung the rope over the spike his dad had hammered into the rock years before.

He couldn't see her now. He clambered from the boat, slipped on the rocks. Called out, but the wind snatched his voice away.

And suddenly there she was, lying not three feet away. Motionless.

He crawled over the slimy rocks, grabbing whatever would keep him from sliding back into the sea, and knelt beside her; he shook her. "Lady? Lady, you gotta get up."

She didn't move.

"Lady. Please. You gotta get up." He pulled on her arm, but she only turned over. She wasn't a lady. She was just a girl. Wearing jeans. Not that much older than him.

He grabbed under her shoulders and tried to drag her toward the boat. She was heavy, heavier than she looked, and she wouldn't help.

And he just kept thinking, *Please don't be dead.*

Then she moved. Her eyes opened, and they were wide and scared. She grabbed hold of him, nearly knocking him over, but together they crawled to where the dinghy bucked like a bronco in the waves.

He didn't know how he got her into the boat, or how he rowed to shore, or pushed the dinghy to safety on the rocky beach. He was so cold he couldn't feel his fingers or his feet. And she'd closed her eyes again. This time he didn't try to wake her; he ran, not home, but across the dunes to Calder Farm, burst into the kitchen, and fell to his knees.

"The beach. Help her." And everything went black.

When he awoke, he was lying in a bed, covered in heavy quilts.

"Go back to sleep. Everything's all right."

Gran Calder.

"Is she dead?"

She patted the quilt by his shoulder. "No, no. You saved her life. You were very brave."

His lip began to tremble. He couldn't stop it.

Then somebody screamed, and she hurried out of the room. He pulled the covers over his head so he wouldn't hear, but he couldn't breathe. Another scream worse than before. What were they doing to her?

He slid out from the covers but he wasn't wearing anything. Someone had taken his clothes. He pulled the quilt from the bed, wrapped it around himself, and dragged it out into the hallway.

Only one light was on, but a door was ajar at the end of the hall. He crept toward it, trailing the quilt behind him.

The girl screamed again. Then stopped.

He stopped too, frightened even more by that sudden silence.

Then a new, smaller cry filled the air.

Chapter 1

Meri Hollis dropped the paint chip into a manila envelope and rolled from her back to sit upright on the scaffolding.

She stretched her legs along the rough wood and cracked her neck. It had been a long day, first standing, then sitting, then lying on her back. Every muscle protested as she leaned forward to touch her toes, but she knew better than to start the descent before her circulation was going again.

While she waited she labeled the newest sample, added it to the file box, and placed it in a bucket that she lowered thirty feet to the floor. She flipped off her head lamp, pulled it from her head, and took a last look at her little corner of the world, which in the dim light looked just as sooty and faded as it had twenty hours, two hundred paint samples, and several gallons of vinegar and water ago.

It had been slow going. The meticulous cleaning of paint layers was never fast even on a flat ceiling, but when you added plaster ornamentation, extreme care was needed. But Meri had finally reached enough of the original ceiling that she was sure it had been painted in the mid-1800s.

It was exciting—especially if what she suspected turned out to be true.

She'd discovered the first fleck of gold that afternoon. Surely there would be more. But further study would have to wait until Monday. She was calling it a day.

Meri stored her tools and slowly lowered one foot to the first rung of the pipe ladder that would take her to the ground floor. Work had stopped in the grand foyer a half hour ago, but she'd been determined to finish that one test section today.

She reached the bottom on creaky ankles and knees, grabbed hold of the ladder and stretched her calves and thighs. When she felt steady she picked up her file box and tools and carried them to the workroom.

Carlyn Anderson looked up from where she was logging in data from the day's work. "You're the last one."

Meri deposited her file on the table and arched her back. "Now I know how Michelangelo felt. Only he ended up with the Sistine Chapel and I got a sooty ceiling in a minor mansion with two hundred plus chips from twenty layers of ancient paint in various hues of ick."

"Yeah, but just imagine what it will look like when it's back in its original state."

"Actually I got a glimpse of it today. If I'm not mistaken, there's gold in them thar hills."

"Gilt?"

"Maybe. It might be a composite. In the state the ceiling's in, it's impossible to tell without the microscope." Meri pulled a stool over to the table and sat down. "Why the hell would anyone paint over a decorative ceiling from the nineteenth century?"

"The same reason they painted over the Owen Jones wallpaper with psychedelic orange."

"Oh well, someone's bad taste is our job security," Meri said. "Is there someone left who can take this over to the lab tonight?" She handed Carlyn the manila envelope of samples.

"I will, but you owe me, since you've blown off karaoke

tomorrow night. And it's Sixties Night." Carlyn went through several doo-wop moves they'd been practicing on their lunch hour.

"Sorry, but I promised Gran I'd come out for my birthday dinner tonight. I'm not looking forward to a forty-minute drive but I couldn't say no. And tomorrow I'm having my birthday dinner with Peter." She yawned.

"You don't sound too excited."

"Well, I did turn thirty today somewhere between layer four—baby poop brown—and layer three—seventies kitchen green."

"You're in your prime."

"I'm slipping into middle age and instead of proposing, Peter decides to go back to law school." Meri slid off the stool.

"Maybe he'll propose before then. Maybe tomorrow night."

"Maybe, but I'm not holding my breath. Don't listen to me. I'm just tired. I've got a great job, great friends, a family who loves me, and . . ." Meri grinned at Carlyn. "Karaoke. Now, I'd better get going if I want to get a shower in before I hit the road."

"Well, happy birthday."

"Thanks."

"Oh, Doug wants to see you in his office before you go."

Meri winced. "We can guess he's not giving me a raise?"

"No, but he should kiss your butt for the extra hours you're putting in gratis."

Meri yawned. "I'd rather have a raise."

"I'll walk you down."

Meri picked up her coat and bag from her locker, and the two of them headed back to the kitchen, also known as Doug's office, to see what the project manager could possibly want on a Friday night.

The door swung inward, but the kitchen was dark.

"Are you sure he's still here?" Meri asked, groping for the light switch.

The lights came on. "Surprise!"

Beside her, Carlyn guffawed. "I can't believe you didn't know what was going on."

Meri laughed. "You guys."

Carlyn pushed her into the center of the room where at least twelve architectural restoration workers stood around the kitchen table and a large sheet cake with a huge amount of candles.

Doug Paxton came over to give Meri a hug. He was a big, brawny guy who had been relegated to ground work after falling through the floor of an abandoned house and breaking both legs and a hip five years before. He'd grown a little soft around the middle, but he still exuded power and good taste. And he knew his way around a restoration better than anybody she knew.

"Happy birthday. Now come blow out your candles."

Someone had lit the candles during the hug, and the cake was ablaze.

"I may need help," Meri said. "And these better not be trick candles." Though she didn't really know what to wish for. She had everything she wanted—a good job, great friends, a loving family, everything else except a fiancé. She was in no hurry, even if she *was* thirty. So she wished that life would stay good and that things would eventually work out for Peter and her and that the project would find the funding it would need for a complete restoration.

"What are you waiting for? Hurry up. The candles are about to gut."

Meri took a deep breath, motioned to everybody to help, and the candles were extinguished. Cake was cut, seltzer was brought out, since Doug didn't allow any alcohol on a site, and

a good time was had by all, for nearly a half hour until Meri
made her apologies and headed for her apartment, a shower,
and a long drive out to the farm.

Traffic was heavy as Meri drove north out of Newport. Gran
lived about a fifteen-minute stone's throw across the bay. But to
drive there she had to go up to Portsmouth, across the bridge,
then south again. So she hunkered down to endure the cars,
the dark, and the rain.

It must have been raining all day, not that she'd noticed,
because the streets and sidewalks were slick and puddles had
formed in the uneven asphalt. She never did notice things
when she was deep into a project. She had great powers of concentration and could spend hours lost in the zone.

Even as a child, Meri would look up from reading, or weed-
ing, or just lying in the sea grass thinking, to find her three
brothers standing over her. "We've been calling you for hours,"
they'd complain. "Dinner's ready." And they'd drag her to her
feet and race her across the dunes to the house they shared with
Gran. When Meri was fifteen, her father was granted a research
position at Yale and the family moved to New Haven, only
seeing Gran on long weekends and holidays.

Meri sighed. Thirty must be the age when you started remi-
niscing about life. She was definitely feeling nostalgic tonight.
Maybe it was because her future was suddenly looking a little
hazy, though she had to admit, Peter's change of plans hadn't
thrown her into depths of despair. After her initial shock and
dismay, her first thought was she would have more time to concentrate on her work without feeling guilty about neglecting him.

Obviously, neither of them was ready for total commitment.
This would give them some time to really figure things out.

As she crossed the bridge at Tiverton, the drizzle became a
deluge, and her little hatchback was buffeted by gusts of wind
that didn't let up until she turned south again toward Calder

Farm. She could see the house across the dunes long before she got there. Every window was lit, and the clapboard and stone farmhouse shone like a lighthouse out of the dark. Way to the left of it, Alden Corrigan's monstrous old house appeared as an ominous shadow.

Meri smiled. Looks could be deceiving. Alden's house was merely untended. It had seen its share of unhappiness like most of the old houses in the area, but it had also had its share of good times.

She turned into the car path and bumped slowly toward the house. Most of the menagerie of animals that found their way to the farm had probably taken shelter in the barn at the first sign of rain. Still, Meri peered through the dark for moving forms and gleaming eyes until she came to a stop at the front of the house.

A silver Mercedes was parked outside. Meri grabbed her overnight bag from the backseat, ducked into the rain, and dashed toward the kitchen door, which opened just as she got there, casting a bright spotlight on her as she rushed inside.

"Hi, Gran." Meri kissed her grandmother's cheek and shrugged out of her dripping jacket. "What smells so good?"

Gran took her coat. "Your favorite, as if you didn't know. Now come inside."

Meri stepped into the kitchen, shaking off the rain. A man got up from the table. He was tall with hair combed back from a high forehead, and smile lines creasing his eyes and mouth.

"Dad!" Meri said. She dropped her case and purse and gave him a wet hug. "I can't believe you're here. Why didn't you tell me you were coming? Is that a new car?"

He laughed and pushed her gently to arm's length, then planted a kiss on her forehead. "I wasn't sure I could get away. Happy birthday."

Gran gave her a pat. "Go wash up and we'll eat."

Meri hurried to the powder room, followed by several cats

that appeared from nowhere for the sole purpose of trying to trip her up on her way down the hall.

Daniel Hollis had married Meri's mother when Meri was three; three sons came at regular intervals after that, and every spare space was put to use as the Hollis family grew.

Now Gran lived mostly downstairs. She was only seventy-five, or so she told everyone, but since she lived alone, they'd all made her promise not to go up and down the stairs, a promise that she promptly broke. When Meri caught her vacuuming the bedroom carpets, she merely said, "I can't live comfortably knowing all that dust is gathering above my head."

When Meri returned to the kitchen, there were bowls of steaming cioppino set at three places, and the aroma of the rich seafood stew filled the air. They'd just sat down when there was a knock at the door.

"Come in, Alden," Gran called from the table. "That man could smell cioppino from the next county."

The door opened and "that man," a tall, ridiculously thin, broodingly handsome forty-two-year-old man ducked in the low door and stood dripping on the flagstone floor.

"Get yourself a bowl and sit down," Gran said.

"Thanks, but I can't stay. I just came to say happy birthday."

Gran gave him a look that Meri didn't understand and Alden chose to ignore. He walked over to Meri and before she could even stand, he dropped a flat gift-wrapped package on the table. "Happy Birthday."

"Thanks. Can't you stay? I haven't seen you in forever."

"I know, but I have a bunch of work to get finished and I'm way behind. You staying for the weekend?"

"Just till tomorrow."

"Then I'll see you before you leave."

"At least wait until I open your present."

She pulled at the string that was tied around the package; the bow released and with it the paper.

"I couldn't find the tape," he said.

"Why am I not surprised?" She lifted out a piece of cardboard, where a pen-and-ink drawing had been mounted. It was a girl, her hair curling down her back, sitting on the rocks gazing out to sea. The rocks were those of the breakwater on the beach between the two houses. The girl looked like her.

"It's beautiful, Alden. Thank you. Is it Ondine?" she asked, teasing him. Taciturn and reclusive, he was best known for his illustrations of children's books.

"Good God, no."

"Oh," she said, surprised at his reaction. "Who then?"

"Just someone sitting on the rocks."

"Ah. Well, I love it. Thank you. I'm going to have it framed and put it on my living room wall in Newport."

"I'd better be going; your dinner is getting cold."

"You're sure you don't want—"

"Can't," Alden said. "But happy birthday. Dan. Gran."

Gran shook her finger at him. But he was gone.

"Well, that was weird," Meri said.

His leaving seemed to cast a pall over the room.

"Let's eat," Gran said.

Meri dug in, but she noticed that Gran merely picked at her food. Dan seemed to have lost his appetite, too. Meri didn't understand. The stew was heavenly, but their lack of enthusiasm was catching, and she pushed her bowl away before it was empty. "Delicious," she said with a satisfied sigh, though it was a little forced.

The atmosphere had definitely taken a plunge since Alden's visit. She wanted to know why. "Is something happening with Alden? Why didn't he stay for dinner?"

"Oh, you know Alden," Gran said and began clearing the table.

She *did* know Alden. They'd grown up together, sort of. He was already a teenager when she was born, and by the time she was old enough to pester him and follow him around, he was in high school.

Gran refused help with the dishes, and Meri and her father traded work stories until Gran returned with a homemade carrot raisin cake and one big candle. "I always keep a box of birthday candles," Gran explained. "But I guess they melted in last summer's heat wave. So you only get one."

"That's fine," Meri told her. "It will make up for the forest of candles on the cake at work."

They ate cake and Gran pulled a festively wrapped package from the shopping bag she'd placed by the side of her chair.

Meri opened it slowly and neatly, a trait that she was born with and was a big plus in her chosen profession, but sometimes made her brothers scream, "Just tear off the paper."

"How are the three Musketeers? Are Gabe and Penny all set for the baby?"

"Oh yeah, for months now." Dan sighed, and Meri knew he was thinking about her mother who had died only four years before. She would never see any of her grandchildren.

"Let's see. Matt just got a raise, and Will is having way too much fun at Georgetown."

"Oh yeah, I got e-cards from both of them yesterday. And Penny sent a lovely card and signed both Gabe and her names."

The paper came off and Meri opened the box. It contained a hand-knitted pullover sweater in Meri's favorite colors of blue, lavender, and burgundy. "It's gorgeous. Did May McAllister knit this?"

"Yes, she did. And she said if it didn't fit just right to bring it by the store and she'd fix it."

"Everything she's ever made has fit perfectly," Meri said. "Thank you so much."

Gran smiled.

Dan stood and pulled a jeweler's box out of his pants pocket. He walked over to Meri and handed it to her, then stood beside her as she opened it. It was a locket of brushed gold. The inside held two tiny pictures, one of her mother and one of Dan.

Sudden tears sprang to Meri's eyes. "Thank you. It's beautiful."

He hugged her. "You're the most precious thing in the world to me and to your mother, too."

Meri smiled up at him as he clasped the necklace around her neck. She was so lucky that this man had come into their lives and took them both into his heart. He'd been more than a stepdad; her real father couldn't have loved her more.

Meri had noticed a cardboard box, a little larger than a shoe box, sitting in the alcove of the antique kitchen hutch. It was just an ordinary cardboard box that might be sent through the mail, though this one was dented and smashed from years of storage.

Now Gran went to the hutch, but instead of retrieving the box, she took an envelope from the top and brought it to the table where she placed it in front of Meri.

"Another present?" Meri asked.

Her father's lips tightened. "Not exactly a present," he said.

"More like a confession," Gran said, and Meri swore there were tears in her eyes.

Chapter 2

Confession? What kind of confession? Meri looked at Gran, but Gran was staring at the letter like it was poison. She felt her dad's hand come to rest on her shoulder.

For an eon Meri could only look at the envelope.

Gran continued to stand on the opposite side of the table, her head bowed. Her father pulled out a chair and sat down next to her. "Open it. And just remember, it doesn't change anything about our family."

With a swift look toward him, Meri picked up the envelope, watching her trembling fingers from a distance like she sometimes did when she was working, suspending excitement or any emotion so as not to rush and chance marring the surface.

On the front was just her name, Merielle. Nothing more. No "to" and "from," no "Happy Birthday." Just Merielle. And the room became colder. She recognized her mother's handwriting.

She turned the envelope over. It was sealed, and she really, really didn't want to open it. Why had her mother left her a letter and why had they waited more than four years to give it to her?

It wasn't as if Gran had just "come across" it while cleaning out the attic. Meri could tell by her face and her stooped shoulders that she had known about its existence. So why wait so long? And why now?

A young tabby jumped to the table, startling them all. He padded over to sniff the envelope. Gran swept him off the table with a brush of her hand. Not gently. Not like Gran at all.

Meri's stomach began to ache.

She tested the seal, then gently worked the flap away from the envelope. It opened easily. Too easily for someone who had mixed feelings about opening it at all.

She pulled out the single sheet of stationery inside. She didn't look up, afraid of the expressions she might see. She unfolded the paper.

Dear Meri.

The rest of the words swam before her eyes as they rested on the upper-right corner. August 2010. A few weeks before her mother died.

Meri sat there staring at the letter, waiting, hoping that one of them would pull it from her fingers. Say it was a mistake, just a joke, because from the few words she made out, this wasn't an ordinary "advice to my daughter when I'm gone" letter.

Dear Meri,

You are the most precious gift God ever could give me. You made Gran's and my life complete after Huey died. He didn't live to see you born, or know the circumstances of your birth, but I know he is looking down from heaven and loving you from afar.

Meri's eyes fogged over. She swallowed hard, brushed at her eyes and read on.

There's no easy way to say this. And I hope with all my heart that you will forgive me, and love me in spite of what I've done.

Of course I'll always love you. But what was there to forgive? Was she the product of an affair while her father was off flying the friendly skies? She would never have thought her mother could be unfaithful, but it happened all the time. She wouldn't judge her.

So I'll just say it as best as I can. Trust your father, Dan, for he has become your real father, and he loves you like his own, as I do.

Meri blinked. *As I do?* What did that mean? Cold began to creep over her skin.

I was pregnant when Huey died. The baby came early and only lived a few hours.

The room went out of focus. What baby? That baby was her. There wasn't another baby. She cut a look toward her father, who tried to smile, she thought, but it just made his mouth look like a straight line. She dragged her attention back to the letter and the words she did not want to read.

You remember Katy Dewar? She's the midwife who lives over by Briggs Marsh. She delivered my baby, a daughter, here in this house. But there was a terrible storm. A teenage runaway took refuge here. She was pregnant and had come looking for Katy to help her. She also gave birth to a girl the same night my baby died. Her baby was strong and healthy. The girl was terribly sick, but she refused to go to the hospital. She was frightened of something or someone;

*she begged us to keep her baby and not to try to find her
family. That baby was you.*

*Unfortunately, the girl died and we buried her and my
baby in the family plot and you became my daughter. Some
may say it was wrong to keep you, but I knew in my heart
I couldn't let you go and I regret nothing. You became my
daughter. You are my daughter. You are Gran's granddaughter. Always remember that.*

Someone sobbed, but Meri couldn't tell if it was her or Gran.
She was not her mother's daughter. Her mother's daughter was
buried at the little church down the road. It couldn't be true.
Meri shook her head, over and over; once she started she didn't
seem to be able to stop.

It wasn't true. She had a birth certificate. *Not yours.* A pass-
port. *Based on a lie.* A driver's license.

Oh, God. It was a nightmare. She would wake up. She had
to. Because if she didn't, it would mean that her whole life had
been a lie and she didn't exist at all.

She read it again. The words didn't change. The mean-
ing stayed the same. She wasn't Merielle Hollis. She was . . .
nobody. They had all known and they had never told her.

Please forgive me. I'll love you forever,

Mom

Not her mother. Her face twisted; she could feel it as if it
didn't belong to her, like a crumpled piece of paper before you
threw it in the trash. Like a crumpled life.

She wanted to crumple this letter and pretend it didn't exist.
But it did exist, and destroying it wouldn't change the truth.
She'd never been one of them. All these years they had known
and let her think she was.

She folded the letter but couldn't get it back in the envelope. Her father—*not your father*—covered her hand with his and took the letter with his free hand. Held hers when she tried to pull away.

"Your mother was uneasy in her soul. She thought you needed to know. I didn't agree. This changes nothing."

Meri shook her head, barely aware of her tears flying onto the table.

"I know it's a shock, but don't think for a second that it changes anything."

"It changes everything."

"No."

"You've all been so good to me. And . . . And—"

"You are my daughter."

"No, I'm—I'm—"

Gran sank into a chair and covered her face with her hands. "God, what have I done?"

Meri pushed to her feet, upsetting the chair. "It's not your fault. It's—" She didn't know what it was. It was devastating. "I—I have to—" There was nothing she could do. She looked blindly at the two people she had loved all her life and felt like an imposter. It had all been an illusion. They had been a family and she had been . . . nothing.

She looked wildly around. Everything looked the same, but everything had changed. "I have to—" *Get out of this stifling kitchen, have to think, have to make it go away. Have to be what I was before tonight. Merielle Hollis.* But she wasn't—and would never be. Merielle Hollis was lying with a stranger in a nearby grave.

She stumbled back, stopped. "I'm sorry." She rushed toward the back door and ran out into the rain.

"Meri, come back."

But Meri ran.

Alden Corrigan stood in the dark in the back second-floor bedroom, resting one hand on the windowsill and looking out at the night. It was times like these he wished he still smoked. Funny, he hadn't had a cigarette in over ten years, but it was still the first thing he wanted when things got tense.

He'd come up to the second floor because he could see the farmhouse from here, though he could only guess at what was going on inside.

He'd been against telling her. It was all water over the dam, years ago. No good would come from dredging it all up now. Dan hadn't been much for it either. But Laura had left that letter, and Gran saw it as her duty to pass it on to Meri.

Stuff like that could tear a family apart. And none of them deserved that. He knew from experience that once there was a rift, it could never be put back together.

Alden shivered. He was half tempted to turn on the heat, but that would be rather like pissing in the wind. By the time it made its way to the second floor, it would be morning and hopefully the crisis would have abated. But hell, it was damn cold for April. And rainy.

Like then. Cold and rainy. When he stopped to think, he could still feel the bone-biting cold, the stiffness in his fingers, the wet clammy skin of the girl's face, pale in the night. That face had haunted him for years. Still came to him sometimes late at night, or when he saw Meri after not seeing her for a while. That jolt of recognition. The remembrance of that night and a boy's small comprehension.

The lights had been on that night, too. That must have been how he made it to the farmhouse. He really didn't remember much about what happened after dragging the dinghy onto shore, until he woke up to Gran saying everything was all right.

God, his dad had been pissed—pissed, relieved, and proud.

He could do that, his dad. A volatile combination of emotions all at once. It was enough to knock you sideways. Alden had always stood a bit in awe of his father. He was hardworking, gruff, stingy with his compliments, but good-hearted in his way.

That night he said, "You did good," before he gave Alden a whipping for taking the dinghy out, not for disobeying him, but for doing something so stupid. It was a small price to pay for that "you did good." And Alden cherished it even now.

Strangely enough, it was the sea that had taken his father's life.

There was a sudden flare of light in the cottage. Alden leaned into the window enclosure. The kitchen door opened and closed. Someone ran across the yard. Jesus. Was she leaving?

He'd known this was a bad idea. Maybe he should have stayed. But he couldn't bear to watch her reaction.

So he watched from the window. She ran past the car and out into the meadow, and he lost sight of her. He panicked and moved toward the door. Hadn't he promised to take care of her?

He'd tried to. But the woman was thirty now, and Alden had thought that boyhood promise had been fulfilled years ago.

He refused to run out onto the dunes like some demented Heathcliff. She'd find her way here eventually. She always did. To rant and rave. To celebrate. To ask advice or think things through. Or just to sit and look out the window to the sea.

So instead of putting on his jacket and going to look for her, he went downstairs to the kitchen to put on water for tea. And to wait.

Meri didn't run for her car or down the road, but across the meadow, brittle and swollen with rain.

She hardly knew where she was going. She just ran, out into

the night, the slashing rain, the biting wind. She ran until her side hurt, until her legs trembled beneath her, and her knees threatened to buckle.

The soil was soft and shifting. She slipped in a depression; her ankle turned and she went down on all fours, let out a wail, and beat the rain-soaked ground. *Why?* She wanted to curl up on the sand and grass and die.

She wasn't who she thought she was. Had never been. They'd all lied to her, year after year. She didn't have a real birth certificate. Everything about her was a lie.

She staggered to her feet, started up again, as if she could outrun the things she had just learned. She knew they loved her and would be worried, but right now she didn't care; she hurt too much.

Meri ducked into the wind and rain, ignoring the pain in her side, and ran until she couldn't take in enough air to keep going. She clutched at her middle, tried to straighten up, and saw the dark shingles and peaked roof of a place she knew almost as well as her own home.

The windows were all dark, except for one light on downstairs. Just one and she knew it was Alden's reading lamp. He'd be sitting there like he did, surrounded by darkness except for that one light.

Did he know? Was that why he wouldn't stay for dinner? Of course he did; coward that he was, he wouldn't even stay to see her exposed. And pain turned to white blazing anger. And it was focused on one place—one person.

She dashed wet strands of hair out of her face, grabbed her side, and staggered toward that one small light. She splashed through deep puddles, slid on mud, tripped over rocks sticking out of the soil, and, finally, stumbled up the stone walk.

Meri banged on the door. She couldn't even hear it over the pounding rain. She banged again, this time with both hands.

The bell hadn't worked in years. Why didn't he ever fix anything?

"Dammit, Alden!"

The door opened so quickly that she fell into the house.

"Well, what an entrance."

Chapter 3

You knew. Didn't you?" She clenched both fists and hit him full on the chest. Hit him again. "Didn't you?"

"Ouch." He grabbed her wrists and pulled her hands away, wrapping her in a comprehensive hug, but she wasn't sure if it was for comfort or to stop her from taking out her anger on him.

"You did know." She butted him with her forehead, the only part of her that was free, then collapsed against him, sobbing. "Why didn't you tell me?"

He didn't speak, just stood holding her as if she were still a little girl. He'd always been there. Sometimes cold and distant, sometimes a safe haven. Big brother, best friend, Dutch uncle, devil's advocate. It had been like that for as long as she could remember.

They stood in the entryway, silent, not moving, until her sobs turned to hiccups, and she began to shake with cold.

"I'll get you some dry clothes," Alden said and dropped his arms abruptly, leaving her alone and appalled at her behavior.

He hadn't turned on any lights and Meri stumbled through the dark toward his bedroom, which had at one time been the cook's quarters, long before her time or his.

She met him coming back.

"Towel on the bed along with some sweats. You'll look ridiculous in them. But I think we could use a little humor, don't you?"

A shrill whistling sound came from the kitchen. "Take a shower if you want. I'll make you some tea." He was acting as if she'd just been caught in an April shower instead of passing through the eye of hell. She stepped inside and slammed the door.

Even that was aborted, since the door was swollen from the humidity and refused to close. It made her laugh, but she quelled it. Laughter was too close to tears. She grabbed the towel off the bed and went into the bathroom.

Meri lost track of time in the shower. The water was hot and the jet was strong, and for a second she forgot that her life had just come tumbling down around her ears. She stood under the spray much like she had run through the rain, mindless, trying to drive the knowledge away. But it wasn't going away—even if she shriveled up to nothing.

She turned off the water and climbed out of the tub. Toweled off her hair, and smelling like Alden's soap and shampoo, went to the bedroom to put on his clothes.

There was something weird about that and on a better day she might have found something clever to say about it, but tonight, she just let it wrap around her. Protective, even though the sweatshirt sleeves were a good six inches too long, and the pants had to be rolled up several times just so she wouldn't trip on them. And apropos of the man who was something between enigma, work in progress, and sage of the ages, he'd left her a pair of wooly socks to wear.

Raw and exhausted, she padded out to the living room, where a tea tray and newly lit fire were waiting. Alden wasn't there, but she heard his voice from the dining room.

She had meant to come out and apologize for treating him

like a punching bag, for being ungrateful and selfish, but the apology died on her lips.

"Why don't I keep her here for a while tonight? Give her a chance to calm down."

She marched over to the archway and ambushed him as he hung up.

"Keep me? Keep me? You make me sound like a child or a half-wit."

"Do I? I just thought that you might want to get a little distance on the whole thing and give them a chance to recover from your outburst. They're pretty upset, and I think we've all had enough drama for one day."

Her eyes filled up again. She didn't think she had any tears left.

"Plus it's still raining and I'll have to walk you home, and then I'll have to walk home again. I've gotten wet enough for you this evening." He walked past her to the coffee table and began to pour tea into two mugs.

Like a slap to a hysteric, his attitude drove any tears away. He always knew just when to administer a dash of cold water, this reclusive, sometimes bitter, man. She probably needed it, but tonight she was too bruised to withstand it; she lashed back.

"Why do you sit around in the dark? You have money." It was a cheap shot, and she didn't expect an answer.

"Not as much as you might think."

It surprised her so much that she blurted out. "Two kids can't cost that much."

He handed her a mug. "When their mother is Jennifer, they can. Besides, this is all I need." He made an offhanded gesture at the room; the couch, chair, and a few tables spotlighted by the fire and reading lamp, the ceiling disappearing into darkness, the windows and French doors framing the night.

When she was a child and Alden's dad had been alive, there

had been much more furniture. Antiques and family heirlooms and all the detritus from several generations of Corrigans.

But Alden had begun minimizing after his father's death, and his ex-wife had helped herself to many of the family heirlooms.

Meri took the mug. Alden's divorce had not been amicable, she knew that. She remembered coming home from college once, anxious to consult him about the internship she was up for. But when she reached the house, she heard them arguing. Yelling, really. Nora and Lucas were sitting outside on the steps, huddled together. There was a crash from inside the house. Nora pulled the younger Lucas to his feet, and they ran toward the beach; Meri crept away and tried to forget.

"Why don't you sit down?"

"What? Oh."

Meri squeezed past the wingback chair, its crinkled leather patched with gaffer's tape. Stepped over the pile of books that littered the floor, and curled up on the couch. It was old like everything else in the room and was beginning to sag. But it was as comfortable as her grandmother's lap. *Her grandmother.* A half sob escaped.

"Enough. You've had your cry; you took long enough in the shower to decipher the Rosetta stone, so you must have had time by now to get your head screwed on right."

"You could be a little sympathetic. It's horrible to show up to your birthday dinner and find out you were . . . you were . . ." She couldn't say it.

"Switched at birth?" he said in sepulchral tones.

"Sometimes I hate you," she blurted.

With the rain pelting against the glass of the French doors, and the waves crashing in the distance behind him, with the fire flickering against his harsh features, he looked like how she imagined Mephistopheles had looked when he pinned Faust to certain damnation.

"Do you?"

She shuddered. "No. But you're not funny. It's too close to a gothic horror story to joke about."

"All we need is a crazy lady in the attic."

"There isn't one, is there?"

"No." He picked up his mug and walked to the fireplace. "Just a few skeletons in the closets."

"In my closet anyway. I just found out I'm not really my mother's daughter. I don't know who my mother is. Instead of proposing to me, Peter's going back to law school . . ." She hadn't meant to tell him that.

"The boyfriend?"

"Not *the* boyfriend, *my* boyfriend."

"You have had an exciting birthday, haven't you?"

She glared at him, a thousand things going through her mind.

"Don't say it."

"What?"

"Whatever you were about to say about me being a big brute, distant and unfeeling, callous and out of touch, and that I never really liked him anyway."

"Well, you didn't."

"I didn't *not* like him."

It had been exactly what she was thinking, even though she knew it wasn't really true. Except about Peter. Alden was worse than her dad about Peter. *Her dad.* Had he known when he married her mother that Meri wasn't really hers?

"I was just going to say that you don't understand."

"Actually I do." He put his mug down and sat down next to her. "You have a family who loves you, no, who dotes on you."

"But—"

"No buts. They adore you. Always have. Always will."

"But I'm not really—"

"Oh, for God's sake, will you give it a rest? Blood is highly overrated. Family is not about somebody who can get knocked up in thirty seconds of poor decision making. It's about who loves you unconditionally for life. When you're good, when you screw up, when you hurt them more than they deserve.

"My mother left my father and me when I was eight. Dad neglected her, so she found somebody else. She had to choose between him and us—him and me. She chose him. That's blood for you. After she left, your mother and Gran became my mother and gran. That's family. Finish your tea. I'll walk you back."

They finished the tea in silence. She knew he was mad at her, but that was because he didn't really understand what she felt.

He put his cup down and stood. "Come on. I'll find you a rain slicker. I think Nora left one that might fit you. She's as tall as you are now."

She put her cup on the tray. "Don't be mad at me."

"I'm not mad."

"You are. I know you all want what's best for me. I know they love me, and I love them." *I even love you, you big bully.* But she would never say so. "I just wasn't expecting this; I wish it didn't have to be so complicated."

Alden passed his hand over his face.

"What now? I said I was sorry."

"Let's just go."

Dan hung up the phone. "That was Alden. He's bringing her back."

Therese held tight to the back of the kitchen chair. She felt old. Maybe too old to face what might lay ahead. And she hated being in the position she'd been placed.

She'd had two choices, either lie to her dying daughter or lie to her granddaughter. What choices. Maybe she should have stuck with the living. Did the dead know whether their wishes were carried out or not? Did they care?

"How can I face her after what I've done? I should never have given her the letter, but I promised."

"I know, Therese. This is what Laura wanted. But for heaven's sake, hide that box. I don't want to put her through any more tonight. She has enough to come to terms with. There's plenty of time for the whole story to come out, once she's gotten used to this part."

Therese Calder slowly shook her head. "No. No more tonight." She turned toward the hutch. God, she wanted to take the contents of that box and throw them into the fire. But it was too late for that. Once you started unraveling the past, you couldn't stop it until you came to the end.

She slid the box toward her. It sagged a bit when she lifted it. It had been hidden away for a long time, and it was carrying a heavy cargo. She looked around the kitchen, suddenly uncertain as to where to put it.

"Here, give it to me. I'll put it in the attic."

"No, not the attic. Put it in the closet in my room." *Where I can watch over it as I have for thirty years.*

They walked silently back over the dunes to the cottage. The rain had let up some, but a fine mist coated their slickers. Alden didn't take a flashlight. Neither of them needed it. Even with the cloud cover they knew their way.

There had been back and forth between the houses for generations. A path had gradually formed from the tramp of years to and from.

What would happen now? Alden wondered. Would things change irrevocably? Would the path grow over? Which one of them would leave first. Him? The woman walking beside him, carrying her wet clothes in a plastic grocery bag?

Thirty years old. It was hard to believe. He still could remember the night she was born, most of it anyway. There were big gaps that he'd never been able to coax out of his subconscious. Maybe he didn't have to know. Maybe none of them did.

He'd been against telling Meri. He didn't like change. Not that kind of change anyway, the kind that brought upheaval as this was sure to do. Would she forgive them for keeping her in the dark all these years? Would she forgive him?

And what would learning the truth do to her?

"What?"

He looked sideways at her.

"What was the sigh for?"

"It was a yawn," he lied. "Sorry. I was up early this morning."

"Oh."

They walked on. Toward the cottage, toward the yellow rectangles of light that could have been taken straight from Arthur Rackham. Hansel and Gretel, the Seven Dwarfs. Only when you got closer did it look like what it was, not a fairy tale, but a New England shake and stone farmhouse, built by pragmatic, hardworking farmers over a hundred years before.

Behind them, his house loomed like a bad memory—a monstrosity left over from the Gilded Age that didn't quite make it to Newport. Now it was a drain on his finances and sorely in need of renovation.

Meri hesitated when they reached the kitchen door. Alden opened it and nudged her inside, shutting the door behind her. Then he shoved his hands in the pockets of his rain slicker and began his solitary walk home.

Was his promise to that poor girl fulfilled now that Meri knew? And when had his promise changed from obligation to joy?

Chapter 4

Meri heard the door close behind her. She'd been hoping Alden would stay for a few minutes at least, to help with the transition or lend moral support. But she should have known better.

Her dad and Gran stood together facing her like a photograph, stuck in time.

Feelings of love and remorse swept over her. "I'm sorry."

"It's all right," her dad said and scooped her into a hug. "We all love you, sweetheart."

"I know, Dad. It was just such a shock. I had no idea at all. And now . . . Well, I just feel like I don't know who I am."

"You're a Calder Hollis," Gran said.

Dan opened one arm and included Gran in the hug. She was small next to her son-in-law and granddaughter. Because Meri *was* her granddaughter—Alden was right. She knew Gran loved her, would always love her; she knew that. The problem wasn't with them; it was with her, and she needed to figure out a way to come to terms with the other stuff herself. But that could take some time, once it had settled in, and she found out the whole story, and found her birth family, and then . . .

The next morning broke clean and sunny. It was going to be a gorgeous day and for seconds after waking in her room upstairs at Gran's, Meri forgot the trauma of the previous night. But even the sun couldn't keep realization at bay for long.

It all came back to her as soon as she saw Alden's sweatpants and sweatshirt lying over the back of her desk chair. She curled up, unwilling to face the day. Face her new status.

Damn Alden and his "switched at birth" nonsense. But it wasn't nonsense. Her mother had taken a baby that wasn't hers and raised it as her own.

It would be laughable if it hadn't been her. And she tried to imagine what she would think if she heard the story of someone else in that situation. Would she shrug it off and think so what? Laugh and say lucky kid? Or dismiss it as a fabrication since it would be impossible to pull off something like that in twentieth-century Rhode Island? Of course that proved not to be the case.

She groaned, then stopped herself, remembering Alden's other words. *They love you even when you hurt them.* And she was not going to hurt them again. They had been good to her all her life. Whether she deserved it or not. She wouldn't repay them by throwing that love in their faces.

Meri dressed in jeans, scrubbed her face, held a cold washcloth over her swollen eyes, covered the worst of the blotches with makeup, pulled her hair, a bit unwieldy from sleeping with it wet, into a ponytail, and went downstairs to face her new life.

Her father sat at the kitchen table, nursing a mug of steaming coffee. Gran was standing at the stove. "What would you like for breakfast?"

Meri didn't think she could eat, but she'd taken Alden's words to heart about hurting them so she said, "Do you still have some of that farm bacon from Scully's?"

Gran's face and body lightened about ten years. "Of course I do. It's your birthday."

Meri poured herself coffee and went to sit at the kitchen table with her father. She slowed down as she passed the hutch and noticed that the cardboard box from the night before was gone.

Had that been a part of their disclosure last night? Would they have shown her the contents if she hadn't run away? Had they changed their minds about showing her the rest? Or was it just a box that had made its way to recycling this morning? Either way, Meri wasn't ready to face anything more today. And really, what more could there be?

"Do the boys know?"

Her dad looked up from his coffee cup. "Not yet, but it won't make any difference to them. They're your brothers. You're their sister. Period."

"Will you tell them, or should I?"

"I will, and I'm sure they'll be calling you."

And what would she say to them when they did?

After a hearty breakfast, which everyone forced down with a smile, Dan collected his gear and threw it in the trunk of his car, along with a plastic container of cioppino.

"Sorry I have to run out on you like this."

"That's okay. I'm going to have to leave pretty early myself. Dinner with Peter tonight."

"How's that going?"

"He's decided to go back to law school."

"Smart move, but how do you feel about it? It's a long haul, law school."

"Yeah, but he won't go until the fall, so we'll have a few months to figure out what we want to do. If—"

"Don't even worry about the other thing. If he loves you, he won't care."

She smiled and wondered if that was true. She thought about

it. Would she love Peter if he told her he wasn't who he said he was? Of course she would. Her dad was right.

It wouldn't matter to her. So why did the circumstance of her own birth matter so much?

"Love you." Dan kissed her forehead and gave her grandmother a hug. "You two take care. I'll call you."

They stood together and watched him drive away. Stood there until he reached the road and drove out of sight.

"Let's get the dishes done," Meri said. "And then I want to go over and say good-bye to Alden and thank him for letting me drip all over his floor."

"I'm sure he didn't mind a bit."

"He's always there, isn't he? I don't mean at home, but . . ."

"Ever since he was a boy. Reliable. Good man. His father was a good man."

They went inside. "And his mother?"

"Alden's mother?"

Meri nodded. "What she was like? Alden said she ran off with another man when he was eight. He never told me that before."

Gran sniffed. "She was a piece of work, that one. Lorded it over the whole neighborhood. Called that old monstrosity 'the big house,' like one of those public television shows." She snorted. "Though Laura used to say it made it sound like the state prison.

"Which would be fitting because that woman made Wilton miserable from the day she married him. Never satisfied, that one, finally left. Frankly, we all thought it was the best thing that could have happened to Wilton and his boy, though I'm sure they didn't think so at the time."

"And Alden's wife?"

Gran ran water into the sink and squirted detergent under the spray. "You remember her."

"I do remember her. She was pretty and kind of distant, I thought. But I didn't pay much attention. I was a teenager, and then I was off at college."

"She was a gold-digging little bitch."

Meri nearly dropped the plate she was scraping into the trash. She'd never heard her grandmother use that word before.

"Like father like son. Alden married one just like his mother. It's amazing the man has anything left. There's some family money, whatever the mother didn't abscond with. His father left him pretty well off."

Therese took the plate from Meri and slid it into the soapy water. "Everybody says he makes good money as an illustrator, but they also say she takes every penny she can screw out of him. Now go get those other plates if you want to go over there before you drive back to town."

A half hour later, Meri was walking over the same meadow she'd run across the night before. Today was sunny, though, and only a few puddles remained to remind her of that headlong reckless flight.

She knew that Alden might be working, so instead of disturbing him by banging on the door—a remembered image she could do without today—she walked around the house to the ocean side, where she could look in the glass of the solarium where he sometimes worked.

His drafting table was set up, and his tools were lined up within reach. He was wearing a paint-splattered dress shirt, open at the collar and sleeves rolled up to the elbow. A curl of dark hair fell over his forehead, the rest curled around the frayed collar.

He looked up, saw her, and smiled.

It caught her off guard, that smile, as it always did. Mercurial and ephemeral. And totally unpredictable.

He tilted his head in question, then put down his pen and motioned her in.

The grasses grew high around the glass room and she had to trample a path to the door.

"I wanted to say good-bye before I go back to town," she said and stepped up to the flagstone room.

The smile was gone; a frown, just as ephemeral, passed over his face. "You're coming back next weekend?"

Meri walked in and stood looking out to the dunes and the expanse of ocean and the black rocks of the breakwater.

She knew he wasn't just asking about her plans for the weekend. "Of course, if I can get away. But work is ramping up. I didn't tell you, but I've worked down to the base level of that wacky ceiling and I think there's gilt."

"Exciting."

"Yeah. A little unnerving. Even if it's real gold, it's probably damaged beyond repair. Though it probably isn't really gilt. I mean, what idiot would paint over gold?"

Alden raised an ironic eyebrow.

"I know, stupid question. It's really amazing that the house has been left unrestored for so long. Maybe because it isn't fish or fowl. Not late enough to be Gilded Age, but not old enough to be Revolutionary. It's amazing though, and it has some beautiful features. Certainly enough features not to be left as a condemned boardinghouse. Now if Doug can just convince the local historical societies and their patrons to support the rest of the renovation. I'm hoping the gilt work will be the carrot."

She blew out air. "Fingers crossed." She stared out at a family of plovers that raced across the dunes. "Thanks for putting up with me last night."

"My pleasure."

She turned and made a face. "Really?"

"Well . . ."

"I know I was a hysterical mess. It was just such a shock. No one ever hinted that I wasn't a real Calder."

"Let's not start that again."

"I'm not. Just thank you. What are you working on today? Can I see?"

"Sure, it's mainly sketches at this point."

Meri leaned over the table, studying the creatures that frolicked across the drawing paper. She looked closer and saw that what she'd first thought were cuddly children's book elves were something darker and more sinister.

"What's it for?"

"If you can believe it, it's for the autobiography of an underground, grunge rock singer I'd never heard of before taking the commission. And wish I'd never heard or read about since. Seriously fucked up."

She laughed. "If those little guys are testaments to his life, I don't doubt it."

"Pretty nasty stuff. That's why I'm out here today. In the sunshine."

"It would give me nightmares."

"It would give anybody nightmares."

"Even you?"

"Absolutely me. This might be the first project I've turned in weeks ahead of deadline, just to get it out of my house."

"Why did you do it?"

"Why do you think?"

"Child support?"

"More or less. Plus Nora will be going to college year after next."

"Doesn't her stepfather make huge amounts of money?"

"He's not touching my daughter's or son's education."

"Ooo-kay."

"Sorry. It's these malevolent creatures. They're in my head today."

"Well, I'll leave you with them. Call if you need me to send a priest to exorcize them."

"Funny."

"Oh," she said. "I loved my birthday present. Thank you."

"You're welcome."

"When I asked if the picture was Ondine, why did you say, God no?"

He shrugged. "Sordid story. Bad outcome."

"I think you should do a nice children's book next."

"I am. A picture book version of the *Odyssey*."

Meri made a face.

"The bowdlerized version."

An hour later Meri was on her way back to Newport. Gran hadn't mentioned the box, which made Meri think it was probably nothing. That was the trouble with secrets. Once you learned one, you expected everything to be related.

She put it out of her mind; she had more urgent things to think about, like what if anything would she tell Peter tonight about her less than conventional birth. She spent the drive home arguing with herself about what and how much to say.

He did have a right to know. Some people might freak, but she didn't really see Peter doing that. Would he be disappointed? Maybe. More likely he would be worried that she had no history of family illnesses or disease, which would be a problem if she or any of their children got sick.

She supposed she'd have to find out who her mother really was, though she was loath to go there. Would Gran and her father and half brothers feel rejected if she hied off in search of her "real" family? But they weren't real. Alden was right; this was her family, and she was grateful and she loved them. And that should be enough.

But was it?

A car was just leaving a permit-only parking space when

she turned onto her street. Meri pulled into it, then just sat in the car, feeling stuck between two worlds, until she realized she was shivering from the cold. She had a world, and she was sticking to it. She grabbed her packages and went upstairs.

Her tiny apartment overlooked the street and could be noisy, especially in the summer. But it also got lots of light. Today it was dark except for one ray of sunlight that slashed diagonally across the polished wood floor. The living area was narrow, just large enough for a coffee table to sit between couch and chair on one wall and an entertainment unit on the other. She dropped her packages on the round dining table, threw herself on the couch, and reached for the remote.

An hour of *This Old House* later she got up.

Meri showered and changed into heels and a little black dress, then changed her mind. She wanted to be frivolous tonight. She went back to her closet and brought out platforms and a red lacy Diane von Furstenberg that Carlyn and she had found at a consignment shop.

Fashion didn't have to be expensive—couldn't be expensive on their salaries—and they spent a lot of fun hours scouring shops for gently worn gems. What would Carlyn say when she found out about Meri's past? Probably think it was a great adventure. Carlyn would never be horrified at anything she did. Would she?

And really, did it matter these days who your birth mother was? Everybody was adopting. *But you weren't really adopted, were you?*

That was what worried her. What was her legal status? She wished she had brought the letter with her, but when she'd returned to the cottage last night, the letter and the box were gone. Gran was looking tired and worried, and Meri didn't have the heart to dredge it up again.

So she'd left her grandmother with a smile and a hug and thanked her profusely for the party and the presents and didn't mention the letter or the box or anything that closely resembled a question about her birth.

There would be time enough for that.

She'd just changed her hair for the third time, opting for a messy ponytail instead of loose and below the shoulders, or pulled back in nacre combs, when the doorbell rang.

She hurried to get it.

Peter Foley leaned against the door frame. Just seeing him made her smile. Good-natured, good-looking, career focused, fun loving—Peter pretty much filled her list of what made the perfect guy.

"Hey, beautiful."

"Hey."

He stepped over the threshold and lifted her into a kiss. She fell into it gratefully. It was so comfortable, so where she wanted to be. For a moment she forgot the rest of the weekend and only looked forward to the night.

The kiss went on for a while and she was considering forgetting dinner altogether and knew he was thinking the same thing.

He broke apart first. "Come on, I had to sell my soul for these reservations." He grinned, a boyish look that made her feel all tingly. "Sustenance before fun."

"I'll get my coat and purse."

The restaurant was crowded, but Peter had managed to get a table next to the rustic brick wall, which gave a little more privacy and cut down on the noise. He always managed those little things. In restaurants, they never sat in view of the kitchen or the restrooms. When someone gave Peter tickets to a Sox game, they were always box seats. He'd only been with Malcolm, Trade and Garrett for six years, but he was the one they sent to benefits and fund-raisers. She'd met him at a Historical Preservation Group benefit two years before.

Meri looked across the table at him, brown hair burnished

red in the candlelight, his smile slightly crooked, and she felt a rush of emotion, a mixture of love and uneasiness.

And she knew she couldn't tell him tonight. That wasn't so bad of her. She had the whole summer. She wouldn't take that long, that wouldn't be fair. But surely he didn't need to know tonight.

Would it make a difference to him? That's what worried her the most. People were adopted all the time—there was no stigma to it—and it wasn't like she was the heiress to a great fortune or an impressive pedigree, just a family of farmers from across the bay.

But what if her mother was someone who could be an embarrassment or, worse, a scandal? Peter was ambitious, but surely her origins wouldn't hold him back, surely he wouldn't hold that against her. Would he?

Maybe the right thing would be to tell him tonight and get it over with. Take the chance that he'd say, "No biggie," and then she could stop worrying about it. But she didn't want to take the chance, not now when her emotions were still so raw. She'd wait.

"I have some news," he said.

She looked up. His expression was hard to read. Excitement? Nervousness?

Was he going to propose after all? In a restaurant?

Meri's heart blipped. She'd been expecting it, sort of, but they had talked about the possibility of law school and all that it would entail. Had he decided not to wait? And tonight of all nights. She couldn't say yes without explaining her new circumstances. But could she sit there over chocolate ganache cake and explain what had happened, when she wasn't sure of all the facts herself?

She swallowed.

He reached for her hand. "Maybe this isn't the right place, but . . ."

Panic rushed up her chest and clenched around her throat.

"I hope you'll be okay with this. I was talking to my uncle in L.A., and his firm has an opening for a paid internship. He offered it to me."

An internship, not an engagement. She was embarrassed by the relief that washed over her. She wouldn't have to explain tonight. "That's wonderful," she said.

"It will give me a chance to get some hands-on legal experience before I start school."

She nodded.

He squeezed her hand; now excitement had overtaken his nervousness. "I accepted."

"That's really great. I loved both my internships."

"The only thing is . . . it starts next month. I gave my two-week notice today."

A utensil clinked against a plate; a laugh, too loud, rose above the other conversations. Every noise seemed amplified, so that she could barely hear Peter say, "I know. It's all happening really fast. But I felt like I couldn't wait."

He was still holding her hand. She considered pulling away. Decided against it.

"I know we thought we'd have the summer to decide what to do, but I can't really turn this down."

"No, of course not."

"But it means I'll be gone for the summer. Which really sucks . . . for us. You could go with me, but the pay isn't that great. It's an internship."

She stopped him. "I know. I understand. It's a great opportunity."

"I can't support both of us if I'm interning, but you could get work. I don't want you to think I want to leave you."

"I don't. And that's sweet. But Peter . . ." She withdrew her hand and patted his. "I have my work here. It's only for a few months. Don't feel bad. I understand."

The waiter hovered by the table ready to snatch their half-empty plates. "Are you finished?"

Meri wondered that herself. "Yes, thank you," she said and leaned back for him to clear.

He removed their plates and returned with the check. Peter stopped to pull out his credit card, and the two of them looked anywhere but at each other until the waiter returned.

They walked out into the night. The night was clear, but colder and Peter's arm around her helped ward off the chill. She'd miss that. She'd miss him.

"Are you sure you're okay with this?"

"I'll miss you, but I'm sure."

"We can still see each other. I'll be back, and you can come visit."

She smiled. "Of course we can. It's all good."

"I love you."

"I love you, too. Things will work out."

They stopped by Peter's car. "So do you want to stay at your place or mine?"

"You know, Peter, I'm really tired. I had a long week and a long night last night. I think I better just get a good night's sleep."

"You're sure? We could get engaged before I leave, I just thought that—"

"There's no rush. It's only three months, and we'll both be busy. Right now careers have to come first." And it would give her time to figure out who she really was. "It'll work out."

Peter sighed. "I guess." He pulled her close. Kissed her, a long kiss, one she fell into wishing, hoping—no, expecting—this to be the one stable thing in her life.

"Sure you don't want to come to my place?" he murmured.

She moved away, tapped his chest. "I'd love to but it's late and we both have work in the morning."

He let her go. "Get in. I'll drive you home."

"Thanks, but by the time you make the loop of one-way streets, I'll be home and in bed. It's just a couple of blocks; I think I'll walk."

He frowned, concerned and disappointed, a little hurt, and she felt a rush of affection for this kind, sweet man.

"You're pissed."

"I am not." She reached up and kissed his cheek. "But I am exhausted. Go to L.A. and become a fabulous lawyer. I'll be here when you get back."

He hesitated. "We could—"

She gave him a playful push. "Go."

He beeped his car. "I'll see you before I leave," he said and got inside. She waved as she tipped her head into the chill and walked down the street. She heard his car speed away.

And immediately had second thoughts. Maybe they should have spent the night together like nothing was changing. But then what? It was better just to get it over with, make a clean break. They might weather the separation. If it was supposed to be, they'd get back together in the fall. Or someday. But someday was a hell of a long way away.

She walked slowly down the street, feeling bereft, at sea. When she reached the block where their favorite karaoke bar was, she stopped. Carlyn would be inside, singing her little heart out. Geordie and Trish would probably be there, too, singing backup without Meri. The four of them were regulars on karaoke night. They even had a bit of a reputation.

Meri chuckled. Some claim to fame. Maybe she wouldn't go home. Maybe she really needed to be with her friends. She stopped on the corner, indecisive. She didn't want to be alone just yet. Didn't want to lie in bed in a dark room and wonder how her life had spun out of her control so fast.

What the hell, a drink, a song, good friends. She started down the street to the club.

Two girls were just finishing up a giggly version of "Signed,

Sealed, Delivered," when Meri walked in. The room was crowded and dark except where the half-moon stage was bathed in yellow gel lights, and she groped her way toward their usual table.

"And now, Carlyn and the Slow Tops."

Carlyn bounced up and turned right in to Meri.

"You came," she yelled over the whistles and cheers. She grabbed Meri and Meri barely had time to drop her bag and throw her coat on the back of a chair before Carlyn propelled her toward the stage.

"Carlyn, I'm not—I don't."

"Tell me later."

She pushed Meri onto the stage. Meri took her place next to Geordie and Trish who stood at the second mic, off to the side.

Carlyn took the main mic and nodded to the deejay. The music began. Carlyn belted out, "Don't take your—"

Meri cringed. Of all the songs, of all the nights. "Breaking Up Is Hard to Do."

Chapter 5

It took an eon with Meri holding on to every last shred of her control before the last "dooby doo down down" faded out. Cheers and whistles followed, while the Slow Tops and Carlyn took hands and bowed. Laughing, they ran off the stage, catching high fives and playful swipes. They fell into their chairs exhilarated, and Carlyn motioned to the waiter for more drinks.

Meri was the only one not laughing. She'd been wrong to try to socialize her way through this mess that was her life. She needed to go home and curl into a cocoon and come out a butterfly. She half smiled at that. Alden could make a wonderful series of drawings of it.

A guy in a Rhode Island School of Design sweatshirt climbed up the two steps to the stage. His cheeks were flushed and he fidgeted behind the mic until the words appeared on the screen. "This is for Hannah," he said quickly. The audience returned a long *awww,* and "Can't Help Falling in Love" started.

Carlyn nudged Meri. "So what happened to Peter? Did you leave him parking the car?"

Meri shook her head. "He went home."

Carlyn frowned at her. The problem with best friends was they had radar for when you weren't yourself. Ha. Not that she'd ever been herself.

"He went home?"

"Falling in Love" continued shyly and off-key behind her.

"And I'd better get going, too." Meri stood up.

"You just got here."

"Long day and I'm beat. I think I'll get to bed."

"It's only eleven thirty," Carlyn said.

The singer wobbled to a breathy finish.

Meri tried to smile, but reached down for her bag so Carlyn wouldn't see her expression twist into pain. Then without looking at her friends, she waved a general good-bye and fled toward the door.

She was halfway to the corner when she heard footsteps behind her. Not a mugger, but her best friend. Meri's instinct was to run, but she would have to face her sooner or later.

She stopped walking and resolutely turned and waited.

Carlyn had come out without her coat, and for some reason that made Meri want to throw her arms around her and thank her for being her friend.

"Okay. What's going on? And don't say nothing. Something Peter did. Or else he'd come with you."

"He's leaving next week, and—"

"Next week? What happened to September?"

"His uncle got him an internship at his law firm until school starts. Paid."

"How's he going to intern and work full-time?"

"He quit his job."

"Holy shit. . . . But that's okay, he'd have had to leave in the fall anyway. Maybe this will give you two more time together to decide what to do."

Meri shook her head. Too much had happened in the last twenty-four hours that she knew she couldn't begin to explain.

"What? Why are you shaking your head? He won't have more time?"

"It's in California."

Total silence while Carlyn's face registered dumbfounded shock. Then comprehension. "Oh, shit. That's a pretty long commute for dinner. What are you going to do? Did he ask you to—"

"Don't look so worried," Meri said. "You're not going to lose your doo-wop backup. I told him to go and have a good time or something like that."

Carlyn frowned, scrunching her shoulders while she peered at Meri.

"You look like a turtle when you do that." Meri's voice cracked.

"You broke up?"

"No. Maybe. I'm not sure. It kind of looks that way."

"I'm so sorry. But it's only for a few months; you'll get back together. You're perfect for each other."

Meri shrugged. Her throat was burning, and her mouth was much too dry to form words.

"Oh Lord." Carlyn shut her eyes and grabbed her head with both hands. "That was absolutely the worst song to sing. Meri, I'm sorry. Sorry, I had no idea. But didn't he ask you to come with him?"

"Sort of."

"And you turned him down?"

"What would I do in Los Angeles? Dig out the La Brea tar pits?"

"Well, there is that. But I'm sure things will work out. Eventually."

"There's something worse."

"What?"

Meri shook her head.

"OMG, you're not pregnant?"

"No, of course not."

"Then what?"

"Nothing. It's nothing. I don't even know why I said that."

"Well, if it's nothing, then come back inside."

"No, I'm beat; really, I just stopped in for a minute. Go back inside; your teeth are chattering."

"You sure?"

"Yeah."

"Then meet me for a run in the morning. Afterward, we'll have waffles and lots of whipped cream at Barney's. My treat."

"That sounds good."

"Ten o'clock at the Ruggles Avenue entrance to the walk. We'll do the north route, loop back and take the forty steps a couple of times, then drown our sorrows in sugar."

"Okay."

"No cancellations."

"All right. I'll be there. Night." Meri gave Carlyn a swift hug and walked away.

"Ten o'clock!" Carlyn called after her.

Meri raised her hand and kept walking.

The streets were pretty quiet for a Saturday night, still a bit wet from yesterday's rain. The buildings seemed swollen and cold, the streetlamps doing nothing to warm the chill in the air. It was only two blocks to her apartment, but she began to rue wearing her platform shoes.

Meri was glad she'd left a light on. Coming home to a dark apartment might have put her over the edge. But she opened the door to a cheery, albeit empty, scene. She hung her coat up in the narrow coat closet, then went through to her tiny bedroom and neatly hung up her dress. And that was as far as she got before hurt, anger, and self-pity took over.

She sat on the edge of the bed that she would be occupying

alone tonight, took off her shoes, and threw them as hard as she could through the open closet door. Then she crawled under the covers, underwear, makeup, and hair band still in place.

And lay there watching the numbers on the digital clock tick by.

Therese Calder woke with a start. The house was dark. She listened for any sound that was different, but only heard the shushing of the sea and the whisper of branches as a breeze wafted through the trees.

She had a compelling urge to call Meri, just to make sure she was all right, but it was after midnight. She'd still be out with Peter. Therese hoped he would be understanding, not be one of those people who turned his back on his friends when they disappointed him. But why should he be disappointed in Meri? How could anyone be disappointed in her?

She was so loving and kind and compassionate.

Therese's conscience writhed under guilt, old and new. For what she'd let happen thirty years ago, and what she'd done only last night. But what were her choices? Let the child be taken by Social Services, placed in some home that might love her but just as easily might have abused her?

In her heart, she knew they had done the right thing. And it wasn't like they hadn't tried to return the baby to her rightful family.

Therese cringed, chastising herself for her half-truth. They'd found the family and the family had not wanted to hear about their daughter or their grandchild, so she and Laura told them that the baby died with the mother. They left their address and phone number. But the people never asked about the grave or contacted her again.

They had erased their daughter from their lives and their love. And after meeting them, the decision to keep Meri had been easy.

God would either forgive her or not. She'd done what she thought best. Both times. And now she would have to act because of those decisions.

The box that belonged to Meri sat on the top shelf of Therese's closet beneath a stack of quilts. But it burned through the closed door like some enchanted thing in one of Alden's fairy tales. She wouldn't be surprised to see it jump down from the shelf and run out of the house crying "Read me. Read me."

She shuddered and nestled down beneath the comforter. How much longer could she live with that box in her possession? It didn't belong to her. It belonged to Meri.

Tomorrow she would call Alden and ask him to drive her to Newport. He hardly ever went anywhere except to take the train down to New York to see his editors and agent, and he rarely went into Newport. She didn't know what was wrong with the man, to live out here all by himself.

It was a comfort to have him nearby, but he should be getting on with his life. He'd been alone for—she thought back—six years? eight? A long time for a man in his prime. Was his marriage responsible for that, or had he been marked by what had happened three decades ago?

She would call him first thing tomorrow. Maybe they would stay and take Meri to a nice restaurant. Alden would see what he was missing and get interested in life again, instead of living with a bunch of imaginary creatures and an old lady for his only neighbor.

She would go back to sleep now. There were no frightening noises outside. The only sounds she heard tonight were the beating of her own heart and the shushing of the waves. . . .

Meri lasted nearly twenty minutes before she had to get up and put her shoes away properly. Sometimes she wished she was one of those people who was überdetailed at work and a slob at home. But she couldn't stand a mess. Which, if she allowed herself to think, was pretty much what her life was at the moment—a mess.

She pushed the blanket away and turned on the light. Rummaged around in the bottom of the closet, until she found the wayward shoes and returned them to their storage box. Looked at the coordinated rows of hanging clothes and had an overwhelming desire to yank them off the hangers.

Step away from the situation. You're about to lose it and that's not good.

Rattled, she stepped back and back, shook herself. Where had that urge come from? It was a dangerous thought. If she didn't stay on an even keel, her whole life might come tumbling down.

She'd meet Carlyn in the morning for a run like always. Do the laundry in the afternoon, like always. Go to work on Monday, continue to work on the ceiling while she waited for the paint analysis to come from the lab.

That ceiling held untold possibilities: colors, patterns, maybe even gilt. It was a mystery to solve, hopefully one that would uncover a beautiful fascinating remnant from a life gone by. Meri shied away from the thought that her own past was a mystery—she wasn't about to chip away at that. She doubted there would be anything wonderful or worth preserving from a runaway girl and an abandoned baby.

But as she brushed her teeth she wondered, what had the girl, her mother, been afraid of, what or whom? Her baby's father, her parents? Was she running from the law, immigration? And just as that glimpse of gilt beneath all those layers of paint had set her blood racing, the desire to find out the truth settled inside her.

She needed to know. She wouldn't hurt her family, the family who raised and loved her, her true family. But surely Gran wouldn't mind if she asked about what had occurred at her birth. Did she look like that girl?

Her hair had always been darker than her mother's, and Meri was taller by several inches. She'd just assumed her father was tall. But they both had blue eyes. The teenager must have had blue eyes. Did they have a picture of her? Did they know her name? *I need to know.* She would learn the facts, then she would leave it alone and get on with her life as Merielle Calder Hollis.

That's who she was. The Calders had loved her and shaped her character and were always there for her. Alden was right about that. It wasn't who birthed you. It was who nurtured you. She was a Calder Hollis, a Calder Hollis.

And those words followed her to sleep.

Sunday was another sunny day. Meri showered, changed into running clothes and shoes, and put her hair back in a ponytail. She filled a waist pack with credit cards, ID, keys, and cash, then added a water bottle and clipped it on. On her way out, she grabbed a fleece jacket in case it was cold.

But it wasn't cold. It felt like spring, and a little surge of optimism swelled inside her as she walked across town to meet Carlyn.

Carlyn was waiting for her at the entrance to the Cliff Walk near Newport's grandest "cottage," the Breakers, built by the Vanderbilts at the height of the Gilded Age.

"Leave that in the car," Carlyn said, indicating the jacket. "You won't need it today." She tossed Meri the keys to her ancient Alfa Romeo and began stretching.

Carlyn and Meri had met over karaoke their freshman year and had been best friends ever since. Carlyn was a business major at Rhode Island College but caught the restoration bug when Meri dragged her to a behind-the-scenes tour of the Breakers. When Carlyn graduated, she turned her back on the financial district and signed on as fund-raiser for Doug's first solo project.

As project manager for the Gilbert House restoration, she

compiled data, kept the project on budget or came up with more funding, logged progress and setbacks, ordered supplies, answered phones, and occasionally went out to get lunch for everyone.

Doug was constantly trying to entice Carlyn to work solely for his projects. She was a gem, both as a preservationist and as a friend. She kept him dangling, mainly, Meri thought, because he was a willing victim to her teasing. Meri knew Carlyn loved the job, and though the pay was poor, it was a lot more satisfying to "crunch numbers for a worthy cause."

Meri tossed her jacket in the front seat and locked the door. When she crossed the street, Carlyn was bent over touching her toes. She popped up, reminding Meri of a jack-in-the-box, though it might have been her reddish hair that began to frizz as soon as it hit the sea air.

Meri quickly stretched, and they started off north along the cliff. The air was brisk and there was a healthy breeze along the water. It was a perfect early spring day for jogging or speed walking or strolling, and the walk was already busy with people.

They began at a brisk walk until they passed the grounds of the Breakers, then broke into an easy jog, running side by side when the walk was wide enough, and single file when passing slower pedestrians. Parts of the walk had taken a beating in the last hurricane, but it was whole again.

Meri relaxed into the pace, breathed in the fresh air and sunlight, and cast occasional glances at the bay that glistened blue in the sun.

Students at Salve Regina were already stretched out on the lawn. Spring break was only a week away and they were getting an early start.

Carlyn suddenly veered right; Meri followed her down the forty steps to a small lookout. By the time she reached the bottom, Carlyn was turning around and heading back to the path.

Meri huffed out a breath, and taking a longing look at the water, began the climb up. Carlyn was jogging in place when Meri reached the top.

"I'm dying," Meri gasped.

"Just another three-quarters of a mile and we'll walk back."

"Right." Meri took a deep breath and started out again. By the time they reached the end of the walk at the Chanler Inn, Meri was wishing she was idly rich and could stop at the luxury hotel for brunch. But the Chanler was not for them. They would do their brunching at Barney's Budget Breakfast and More.

Barney's had great food. And their kind of ambiance: noisy, fun, and upbeat. Barney was actually a sixtysomething-year-old woman, with gray hair braided down her back. She'd lived in Newport ever since as a hippie she'd ridden into town on the back of a Harley and decided to stay. Her waffles could not be beat.

When they finally reached the end of the walk, Meri was still on her feet mainly by keeping the image of a double cappuccino like a dangling carrot to keep her going. Carlyn immediately started stretching, while Meri huffed her breath back to normal.

Well, Carlyn didn't spend hours a day crunched up on a scaffold thirty feet above the floor. She went to Zumba class on Wednesday nights and spinning three times a week. She was a demon.

Meri counted carrying laundry downstairs to the basement and walking to the corner market as major aerobic exercise.

Carlyn barely waited for Meri to catch her breath before she started back the way they had come. At least she'd slowed to a power walk. Meri dragged herself beside her.

"You look beat," Carlyn told her. "You need to get more exercise."

"Tell me about it."

Carlyn slowed to a normal walk. "So want to tell me what happened with Peter?"

"Just what I told you. He's got an internship in L.A. He quit his job and is leaving next week."

"I can't believe he's just leaving like that. What about the two of you? We all thought you were going to get married."

"So did I. Actually, I'm pretty sure he did, too."

"But he's still coming back east for law school, right?"

"I guess."

"So it's not over."

They'd slowed to a pedestrian walk. Meri shrugged. "Well, I sort of gave him his freedom."

Carlyn stopped outright and spun Meri around. "You dumped him?"

"No," Meri said, stepping aside for a runner to pass. "I just told him to go and—hell, I'm not sure what I said or why. Suddenly I just felt like it was out of my control. I didn't want to go to California and he didn't want to stay here. And if we can't even decide between us, if neither of us is willing to make a sacrifice, maybe it's not the right relationship."

They'd started walking again, but again Carlyn stopped. "Of course it is. You guys are perfect together."

"I thought so. But actually it's a good thing."

"Okay, you're losing me. Come on." She dragged Meri over to a bench and sat her down. "Spill."

"It's not about Peter."

Carlyn rolled her eyes.

"Really, it isn't. Something happened. To me. I mean, I found out something this weekend."

Carlyn's face changed to apprehension.

"Oh, nothing bad. Nothing life threatening. But something about my past that . . . Oh hell, Carlyn. I was adopted."

Carlyn's mouth fell open. "Adopted? Wow. And you just found out this weekend?"

Meri nodded.

"That is so weird. Why wait until now to tell you? They did tell you, right?"

"Sort of. My mother left me a letter." Meri pulled her feet up and hugged her knees.

"Okay, that's weirder than just weird."

"My dad—my stepdad—was there and Gran. They both knew, had known for a long time I'm pretty sure. The letter was from right before my mother died. I guess she didn't want to die without telling me."

"Okay," Carlyn said slowly. "It's weird. But does it matter? I mean it doesn't change anything about you . . . except maybe your blood type." She grinned, and Meri felt "normal" for the first time since she'd found out about her birth. But it didn't last. It wasn't just that she was adopted. She was pretty sure she could get past that. But it was the other thing.

"Are you freaked? You shouldn't be. I mean, I know it will take some getting used to. But does it really change anything? You have a great family, and they haven't changed."

"That's what Alden said."

"Your neighbor out in Compton?"

"Yeah. He said my family loved me, and that was all that mattered."

"Sounds like a pretty smart old dude."

"Yeah, but there's something else." Should she tell Carlyn the whole truth? It would leave her vulnerable if it got out. Would there be legal ramifications? What could possibly happen? Her mother was dead, and Meri could hardly be held responsible. But Gran. What could they do to Gran?

"What? Go on and get it out. And we'll figure out how to deal."

Meri hesitated. Took a breath. If she couldn't trust Carlyn, there was no one on earth she could trust. "I'm not sure the adoption was legal."

Chapter 6

Whoa. You mean like black market kind of stuff?

"No. Not exactly."

"Not exactly, how?"

"I don't know if I should tell anyone."

"Cross my heart and hope to die if you leave me dangling at this point."

Meri smiled. She was so fortunate in her family and in her friends. She knew that. She'd come this far. And maybe Carlyn would have some advice.

"I don't know all the facts. I was so blown away, I just fled back here without asking too many questions. I know I have to, but—" She shivered.

Carlyn dragged her to her feet. "Talk while we walk. I'm feeling the need of a triple-double shot something." She slipped her arm into Meri's. "Start from the beginning."

So Meri told her about the letter. About her mother's dead baby. About the teenager whose baby lived. How she was that baby and her mother's baby was buried with the teenager.

"Holy crap," Carlyn said when Meri had come to the end of

her explanation. "I'm buying breakfast. Are you going to try to find your birth family?"

"I don't know. I have to talk to Gran. See what she remembers. But, Carlyn, don't say anything to anybody. What if my mother and Gran broke the law? Could they send Gran to jail?"

"Jail? Surely not. Do you think they could?"

"On your left," someone called out.

They automatically moved aside and waited for a group of joggers to run by them.

"Maybe you should ask—" Carlyn stopped, frowning. "Did you tell Peter? Is that why you broke up?"

"No. I was deliberating whether to tell him when he told me he was leaving for L.A. It made the whole question academic at that point."

"Maybe you should ask him. He worked in the legal department. He's going to study law. Maybe he can do some research."

"No. I shouldn't have even told you. It puts you in a really awkward position. I know. But—"

"Stop. That's what friends are for."

"But you have to promise not to tell. Unless you're under oath. Please."

"Of course I won't tell. I'll even plead the Fifth." They started walking again. "Are you okay with all this?"

"I don't know. At first I didn't believe it. Then I was shocked. And hurt and angry and confused. But two days later, I'm jogging with you. And life goes on. It wasn't like it was my fault. And I know my family loves me and would do anything for me. I'll come to terms with it. I just hope it doesn't come back to bite us all in the butt."

"If it hasn't by now, I doubt if it will."

"Famous last words."

"Just don't go stirring things up. Though I guess that's a stupid thing for me to say."

"Why?"

"It's kind of your life's work. Uncovering the past."

Alden had just reached in the freezer for the coffee when his cell phone rang. He checked caller ID and answered it.

"Daddy."

"Hi, honey; you're getting an early start."

"We're going to church." Nora dragged out the last word. "Are you sick? You sound hoarse."

"I'm fine. I haven't had my coffee yet."

"It's almost eleven o'clock." A pause. "Were you out late last night?"

"I was up late working."

"Oh. You know, you should really get a life."

"I have one, keeping you in designer jeans and Lucas in computers."

"I mean a real life. Anyway, I have a proposition for you."

"Am I going to like it?" He measured coffee into the coffee filter.

"Of course. I want to come there for spring break."

"Great. When is spring break?"

"It starts this Saturday."

Alden shook the fog out of his brain. "I thought you all were going to Boston next week."

"*They* are. I don't want to go. Please let me stay with you."

Between her age and her normal personality, Nora could often be dramatic, sometimes jaded and worldly, but today she sounded like his little girl. "What happened?"

"Nothing, I just want to come home. Please. They're just doing stuff for Henley." She drew out the name of her half brother. "He's such a butthead. They're just making me go so

I can babysit when they want to go out. They already treat me like Cinderella. And after the baby comes, it's just going to be worse. *I* don't have a life."

Another baby.

"If it's okay with your mother and Mark, I'd be glad to have you. What about Lucas?"

"They bribed him with the computer museum. He's such a geek. Make her let me come. I don't care about computer museums or their 'family time.'" The last two words dripped with teenage disgust. She was obviously quoting. "They can have their stupid family. Lucas and I are just an afterthought. Not that he even notices."

Alden wanted to tell her he was sure they both loved her and Lucas. But he wasn't sure. And he didn't want to make light of something that was upsetting her.

He passed a hand over his face. His unshaven face. "Look, I'd love for you to visit, anytime, but not if it's going to cause dissension in the family."

"Not you, too. Please, Daddy. Please. At least talk to Mom."

Alden heard another voice in the background, a voice he knew. "Nora? Aren't you ready yet? We're going to be late for church."

He turned on the spigot to drown her out. Poured water into the coffeemaker and turned it on.

"Oops, busted." Nora moved the phone away and he heard a muffled, "I'm talking to my father," delivered in her "officious" voice. "I'm going *there* for spring break."

"Give me that." A scuffle and Jennifer took the phone. "What's going on? Did you instigate this?"

Jennifer. Still looking for an argument. Anger swelled inside him. He knew it was a purely reflexive reaction. Life with Jennifer had been one long argument from the minute they'd driven up to the house, the moment she realized she wasn't going to be living in the lap of luxury in a Newport-style mansion, but in an old house in need of repairs. How had she gotten it so wrong? Certainly not from him.

"Well? I'm waiting for an answer."

"Nora would like to come here for spring break."

"Did you put her up to this?"

"He didn't. *I* called *him,*" Nora said from the background.

"Nora, go downstairs."

"This is the first I've heard of it. You can send both of them if you want." He stopped himself before he said he would take them anytime. She would never let them come for a visit if he did.

"This was supposed to be a family vacation, and she's done everything she can think of to make life miserable for everyone."

Do not engage, he told himself. Argument never did any good. Their arguments had once led to great sex, but even that had paled after the first few months. Now, he just didn't care.

In the background he heard Nora yell, "I'm going to Dad's."

"Fine, suit yourself. I've had it with you. We'll drop her off on our way."

"When are you—"

She hung up before he could ask when they would arrive. He got down a mug and poured coffee into it. He'd better get some work done. It looked like he was going to have a visit from his daughter.

Therese was sitting at the kitchen table, drinking coffee, and deliberating about whether to ask Alden to drive her into town, when there was a knock at the back door. She smiled, knowing who it was, but she also felt a secondary moment of panic. Once the decision was made, there was no going back.

The door opened and Alden stuck his head inside.

"Come in. Pour yourself a cup of coffee." Therese pulled

her own mug closer and wrapped both hands around it. It was comfortably snug in the kitchen, but she couldn't seem to get her hands warm.

She watched Alden shed his windbreaker and hang it over the back of the chair. Watched his back as he reached in the cabinet for a mug, poured out coffee. When he turned to come back to the table, he stopped, tilted his head in the way he had, then came over to sit opposite her.

"Therese, are you feeling okay?"

"Yes." Physically, anyway. But for the rest of it . . . "I have something on my mind."

Alden nodded.

"There is a box. Laura left it for Meri." She looked up from her coffee to find Alden watching her. She could never tell what he was thinking. It was like his thoughts were so deep inside him that they had a hard time coming out. But she knew they were there.

When she was a girl, there had been a boy like that in her class at school. He sometimes came to help out at the farm when it was still a working farm. He pretty much kept to himself, even though he knew Therese from school.

She'd asked her father why he never said much.

"He's a deep one," her father said.

Alden was another deep one. God only knew what lived in his brain along with all those fanciful creatures he drew, sometimes beautiful and colorful; sometimes black and frightening, bringing a chill all the way up your spine.

He'd been such a loving boy and like a big brother to Meri, patient and kind even though he was twelve years her senior. Then he married that awful women. Therese thought she must have squeezed all the love right out of him. But he was loyal. And he loved his children. And the Calders. And especially Meri.

She swallowed. "I wanted to ask you if you would drive me to Newport to give it to her."

His eyebrows dipped. "Mind if I ask what's in it?"

Therese shook her head, took a breath. "Just some things Laura wanted Meri to have. Mementos. Letters from her father . . . that is, from Huey to Laura. A few papers." She paused. "A diary."

She hadn't realized that she was no longer looking at Alden until she heard his intake of breath. Then she forced herself to look him in the eye—those dark gray eyes under black lashes that had made him such a beautiful boy. When had those eyes become so unfathomable?

But she knew the answer: the night they had placed a grown man's burden on his young shoulders, the night he'd sworn to keep their secret.

A sound escaped from somewhere deep inside her. Alden was on his feet and coming to her. "Gran," he said, just like he was still a boy.

She held up her hand warding him off; she didn't deserve his sympathy, his concern. He'd lost his innocence of the world that night, and it was partially her fault.

He ignored her, dragging a chair over and sitting down; he wrapped his arm around her and pulled her close. "It's all right. It will be all right."

"So you will take me?"

"No."

She pulled away. "Then I'll take the bus."

"Gran, listen to me. Wait. Don't make her assimilate this all by herself away from us."

"Alden, I know you want to protect her, you always have. But it might be easier if she doesn't have us looking over her shoulder, pressuring her. I may be selfish, but now that it's started, I want it done. Not for myself. I would rather have taken this to the grave with me. But I didn't, and now that she knows, it has to finish, if any of us, especially Meri"—*Or you*—"are going to get on with our lives. Whether she accepts us or rejects us, we can't keep her bound by this secret any longer."

"It might be easier on her, but what if she—" He stopped abruptly, but she knew what he would have said.

"If she doesn't want us?"

He looked bleak. Alden, maybe more than either Laura or her, was tied firmly to Meri, whether he realized it or not. Once this was done, he would be free, too.

Alden straightened in his chair as if resolved. "I have to go to the city tomorrow to turn in some pages and talk to my editor. I'll stop by her work on my way. I was going to anyway."

"You're a good boy."

He lifted an eyebrow and she realized her mistake. For a minute she'd been somewhere else, sometime long ago. "A good man."

"I was coming over to tell you. Nora is coming for spring break. She'll be here on Saturday. I was going to ask Meri if she had some time to maybe show her around, or do something with her. I have a lot of work to do next week, and she gets bored quickly.

"I'll ask Meri if she can come this weekend. That way she can read everything here, and if she has questions, you'll be here to answer them."

Therese shook her head. "I thought about this all night. It's better for everyone if it isn't dragged out. She has a right to know it all. Am I being selfish to want this finished?"

"No. Of course not; you've never been selfish, ever since I've known you. Am I?"

"You? Why would you say such a thing?"

He bit his lip, then asked quietly, "Am I in the diary?"

Therese patted his hand, understanding dawning. "Perhaps."

He pulled his hand away, braced his elbows on the table, and lowered his head to his hands.

"What is it? You only did good things."

"I didn't tell her. All these years I never told her. I never told anyone."

Therese rubbed his back, just like she had the night Meri was born as they waited for Wilton to pick him up and take him home—a boy with an awful burden thrust upon him.

She'd known even then Alden would never break a promise, but she drew the line at making a boy lie to his father. So she told Wilton the whole story. How Alden had saved the girl and the baby. How the girl had made him promise not to tell anyone about her or Merielle.

They didn't know then how desperate the girl was. They thought it was just exposure to being out in the rain, that she would come around. She'd see her baby and feel better. The night Meri was born, they'd let Alden in to see the baby, and she asked to speak to him alone. Therese shouldn't have allowed it. But she didn't have the heart to deny the girl's request.

So she and Laura had retreated to the hallway and stood listening behind the closed door. He'd promised to take care of her baby. And he had—for thirty years. "It won't make a difference to her."

"Won't it?"

"Well, perhaps she'll be a little miffed at first. But when she thinks about it, she'll be grateful."

"Which is just what I'm afraid of. But if you want me to take the box, I will." He stood up. "Where is it?"

Therese pushed herself up from the table. She felt weak and old and guilty. New guilt heaped on the old. Once again she was asking Alden to do something she had hoped they would never have to do.

"It's in here," she said and walked out of the kitchen.

Meri and Carlyn stuffed themselves with Belgian waffles, covered in fruit and whipped cream, and drank two cappuccinos apiece as they carefully avoided more talk about the past. But Meri could feel the bond between them had grown stronger. And she trusted Carlyn with her life.

She just hoped that she was as good a friend to Carlyn as Carlyn was to her.

They parted on the sidewalk outside of Barney's, Carlyn off to the lab and office to catch up on paperwork, and Meri to do laundry.

Life goes on, Meri thought as she carried work clothes, sheets, and pillowcases down to the basement. As she shoved clothes into the washer, she was hit with an image of the past weekend: her dad clasping the locket around her neck, a picture of him and her mother. She knew it was his way of telling her that nothing had changed, that he claimed her for his own. And she had to believe him.

She did believe him and that grounded her more than anything else. Alden was right, as he often was, damn him. Indiscretion in the backseat of a Chevy did not make a mother or a father.

And Meri realized, not for the first time, just how lucky she was.

Her cell rang as she was folding pillowcases. Will, the youngest Hollis. Guess the word was out.

"Yo, sis. Whatcha doing?"

"Laundry. How about you? Studying by any chance?"

"I'm watching a *Star Wars* marathon. For my film class."

"Uh-huh."

Heavy sigh across the connection. "And then I'm going to the library to study for my biology final."

"Finals already?"

"Yep, then I'm headed south for some fun in the sun. Uh, unless you need me to do anything."

God, she loved her brothers. *Her brothers.* "I need you just to be you. Go have fun, but first try acing your exams."

"Will do. Gotta go. Love you."

"Love you, too." They hung up. Meri wiped away a tear. Awkward and obvious. She couldn't remember the last time her youngest brother had said he loved her.

She finished folding the laundry and carried it upstairs to wait for the other two to call.

She didn't have long to wait. She'd barely gotten her underwear back in the drawer when her dad called to let her know he'd told everyone. Matt's call followed almost immediately. Gabe and Penny called together, then Penny called back on her own to offer girl time. Another call from her father to see how she was. They'd all obviously been communicating. The last one was from Gran, sounding so tired and frail that Meri was tempted to drive back and take Monday off.

They were all filled with love, reassuring, and insisting that nothing was any different than it had always been. They were wonderful and it was exhausting.

She went to bed and the calls played over and over in her mind. They loved her, she had no doubt of that. But it was still a lot to take in.

Meri awoke Monday morning, dragged out and not ready to face the world. She contemplated calling in sick, but that was crazy. She needed to get some distance on this, and work would get her back on an even keel. Work was the one thing she could lose herself in, where she wouldn't have to think about anything that was happening in her life.

So what if cleaning away layers of paint with a solution of vinegar and water was on the tedious side. Today she was thankful to be studying someone else's past rather than her own. She was heartily sick of thinking about herself.

Fortunately her ceiling had been pronounced lead free, unlike the walls she had taken samples from wearing toxin-resistant overalls, latex gloves, and a respirator. By now most everything on the first floor was close to being documented. She'd started alternating between sampling and cleaning. With most of the sampling finished, she could concentrate solely on her ceiling.

If they passed the next lead and asbestos test, they would be home free. At least with the ceiling declared lead free, she wouldn't have to suit up; and it meant that there wouldn't be that many layers of paint to clean away before getting to the original pattern.

Last Friday had been the first day she'd begun to have an idea of what it might look like. She'd started at one edge of the circular area last week and was working a grid toward the center in order to reveal more of the full pattern.

This was hindered because the ceiling was embellished by ornamental plaster decorations, their intricate designs made more difficult to discern by the sloppy overpainting, and the cleaning had to be executed gently to avoid breaking off delicate details.

The morning passed quickly; she was back in the zone as more and more of the pattern revealed itself. She hardly thought about anything but what the ceiling would look like when she was finished. And then she'd knock on the wooden scaffolding that they would get the rest of the funds needed to bring the house back to its former glory.

She lost track of time until Carlyn yelled, "Hey, you," from below her. "It's almost two. Come have lunch with me."

Meri had been ignoring the rumblings in her stomach for the last hour. She'd had a carton of yogurt at six that morning while she read the latest issue of *Preservation* magazine. That was hours ago. She hadn't brought lunch.

"Can you order—"

"Already did. Now come down."

Meri secured her tools and climbed down. The woodworkers were already back at work after their lunch break. The paint had been stripped under the careful eyes of the EPA several weeks ago. Beneath it, golden oak window and door frames were being repaired or replaced with the help of several interns.

She cleaned up and joined Carlyn at the kitchen table. Doug's desk, which occupied the far corner, was piled high with papers, but it was missing their director.

Meri and Carlyn had the kitchen to themselves.

"So what's new?" Carlyn asked.

Meri gave her a look. "What's for lunch?"

"Turkey and Swiss on a croissant, and roast beef and brie with mustard on an egg roll." She slid the roast beef toward Meri. "And spring mix salad to get in our green quota." She pushed a Styrofoam bowl across the table, then reached in the fridge for two bottles of water.

Meri unwrapped her sandwich and glanced at Carlyn. "You look tired."

"Probably from spending most of yesterday looking for ways to squeeze more than a hundred pennies out of every dollar."

"Are we going to run out of money?"

Carlyn finished chewing and wiped a smear of mayonnaise off her mouth. "You should know by now we're always on the verge of running out of money. The powers that be weren't sure Gilbert House was worth the expense. Fortunately for us Doug is a master fund-raiser." Carlyn looked past Meri to the doorway. "Hello." In a lower voice she said, "TDH alert in the doorway."

Tall, dark, and handsome alert. Meri couldn't resist. She turned to see who it was.

"Good God, Alden!" She stood and knocked over her water. "What's happened?"

Chapter 7

Alden held up both hands. "Nothing's wrong. Everybody's fine."

Meri slumped with relief and began mopping up the spill. "Then what are you doing here?"

He was wearing black jeans with a black sweater beneath an incongruously expensive country jacket. A Blackwatch plaid scarf hung from his neck. Definitely dressed for success by Corrigan standards.

"Meri!" Carlyn scolded.

"I mean, I'm really glad to see you, but you don't normally come to town. And never all dressed up." She tossed the wet napkin toward the trash can. It made it halfway and splatted on the floor.

"I was on my way to New York and thought I'd drop by."

Meri looked at him speculatively.

"Hi," Carlyn said behind her.

Meri took the hint. "Alden, this is my friend, colleague, and partner in karaoke crime, Carlyn Anderson. Carlyn, this is my neighbor, Alden Corrigan."

"Alden? You're Meri's neighbor? I wondered why we've never met before." Carlyn shot Meri a speaking look.

Alden shifted on his feet, looking ready to bolt antelope-like down the hall. "I don't get into town much. Meri, can you walk me out to my car?"

"You're leaving already?"

"I've got a three-forty train."

"You're not driving?"

"No."

"And you just 'stopped by' on your way to the train station in Providence?"

He shrugged.

"That's two hours out of your way, Alden. Fess up. What's wrong?"

"Nothing. I told you. But can we just talk for a minute? I have a favor to ask. Two actually."

"Don't mind me," said Carlyn and got up from the table.

"Don't get up," Meri said. "We'll go outside."

Carlyn sat down, but her look told Meri that she was going to pump her for information as soon as she got back.

Meri looked at Alden as she walked out the door. *TDH*. He was definitely tall and dark, and he *was* good-looking, but a little old for Carlyn. Or maybe not too old, but way too serious. She smiled at him.

"What?"

"I was just trying to imagine you at karaoke night."

He smiled somewhat ruefully, shook his head.

She punched his arm. "What's the favor?"

They were walking down the center hall toward the back door. He stopped in the alcove of the back staircase.

"First, how are you?"

"I'm fine. Well, I'm trying to not think about any of it. Did Gran make you come all this way to check up on me?"

"No. But she *is* worried, and she feels bad for having set this whole thing in motion. She said you sounded upset when she called you last night. I hope you're not upset with her."

"I didn't sound upset." She'd made a point of being upbeat because Gran had sounded upset. "And I'm not upset . . . not exactly," she added truthfully. She had no idea how she could carry on a normal conversation with her grandmother, not after this weekend.

"Meri . . ." He reached for her arm, started to speak; dropped his hand. "Call her, okay? And let her know you don't hate her."

"I don't hate her; how could she even think that?"

"Just let her know, okay?" He gave her one of his piercing looks, what she'd dubbed his Darth Vader look when she was in her teens, though he'd pointed out that no one ever saw Darth Vader's eyes.

"Okay. I'll call her tonight. What's the second favor?"

"Nora's coming to spend spring break with me."

"Great."

"I know you're busy, but do you think you could come out for the weekend and say hello? Maybe arrange to do something with her once or twice? Show her around Newport or take her shopping or something, my treat. Just so she won't spend seven days in her room texting the friends she's pissed she had to leave."

"And keep her out of your hair, so you can work?"

"No. It's just she's having trouble with her mother at the moment. Actually with the whole living situation. I thought maybe she might want to talk. To . . . someone."

"Not you?"

"Evidently I wouldn't understand. I guess I'm not that good with teenagers, not hot or cool or whatever."

"That is so much bull; you've always been goods with kids, and . . . adults who sometimes act like kids."

He smiled at that. "That's different. You're not my daughter."

"And thank goodness for that."

"Actually she asked if you were going to be out at the farm. She says I'm too overprotective."

"When is she coming?"

"Saturday."

"Sure. I'll come out to see Gran, try to work things out with her. Then see what Nora is interested in doing. Maybe she'd like to come stay in town for a night or two and Carlyn and I'll show her a good time."

She had to bite her lip to keep from laughing at his expression.

"That won't be necessary."

She couldn't help it, she cracked up. "What kind of good time do you think we'd show her?"

"I shudder to think; could we maybe stick to shopping and pizza?"

"Sure. Now do you have time to see what I'm working on before you go?"

"Always."

Constraint broken, she linked her arm in his and led him to the front foyer, then maneuvered him to the opposite wall of where she'd been working. "It's hard to see all four feet by four feet of it, especially with the scaffolding in the way. One day we'll hopefully be able to afford a hydraulic lift. But look." She moved in close to get his perspective and pointed to where the dull blue, green, and deep red colors were framed by an amorphous edge of modern paint.

He studied her little patch of work like it was the work of a great master. He always took an interest in what she was doing. Actually he always took an interest in everything. How could Nora possibly be bored with him?

Impulsively, she reached up and kissed his cheek.

He laughed quietly. "What was that for?"

"Just because. And now that you've been appropriately appreciative, you'd better hurry or you'll miss your train."

She walked him to the back door again.

But when she would have left him at the door, he took her elbow. "Come out to the car with me. Gran sent you something."

Meri hesitated, looked at Alden but as was often the case, his face was unreadable. "Please tell me it's leftover cioppino."

"Come." He led her over to his ancient Volvo station wagon, unlocked the back, and handed her a cardboard box. She had to force herself to take it. It was the same box she had seen on the hutch the night of her birthday dinner. The box that they had meant to give her then and changed their minds? She looked a question at Alden.

"It's things your mother . . . Laura . . . saved for you."

"Oh."

"Put it in your car. You can look them over after work."

"Do you know what's in here?"

"No."

"You didn't peek?" she asked, trying to add a little levity to the situation.

"Of course not. It's for you. I have to go."

She forced a smile. It didn't fool either of them.

"Saturday. Don't forget."

"I'll be there." She watched him get into the car and waved as he drove out of the parking lot. Feeling suddenly alone, she put the box in her car and locked it, something she rarely did on-site. Then, leaving her questions securely locked inside with the box, she returned to the kitchen where she knew Carlyn would be waiting with a million questions of her own.

She was. As soon as Meri walked through the door Carlyn said, "That's your elusive neighbor? No wonder you've never let me meet him. The way you talk about him I expected to see an old geezer, not a hot stud."

Meri laughed. "He *was* looking awfully GQ today. He can pull it off when he tries." She sighed. "He just doesn't usually try. Most of the time he runs around in holey paint-smeared jeans and shirts with frayed collars, also paint smeared."

"I don't know, I'm getting a good visual on the holey jeans part. I take it he's a painter."

"An illustrator, book illustrator, and a lot of the smears are colored ink, not paint."

"I didn't know people actually still drew pictures for books. I thought it was all done on a computer program."

"He does that, too, but he doesn't like it as much as getting down and dirty."

Carlyn raised her eyebrows. "So what does he do for fun?"

"Alden?" Meri thought about it. She couldn't really think of him having a rollicking good time. Maybe that's what he did on his trips to Manhattan. But she didn't want to "get a visual" about that. "He takes his sailboat out when he's not on deadline."

Carlyn deflated. "I get seasick. What else?"

"You know, I'm not sure. He's always going into Manhattan to see his agent or editor to turn in his work."

"Manhattan is good. What else?"

"I don't know. I'm sure he has a life, but I don't see him that much anymore." And she certainly didn't ask him about his "life." "And when I do see him, we don't talk about stuff like that. Except neither he nor my dad are in love with Peter. Do you think they know something I don't?"

"Just overprotective. Dads do that." Carlyn shrugged. "I guess maybe neighbors do, too."

"His family has lived next door to us forever. He's like one of our family."

"Well, I wouldn't mind putting him in my family. Is he married?"

"Divorced." Meri eyed her friend. "Are you seriously interested?"

"Well, I wouldn't say no if he were interested back. Kids?"

"Two teenagers."

"They live with him?"

"No. But you might meet one of them next week."

"Can't wait." Carlyn crumpled up her sandwich wrapper and tossed it at the trash can. It arched gracefully into the center of the circle. Carlyn pumped both fists in the air. "Booyah. Two points!"

She snagged another bottle of water. "Back to the grind. Thanks for introducing me to your neighbor."

Meri waited until she was gone, then poured herself a cup of hour-old coffee. Why had Alden and Gran waited until today to give her that box? Why not Friday night? Because they didn't want to be there when she learned the rest? The rest of what? Her birth mother died. They switched the babies. Meri lived.

For the first time since learning of her birth, she really felt cut adrift. Had she disappointed them all with her reaction? Had she planted a seed in their minds by the way she acted? Did they think that she didn't want to be a part of their family? Or worse, had they decided they didn't want her?

And why today of all days did Alden have to leave for the city?

Therese watched the clock on the oven. She had hoped that Alden would call once he saw Meri, but maybe he didn't have time. Maybe he hadn't gone to Newport after all. Maybe he despised her and threw the box in the bay.

And maybe that's what she should have done years ago. But it was too late. Too late to change the past. Too late to make amends. From here on out they would be feeling their way, and she prayed fervently that she hadn't ruined her granddaughter's life. For granddaughter Meri was and would always be. No matter what happened.

When it was six o'clock, she stopped waiting for Alden's call.

She made some buttered toast and tea for her dinner, carried them into the parlor, and ate while watching the nightly news.

It was after six when Meri finally quit work. She was ridiculously stiff, but she'd thrown herself into her work on the ceiling with renewed energy. She would need another area twice as large before there would be enough to show the before-and-after for the fund-raiser that was being planned for late summer.

She'd already discovered a border that probably ran the circumference of the ceiling. Tomorrow she would move toward the center of the ceiling and uncover a new piece of the pattern. On the ceiling as well as her life.

Her work had to be coordinated with the other projects. Like a finely honed machine all the pieces had to come together in a specific way. You couldn't refinish the hardwood floors until the scaffolding was taken down and the walls had been shored up where needed and repaired. The ceiling, the floors, the woodwork—every aspect had to be scheduled according to an overall plan. Discovery and analysis were important, but the workers who performed those steps had to allow time for the paint restorers and muralists to come in and renew examples of the interior to show potential patrons.

Then the whole process would start over again in full. The whole ceiling would then be cleaned. The entire foyer would be repainted in original colors, the woodwork polished, and the floors revitalized. And the process would be repeated in every room.

Meri worked late, then wandered through the rest of the first floor to see what progress the other workers were making. She was procrastinating, she knew. As much as she was curious about what was in the box sitting out in her car, she was afraid to find out what it contained. But she couldn't put it off much longer. Gran was probably sick with worry. Alden hadn't looked too happy about it either.

At least he had the city to distract him; Gran was sitting in the house all alone.

Carlyn was still plugging away at her computer when Meri left. She looked up when Meri waved good night and went back to whatever she was doing.

Carlyn could be working for more money in a comfortable office instead of being surrounded by dust and hammering and skill saws, not to mention potential lead poisoning. But she liked to be where the action was, even if her desk had been scavenged from the curb, and the power was constantly going off while wires were rerouted, or some questionable hardware was exposed. Their project wasn't a high priority on the historic restoration list.

Plus Meri suspected she was just a little enamored of Doug. Which was funny. A teddy bear Doug might be, but Carlyn usually went after hot bodies. Even so, Meri noticed that her friend tended to brighten whenever he entered a room.

Unfortunately Doug was happily married.

She shrugged. Everybody's life was complicated in one way or another. It was time to get hers back on track.

Meri drove home with that damn box sitting on the passenger seat beside her. She fought the urge to just sit in the car and look inside. It might be awful or totally benign, but either way she'd rather be in the privacy of her own apartment when she found out.

Ten minutes later Meri sat on the couch, feet together on the floor, hands in her lap, studying the crumpled cardboard box like it was the Ark of the Covenant. Slowly, she pulled it forward and carefully lifted off the top.

At that point she decided she needed a glass of wine. There was just enough pinot grigio for a half glass left in the bottle in the fridge. She brought it back to the couch. Sat down. Looked in the box. Saw a stack of her report cards, secured by a rubber band.

Maybe this wouldn't be so mind jarring after all. Mentally crossing her fingers, she lifted them out. The rubber band fell away.

Her mother had saved every report card from every school year. She looked at a couple. Straight As. She hadn't received a B until fourth grade in geography. She remembered it perfectly and actually smiled. She'd been shocked when she opened it and saw that big fat B. She'd been mortified to take it home. She'd sat by herself on the long bus ride home and hung her head when she handed it to her mother.

Her mother had been sympathetic. Gran said, "The world's too big to know everything. Don't you worry about it."

And that was that. Though she did put in extra study time on that subject and aced the next marking period.

She put the cards aside and lifted out a pair of baby shoes, white and tiny, with a handwritten card inside: *Meri's first shoes.*

Fireworks went off in Meri's heart. She was loved, she knew it, but it wasn't until she saw those shoes that she understood. She held them, tiny and a little brittle from years of storage. They had a little strap with a tiny nacre snap on the side. She placed them in her lap while she looked at the rest of the contents. Letters from Huey to her mother when they were in college. A jewelry box and a man's wedding ring. Huey's. The man who should have been her father.

So she might never know who her real—no, not real—her birth father was, but she thought Huey would have loved her. And she knew Dan did. She was a Hollis. Now she just had to keep saying that until she completely believed it. Because whenever she stopped and wondered, a niggling fear took a bite out of her peace of mind.

She took out a white paper doily from her parents' wedding reception, *Huey and Laura Rodgers, June 3, 1983, Christ Church*. A photo of her father—she stopped herself—a photo, creased and worn from much handling, of Huey Rodgers on his graduation from flight school. A dried corsage from Meri's senior prom folded inside a piece of waxed paper. A dance card from somebody's sweet sixteen party.

All this time she had thought her dad was dead, that he had died before ever seeing her. Dan was the best father anyone could have, but a question started deep inside her mind and gradually worked its way to the surface. But what if her biological father wasn't dead? Did he know about her?

Was that why her birth mother had run away? She was afraid of him? An involuntary shudder racked Meri's body. Maybe it was better not to know.

She took out a large plastic baggie, sealed and resealed with tape. She had to stop to find scissors to open it. She didn't want to force it open and take the chance of tearing any of the contents. Long years of training had engrained neatness and methodology in her until it was second nature. And though part of her wanted to tear through the plastic, she took her time removing the tape, then carefully slid the contents onto the table.

On the very top was a photograph of a girl and a boy at the beach. Not Huey and Laura. The runaway? Prepregnancy days. They were young, happy, without a care. What had happened to end that happiness? Meri flipped the photo over. No names, no place, no year, just blank white backing paper, yellowed with age. She turned it over and brought it closer to the light, peered at it as familiarity settled on her. And a little disbelief.

Meri set her baby shoes aside and went into the bathroom to look in the mirror, looked again at the photo and again at herself. She looked like the girl. Now that she saw her photograph, she understood why she'd looked just a little different from her half brothers.

She always figured it was because she had a different dad.

She did, and also a different mother. Her mother smiled at her from the photo. Dark hair pulled back on one side. The straight nose, the blue eyes just a little more almond shaped than her mother Laura's eyes. She couldn't tell about the height. The boy stood half a head taller, but there was nothing to judge by. But she recognized Easton Beach. It was less than ten blocks away.

Could they possibly have lived right here in Newport? No, that was crazy; they must have been on vacation. That was it. Vacation and then when she got pregnant, she came back because . . . the boy lived here?

Had her mother's parents searched for her? Had they been inconsolable not to know what happened to her? Why was she buried in the Calder family plot?

Something between anxiety and anticipation pulsed through Meri's extremities. She tried to tell herself it was just the day's coffee at work. But she knew what it really was. A similar feeling had pulsed through her just the other day at work when she lifted her cleaning cloth and saw gold.

Meri went back to the living room and propped the photo against a malacca box she had found at an antique store in Portsmouth. She continued to pull things out of the cardboard box. A death certificate. Baby Rose's. Rose Jones. Mother: Riley Jones. Father: unknown. The certificate had been put in the bag with Riley's possessions—if Riley was her real name; certainly Jones wasn't.

A key ring with a circular medallion, yin and yang, enameled white and black. A cheap bracelet like the ones you won at a carnival or got out of a machine. Two house keys. No car keys.

No driver's license. Maybe she hadn't been old enough to drive. That was a daunting thought. A teenage runaway. Where were her parents? Why hadn't they come to take her home? Had they given up hope of ever finding her?

Meri yawned and glanced at the clock. Had she really spent almost an hour looking at a few trinkets and mementos?

She had so many questions. And at last, hopefully she would learn some of the answers. Because when she returned the things to the bag and moved it from the box, she caught sight of one last item.

She knew what it was, the thing she had been anticipating and dreading, a small notebook, black marbled like the ones you used in school. And she knew what must be inside.

Chapter 8

Meri took a sip of her wine, which was now room temperature, and reached for the notebook. She held it in both hands, just looking at it, knowing that once she opened it she would have to follow it to the end. Then laughed at herself. It might be one of her early essays left over from school.

She opened it to the first page.

It was her mother's writing—not hers. Never the neatest, it was so familiar to her that she could almost feel her mother's presence. Nonsense, of course, but this whole past weekend had been so gothic and weird that she just fell into a mood and wondered if she would even be surprised if her mother materialized right there in her living room.

And a thought struck her so off topic that it took her breath away. Was this Alden's world? Every day surrounded by the fantastic, the frightening, unreal creatures that populated his pages, the faeries, the ogres, the ghosts? Did they also infiltrate his brain, become a part of his life, his way of thinking? Things that had to be tamed, accepted, or driven away.

Because the bizarre things she'd confronted this past weekend were enough to rock her world. Of course hers were real, and his weren't, were they?

She'd have to ask him someday. Right now, she had her own demons to deal with.

She flipped through the pages. It wasn't like true diary entries, but half sentences on one page, a short paragraph on another. Sometimes a whole page or several that flowed together in a long stream of writing. And it seemed to skip back and forth from things as they happened, to her mother's memory of things that had passed.

There was a lot. Every page but the last few were filled with her mother's loopy scrawl. *Why did you have to get sick? Why didn't you tell me all this before you died?*

Meri riffled through the pages looking at dates. At first the entries were close together. And started with the night of Meri's birth. Then the dates tumbled from past to present without obvious reason, a burst of entries followed by long silence. Sometimes a year went by before she wrote again.

Until the last fifteen pages. There the writing became weaker, stretching out on the page then cramming the letters together as if the words were racing to the end, as if they were afraid time would run out before they were finished. As it had.

The last entry ended with *more later if I can*. It was dated two days before her mother died.

Meri turned back to the front page. Took another sip of wine.

There was a long inscription on the top margin, as if written as an afterthought. As a prologue?

The script was so faded that she had to move to the chair that sat beneath the reading lamp. She turned it to full wattage and squinted at the script.

I know I have to put this down on paper. So much has happened that already it is hard to remember how things came about. But they did. And one day it might be important.

April, 1984

I guess it really started the night we heard on the news that a plane had gone down, a passenger plane, the same airline Huey flew for. His flight. It started that moment, the pain. Way before they officially notified me I knew the truth. Huey was dead along with his crew and eighty passengers. It was a mechanical failure, there would be an investigation. I would be remunerated.

Remuneration. It was too soon for my husband to die. It was too early for the baby to come. But he did, and she did.

For two months I lay on my back trying to save the only thing left of my marriage while inside I raged against being left alone after two years of happiness. I loved Huey and I swore I would never love anyone else, except this baby if God would only let me keep her.

But he didn't. She just came, hardly with a pain, or a cry, no time to even get to the car much less to the hospital. Katy Dewar came from over at Briggs Pond. But it was too late when she got here.

Meri wiped tears away, reached for her wine. Surely this was more than any daughter needed to know.

I went a little crazy. I wanted to die, what was left for me? Huey gone, my little girl gone. We would have named her Rose. They let me hold her for only a second. Then took her away. I begged for just a few more minutes, but Katy said there were things to be done. Rose was never even put in the crib that Huey and I found in Grover's junk store and refinished together. I never saw her again. Little Rose. We buried her a few days later. But that was after the storm came.

Meri shook herself. This was more than she could stand. She closed the book, got up, and went to the window to stare out. The street was quiet. It was late and off-season. Everyone was in bed, getting a good night's sleep before work the next day. Where she would be tomorrow, up on that scaffolding cleaning away paint like nothing had happened.

Her eyes were gritty and her stomach burned. She needed tissues, water, and something to eat. She went to the kitchen and opened the fridge.

Empty, except for a six-pack of water. She took a bottle and closed the door. Looked in a cabinet and found a nearly empty jar of peanut butter, no crackers, no bread. She got a spoon and carried the peanut butter and bottle of water back to her chair.

They tried to take me to the hospital but I fought them off. Why take care of me? There was nothing left to me. Nothing. Empty. Crazy. I could see them looking at each other, Katy worried, Mother worried and scared. I heard Katy say she wouldn't leave until I was "out of the woods."

The next afternoon, or maybe the next, a storm came in, a big one. One minute it was sunny and then black. The wind howled, just like I felt, and the rain came so hard you couldn't see across the yard.

It was warm and bright inside though. All the lights on, not even flickering as they did in most storms. I just thought of that now. Why didn't the lights go out? Mother had forced me to the kitchen to eat some soup she had made. Katy helped me to my chair. I didn't need help. I wasn't physically sick, my heart was broken.

Mother had just filled the bowls when there was a pounding on the door. At first I thought it was the wind, or a tree branch, but Mother rushed to open it. And little A from across the way fell inside to the floor. He was soaked and freezing. He tried to say something, but his teeth were chattering so hard we couldn't understand him.

"Is it your father?" Mother asked. He shook his head. "Her. On the beach. Help her."

God, I'll never forget his words or the look of sheer terror on that boy's face.

Meri sat up. Little A? Who was little A? But she thought she knew. What other A lived in the only house across the way, but Alden? She read ahead, wondering where all this was going. There was some more writing that was indecipherable, but she just skipped over it. She'd go back later and read every word. But for now . . .

K, who's a sturdy woman, told me to gather some heavy blankets and she carried him upstairs. When I reached the bedroom where she'd taken him, he was already under the covers. We piled on more blankets. K told me to watch him, and she and Mother hurried away. He was so pale, I just fell down on my knees like a child and prayed that he wouldn't be taken, too.

The passage ended. Meri turned the page.

My God, she's a mere child. Not much older than A. She wasn't anyone from around here. I couldn't imagine why she would be out here alone and on the beach.

She was awake but could barely stand, and K and Mother had to practically carry her up the stairs. I went to get a nightgown for her and when I came back, she was sitting on the bed wrapped in a blanket. When she raised her hands to put on the nightgown, I saw and understood.

She was pregnant. Very pregnant. And my heart broke

all over again. Even as I looked enviously at her huge round belly, she doubled over and screamed. I recoiled, I admit it. But only for a moment, then I prayed that she would deliver her baby safely and it would be healthy and it would live.

They laid her back on the bed, just as another cry was wrenched from her.

I'll call for an ambulance, Mamma said. K lifted the nightgown, pushed the girl's knees up, and said, No time.

And that's when things began for me. When my will to live came back again.

Everything began happening at once, and not easy. Not like with me. Not just an exhale and she was gone. But with flailing and screaming. The baby came quickly. Katy said she must have been in labor for hours. It was horrifying to consider. Out in the storm and in labor. I hope when A wakes up, he can tell us what happened.

He did wake up. The baby came on the most bloodcurdling scream you've ever heard, and I remember thinking this girl never had Lamaze classes. It was a stupid thing to think at a time like that, but that's the way the mind works sometimes.

Katy did what midwives do and swaddled the baby in a blanket that had been heating on the radiator. I was holding the girl's hand; she'd been clutching it so hard that it hurt, now it lay still in mine. But she was breathing.

The door burst open and A stood there wrapped in a quilt. "Don't hurt her!"

K came to him and leaned over and braced her hands on her knees to look him in the eye. "She's fine. That was good screaming. She's had a baby. Do you want to see?"

He nodded. I remember his cheeks were flushed, but the rest of him was shockingly pale. The quilt trailed behind him as he followed her over to the crib where my baby would never lie. Now a healthy baby lay there.

He peered down at her then looked at me. "Is that your baby?"

Tears just came to my eyes and I couldn't speak.

"Hush, child," Mother said.

He frowned at her, puzzled, looked back at the baby. "What's her name?" he asked. And from the bed where the girl lay almost motionless came one word. Merielle.

Meri wiped away a tear, emotion for all those people filling her and spilling over. And the dawning of the enormity of what they had done and were about to do made her want to fling the book away. But she couldn't stop reading. Her head was aching, and she felt sick to her stomach. She was stiff from sitting at weird angles while working on the ceiling all day, then sitting tensed and balled up in the chair reading this account of her birth.

And she had to get to work tomorrow. Reluctantly, she put the book back, covered it with the other items that had come with it, and carried it to her bedroom. Looked around and finally put it on the top shelf of her closet.

Meri quickly got ready for bed, crawled beneath the covers, and remembered that she had promised to call Gran. It was way too late. It would have to wait. She lay back, forced her muscles to relax, and let her thoughts unwind. She was thinking of her mother Laura and her mother the teenaged girl and wondering, as her eyes finally closed on sleep, how and why Alden had been there when she was born.

Alden sat in the near darkness of the hotel bar, nursing a drink he didn't want. The rock star's creatures were rolled up in his editor's office waiting approval from said rock star. Alden thought he would feel lighter, less moody when they were gone. Work could do that to you. You got so involved in the process, the development, that you took on the character of the work. Everything seemed to fall apart since he'd started on the nightmare souls that peopled the man's memoir.

He didn't even know why someone like that would want to remember the life he led. Actually he was amazed that the man had any memory left at all. From the accounts of his life with drugs, drink, and indiscriminate sex, he should be dead.

But now that the nasty little creatures were literally out of his hands, Alden didn't feel a whit better. Possibly because of all the other stuff that was going on in his life.

He couldn't shake the memory of Meri, drenched in the rain, body shivering and face etched in anger. He'd been totally out of his element. Before then, things had always been what they were—comfortable in some ways, open-ended and frustrating in others.

She'd been mad at him before, countless times, over various things he did or didn't do, did or didn't think, but this was the first time her anger had frightened him. Because it was just the beginning.

She was probably sitting in her apartment right now. Reading the damn diary. Finding out about his part in the whole drama. Though frankly he had forgotten most of it.

He glanced at his watch. If he hurried, he could catch the last train back to Portsmouth. But he'd agreed to meet Paige Whitaker for a drink and whatever came after, usually her apartment or his hotel room.

He'd called her to let her know he would be in town. He thought it would be good to take his mind off everything. But now he wished he hadn't.

He looked at his watch again. It was too late to cancel. She'd be here any minute. Even as he thought it she appeared in the doorway. The brighter light of the lobby silhouetted her; she was tall and slim, with hair sleek to her shoulders. Nice woman, smart, inventive in bed, not interested in monogamy or commitment, which worked for him. But tonight for the first time in the year or two he'd been seeing her, he was struck by how much she resembled Meri.

God, was he attracted to her because somehow she reminded him of the child he'd promised to protect, the woman she'd grown up to be, or was it just a play of the light because he had Meri on his mind?

Paige saw him, smiled, and made her way across the room. He gulped down the rest of his drink and stood up. "Paige. You look wonderful."

Meri knew she'd been dreaming when she woke up shivering, with the covers tossed to the floor. She pulled them back onto the bed and curled up beneath them, determined to go back to sleep. It was still early, too early to get up and face a day of intricate detail work.

But it was a no-go, and after forty minutes of unsuccessful willing herself back to sleep, she got up. She showered and dressed and spent a long time staring into her closet at the box on the top shelf. She was tempted to take it down and read a few more pages, but she knew once she started, she wouldn't want to stop, so she closed the closet door. The past could wait until tonight.

She drove to work and arrived so early that Doug was just getting out of his car when she drove into the parking lot. He waited for her to get out and they walked into the house together.

"You're early."

"Wanted to get an early start. You're awfully dressed up."

He was wearing a suit and a striped tie, the same striped tie he dragged out for meetings and benefits unless it was black tie.

"Meeting this morning. I was just picking up some notes."

They walked inside together. Doug turned up the thermostat and the radiators clanked to life. In a couple of hours it might actually be warm enough to work. April in Newport was turning into spring but the nights were still cold.

Doug gathered up a pile of papers, stuffed them into a battered attaché case, and left again.

Carlyn came in while Meri was making the coffee.

"What's going on?" Carlyn asked while she shrugged out of jacket and gloves. "Why are you here so early?"

"Got up early. Anxious to get on with it."

"Where was Doug going?"

"He said he had a meeting."

"Good." Carlyn dropped her briefcase on the kitchen table and reached for two coffee mugs. "I just hope he comes back with some good news."

"He didn't seem very happy this morning, and neither do you. What's going on? Something with the project?"

"Well, between you, me, and the fence post, we're spending money faster than I'm finding it for him. He's talking about cutting down to four days a week. Which means less pay for everyone."

"But good weather is on its way, which means we won't have to use heat; that's got to cost a bundle."

Carlyn merely nodded.

The coffeepot beeped. Meri poured coffee into the mugs and handed one to Carlyn.

"Thanks." Carlyn took a sip. "It's just that there are a bunch of big projects at the moment. They, of course, get first dibs on the available grant money."

"You've been doing a great job of finding cash."

"Thanks. I'm working on it, constantly. But I'm behind on the rest of my work. What we need is either a full-time fund-raiser or a secretary/archiver."

"What about an intern?"

Carlyn gave her an are-you-out-of-your-mind look. "An

intern could archive while I fund-raised, but by the time I taught the person the system, we'd be out of money again."

"Catch twenty-two," Meri said sympathetically. "Well, then I'd better get started and try to ramp up my work rate."

"Did you bring your lunch?"

"I haven't had time to get to the store."

"Me neither. I'll order something from Grady's; know what you want?"

"Nope, anything's fine."

"Noon okay?"

"Perfect. Now I better climb up my stairway to heaven if I'm going to finish this grid before the weekend."

Meri worked methodically for the first few hours. By late morning she'd completed the first square of the grid, and she began on the next. Her fingers were sore from the cleaning, which involved pressing just enough to remove the outer layers without destroying the original and using a dull blade and brush to remove the paint stuck in the crevices of the ornamentation. She'd said she'd ramp up her speed, but it was impossible. Any faster and work became sloppy, and there was no place for that in restoration.

But she could already tell that it was going to be a beaut. And with the discovery of the Owen Jones parlor wallpaper and the woodwork, there should be enough to garner interest from potential patrons. From Doug's mood, and what Carlyn said, they needed all the help they could get.

Meri was finishing a particularly stubborn spot when she noticed a hairline crack in the paint job running away from the center medallion. She didn't think much about it; old houses settled, cracks formed. It was the nature of things.

But a few minutes later, the inch-square section she'd been trying to clean crumbled and fell, taking a larger piece and several layers of paint with it. She just managed to catch a handful before it hit the scaffold's floor. She gently laid it on a piece of cardboard and turned on her flashlight to take a look.

And saw what she least wanted to see. The underbelly of the paint was cratered with bits of white plaster and black specks of mold. Evidence of past or present moisture. Enough to grow mold.

"Damn," she said out loud. She bagged the piece and sealed it, then maneuvered to get a better look at the ceiling. She slowly ran the light over the crack and surrounding area peering closely at the paint, poking and prodding with her finger. Everything seemed dry enough; the paint was hard and there didn't appear to be any other weak or soft patches around the crack.

It was probably from an earlier leak somewhere. Hopefully it had been repaired. But they would have to make sure and that could take up precious time they didn't have.

Evidence of moisture could be linked to a burst pipe, a flood on the second floor, a slow leak, or gutters that had probably not been cleaned while the house sat abandoned or even while it was a boardinghouse. It could be from the roof, or loose chimney flashing. Whatever had caused it, finding it and fixing it would be a pain in the butt.

She would have to take the fallen piece down to show Doug. Hopefully they wouldn't have to call in the EPA again.

It was close enough to lunchtime to take a break. She put away her tools and double-checked her workspace. God forbid a truck rattled past and sent an X-Acto knife hurtling down on the heads of her coworkers.

Holding the dubious specimen, Meri climbed down to the first floor and made her way back to the kitchen. No one was there, so she left the bag on Doug's desk and went to clean up for lunch.

When she came back, Carlyn was paying the delivery boy.

"Add that to what I owe you from Friday," Meri said and started pulling food out of the bag.

"Hungry?" Carlyn asked.

"Ravenous. I managed to miss dinner and breakfast this morning. I really have to get to the grocery store tonight."

"You're not broke, are you?"

"No. I have money, just no time." *Or inclination,* Meri thought. Yesterday she'd dreaded seeing what was in the box her mother had left, and today all she really wanted to do was get home and read more of the diary.

Doug came in a few minutes later, looking harassed and disheveled. No wonder Carlyn was carrying a torch; he was completely adorable.

He poured himself a cup of coffee, but instead of carrying it over to his desk, he sat down at the table with the two of them and heaved out a sigh.

Meri pushed the sugar container toward him. He poured a stream of sugar into his cup. He seemed so distracted that he might have just kept pouring if Carlyn hadn't snatched it out of his hand.

He grumbled to himself.

"What's the matter, boss?" Meri asked.

Doug scrubbed his face then looked over his fingers at her. "Where do you want me to start? The part where we're over budget and we haven't even come close to finishing the projected work for the quarter? Or the part where we lost the Lendenthal grant to the Hopkins House?"

"Ah, crap," Carlyn said. "Nasty break."

Doug rumbled some more.

"Well, we'll just have to plug along," Meri said, trying to be optimistic and wishing she didn't have to inform him of the envelope sitting on his desk.

"It's not you. It's everyone. Not that any of you are working too slowly. I only hire the meticulous best. I'm not going to start cutting corners now, and I'm not going to paint the whole damn house white."

"Uh-oh," Carlyn said. "You've been talking to Sweeney again."

"It's not her fault. She's juggling a list an arm long of people wanting grants to restore."

"I'm working on getting some corporate sponsors."

"And don't think I don't appreciate it. Ah, what the hell, we'll see it through. Somehow."

"We always do," Meri said. She stood and gathered up her trash then stopped. "But I have to warn you, we may have a bit of a problem with the ceiling."

"Oh God, what now?"

Meri walked over to the desk and lifted the envelope. "This fell off the ceiling while I was working this morning."

Doug took it, turned on the desk lamp, and pulled out a jeweler's loupe. "And this just broke off?"

"Yeah, no warning; everything felt solid. It was near a settling crack but nothing to indicate the paint or the plaster were compromised."

"Damn."

"It didn't look too bad. I'm going to do a few random samples this afternoon, just to check it out. Hopefully it's an isolated occurrence, and if need be, we can just inject some adhesive . . . fingers crossed. I'd hate to lose too much of the original pattern until we get a good schematic of it."

"Me, too. Do what you need to do. Wear a ventilator."

"Doug," Meri whined, knowing he was right and that she'd been lucky so far not to have to totally suit up.

"Do it."

"I could have been a dental assistant and done all this work right side up—and wear makeup."

Doug cracked a smile. Mission accomplished.

"Just do it."

Meri saluted. "Aye, aye, Captain."

"And a hard hat," he called after her.

As Meri reached the hall her cell rang. She fished it out of her pocket and checked caller ID. Her heart gave a painful thump. *Peter.*

She listened to it ring, while adrenaline coursed through her. What if he'd changed his mind? Wanted her to come to California with him? Or maybe he'd decided not to go. She wasn't ready to tell him her history, but she couldn't not tell him, if they wanted to stay together.

The phone rang again; one more ring and it would go to voice mail. She pressed answer. Took a breath. "Hi."

Chapter 9

I can't stand this."

No hello, no whatcha doing? And Meri didn't know what to say. So she waited.

"Can we please talk? I realize that I should have waited until after dinner to spring the whole California thing on you, but I was so excited. Let's have a drink tonight or I could come over and bring a bottle of wine."

No, not at her apartment. Not with the diary in the next room. She needed time. And she needed to finish the rest of the entries or at least the ones from that year before she could decide how much to tell him or Carlyn—or anyone.

"I can't tonight."

"What about tomorrow or Thursday? I have to drive out to see the parents for the weekend."

"I—"

"Come on, Meri. Let's just talk. Things happened too fast. I miss you already. I'm not willing to give up just because I'm gone for the summer." Pause. "Are *you*?"

Of course she wasn't, but how did she say, *It's not you, It's me,* without sounding like every television serial out there. But it was true. What was she afraid of? If she loved and trusted him, wouldn't she want to tell him? "How about tomorrow after I get off work? But let's meet at Grady's. It will be quiet and we can talk."

"Good. You want me to pick you up?"

"No. I'll meet you there. I'm not sure if I'll be coming straight from work or not."

"Things picking up around there?"

She had to smile; things didn't pick up in the restoration world, they just plodded along like the proverbial tortoise, enjoying the process, reveling in the minutiae of discovery, until the final reveal. Or until the money ran out.

"Pretty busy. See you tomorrow."

She stopped by the equipment room and checked out a respirator. Her hard hat was already on the scaffolding platform. She hated using it. Between the hat, the ventilator, the head lamp, and the light scope, it put too many obstacles between her and the study area.

On the other hand, she didn't want the ceiling coming down on her head, or to risk breathing in mold or lead dust.

Before she climbed up, she stopped to chat with Joe Krosky, who was working on the parlor walls. Joe was an intern from University of Rhode Island, but not your typical intern. He was taking a break from Ph.D. work in molecular biology. His hobby was renovation.

He was one of those perennially energetic people, who bounced on their toes while attempting to stand still. Only when he was working did he seem to enter some Zen state of quietude. He always wore the same thing to work: white painter's overalls and a bright red bandanna securing his bushy carrot-red hair.

"Any mold?" Meri asked as she watched him meticulously trace the wallpaper pattern near the arched doorway.

"Nope, but I shudder to think what's been chewing on the woodwork."

Meri did shudder just thinking about it. "I'm sure whatever it was, is gone."

"I hope so. I keep expecting to turn around and find an audience of rodents sitting up on their hind legs ready to applaud."

"With little top hats and white shirt fronts?"

Joe bounced on his toes. "And spats." He went back to work, serenity returned.

Meri went out to the foyer and climbed up the ladder.

She spent the afternoon inspecting for mold, loosened paint, and weakened plaster. It was boring work, so she was surprised when Joe called up to say work was ending early and Doug wanted them to come down to the kitchen.

Meri pulled off her respirator and leaned over the edge of the scaffolding. "Please tell me someone's having a birthday."

Joe shook his head, sending dust from his red bandanna. "Maybe we got a another grant. That would be cool."

It would be a godsend. But Meri wasn't optimistic. She just hoped it wasn't bad news.

Joe waited for her to pack up and climb down, and they followed the others in the exodus to the kitchen.

They were the last to arrive and the kitchen was filled with anxious faces, a far cry from the celebration of only a few nights before. And Meri got a sinking feeling that all their lives were about to change and not for the better.

Doug seemed to have aged since lunch, and Carlyn looked grim. What could possibly have happened in the last few hours?

Doug cleared his throat, a rumble that rolled through the uncannily quiet room. "You've all been doing a dynamite job," he began.

"Uh-oh," Joe said in Meri's ear and began to bounce.

"But I'll just say this straight out. We lost the Lendenthal grant."

A general whisper of disappointment.

"There are other grants," Lizzy Blanchard said. She'd only been hired three weeks before; this was her first job as a journeyman glazier.

"There are," Carlyn said. "And we're working on getting them. And we're still in the running for two smaller grants."

"But," Doug said, "in order to keep working at all until we raise more money, I'm afraid . . ." He paused as if the words literally stuck in his throat. "I'm going to have to cut back on staff."

This was met with total silence.

Someone whispered, "We're getting laid off?"

"Good thing I'm a volunteer," Joe said brightly and bounced even higher.

Doug nodded, attempting a smile and failing.

"What if we just cut back on our hours?" The master carpenter, a man well into his sixties, had been laid off at his last renovation for the same reason. Money was tight everywhere. "I'd rather work for less than go back to kitchens and closets."

That got some sympathetic nods.

"Carlyn and I have been going over the books. It might be possible to move to a four-day week and rotate hours, if everyone is willing or can afford to do that. Those of you who can't, I totally understand."

Doug heaved a sigh large enough to fill the room. "The project has just had more problems than we'd foreseen. It will be a beauty in the long run. I'm sure of that. Just not sure how long the long run is going to be at this point."

Carlyn exchanged looks with Meri. She looked like she might burst into tears. Meri pretty much felt the same way. It was selfish, she knew, but with her personal life in upheaval, the question of her birth looming in the unknown, she'd been clinging to work to keep herself sane.

But she couldn't work for free; she was barely making it as it was. Still, she was excited about her ceiling. She liked working for Doug and spending work time with Carlyn, Joe, and the others.

Doug had put together a great crew. Students and volunteers, craftspeople on their way up or happy to be part of a small operation rather than one of many at a large firm. Artists, painters, gilders, glaziers, masons, all who came in on a need basis, because they respected Doug as a conservator.

He had a knack for discovering ugly ducklings and bringing them back to unexpected beauty. He took on projects that others turned up their noses at. Consequently, in spite of his successes, he was always working on a shoestring budget.

Meri had a few months' worth of rent saved. And if it came to it, she could give up her apartment and commute from Gran's. Would she do that? For one project?

For this project, she thought she might.

"So think about it for a day or two. Then I'll talk to you all individually. Whatever you decide, I understand. Now everybody go home and try not to worry."

The group reluctantly filed out of the kitchen. Some headed back to their stations to finish up for the day, and maybe for the project. Some went straight to the parking lot, probably to discuss what to do or to hit the want ads.

How had things gone so bad since lunch? Meri hung back until only she and Carlyn were left.

"Give me the worst," Meri said.

"The backers are wondering whether the house is worth the restoration."

"Hell, yeah," Meri said. "Underneath the crap is a gem, I feel it."

"So does Doug. Not everyone has his confidence."

"Well, we'll just have to show them, won't we."

"That's what I told him." Carlyn shrugged. "He feels like it's his fault."

"That's our Dougie." Meri sighed, trying not to think what

this might mean for her. "Well, I'm going to stay as long as I can. I can do double duty at the lab and help with the layer analysis. I don't think I can speed up the cleaning. All that decorative molding has been globbed with paint layers, and it's slow going. But I'll get down to the original pattern. Hell, I'll even do the tracing."

"At the rate we're going, you may have to do the painting and gilding."

Meri held up her hand. "Not my forte, I'm afraid. But tell Doug I'm in for as long as I can afford it."

"Thanks."

"I take it you're staying."

Carlyn shrugged. "As long as I can afford it."

Meri climbed up the scaffolding once more to catalog her findings of the day and retrieve her tools and equipment. She returned the respirator and hard hat to the equipment room, did a quick cleanup of hands and face, and carried her notes to the workroom where she logged them in the daily ledger. Doug wasn't around and neither was Carlyn, but Meri guessed they were somewhere in the building regrouping and brainstorming about additional means of income.

Joe stuck his head in the door. He'd donned his leather jacket. A cardboard tube stuck out of the messenger bag slung across his chest. "I'm dropping by the lab on my way home. Got anything that needs to go?"

"Joe, bless you. Yes. Just this one sample." Meri found the moldy plaster sample and quickly scribbled a note to Lou, the lab intern, to bump it to the front of the queue. Joe carefully placed the sample in the messenger bag and bounced his way out to the parking lot.

A few minutes later she heard the rumble of his Kawasaki as he turned into the street.

Now that it was the end of the day, Meri was anxious to get home. On her way to her locker to get her coat and bags, she heard voices coming from Carlyn's office. "Good night, all," she called.

Doug's shaggy head appeared, Cheshire cat style, in the doorway. "Carlyn told me you'll stay. Thanks."

"My pleasure. I'm the last one, I think. See you tomorrow."

She'd been absorbed in her work all day, but as soon as evening came on, Meri's mind turned to the diary waiting to be read. Suddenly anxious to get home and to the diary, she hurried through the house to the back door and was almost jogging as she reached her car. But once in the car, she remembered she had to get to the grocery store. The cupboard was beyond bare; she didn't even have enough dish detergent to wash a plate even if she could find something to put on it.

She pulled down the visor and took a quick look in the mirror. She wouldn't be going anywhere without a shower. Even the most dedicated restorer wouldn't show up at the Stop & Shop the way she looked.

Tomorrow for sure she'd go. Tonight, she'd have to order in.

Therese wanted to call Meri. She wanted to know she was okay and to learn whether she had looked in the box or read the diary. She hadn't read it herself. But Laura said it was there, and that she had written it first to keep herself sane, then to explain to Meri what had happened. And third, in case there were any legal ramifications, she wanted just what had occurred down in writing.

Therese had asked, what legal ramifications? A baby died, a baby was born, and a baby was given a loving home. There had been no question as to what to do. Anybody would have done the same.

She was a farmer's wife and farmer's daughter; when a calf lost its mamma, you fed it, gave it a home. Therese wasn't so naive, however, as to think it would be the same with humans. They should have taken Meri to Social Services and filled out a form to foster her—and take the chance of losing out to some couple who would starve her and mistreat her, and do horrible things to her, just because they wanted the money the state would pay them.

Therese knew about these things. Her best friend in school had been fostered out with her two younger brothers. They were split up. She lost track of them. She never saw her friend or her brothers again. But she heard the youngest had been arrested and died in a fight in jail.

That's what fostering could do to the young and the helpless. Not always, but you never knew. Maybe the other two were lucky and went to families who loved them. Maybe they had even made a good life for themselves and were happy.

But neither Laura nor she had been willing to take a chance with that precious baby who was left in their care.

Therese took a wet cloth to the kitchen table. She'd cleaned it already after lunch, but she cleaned it again, just to have something to do. But she kept one ear out for the telephone.

She didn't expect Meri to call. She was busy. And Therese figured Alden had been too busy to call, too. Sometimes she hated being out here all alone, and not knowing what was going on with the rest of her family. Her side of the family were spread out over creation, but the Hollises, they stayed in touch.

But they were all busy with school and business and babies on the way. Babies had a way of taking over your life. And it shouldn't be any other way. If they could just stay innocent forever.

"Old woman," she scoffed. She was well over eighty, though vain person that she was, she always lied and made herself younger. She usually didn't feel old, but tonight . . . Tonight she felt her age and more.

She looked out the window. She knew Alden wouldn't be back today. Maybe tomorrow.

She'd bake a nice cherry pie; she still had two jars from the batch they'd put up last July. She'd have it ready when he got back, just as a thank-you for taking care of Meri.

That's what she'd do. Make a pie.

She got down the yellow Fiesta mixing bowl, then went to the pantry for the flour and Crisco. She'd bake a pie and everything would turn out all right.

Meri and the delivery boy arrived at her door simultaneously. He waited for her to rummage in her purse for his payment, handed her the bag of food, and left before she'd even found her door keys.

She would have been better off saving her money and having a can of soup. Only she was fresh out of soup and the pad thai aroma coming from the bag as she carried it upstairs was enough to make her salivate.

But not enough to make her forget the diary.

Meri stopped in the kitchen long enough to get a bottle of water, then placed the bag and the water on the coffee table and went to get the diary out of her closet.

> *She says her name is Jane, though neither Mother nor K believe her. She says she went to see K, but she wasn't home. A girl there, her apprentice I imagine, told her K had come to Calder Farm and might not be back for a while. So she hitched a ride. Hitched a ride in her condition! They brought her as far as the crossroads. But she got confused, didn't know which house, and decided to end it all.*
>
> *End it all. How could she even contemplate doing something like that and taking another helpless life with her? We were all horrified when she said that, and I confess, at that I felt a red hot anger. I think I wanted to kill her for even contemplating doing such a thing, much less carrying it out,*

when I would give anything to have my baby here safe and sound.

She went out to the breakers, but couldn't go through with it. She saw our lights on and decided to try to come here, but the rain started and the rocks were slippery and she couldn't get back to shore. Then she saw the dinghy and called for help.

She looked toward the boy when she said that. "You saved me," she said. And I think how the ocean could have taken all three of them. Two innocents and this girl. Maybe she too is innocent. It's hard for me not to feel bitter, I admit. I put it into words on paper and hope that I can get past my feelings and try to help her.

She's sleeping now. As we were tiptoeing out of the room, she roused, told the boy to come back, which he did. She held his wrist and looked at us huddled by the door like the three witches from Macbeth. She was waiting for us to leave. What could she possibly have to say to a boy that young beyond thank you? She didn't need us to leave to say that. She had already thanked each of us. Mother and K exchanged looks, then we all left the room.

She's polite and well bred; you can tell that even in the state she's in. But she's frightened of something or someone and she won't tell us where she came from or who she really is. Hopefully she will learn to trust us.

We didn't go downstairs but stood just on the other side of the door, our ears pressed to the wood. At first we heard only murmurs. Mother put her fingers to her lips and we leaned against the door, all three of us. But all we heard was Jane say, "Promise me," and the boy reply, "I promise."

It isn't right, Mother said. That a strange girl with an un-known past and an unexplained baby would be demanding promises from a boy not yet thirteen. But what could we *do? A didn't say a thing when he came out still wrapped in that quilt, clutching it so tightly that his knuckles were white. He was deathly pale himself, except for the flush of his cheeks, which I hope isn't the onset of a fever.*

I wanted to touch his hair, push the curls from his forehead where his hair has begun to dry.

Whatever the girl made him promise, it has frightened him. What on earth could it be?

Meri's hand went to her throat. Alden had been there. It was his dinghy that the girl saw. She'd hailed him and he'd gone to her. Somehow he had gotten close enough to the breakers without capsizing the boat and got her to shore. But he hadn't been able to get her to the house, so he had run for help.

Meri wiped at her face and realized that her cheeks were wet from tears she hadn't felt fall. Just the tightness in her throat. They'd all known and conspired to keep her past from her. She knew it was because they loved her and wanted to protect her. But she wished, really wished, that her mother had told her sooner, because right now she could use her mother's love, her reassurance, her touch, a kiss on Meri's cheek, a comforting hug.

Instead she got pad thai.

Mother took the boy downstairs. She called his father and W is bringing him dry clothes. I don't know what he must think. Mother will tell him what she thinks best, though I'm afraid he will go hard on the boy. He's old school about sparing the rod. Not that he's abusive. He's just firm.

Meri mechanically lifted a mouthful of noodles to her mouth. It was like reading a novel, not like a real diary. But it must be real. Her mother had a fanciful streak, but not this fanciful.

*Wilton came and while A went to change, Mother ex-
plained what had happened as best she could. Wilton and
the boy left together.*

Meri turned the page. The next entry was the following
morning.

*"Jane" is gone! When I came to wake her for breakfast,
her bed was empty, her clothes gone. She left a scrap of
paper that said keep my baby forever, please.*

*She didn't have extra clothes, or a heavy jacket, and the
weather has turned unseasonably cold. And she left her
baby. Merielle. How could she do such a thing?*

*Mother wanted to call the police, but K stopped her. She
explained that they couldn't start searching until forty-eight
hours had passed and we'd do better to start looking for her
ourselves. We all went out to search, K to the dunes and the
breakwater beach, Mother out across the fields.*

*They made me stick close to home, because I wasn't fully
recovered from—I can't even say it. And someone had to
stay with the baby. But I searched the house, the outbuild-
ings, calling the girl's name, but she never answered. Maybe
she was hiding and didn't trust us to help her. What could
make a girl so frightened? Unless she had broken the law.
Or she'd been abused.*

Meri knew it had been coming, that possibility that her
mother had been abused. Somehow she thought it would be
easier to know her mother had robbed a bank or even killed
someone than to learn she'd been raped by someone in her
own family or a family friend, even a stranger. That would be
an awful end to a life.

An awful beginning for a baby. She shuddered. And fervently hoped that this question would eventually be answered

by the diary. Because if it weren't, she didn't know how she would reconcile herself to not knowing.

> *The baby, Merielle, precious little Meri, began to cry. I lifted her out of the crib and my milk let down. I was surprised. My blouse was wet from it. I didn't think about that. I sat in the rocking chair with her and she nuzzled my breast. I didn't think I would have enough milk, but she latched on and pulled and pulled until she fell asleep.*

Meri dropped the book on the coffee table. *TMI, Mom.* She went to the little kitchen and looked in the fridge. Nope, still nothing there. She heartily wished for a glass of wine but settled for another bottle of water. She was tempted to go to the store. But she knew she couldn't leave until "Jane" was found and Meri found out what happened to the baby.

She froze with her hand reaching for the water. Really? Find out what happened to the baby? The baby was her. She knew what happened to it; it grew up as a Calder. What she needed to know was why.

She returned to the couch, picked up the diary, and found where she'd left off.

> *I held her while she slept. I didn't want to put her down. I didn't think I would be able to put her down. Because weird ideas were filling my mind. And while Mother and K were searching the fields for Meri's mother, she became mine.*

Meri read the words. Reread them. Maybe she didn't know what happened at all. Maybe she didn't want to find out. And the questions she had been suppressing for days shot to the surface of her mind. How had the young mother—her mother—died? Why was she buried in the family plot? And how far would Laura Calder go to keep her baby?

Chapter 10

Meri glanced at the clock. No way was she going to get through this diary at the rate she was going. She couldn't keep reading and be useful at the project tomorrow. She couldn't do that to Doug, not if they were going to be forced into a mandatory Fridays-off schedule.

She could take it to work with her and read it on her lunch break, but how would she explain what she was reading to Carlyn or anyone else?

She would have to tell Carlyn eventually, but not until she knew the whole story. At least as much as was known. And to do that she needed to talk to Gran and confront her reticent neighbor about what his place was in all of this, how he'd found her mother and saved her, and why he'd never told her what he knew.

She went back to reading, this time skimming the least pertinent passages. She'd go back over it on the weekend, but right now, she just wanted to know what happened to "Jane."

Katy has gone home to deal with the birth certificates. There was much discussion about what to do. They must be filed eventually. She's holding off in the hopes that "Jane" comes back for her baby. But there has been no sign of her. We listen to the news and called the hospitals, but no one fitting her description has been found. I hope she's okay.

Wilton came over today while Mother and I were sitting at the kitchen table having a cup of tea and Meri was napping. He and Alden had been out on the breakers and found a backpack. It had gotten wedged in the rocks. It has to belong to her. He dropped it in the sink since it was pretty sandy and wet, nodded, and left. He didn't give us time to say thank you or ask about Alden.

It's a sad commentary on a young life: a pair of jeans and a pullover, a rolled-up sweatshirt, a picture of a boy with no name on it, and a sodden picture book of mythology. So sad. Mother plans to press it in hopes of saving some of the pages. And at the bottom was a wallet, no credit cards, and very little cash. There is a student ID. Riley Rochfort. Rochfort. Everyone around here knows that name.

We have promised not to look for her family or return her baby to them. She even wrote out a simple "adoption" paper, which comes nowhere near being legal. She wouldn't say why she is so adamant that they not find her or learn about the baby. But one thing I know. This is not the spiteful revenge of a spoiled teenager. I can only guess why she is so afraid, and that brings out exaggerated nightmares that I fervently hope are not true.

This much I know. I won't give up this baby to people who will harm her, neglect her, or toss her into the Social Services system.

Meri's eyes ached from reading the faded writing. It was almost midnight. She should go to bed. She stretched out her arms, cracked her neck. And continued reading.

They found Riley this morning. We heard it on the news;
we hoped that it wasn't her. A young girl stepped in front
of a tractor trailer. The driver tried to swerve but it was too
late. They say she died instantly. Wilton drove Mother to the
police station and she identified her. Oh, Riley, why did you
do it? We would have taken care of you and the baby. Why
did you have to run away?

Meri stopped reading. Riley had stepped in front of a truck. On purpose? An accident? They would never know. *She* would never know. And suddenly it didn't matter what happened next. Her mother had left her and stepped in front of a truck. Good God. If her life was so bad, why hadn't she just gotten rid of the baby? *Rid of me,* Meri amended. And she had to admit she was glad Riley hadn't taken that option.

Meri put the diary down. She was maxed out. She'd learned the gist of what she wanted to know. The rest could wait. She returned the diary to the box and the box to the closet. She got ready for bed, but she didn't go to sleep. Riley Rochfort. Her mother. It was an unusual name—except in Newport circles. The name belonged to one of the minor gilded satellites, a contributor to restoration projects and on the boards of several philanthropic organizations.

Those Rochforts were a local family with a lot of clout. Was Riley one of them? Maybe the diary would tell her. Or maybe her grandmother would know. If not, there was always Google.

Meri settled down, determined to sleep, but sleep eluded her until the sky lightened into dawn. She knew how Pandora felt when she opened that jar and released all the evils on the world. The questions that whirled around in Meri's brain might easily be her undoing. Where the answers led might be worse than not knowing.

When the alarm went off at eight o'clock, Meri dragged out of bed and went to work.

Coffee was made, but there was no sign of Doug or Carlyn. Meri poured herself a half cup, not wanting to jangle her nerves more than lack of sleep and stress had already done, and lowered herself into a chair.

Between standing or sitting for hours a day with her neck crooked upward, and spending nights hunched over the diary, she ached in places she couldn't even remember aching in before. Add the lack of uninterrupted sleep and she felt—and probably looked—like the living dead.

She'd attempted makeup this morning, but it hadn't done much to conceal the dark circles under her eyes.

"Unlike my ceiling," she groused.

"What about your ceiling?" Carlyn struggled through the doorway, holding two heavy file boxes.

Meri pushed the chair back to help.

"Stay put. I'm almost there." Carlyn staggered over to the kitchen table and dropped the boxes. She pressed both hands to the small of her back and stretched. "And before you ask, yes, there are more, but I think I'll wait for an intern to show up."

"So what's in them?"

"Doug's files. His wife has decided to renovate his home office and turn it into a den." Carlyn squawked out a laugh. "Are you ready? At work or at home, the poor guy can't get a decent place to park his butt."

"Exactly how many are there?" Meri asked, frowning at the corner that held Doug's curbside desk and a mountain of books and files tipping precariously into the room.

"He'll have to move upstairs to one of the empty rooms. He likes to be where the action is, but I'm not giving up my office. Besides, he wouldn't have enough room there. I'll fix it up nice . . . enough."

She stopped, looking at Meri for the first time. "Wow, who beat you up?"

"That bad?"

"Honey, please tell me you and Peter reconciled and were burning up the sheets all night, and that you're not staying up worrying about"—she lowered her voice—"the adoption thing."

"No Peter, though I'm supposed to see him tonight."

"It's the other?"

Meri nodded.

Carlyn pulled out a chair and sat next to her. "You want to talk about it?"

"Not yet. I'm still trying to assimilate it all."

"Well, it doesn't change a thing about you." Carlyn leaned over and pulled Meri into a hug. "You are who you are and we love you."

"Thanks," Meri said, hugging her back. She felt very close to tears. "Well, I'd better get to work." She stood and gave Carlyn's shoulder a squeeze. "Thanks, girlfriend."

Meri checked out a respirator and a hard hat, filled a large container with the vinegar-and-water solution that she used to clean off paint, and climbed the scaffolding to the ceiling.

The section she had cleaned was promising, but depressingly small compared to the area still covered with paint, soot, and grime. She needed a section at least twice as large in order to show the pattern in situ and how it would look when the restoration was finally completed. And a flash of brilliant color and gold ought to garner some enthusiasm for completing the project. Not that she'd seen any more gold since the first day. Probably destroyed, if it ever existed. But maybe, just maybe there was enough left to imagine the original.

She'd lost precious time looking for mold yesterday. The only place she hadn't looked was underneath the medallion.

Mold could undermine all their work. It destroyed surfaces and made layers unstable. Not to mention its toxicity. But mold around electricity meant moisture, which could be dangerous. There was no lighting fixture associated with the current medallion, but houses of that period generally had chandeliers. She'd have to look.

Besides, Meri was really hoping the original medallion had been smaller and more proportionally correct, and that removing the replacement would reveal some intact design of the original ceiling, not a black mess that would have to be destroyed.

She would need help to remove it, but first she would score the seam so that it would come away cleanly without cracks and tears that might destroy any of the original pattern that might be underneath.

Meri stood beneath it, a giant wart that been painted in several layers of oil-based psychedelic colors before being covered in latex white. When she'd first sounded it weeks before, she'd been hoping for a later date foam replacement that would be much lighter and easier to remove. But no such luck. It was plaster. And heavy. At least she wouldn't be responsible for cleaning it.

It would be sent straight to the salvage yard.

She strapped on the ventilator and applied a mild solvent around the edges of the medallion. Then she went back to her cleaning while she waited for the solvent to soften the outermost layers of paint.

By the time Meri broke for lunch, she was feeling a little wonky. She hadn't eaten breakfast and she hadn't brought anything for lunch.

She had a headache, probably from the respirator and hard hat. She left them on the scaffolding and climbed down. Joe was already back at work and two of the interns who were repairing woodwork were consulting about a windowsill.

By three o'clock Meri was back on the scaffolding. She

cleaned off the solvent and soft paint and sealed the goop in a plastic bag. There were still layers of hard paint left. She could apply more solvent, but that meant that she would have to wait until tomorrow to have it removed. And she really didn't think that would be necessary. The worst was gone and now only dried cracked paint remained.

She laid out various size knives and putty knives and took a good look at the painted medallion.

She was itching to find out what was beneath it. Would it be raw plaster or possibly a preserved pattern? Hopefully, not any forgotten live wires.

Meri began carefully scoring a line around the base of the medallion.

When she finished scoring the entire circumference, she went back and began to carve out an angled cut to loosen it from the last few layers of paint.

She changed to a heavier-weight utility knife and made a shallow cut at an angle to the scoring. Then she lifted out a small section with the tip of her knife and continued to make another cut and another until she'd cut out a third of the circumference. Each time she cut, she tested the medallion, checking for any movement that might indicate weakness in the attachments.

Everything went fine until she was a quarter of the way around. When she made the next cut, a sprinkling of paint flaked away. Not a good sign. It could mean poorly laid plaster or possibly more water damage. She slowed down, cutting and testing the weight with her free hand.

After the first sprinkle of plaster, it seemed solid enough. She continued around the edge of the medallion. When she was halfway around, she felt a slight shift.

At first she thought she'd imagined it, then without warning, the whole medallion fell in a screech of rusted bolts and falling plaster.

The knife flew out of her hand as she reflexively grabbed the medallion with both hands, attempting to hold it in place and prevent it from breaking into pieces. Plaster dust and paint chips rained down on her head, clogging her nostrils and blinding her.

"Heads up!" she screamed as plaster fell onto the scaffolding and down to the floor.

She could hear urgent voices and running feet below.

"Meri! Meri! Are you okay up there?"

She coughed and tried to clear her throat, but it was filled with dust. "Yeah," she said hoarsely. "But the center medallion just came loose. I'm trying to hold it in position, but I need help."

"I'm coming up, don't move." Doug's voice.

She coughed and spit out plaster. "No, I'm fine. You stay there. Send me a couple of interns." Her arms were getting tired, and her legs had begun to shake, but she didn't know what, if anything, was holding the medallion to the ceiling.

Footsteps clattered on the ladders, and two pairs of hands relieved her of the weight.

"Careful," she said. "I don't know what's under that. There may be wires."

The two interns held it steady as Joe Krosky reached the top and hurried over with a high-beamed flashlight. "Wires are tied off. Lower it gently. Gently now."

The two men lowered the heavy plaster decoration while Joe grabbed one of Meri's knives and cut the final adhesions of paint away. They moved it away and deposited it at the end of the scaffolding.

"Meri!" Joe said. "You're bleeding."

She'd been vaguely aware of a searing pain in her left hand, but she'd forgotten about it as the medallion was lifted away to reveal gold.

"Meri!"

"What's going on up there?" Doug's voice from below.

"Meri's hurt," Joe said.

"I can see the pattern," Meri called down to him. "It's real gilt. I'm sure of it."

"Meri, are you okay?" Carlyn's question seemed to come from far away.

Joe had moved up to her. "What did you do to your hand?"

Meri lifted her hand and tried to focus on it through a haze of plaster dust and fog. Blood was oozing across the fine layer of dust that coated her hand, turning it into a pink paste. Fresh blood dripped down her arm, soaking the sleeve of her sweatshirt. At first it didn't register, then she realized it must have happened when she dropped the knife.

Now the pain came with a vengeance. "Better tell them to put a tarp down. Don't want to drip on the floor."

"Forget the floor. Let me see."

She held up her hand.

"Joe, what's happening up there? Is Meri all right? Should I call an ambulance?" Doug's voice was strident.

"Stay put, Meri, I'm coming up." Carlyn started up the ladder.

"Do you think you can climb down?" Joe asked

"Of course. But I need something to keep the blood off the floor."

Joe looked around. Found nothing. Pulled off his hoodie. "It's not too clean."

"Kind of academic at this point. Thanks," Meri said. She wrapped her hand in his sweatshirt. "This will do until I get down. I'll buy you a new one."

"Don't worry about it. I'll help you down."

Carlyn met her as she reached the ladder. "Turn around. I'll spot you on your way down."

Meri tried to nod, but the movement made her dizzy. She was definitely going to need help getting down.

She grasped the rail with her right hand, reached her foot for the first rung. Joe hovered over her like a redheaded gargoyle. She reached for the next rung and felt Carlyn's hand on her butt.

"I've got you, just one step at a time."

It seemed an eon before Meri had both feet on the floor. She cradled her arm in her good hand. "Doug. Look up. The ceiling."

Everyone looked up, including Meri. She swayed on her feet.

"We're taking you to the hospital."

"Sorry to cause such a fuss." Was she slurring her words?

"Now." Doug wrapped his beefy arm around her waist.

"I'll get your purse and coat." Carlyn took off in a blur.

"Don't let me drip on the floor," Meri said and let Doug lead her away.

The emergency room nurse took one look at Meri and ushered her through the door that led to the examining rooms. Carlyn was allowed to come with her, but Doug was left dealing with insurance and pacing in the waiting room.

"Do you want me to call your grandmother or your dad?"

"No. I don't want to worry them." Her hand was beginning to throb, and there was fresh blood seeping out of the towel that somehow had replaced Joe's sweatshirt. She was worried enough for everyone. What if the knife had hit a nerve?

"Didn't you have a date with Peter tonight?"

"Oh God, I forgot."

The curtain that surrounded the gurney opened and a man wearing a white coat and stethoscope entered.

Must be a doctor, Meri thought. Her brain seemed to be slowing down. She grasped weakly at Carlyn's arm. There was something she meant to say, but she couldn't remember.

The doctor introduced himself. His name flew right over her head. She squinted at his name tag. Couldn't read it.

Carlyn touched her arm. "I'll take your phone and call him, okay?"

Meri nodded. "Tell him something's come up; I'll call him later."

Carlyn nodded and left; she was replaced by a nurse in blue scrubs.

"Let's see what we have here." The doctor began unwinding the towel. Meri had to force herself not to pull away. The pain was getting pretty bad. She caught herself rocking back and forth like a dinghy moored on the breakwater.

The doctor said something, and the nurse moved away. She handed him something and brushed at Meri's hair. Particles drifted to her shoulders and to the gurney.

"How did this happen, hon?"

"The medallion fell."

"The what?"

The doctor and nurse exchanged looks.

"The medallion," Meri explained. "It fell and—I—dropped the knife. I guess it cut my hand."

The doctor tossed the towel away. "I'll say it did."

"Is it bad?"

"Well, let's just take a look, shall we? First we'll need to clean up the area around the wound."

The nurse began to swab Meri's palm.

"I'm going to give you a local anesthetic. You might feel a little sting. Think of something pleasant, the ocean. It will only take a minute."

Meri flinched at the sting.

"So," the nurse said cheerfully as she continued to clean Meri's hand. "Is this plaster dust? Are you renovating?"

"Yes," Meri managed.

"We turned our attic into an extra bedroom last year. My husband was covered in paint and plaster for weeks on end. But it sure makes a difference, doesn't it?"

Meri nodded, jerked her hand back as the doctor pressed the skin around the wound.

"Did it hit anything?" Meri asked.

The doctor looked up. "Move your fingers."

Meri did, watching to make sure she wasn't having one of those ghost reactions and that they were really moving.

"I'd say you're a very lucky girl. A few stitches and in two or three weeks you should be good as new."

"Two or three weeks?" Meri's head cleared.

"For a full recovery. Just take it easy until then. Are you left-handed?"

"No."

"Good, then you can just baby this along for a while. When was the last time you had a tetanus shot?"

"I'm up to date on all my shots." In her profession it paid to keep current.

"Excellent. Now this might hurt a little. . . ."

Chapter 11

Carlyn returned to the room as the doctor finished with the stitches.

"I'm putting you in a wrist splint to keep the thumb stable."

Meri and Carlyn watched him fit the splint, then wind gauze around Meri's hand until it was unrecognizable. He finished by rummaging in a drawer and pulling out a plastic bag that contained a sling. He fitted it around her neck.

Meri stared at the sling and gauze and tape, her heart stammering. "How long do I have to wear this?"

"It's just a precaution to prevent you from opening the stitches. You can change the bandage in a few days. Do you have someone who can help you? If not, you can come to my office."

"I can," Carlyn volunteered.

He handed Meri a prescription. "Take these for pain if you need them. You're good to go then."

"Can I go back to work?"

"If you don't use your hand—at all. But no going up ladders for a few days."

Meri thanked him and slid off the table.

"Did Doug go home?" Meri asked as they walked back to the waiting room to be discharged.

"No way. He's like an expectant father out there."

"My hand looks much worse than it is," Meri complained. "He's going to freak."

"Don't worry about Doug. He'll cope until you get back."

"It's a good thing it's my left hand."

Doug was waiting for them and so was Peter . . . and Alden.

"Not my fault," Carlyn said under her breath. "I called Peter to cancel and he wanted to know why. I tried to downplay your accident. Guess it didn't work.

"And I called your neighbor because I thought someone in your family should know in case you needed help with insurance or something. And I didn't want to worry your gran. I told him he didn't have to come."

All three of the men looked up at once. Doug was so pale that Meri was afraid he might faint. Peter and Alden hurried toward her. Well, Peter was hurrying. Alden never seemed to rush, though he was having no trouble keeping up with Peter.

Peter nudged Carlyn out of the way and put his arm around Meri's shoulders. "Thank God you're all right. I came as soon as Carlyn called."

"Thanks, but I'm . . . fine. I think."

"Do you have to check out? I'll drive you home. Or maybe you should stay at my place tonight."

"She'll be coming home with me," Alden said at his driest. "Her grandmother insisted that she recuperate at the farm."

"I can take care of her," Peter said defensively.

Which for some reason made Meri smile.

"I'm sure you can. You can visit her at the farm this weekend."

"I'm going home to my apartment," Meri said.

Both men turned on her.

"I'll drive you," Peter said.

She waited for Alden to counter with something, but he just stood there.

And suddenly Meri knew where she wanted to be. At home with Gran.

She turned to Peter. "Thanks, but I think I better go set Gran's mind at ease. She'll worry all week if she doesn't see for herself."

She didn't miss the look that Peter shot Alden, but in true Alden style he totally ignored it.

"If you're sure."

"I'm sure, but thanks."

"Should I cancel my trip this weekend?"

"No. Visit your family. I'll be back in town when you get back."

"Okay, then." He leaned over and gave her a meaningful kiss, in case anyone was wondering about their relationship. "Take care of yourself." He turned and strode out the double doors to the parking lot.

Alden slipped the prescription slip out of her hand. "I'll go get this filled for you. Sit down."

"Thank you." She didn't sit down but went over to Doug who was standing on the sidelines.

"I'm really sorry about the medallion."

"Don't worry about it. As long as you're all right. What did the doctor say?"

"Not to climb any ladders for a few days. I can help Joe with the wallpaper tracings. But did you see the ceiling? Was I right? Is it gilt?"

"Yeah, they called over to say there *is* gilt, and the whole pattern under the medallion was intact."

"That should make life a little simpler," Meri said.

"Yeah, a big find." Doug whooshed out a breath. "Meri, you scared the crap out of me."

Meri was sure he was reliving the fall that had put pins in his legs and kept him on the ground. "I'm fine. I should have shored up the medallion, but it seemed solid."

"The bolts were rusted through. It would have come down on its own. Only the paint was holding it up. It was your daring save that kept it from falling on everyone's heads."

She lifted her bandaged hand. "Sorry, this is going to slow down the ceiling cleaning a bit."

"It can wait. Actually I've canceled work for Friday. We'll be moving to four-day workweeks until further notice."

Read, *when we get more grant money.* It was a catch-22. You couldn't get money unless you had something to show and you couldn't get things in shape to show without the money to do it.

"So take tomorrow off and come in on Monday, unless you need more time."

"I won't. And, Doug, don't even think about replacing me."

"Are you kidding? You're the most well-rounded, meticulous technician I have. And I'm not giving your ceiling to anyone but you."

Alden returned carrying a white pharmacy bag and a bottle of water. "You might want to take one of these now." He opened the bottle of pills, poured out a capsule into his palm, and handed it to her. He opened the water and handed that to her.

She didn't even think about protesting. She felt pain all the way up her arm. She put the pill in her mouth, reached for the bottle, swallowed it, and handed the bottle back to him. She felt frustration boil up inside her. She couldn't even screw on a bottle cap. How the hell was she going to do things with one hand bound up like a sausage?

Carlyn handed Alden Meri's purse and work bag, then helped Meri to put one arm in her jacket. The other side, she draped over Meri's shoulder.

"Thanks, girlfriend."

"No problemo. Your phone is in your bag. I'll call you to-morrow. Take good care of her. I need her for karaoke." Carlyn grinned.

"I will," Alden said and steered Meri toward the exit. "You okay? My car's in the lot. I can bring it around."

"I'm fine. You didn't need to come fetch me. I'll be perfectly fine at home. Carlyn or Peter could have driven me."

Alden gave her a look. "Carlyn maybe."

"I take it back; you're worse than Dad when it comes to Peter."

"Did you want to go with him?"

She didn't have to think about her answer. "No. I wanted to go with you. Does Gran even know about the accident?"

He grinned. "Not yet. I wanted to see for myself."

"Sneaky. But I'm glad you came. I want to go home. To Gran's. But can we at least stop by my apartment so I can pick up some things?"

They walked to the parking lot, Alden on her good side and standing so close that she had to stop and say. "Don't hover. I'm fine." She smiled at him. "I'm sure Gran will fuss over me enough for the both of you."

He backed off. "I wasn't hovering, just being alert."

"Ah."

By the time they had parked, and Meri got out of the car, she welcomed Alden's "hovering." She was feeling no pain, liter-ally and figuratively. It must be the pill. She didn't like pills, because it was hard to work efficiently or safely on drugs. She never even had a glass of wine at lunch on the rare times she had a real sit-down lunch in a real restaurant.

She managed to find her keys with one hand but when she tried to fit the key to the keyhole, the keys fell from her hand. Alden scooped them up and opened the door. He held on to her going up the flight of stairs and then opened her apartment door.

"Sorry," she said. "I seem to . . . It's the drugs."

"You'll be okay."

"I know, I'll just pack some things for the weekend."

She let her jacket fall off her shoulder and worked her arm out of the sleeve. "Pain in the butt," she mumbled.

Alden took the coat.

"I'll just be a minute." She went into her bedroom and pulled her suitcase from under the bed and put it on the mattress. She managed to unzip it with one hand. She had more trouble with the two knobbed drawers of her dresser but refused to ask Alden to help.

A girl had her pride. She grabbed two pairs of jeans, a pair of sweats, some T-shirts, sweaters, and underwear. But when it came to shoes, she ran out of steam. She needed a little break. She sank down on the mattress next to her suitcase.

And the box, she'd need to take the diary . . .

Alden sat on the couch listening to Meri mumble and make noise as she moved slowly about her bedroom. She was probably having trouble packing with only one hand. But he made himself sit where he was, determined not to hover.

Did he really do that? Nora had accused him of being overprotective just a day or two ago. Well, fathers were supposed to be overprotective, especially if their daughters lived a hundred miles away and they rarely knew what was going on in their lives.

Meri wasn't his daughter, but he had promised to protect her—and he'd taken that promise seriously. He breathed out a laugh, thinking of his younger self, coming to the farmhouse every day after school to see the baby. Spending the weekends with the Calders, asking questions, and worrying if Meri started to cry or threw up her milk. That must have been when he'd learned to hover.

And he hadn't stopped, he guessed. Though he'd tried. Even

as a teenager, he was busy, did regular teenage things, except for spending a lot of time drawing and taking art classes, but he still made sure everything was fine with Meri. She was an inquisitive little thing and couldn't wait to go to kindergarten. She'd bring him things she'd found in the dunes, or lug the big mythology book over and put it in his lap and climb up after it to be read to.

It never occurred to her that an adolescent boy wouldn't want to read to a kid. Actually it hadn't really occurred to him, either. She cried when he left for college. After that he only saw her on breaks, but she was busy then, too, popular and always doing some project or other or hanging out with her friends.

Then life happened: he moved to Manhattan, started getting freelance jobs, met Jennifer, got married. By the time Alden had brought his daughter and pregnant wife to live at the beach house, Nora was two and Meri was old enough to babysit.

Enough of the past. He stood up, listened. Things were suddenly very quiet in Meri's bedroom. "Meri?"

No answer.

He went to the door. "Meri?"

She was sprawled crosswise across the bed, her right hand in her suitcase as if she'd just put something there and fell asleep.

Quelling panic, Alden stepped inside and went to the bed. He watched as she exhaled. She was fine. She'd fallen asleep. *Must be the pills,* he thought.

He lifted the suitcase from the bed and put it out of the way. Took one look at her work clothes and plaster-covered hair, and thought, *What the hell, sheets will wash.* He untied her sneakers and slipped them off.

Meri roused enough to get under the sheets. As he pulled the quilt over her she opened drowsy eyes.

"You saved me."

"No. I just drove you home from the emergency room."

"No. You saved me." She smiled slightly and fell back to sleep.

It looked like they wouldn't be driving back to Little Compton until tomorrow.

Meri woke with a start. Light was coming through the window. She felt dirty and thirsty, and there was a throbbing pain coming from her left hand. Then she remembered the accident: going to the emergency room; Alden, Doug, Peter, Carlyn; Alden driving her home. They were going to Gran's. She wasn't at Gran's. She was at her own apartment.

And she smelled coffee.

She pushed the quilt back and sat up, sending rays of pain up her left arm. Well, she could get used to it. She wasn't taking any more of those pills. Maybe a half if things got worse.

Coffee would be good. Meri pushed herself to her feet and realized that she was still wearing her work clothes. She walked out to the living room.

Alden was standing at the window holding a mug of coffee.

"Did you stay here all night?" she croaked. Her throat was hoarse from the plaster dust.

He nodded. "How do you feel?"

"Fine. Where did you sleep?"

"In the chair."

"The couch pulls out to a bed."

"No big deal."

"Well, thanks." She went over to the kitchen and found a mug already placed next to the coffeepot. She poured herself a cup and sat on the couch.

Alden turned from the window. "There isn't anything in your refrigerator but congealed pad thai."

"I've been too busy to shop."

"And too busy to eat?" He raised his eyebrows as he gave her the once-over.

She shrugged. Or at least tried to. It seemed like every time she moved, it set off a new jolt of pain. "You shaved."

"Found a package of disposable razors under the sink."

She understood his expression and she wasn't in the mood for any aspersions cast on her relationship with Peter. "Well, good for you."

"Finish your coffee, and I'll take you somewhere for breakfast before I take you home."

She considered protesting but just didn't have the energy to fight. She rarely won when Alden really set his mind on something.

"On second thought, maybe we'll just stop for bagels and eat in the car."

"I'm fine, really."

Another lift of his eyebrows sent her into the bathroom to look in the mirror. She didn't look fine. She was a walking disaster area. Her hair, face, and clothes were smeared with dirt, blood, and plaster dust. She couldn't go to Gran's looking like this.

She grabbed a washcloth and turned on the water. Alden called, "Don't get your stitches wet."

Meri scrubbed her face with one hand. When she'd gotten as clean as possible, she opened the door and came out.

"Alden, I can't go looking like this."

He shook his head, his lips working until he burst out laughing. "Sorry, but you do look a bit like one of my more imaginative illustrations."

"The poor little match girl?"

He shook his head again, trying not to smile.

"You'll have to wait while I take a shower."

"You can't get your hand wet."

"I'll hold it out of the shower curtain or put it in a plastic bag; I must have one around here somewhere."

"Or you can wait until you get home where I'm sure there

are plastic bags, and there's a walk-in shower. And Therese can hand you soap and stuff."

She looked back at the bathroom, so close and yet so far . . . "I don't suppose you—"

They looked at each other for a long second, then Alden slowly shook his head.

"She'll freak when she sees me. At least let me stick my head under the faucet. I'll only use one hand. Are you in a hurry?"

Alden sighed. "Come over to the sink. Where's your shampoo?"

"In the rack on the tub."

She moved the coffeepot out of the way and turned on the water.

Alden came back with shampoo, conditioner, and several towels. He rolled up his sleeves, then rolled up a towel and put it on the counter for her to use to cover her eyes. She leaned over and rested her head on the edge of the sink, flooded with memories of standing just like this while her mother or Gran washed her hair in the kitchen, then sat her down at the table to comb out the tangles.

A sense of love swept over her for her family, for the life they'd given her. For Alden promising to take care of her. She vaguely remembered trying to ask him about that last night, but it was elusive. Maybe she had just meant to. There would be time this weekend, maybe even during the ride to the farm.

Long fingers pushed her hair forward and she felt water run off her neck and ears.

"Too hot?"

"No. It feels wonderful."

She felt the cold of the shampoo smelled the sweet scent of citrus as Alden scrubbed the tangled mass gently with both hands.

Meri gave in to the rhythm of his hands, the drag of his fingers. There was something soothing about a shampoo. Like a lullaby. She sighed. "Wonderful." *Sensual. Sexy.*

He yanked at her hair and the feeling shattered.

"Did you say something?"

"Uh-uh. I don't think so. Did I?" Did she? She was still loopy from that pill. She sighed as Alden began to scrub again. Harder this time.

"Ouch."

"Sorry, it's pretty tangled and I haven't had to do this in a while. Plus dried plaster is a lot harder to get out than Play-Doh."

She turned her head to look at him. Water and soap ran in her eyes.

"Hold still."

"You used to wash Nora's and Lucas's hair?"

"Sometimes." He turned on the water and let it run. She could feel him testing the temperature. Then he began rinsing the suds from her hair.

"Did you ever wash mine?"

"No."

She thought of what he must have missed when Jennifer took the children so far away from him. And she made a promise to be a good friend to Nora when she came and to try to help her over any rough spots she might be going through. And she'd be a better friend to Alden. A real friend. A friend with—Her thoughts fuzzed over. Damn that pill. A friend. A really good friend.

Alden turned off the water and squirted conditioner into his palm, fingered it through her hair. Stopped when he reached a tangle and eased the knot away. He was full of surprises, this man. He was a natural at taking care of people.

Another rinse and Meri was beginning to feel a little dizzy when Alden flapped open a towel and wrapped it around her head. She lifted her head up until she was standing.

"I did the best I could. It should be presentable."

"Thanks. I appreciate it. Really."

He collected the shampoo and conditioner and the used towel and carried them back to the bathroom, while Meri went to change clothes and look for a comb. She managed to get on clean jeans, all but the button and zipper, and after a few frustrating tries, she decided to just cover it up with a long sweater. Only the sleeves wouldn't go on over her bandage, so she had to rummage through the closet until she found a sweatshirt with the cuffs cut off.

When she came back from her bedroom, Alden was throwing the carton of pad thai into the garbage can.

Meri stood combing her hair and watching him. He realized she was there and stopped. "I assumed you weren't planning to take that with you."

She shook her head, felt the room spin a bit, and sat down in the nearest chair.

"Maybe you should take another one of those pills."

"No. They make me dopey, and I don't want to be dopey." She stopped, smiled. "Any dopier than usual. I'll just take some aspirin for now. Though I could use something to eat."

He tied off the plastic garbage bag. "Are you ready then? We'll call Gran from the car and let her know we're coming."

"Almost. I just need to get some shoes and . . . something else."

She went back to her bedroom and shoved her feet into some moccasins since she wasn't about to wrestle with laces or ask Alden to tie her shoes. She'd imposed on him too much already.

She found her suitcase on the far side of the bed threw a pair of boots and sneakers on top and shut it. She lugged it to the door and remembered the box, still on the top shelf of her closet.

Getting it would be tricky, but she wanted to take it with

her. She'd have to ask Alden for one more favor. And besides he'd already seen it. There was nothing to be furtive about.

He was wearing his jacket, and he got the box down without comment, found a shopping bag from a local boutique, and placed it inside without a word. Then he picked up the bag and the suitcase and carried it to the front door where the trash bag was sitting.

He helped her into her coat as best he could. Meri slung her purse over one shoulder and followed Alden, her luggage, and the trash bag out the door.

Meri was surprised when they walked out into sunshine. Alden stopped to dump the trash into the outside bin, and Meri got a sudden pang of guilt that came from nowhere for no reason though she thought it might have to do with Heathcliff and taking out the garbage.

And as unreasonable as it was, she just hoped Peter never found out that instead of driving Meri straight to Gran's, Alden had brought her here and stayed the night.

Chapter 12

I think I'd better call Gran and warn her I'm coming."

"Good idea." Alden waited for a car to pass then pulled out of the parking place. He glanced down and watched Meri rummage for her phone. She swiped her thumb to open it and called.

He could feel her watching him as she waited for Therese to pick up. He hoped to heaven she wasn't going to want to talk on the drive to the farm. He wanted to be on his own territory when she started pumping him for the details of the night he found Riley Rochfort on the breakwater, pregnant, sick, and hysterical.

"I'm fine," Meri said. "I cut my hand, nothing serious, but I'm taking a couple of days off, thought I'd come out and spend them with you."

He could hear a voice at the far end but not words. That was fine. He planned to drop Meri off at Gran's door, then get the hell out until the women had a chance to talk things out.

He stopped at a light. Meri hung up. "So . . ." she said and turned toward him.

"Want to stop for breakfast somewhere or just at a deli."

"Just at the deli, if that's okay with you. I know you never eat breakfast, and I'm anxious to get home."

"Fine with me." He drove to a deli near the highway and double-parked, leaving Meri in the car. He came back a few minutes later with a large paper bag.

As Meri unloaded the bag, Alden pulled into traffic.

"I hope you're going to eat some of this," she said, taking things out of the bag and handing him one of the coffees.

He'd bought her a bagel, fruit salad, a yogurt, orange juice, and coffee, hoping it would keep her busy and away from conversation.

Of course he hoped in vain.

As soon as she'd eaten half of the bagel and they weren't even to the bridge, she said, "When were you going to tell me about my mother?"

"We already discussed this. Your mother is Laura Hollis. Your dad is Dan. And you already gave me a hard time about keeping what I knew from you." He kept his eyes on the road and cursed the slow-moving traffic.

"You didn't tell me you were there in a ringside seat."

He ignored her.

"That you actually pulled Riley from the breakwater and saved her life—and mine."

Alden gripped the steering wheel, pretending he hadn't heard her.

"Won't you tell me?"

"Yes, but not while I'm driving."

"Fair enough. But you were there when I was born."

"Yep. Saw you two minutes after you came into this world."

"I hope not naked."

He felt her smile. "No, they had you so swaddled up you looked like a jellybean." He glanced at her. "But there were plenty of other times . . ."

"Alden!"

"What can I say. You were a free spirit. I can't tell you the number of times you'd escape out of the back door, *sans* diaper, headed for the dunes. It was very embarrassing."

"Not for me . . . evidently."

"For me. I was a teenager. Those kinds of things are monumental. More than one time I had to carry you back to the house kicking and squirming. One time you peed on my shirt."

"No. You never told me that."

"It was good training for fatherhood; by the time Nora came along I was impervious to disgusting baby emissions."

She threw a grape at him.

He batted it away.

"Alden, does it really not make a difference?"

Like a light switch clicking from on to off, she'd turned serious.

He looked over to her and tugged a piece of hair curling at her shoulders. "Not in any way."

She fell silent after that. Alden didn't know if it was because her hand was hurting or if she was lost in her own thoughts. He wasn't about to ask.

He knew he'd have to tell her the whole story of his involvement, detail by detail; she was like that. And God knew he'd done the same thing, over and over until it became a kind of story, a fiction separate from himself and reality.

When Alden looked again, Meri's eyes were closed. Hopefully she'd fallen asleep. He was tired; sleeping in a chair just didn't cut it and he'd been drinking coffee since earlier that morning. Enough to give him the shakes or maybe it was just nerves.

He laughed at himself. He'd been a kid, he'd made a promise, which he had kept. How could she fault him for that?

Meri roused when Alden turned into the lane that led to their houses. "I can't believe I fell asleep, after sleeping all night. Sorry."

Alden looked straight ahead. "You needed it."

She covered a yawn with her bandaged hand. "You're not off the hook, you know. I still want you to tell me what happened."

"I know. Why don't you finish reading the diary first." He glanced at her, but not long enough for her to start asking questions. "Or have you finished?"

"Not yet. But . . . you knew there was a diary?"

"Therese told me a few days ago."

"And you brought it to me."

"Hmm."

"Did you read it?"

"Of course not."

She laughed slightly. "Don't get all indignant. You're in it."

"I figured as much." And he wasn't sure why that bothered him so much, except that he didn't want anything to change between them.

"You saved my— Riley and you saved me."

He flinched. No one had spoken that name for decades.

"What's the matter, Alden? Why didn't you tell me all these years?"

And here it was. "She made me promise."

"You were a boy."

"A promise is a promise."

They'd come to the farmhouse, and Alden stopped the car at the kitchen door. Therese was already standing in the doorway. She must have been watching for them. Meri turned to say something, but Alden jumped out of the car and began unloading her things.

Meri got out and hurried to hug Gran. "I'm fine. So don't look so worried."

Alden slipped past them into the house.

They were just coming inside when Alden returned to the kitchen. "I put your things in the hallway."

"Thanks."

"Thank you for bringing her home," Therese said. "Would you like something to eat, Alden? Coffee?"

"Thanks, but I have to run."

He headed for the door. Meri followed him and stopped him before he could get away.

"You'll have to talk to me at some point."

"I know. But there's plenty of time. Talk to your Gran first." And he left her standing in the doorway. Like the coward he was.

I hope what you learned last weekend isn't responsible for your accident," Gran said as she put a cup of chamomile tea on the table at Meri's good elbow.

"No. It was the fault of some rusted bolts. Promise."

Gran fidgeted. "Did you read the diary?"

"I've started on it. Mom's handwriting was never the best, and it's faded over the years. I've gotten to where you had to identify Riley at the . . ." Meri couldn't continue. It sounded like a novel, not her life.

She changed the subject. "There is so much going on at work; the project is running out of money. We've had to move to a four-day workweek, so that's why I decided to come home and stay with you."

"This is where you should be." Gran straightened up. "You just rest for a while."

"Thanks." Meri's hand really hurt, but she'd opted for ibuprofen instead of the prescription painkillers because she wanted to read more of her mother's diary. And then talk to Gran. And then talk to Alden.

She gave Gran a quick hug and went into the living room. Gran had piled cushions against the arm of the sofa and Meri settled into them, pulled an afghan over her knees, and opened the diary.

> It's hard to fathom but no one has come to claim that poor child. She's lying in the morgue like a Jane Doe. But we know who she is. Or was. And Mother has convinced me that we should approach her parents; surely they must be out of their minds with worry, wondering where their daughter is.
>
> Mother gave her name to the authorities. She didn't mention Meri. We don't want to lose that child to bureaucratic red tape. She wants me to return Meri to the family, but I reminded her that we promised Riley to take care of her. Mother is uneasy. She's afraid that we've broken the law. I don't care. I won't let harm come to this precious baby.
>
> Mother calls every day to see if the body has been claimed. And the answer is always the same. I know the family is in town, that the police have contacted them. What are they waiting for?

Meri was half aware of Gran coming into the archway then leaving again. What Meri really wanted to do was to get through the diary and pick her grandmother's brain for what really happened in chronological order. If Gran could remember.

> Mother insists we go to meet with the family. Insist they acknowledge Riley and the baby. I argued until I was hoarse, but she's adamant. I finally agreed, but I insisted we not take

Meri with us and not mention her until we were sure they would treat her right.

Mother made an appointment with them for three days from now. She told them what we wanted, and she said they almost refused to talk to her. I told Mother they must be monsters. But she said they probably thought we were running some kind of scam.

For being a farmer born and raised, my mother has some uncanny street smarts.

The next page was blank as if left for the passage of time, and when Meri turned to the next, it was several days later.

They tried to pay us off!

They accused us of lying, told us that their daughter had died on a trip to Europe and was buried over there in the family private cemetery. And how dare we attempt to extort money from them with these cruel lies. We were stunned. It was a bald-faced lie, and we all knew it. But the man and his wife didn't waver. Just acted all starched up and looked down their noses at us like we were vermin that somehow had skittered into their grand mansion.

They threatened to call the police and, bless her, Mother said as cool as anything, Please do, they've been trying to contact you for days. I wanted to applaud.

They backed down then and Mr. Rochfort did try to buy us off. Which put Mother's back up. I have to say, I've never seen her so fierce, and I was proud to stand beside her. I wasn't nearly so brave. And then she said something that floored me. She told them we wouldn't be bothering them again and that Riley and her baby were both buried in our family cemetery if they would like to visit.

Mrs. R flinched at that, and I had a hard time not bursting into tears, thinking of those lost lives. He said they wanted to hear no more about "this girl," as he called her, or her bastard child, pretending that they weren't his own daughter and grandchild. But he didn't fool anyone in that room. Mrs. Rochfort just stood beside him, letting him talk for her. And I swore then and there they would never get Meri in their clutches. One glance at Mother told me she thought the same.

The servant showed us out. I was more than ready to go. As soon as we were on the street, I asked Mother why she had lied about Riley being buried. She just patted my arm and said, she will be. She went down to claim the body that afternoon.

We buried Riley today next to little Rose, just Mother and me and the Reverend Thomas. We only told him part of the story, that she was an unclaimed runaway, and we would be happy to give her our name. So she was buried as Riley Calder. I'm afraid I've broken the law but I don't see any other way to proceed. Or maybe it's that I don't want to. I don't think I could let go of little Merielle under any circumstance. She's as precious to me, more so, than the premature child that lies next to Riley Rochfort in hallowed ground, a comfort to each other.

Mother arranged it all. I'm so awed by her strength and willingness to take in this child. But when told her so, she said, don't be ridiculous. How could we ever give this baby up?

Meri, you should grow up knowing how much you are loved. You are truly my daughter and Mother's granddaughter and to hell with anyone who tries to prove differently.

Meri's eyes were getting tired and her hand was hurting, and she was half tempted to take one of the prescription pain pills.

She skimmed over the next few pages in hopes that more pieces would fall into place, but they were all about taking care of the baby. Only one passage brought her out of her descending lethargy and made her forget all about her hand.

Alden comes every day to see Meri. He's such a serious boy. He'll sit by the crib just watching her. Yesterday she smiled at him, but instead of making him smile, it seemed to make him more unhappy. I think something is worrying him, but he won't say what.

Today I found him standing over her while she slept, tears falling on the blanket. I asked him what was wrong? At first he only shook his head, then blurted out, "Did I kill her?"

I was stunned. Fortunately, Mother was in the room and she took charge of the situation. Sat him down and asked him what that nonsense was about. I guess trying to spare him, no one had told him about Riley being killed on the highway. He was so afraid he had killed her by dragging her into the dinghy then leaving her on the beach to come get help.

It took much persuasion to dissuade him that it wasn't at all his fault and that he had been brave and managed what few people would or could have done. Then Mother gave him a softened version of what really had happened. It seemed to make him sadder. And I nearly cried myself when he asked in this quiet little voice. "And she left her baby?" Mother soothed him and after a while he returned to the crib and played with Meri until Mother told him it was time for him to go home. He leaned over and kissed Meri, and I heard him whisper. "Don't worry, Meri. I'll take care of you. I promise." Mother and I looked at each other but said nothing. But we both watched out the window until he was home. He seemed less worried, but I'm afraid this whole incident may have scarred him for life.

Meri closed the diary. No wonder Alden didn't want to talk about the past. Even reading about it seemed too intimate, and in a way she wished she hadn't. She had never questioned his place in her life. He'd just always been there.

She knew she'd always been demanding of his time. When Gran or Wilton took her to Alden's football games or soccer tournaments, she'd whine and pout when he went with his friends afterward instead of coming home to play with her. Sometimes he did go home with her when she became too demanding, and now she burned with embarrassment. Even when he was away at college, he always called or wrote her silly little notes.

When she was in college, he was the first person after Gran that she wanted to see when she visited. How selfish she'd been. His marriage was falling apart and she'd wanted him all to herself.

It was normal to her, something she took for granted. But since having brothers who barely took time to text or phone or visit unless they had dirty laundry to bring home, she understood now how unusual his dedication had been. But again she had taken it for granted . . . until now.

Even now he was still taking care of her. Meri let out a breath. She'd have to tell him that he didn't need to feel responsible for her anymore. She could take care of herself. She knew she had to tell him, but already she felt a little bereft. Once she acknowledged it, could things ever be the same between them?

She reluctantly turned the page, but the rest of the diary seemed to be about her growing up and continued sporadically through the first couple of years and finally ceased all together. Meri had a feeling the writing stopped with the appearance of Dan Hollis.

Her grandmother said they would talk after dinner if she felt like it. She'd tried calling Alden to invite him to dinner, but "The man has his phone turned off."

"He must be working," Meri said.

"He works all the time."

"Shall I walk over and ask him?" Meri asked.

"No, no. You just stay put and take care of that hand. I'll go."

But Meri insisted she felt fine. Besides, she wanted to talk to Alden alone.

Around five Meri set off across the dunes, wondering if she had been too precipitous about wanting to talk to him. What would she say? What she was really afraid of? *I know you promised to take care of me. I hope that's not why we're friends.*

He'd probably look at her like she was crazy. Chances are there were times when he didn't even remember making that promise. Kids did stuff like that all the time. And he hadn't always taken care of her. He'd gone to college, moved to Manhattan, so there were years they'd hardly seen each other except at holidays.

By the time she walked over the dunes, Meri had talked herself out of the whole assumption. She'd blown the whole thing out of proportion. He'd promised as a boy, and it was vain of her to think he was still keeping that promise out of an exaggerated sense of duty.

Because that would mean that their whole relationship was built on something that had nothing to do with her. That she couldn't—wouldn't—believe. He was older. Naturally he would have looked out for her, just as she looked out for her younger half brothers. That was perfectly normal. Surely he had forgotten his promise a long time ago.

And most of her believed that.

Regardless, she wasn't to find out that night. The house was locked up; not even Alden's habitual reading lamp lit the interior. She even walked around to the garage, an unattached wooden building that looked as if a brisk wind would knock it over. It was empty, except for two dinghies propped against the wall.

Just as well, Meri thought as she trudged back across the dunes toward home. Her whole arm was hurting now. It was obvious he didn't want to talk. Or maybe he was just busy getting ready for Nora's visit. He probably had shopping to do. Plans to make. And Meri had to confess, the walk had exhausted her; she was too tired to learn any more tonight. She'd eat dinner with Gran, then pop one of those pills and go to bed early.

She had two more days to find out the whole story, or at least all of the story that anyone knew. Then she remembered that Nora would be arriving sometime tomorrow. That too was okay, because the longer she waited, the longer she thought, the easier it was to make herself believe she didn't need to know the real reason Alden had always been her friend.

Chapter 13

By the time Meri returned home, her feet were dragging, her hand was throbbing, and pain shot up her arm in bursts like electrical shocks. She hoped that didn't mean something was wrong.

"Probably just means you're doing too much," Gran told her and made her sit down while she inspected the bandage and her arm. "I don't see anything unusual, but if it's not better in the morning, we can drive in to the doctor's. What I think you should do is take one of those pills the doctor gave you and go to bed early."

Meri nodded. She forced down some baked chicken and didn't protest when Gran handed her a pill and a glass of water and helped her upstairs to her room.

She fell asleep almost immediately but was visited by such dreams of storms and demons that they could have rivaled Alden's drawings. She was surprised to open her eyes to sunshine the next morning.

She lay there blinking in the light, wondering if she should just take the day off, not worry any more about her past, concentrate on the present, maybe even contemplate her future. She hadn't talked to Peter since the night at the hospital, and she didn't want him to think she was neglecting him. (Or that she had chosen Alden over him.) She hadn't. She just wanted to go to Gran's where she knew comfort and acceptance, even now.

She would call him later and make amends. This morning she would talk to Gran and to Alden, but later. Right now she could use some catch-up sleep. She began to drift off, then jerked awake. Nora was coming today. Alden didn't say when. If Meri wanted to talk to him before another week went by, she had better get up and do it now.

Not that she'd figured out what she wanted to say. Mainly just that she knew what had happened and to thank him. Which seemed kind of like being a day late and a dollar shy, but it needed to be said. The consequences be damned.

She settled for a sponge bath. Later she would use Gran's walk-in shower downstairs. Her mom and father had insisted on installing a full bathroom off her grandmother's bedroom.

Maybe with Peter gone, Meri should move back in with Gran, help out with her chores and the house and be company for her. She'd hate to give up her apartment, but when she thought about what Gran and her mother had done for her, Meri knew it was the least she could do. She owed everything to them . . . and to Alden.

Meri dressed in jeans and a sweater, though she couldn't manage the stiff buttonhole and had to ask Gran to do it for her. Gran insisted that she have at least some oatmeal even though the pills had taken her appetite away.

So while Meri forced coffee and oatmeal down, Gran sat down with a cup of coffee and answered all her questions.

Most of what she remembered coincided with what Laura had written in her diary. Some of it veered away, until the part about Riley's handwritten will.

"Can we get in trouble for what happened? The authorities wouldn't come after us now."

Gran smiled. "You mean me and Katy?"

Meri said nothing, not looking at her grandmother, but tracing a pattern with her spoon in the surface of the oatmeal.

"Well, Katy's got a bit of dementia, I'm sorry to say. Got a full-time caregiver. She's not done yet, but she does have moments of forgetfulness. I doubt if they could get anything out of her if they asked. Katy, bless her, is sly like a fox.

"As for me?" Gran shrugged. "I stopped worrying about that the first time you smiled at me.

"We *were* worried about what they could do with you and to Riley. That was her name, Riley."

Meri nodded.

"She was feverish, weak and sick, but her mind was still sharp, so there was no thinking she wasn't in her right mind. She insisted we get paper and pen and write her wishes down. She dictated it out in a voice so weak and thin I worried that she'd have the breath to finish it. 'I bequeath my baby girl, Merielle, to Laura Calder Rodgers. (That was your daddy's, I mean, Huey's name.) I know she will love her and do right by her. She's her mamma now.'

"What kind of craziness was that? We let her write it, and Katy Dewar and I witnessed it, just like it was real. Though I doubt if you can bequeath another human being. We were just humoring her. She was worried, afraid, kept saying they were going to kill her. We didn't think anyone would really want to kill her, but we let her sign it, and then we signed it and put it away in an envelope just to calm her down.

"Of course, after Laura and I met the family, there was no question of giving you back. I'm sorry to say this, but I've never met a colder, more self-righteous couple than the Rochforts. Some story about Riley dying in France and being buried in the ancestral plot.

"I don't know if anybody believed them, but they took off

after that to spend the rest of the spring in Europe, didn't come back until the following fall."

Her grandmother slapped the table lightly with both hands. "And we've never looked back." She started to rise.

"Just one more thing."

"I'm listening."

"Did Riley step out in front of that truck on purpose?"

Therese sat back down. "No, we don't think so. We were all feeling more than a little guilty, so we contacted the driver of the truck that hit her. One of those big trucks from the mattress store.

"He didn't think she did it on purpose, least that's what he said. He said she wasn't even looking when she stumbled into the road. She didn't see him coming. He tried to swerve, but it was just too late.

"Poor man broke down and cried. So did I. And it's something we all will have to live with for the rest of our lives.

"Selfish creatures that we were, it did set our minds at ease. She wasn't trying to kill herself; she was going somewhere or running away. We'll never know, I guess. We told her we would love and protect both of you, and I thought she believed us. I don't know why she ran. It was just an unfortunate, unfortunate accident.

"Now enough of the past. You just spend the day relaxing."

Meri stood and put her bowl in the sink. Then she leaned over and kissed her grandmother. "I'm glad you kept me."

"We never thought of doing anything else." A worry line creased Gran's forehead. "One more thing—we all understand if you feel the need to make contact with your other family. It's only natural and we won't feel slighted in the least. You will always be ours no matter what you do, even if you decide to go back to them."

"I would never, not after what I read about them, not after

what they did to Riley." Meri was curious, but there was no rush. She'd gone thirty years without contact or even knowing of their existence. Someday maybe, but she was in no hurry to do it now.

"Gran?"

"Yes, dear."

"Mom wrote about Alden's part in all of this. She said she thought it might have damaged him, scarred him for life, I think she said. Did I do that to him?"

"Lord, no. It could have cost him his life, having the boat out in that weather. But it's a good thing he did. He saved Riley Rochfort and he saved you."

"And he's watched over me ever since."

Gran pushed out of her chair. "In the same way he watches out for me and your mother. The same way we watched over him. He may have lost his innocence younger than need be, but he's not anything but a fine man and a loyal one. Don't you forget it."

Meri was a bit taken aback at her grandmother's vehemence. Almost as if she were defending him, which she didn't need to do at all. Meri was acutely aware of what she owed to their neighbor and longtime friend.

It was about time she told him so. And before he was distracted by Nora's arrival.

Meri put on a jacket, told Gran where she was going, and struck off across the grassland. It was a walk she had taken hundreds, thousands of times in all kinds of moods and in all kinds of weather. But today the sun turned the old grasses gold, reflecting off the new, delicate shoots with a vibrancy that felt fresh and new—new and wonderful.

The sky was blue, a different blue from the sea, which she could glimpse through the bluffs. She didn't hurry but took deep breaths of the fresh air, hyperaware of being outdoors, and not balanced on a scaffolding high above a dusty wooden floor, breathing in paint fumes and chemicals. And a huge weight seemed to fall from her shoulders.

This is who she was, Meri Calder Hollis, architectural restorer, and a part of this land as sure as if she were the blood progeny of Cyrus Stillman Calder, gentleman farmer.

There wasn't much sign of life, when Meri arrived at Alden's house. But with the brilliant daylight, he was bound to be at work in the sunroom. She followed the trampled grass from her last visit and let herself inside.

He wasn't there; she called out, but there was no answer. But his worktable and pens were set up, so he must not be far away.

She walked across the room and stole a look at what he was working on. And stopped. He was working on a children's *Odyssey* and this must be a siren calling Odysseus to his doom. He'd borrowed the breakers from their own beach. The boulders were dark and slick in a storm, the sea churning around them. And in the distance a boat, a ship, not a dinghy, was being drawn inexorably to its doom.

But it was the figure standing at the crest of the rocks, her arms extended, beckoning, that held Meri spellbound. The gown of rags whipped in the wind, and her hair lifted wild, coiling with a terrible beauty. And most frightening still, it was her own face that stared back at her.

The glass door opened and Meri started.

Alden came in from the outside, his shoes in his hands. He tossed them on the mat by the door and stopped as Meri stepped out from behind the board.

"Meri." His hair was windblown much like the siren's. As she thought that, he thrust his fingers through it, pushing it out of his eyes. "What are you doing?"

"Looking at your latest. It's . . ." She grasped for a description.

"Not finished." He strode past her and covered it, then turned to her. "How are you feeling?"

"Is that me?"

He didn't pretend not to understand. "No."

"Her?"

"It's a siren. I told you I was working on an Odyssey."

"Is that the way you feel, that she—we—lured you to your . . . what . . . death of childhood, innocence?"

"I think you'd better take it easy with those pain pills. You're talking nonsense."

"Is that what Riley was to you? A siren?"

He looked at her long and hard, long enough to make her squirm beneath his gaze.

"Is it?"

"No."

"Is that the way it happened that night? Did she wave you down, tempt you to the rocks?"

"Stop it."

"I don't want us not to be friends. I just want to understand."

They were interrupted by the sound of a car.

"It's Nora."

Nora, who Meri would love to run out and greet, and Jennifer, who she wouldn't mind avoiding for the rest of her life, and she guessed from Alden's body language, he felt the same.

"I'd better get home. You and Nora are invited for dinner tomorrow, around six? Unless you have other plans."

He shook his head, but he was tucking in his shirt, already headed through the house to the front door.

Meri let herself out the back, still shaken by the picture and determined to get away unseen. She would take the long way back. It was the least she could do to avoid any meeting with Jennifer. The woman had never liked her, probably because Meri had witnessed some of her worst moments.

Meri followed the path down to the rocky beach. She'd always loved the rugged shoreline that joined the two properties. Part pebbles, part coarse sand and the occasional boulder at the base of barren bluffs and dunes that rolled into a grassy meadow, it was the best of all possible worlds Meri had always thought.

She stood balanced on the rocks close to the water as the wind whipped her hair about her face. And she had a sudden whim to climb out on the breakwater. But she didn't give into it. She had no intention of doing anything that would slow her recovery time. She wanted to get back to that ceiling ASAP.

But she did stop to imagine what Alden saw when he looked out to the boulders. Well, she had seen it, hadn't she? Just now in his studio.

She moved on, carefully stepping across the shifting stones until she came to the oval of coarse sand they all considered the beach. It was about fifteen feet long and ten feet deep, beneath the bluffs on one side and protected from the tide and waves by the breakwater.

She didn't linger today, but climbed the narrow path through the beach roses and dune grass and over the bluffs to the meadow. She could see a minivan stopped at Alden's house. She turned and made her way back to Gran's.

Alden stood in the yard watching as three car doors opened on the late-model minivan. Nora practically fell out of the back, but Mark was the first to reach Alden. He stuck out his hand, and they shook hands like two business associates in the board-room.

They let go just as Nora launched herself at Alden.

"I'll get her stuff," Mark said and stepped away.

Nora threw her arms around Alden, whispering, "Thanks for letting me come."

Jennifer appeared from the other side of the car. For a change she looked less than put together, though she was putting on a good front. Not that it was easy; her face was more rounded than usual, and her pregnancy showed tastelessly beneath a tight tank top and sweater. As far as he was concerned that look didn't work on young mothers, and Jennifer was pushing forty. This surely had to be her last baby.

"Well, here she is," she said without preface. Alden's arm automatically tightened around his daughter.

Nora made the sign of the cross. "Yes, you can go now with a clear conscience."

Jennifer glared at Nora, then turned it on Alden. "See what I mean."

Alden refused to rise to the bait.

Mark came back with a huge suitcase and stuffed backpack and put them down at Alden's feet. "We're very disappointed in her behavior," Mark added, in his jovial superior way that made Alden want to deck him. But mainly he just wondered where Lucas was. And why he hadn't gotten out of the car, at least to say hello.

As he thought it, Lucas appeared in the car door, slid down to the ground, and walked slowly toward him. He'd hit puberty since Alden had last seen him, and he felt a clunk in his gut, to see his son looking pretty much like Alden had looked at that age, when until now he had always resembled Jennifer. He was tall, skinny, uncomfortable in his skin, and evidently not wanting to see his father.

He stopped when he was about four feet away, the center of everyone's attention.

What the hell? "Hey, Luke, I hear there's a dynamite computer museum in Boston."

His son looked miserable.

Beside him, Nora cleared her throat. "Maybe Dad would like a hello."

Lucas glanced at Jennifer and Mark again, then walked forward and gave Alden a stiff one-armed hug. "Sorry, Dad, do you mind if I go?" he mumbled.

Alden gave him a reassuring squeeze. It felt damn good to

have both children in his arms for even a second, one desperate to stay and one clearly wanting to leave. "It's fine; have a blast."

He heard the whoosh of relief. Then Lucas moved away.

There was a whine from the car. "Mommy, I want to go."

"We have to leave; we're already late having to go out of our way just to drop her off."

"Well, don't let us stop you," Alden said. "Don't feel like you have to hang around just to be polite."

It was a cheap shot, but Jennifer always brought out his worst. It earned him a snort from Nora, and a suppressed smile from Lucas, which relieved his mind, though he did intend to get Nora's take on what was happening with her brother and the family.

"I hope you're satisfied, Nora." And to Alden. "See if you can do anything with her." Jennifer's Nikes slipped in the dirt and she stalked to the car. She was off her game, or else she would have remembered not to waddle. Alden shook hands with Mark for the second time, this time more enthusiastically, grateful that he would be the one stuck in the car with her for the next few hours; hell, stuck with her for life.

Only Nora and Lucas remained. Nora triumphant, Lucas wavering.

"Lucas," Jennifer called from the car.

Lucas startled. Took an awkward step forward. "I love you, Dad," he breathed, before he hurried back to the car.

Alden and Nora, still attached like a barnacle to his side, watched the van drive away.

"Thank you, thank you, thank you," Nora said.

"You're welcome, welcome, welcome, I think," he answered. "What was with Lucas?"

"Oh him, he's conflicted."

"About?"

"His loyalties. You know. He feels he owes it to them because they pay for everything, but he's afraid that you'll think he's a traitor, you know, to you." She sighed. "Don't get all weirded out by it. He'll grow out of it. Plus he's one of the guys, sort of. They're all guys, Mark, Henley, Ryan—even the next one is going to be a boy. They've already named it. And talk to it. Blech. Little Mason," she drawled. "It's disgusting."

Alden laughed. He'd missed her refreshing view of the world. But he was a little worried about her assessment of her brother's feelings, her use of words like *conflicted* and *loyalties.* Either someone had been seeing a therapist or Nora had been watching too much afternoon television.

He took her bag and backpack and they went into the house.

Nora stopped inside the doorway. "Dad, it's like a mausoleum in here."

"Because I don't use this part so much. I've turned the solarium into my studio. You want to stay upstairs in your old room or downstairs?"

She looked at him and he realized how long it had been since they'd actually spent time here. Recently he'd been going to New Haven to see them because they were both busy with way too many activities if you asked him. Twice he had taken them to Manhattan for a weekend. Now he was hit with a searing desire to have them back home.

It was followed immediately by the knowledge that Jennifer would never allow it. He'd been a fool to let her have custody. Everyone convinced him they were better off with their mother, that his lifestyle wouldn't give them the best opportunities. And he'd been stupid enough to believe them. Now he had a daughter who caused trouble and a son who seemed to jump at his own shadow.

"Yoo-hoo, Daddikins, come back."

"What?"

"You just checked out for a sec. I don't blame you. I don't know why you ever married her. She's not very nice."

He should have said, *don't talk about your mother like that,* but it was true, Jennifer was not a very nice person. At least she hadn't been with him; he'd hoped that Mark would make the difference for his kids' sakes. "I got you and Lucas out of it, didn't I?"

"Well, there is that. So why wouldn't I want to stay upstairs?"

Alden shrugged. "No reason. I've just moved down to Geraldine's old room."

"Fat Gerry, the cook? Why?"

"Don't know. Just seemed easier."

"I'm staying upstairs in my old room. And I get that you might not want to stay in the, um, connubial bedroom, but there are eight other bedrooms to choose from."

"Did anyone ever tell you, you've got a mouth on you?"

She grinned. "All the time. Come on. Let's check out upstairs." She stopped, looked him up and down, an evil glint in her eye. "If you're not too decrepit to make it up the stairs."

"Race you."

She won easily. And waited for him at the landing like a triumphant, dark-haired Valkyrie. Alden made a note of that look; he could definitely use it for something.

"Okay, I'm a bit out of shape, and I did have extra baggage." He dumped the suitcase and backpack on the floor. "Both of which seem to be filled with rocks."

"Mainly stuff, not too many clothes, I'm afraid. I thought maybe you would ask Meri to take me on a shopping spree, wonderful father that you are. Is she around?"

"Actually, yes. She's even here this weekend. But she injured her hand. I don't know how up she'll be for shopping till you both drop."

"How did it happen?"

"Something about a ceiling medallion. You can ask her when you see her. We're invited over for Sunday dinner."

"What are we going to do today?" She pushed her bedroom door open.

"Whatever you like."

"I want to unpack, find you a room to stay in, have lunch . . . can we go for pizza? And is the sailboat still in dry dock?"

"Got it out, knew you'd want to take her out."

"Then I don't know, maybe we could just pick something up for dinner, watch pay-per-view and just hang out."

"Sounds like a plan." Actually he was flattered. She wanted to hang out. With her old man. Pretty cool.

"Maybe after lunch, I'll go say hello to Meri."

Meri awoke from an unintentional nap to total quiet. She'd meant to help Gran clean the house, but here she was stretched out on the sofa, with an afghan that Gran must have put over her.

She had one more day to get back to normal and ready to work. Even with one hand. She'd have to stop those pills and grit it out. They made her too loopy. And she needed all her faculties when climbing back on that scaffolding.

Meri knew that beneath her drug-induced stupor she was anxious to see what the medallion had uncovered, if she weren't so damn lethargic.

She forced herself to sit up, then put her feet on the floor and stood. Immediately, she was inclined to sit back down but reminded herself it was just the drugs and they would wear off soon. She went to the powder room and splashed cold water on her face.

Gran was sitting at the kitchen table with a cup of tea. The kitchen was spotless, more spotless than it usually was.

"Why didn't you wake me? I meant to help with the house-work."

"You needed your rest. Tea?"

"I'll get it." Meri detoured to look out the door to the house across the meadow. "I wonder how it's going over there."

"I'm sure it's fine. Alden took the car out awhile back, but they came back after about an hour."

"Probably went for pizza."

"Most likely. Well, I'm glad Nora's here. That family—they hardly stayed long enough to dump her and her suitcase, before they drove away." Gran pushed the sugar bowl toward Meri. "Good riddance."

"No one liked Jennifer, did they?"

"She made it hard for anyone to like her. Airs, that one." She tsked. "Men. Never do have a lick of sense when it comes to women."

Well, Alden didn't seem to. And neither, according to Gran, had his father. "Dad didn't do so bad."

That made Gran smile. "Yes, he did very well, marrying your mother."

"Yes, a very good choice," Meri agreed. "I think I'll make some toast. Do you want anything?"

"No, dear, but I'll get it for you."

"Thanks, but I better learn how to work with one hand for a while."

It took some doing, but Meri had finally sat down at the table with her toast when there was a knock at the back door; the door opened. "Gran, Meri, are you guys home? It's me, Nora."

"We're in the kitchen," Meri called. "Come on in."

Meri and Gran both stood to greet her. A whirlwind blew into the room.

"Lord, child, you've grown," Gran said as she was enveloped in Nora's hug.

"Take after my papa." She pronounced it like an actress on the BBC.

"Hey, Meri." Meri got a brief hug. "That looks pretty serious."

Meri held up her bandage. "Looks worse than it really is. I'll be back to work on Monday. But look at you."

Nora stepped back and struck a pose. She was tall like both

her parents, but she'd always been a more delicate version of Alden. Now her black hair was short and spiked, and her straight boyish figure had some added subtle curves. She wore makeup but not overdone, tight jeans, a sweater with dolman sleeves that looked designer; no grubby teenager or Goth girl there.

"We're having tea. You want some?"

"Thanks, but I just stuffed myself at Sakonnet Pizza. You guys go ahead. I'll just hang." She pulled out a chair and sat down. And smiled until the other two did the same.

"Dad's taking me sailing in the morning. He said you're welcome, but he doesn't think you should risk getting your hand wet."

"And he's right," Gran said before Meri could answer.

"He's probably right. This is so stupid."

"Do you think maybe you'd feel like taking me shopping one day? I didn't bring a lot of clothes."

"Sure. I have to be back at work on Monday."

Gran frowned.

"Doug's counting on me. And there's plenty of work I can do one handed, though I'll probably have to ask Alden to take me to the bus."

"I'm sure he'll take you to Newport," Gran said.

"I might ask him to," Meri said. "And, Nora, if your dad says it's okay, I thought he could bring you into Newport on Thursday after work. You could stay over with me and we could do Newport on Friday, get some shopping in, and hit the karaoke bar with Carlyn on Friday night.

"We can come back here for the weekend so you can spend more time with your dad before you have to leave. What time are they coming back for you?"

"Um." Nora glanced at Gran, then Meri. "Actually, they're not."

Chapter 14

They're having your father drive you back?" Gran asked. Meri could tell by her tone, she was thinking how selfish that was, when they could pick her up on their way back to New Haven from Boston. Meri agreed, though it would give father and daughter that much more time together. "They're not making you take the train?"

"Actually no, the thing is . . . I'm not going back at all."

After a stunned few seconds, Meri ventured, "They've agreed to let you stay here with Alden?"

Nora ran her finger along the wood grain of the table. "They don't exactly know it yet."

"Ah," Gran said. "And how does your father feel about this decision?"

"Well . . ." Nora breathed out a dramatic sigh. "I haven't exactly told him, either. Actually, I thought you two might help me convince him when we come for dinner tomorrow."

Alden had said he was worried about her. Meri thought that was the main reason he had asked her to spend some time with her, when Meri knew he'd rather have every second with Nora to himself. Well, she would do her best.

"This is kind of sudden, isn't it?"

"Not really."

Gran went to the cupboard and brought down a tin of homemade cookies. When had she baked those? Meri wondered. She hadn't even smelled the aroma lingering in the air.

Therese put the tin on the table, and Nora absently reached for one. Chewed and sighed. "I've been thinking about it for a while. It's a good idea. Once you get over the shock you'll see what a great idea it is."

Meri thought their shock would be minor compared to Jennifer's or Alden's.

Nora had devoured her first cookie and started on the second. Gran went to the fridge and poured her a glass of milk.

Meri wondered what had happened at home to make Nora want to come back here. New Haven had to be more exciting for a teenager than living out here and going to school in Tiverton. How on earth would Alden juggle his work with living with a teenager?

"Did anything specific happen?"

Nora shook her head, but she didn't look up. Meri's stomach fell sickeningly as she thought of another teenager who had sought refuge here. Surely nothing bad had happened to Nora. Jennifer might be a selfish, demanding witch, but Meri didn't for a minute think she would put up with Mark acting inappropriately with Nora, whether physically or verbally. Though she might dish out some of that abuse herself.

To be fair, Meri didn't think Jennifer would ever hurt Nora or Lucas. They were her children as much as Alden's. Maybe it was a case of a teenage girl overreacting to some punishment or being grounded, the modern running-away-from-home story.

"You would miss your friends," Gran added. "Though we would be very happy to have you near."

"I don't have that many. And the ones I do have are 'undesirable' and 'inappropriate.'" The way Nora dragged out the two words, Meri knew she was quoting someone. Probably Jennifer or Mark.

"So when do you plan on telling everyone?" Meri asked.

Nora shrugged. "I thought you could help me broach it with Dad. And then I was going to have him tell Mom, though maybe that's not such a good idea. She'll say no, just to bust his—" She glanced quickly at Gran. "His chops."

Meri thought her first statement was closer to the truth of the matter. "So who is going to tell her?"

Nora frowned at Meri. "Not you."

Meri slumped with relief that she wouldn't be asked to deliver that message, which of course would be ridiculous.

Nora switched her attention to Gran. "I thought maybe you could tell her that I was looking ill or something and needed the bracing sea air for a while, then it will be summer and Daddy can demand to have us for those three months, then . . . well, I'll worry about that when the time comes."

Gran crossed her arms and frowned at Nora, though Meri could tell she was fighting a smile. Nora always knew how to finagle what she wanted from Gran.

"You discuss it with your father, then he and I will talk." Gran shook her finger at Nora. "But that's only if you're not doing this out of spite."

"Cross my heart," Nora said, suddenly sounding much younger. Meri had to remind herself that just because Nora was precocious and dressed like a self-assured young woman, in other ways she was still a child.

"Besides, Dad needs me."

Gran raised her eyebrows. "Your dad loves you and loves having you with him. But he takes care of himself just fine."

"No, he doesn't. He's living in the cook's quarters. And I bet he hasn't been on a date since our mother left."

Gran and Meri both laughed at that.

"At least not that he's telling you, young lady." Gran pointed a finger at her. "Now, we'd all be glad to have you stay, but you be sure it's for the right reasons."

Nora stood and carried her glass to the sink. "I'd better get back." She bit her lip. "Meri, are you serious about me staying over in Newport?"

"Absolutely."

"Great. See you tomorrow, I guess. I'm making him move back upstairs while I'm here. Too weird." She kissed Gran on the cheek and waved her fingers at Meri. "Thanks for the cookies and milk." She went to the back door, hesitated, and turned back to them. "I'm not going back no matter what they say."

Meri and Gran looked at each other when she'd gone.

"What do you think that was all about?" Meri asked.

"I'd say that either they didn't let her do something she wanted to do and she's pouting, or missing her father, or . . . they're not treating her as they should."

"Why wouldn't they?"

"Well, I'm not saying that this is what's happened. But Jennifer and Mark have a whole new family. I never understood why Alden let her have sole custody of those two. It was just like he lay down and let her walk over him on her way out. She was always so selfish. And she never really seemed to care that much for her children unless there was an audience. I imagine she demanded custody just to get back at Alden."

"Why?" asked Meri. "People get divorced. What could he ever have done to her that makes her so hateful? I know, stupid question. I remember coming home a couple of times and hearing them yelling at each other and throwing things."

Gran nodded.

"I don't think I've ever heard him yell since."

"Or before," Gran added. "There was something about that woman; they were like oil and water. Good riddance, I say."

Meri smiled. Gran always dismissed Jennifer with a "good riddance," and Meri was inclined to agree with her. Especially after seeing Nora so adamant about not going back. Not whiny or pouty at all, but determined. Should be interesting.

Sunday morning broke sunny, cool with a hint of breeze. *A good day for sailing,* Meri thought, a little disappointed that she wasn't going, too. But Alden was right. Even if she put a bag over her hand, it was stupid to take chances when there was so much work to do. Besides, she had something else she wanted to do before their Sunday dinner.

"I'd like to see my mother's grave. Both of them," Meri told Gran over breakfast.

Gran nodded and forked a waffle onto Meri's plate, which was already holding several slices of thick bacon and scrambled eggs.

"I'll drive you after breakfast."

Meri thought she was perfectly capable of driving herself, but maybe not, and she wouldn't spurn Gran's offer, not when things were so tenuous.

But were they? Hadn't they already settled back to normal? With Gran feeding her and sitting around the kitchen table just talking, it was like nothing had changed, and yet . . .

Maybe they hadn't changed for anyone else. But they had for Meri. She ached for that poor girl who was her mother. Frightened and alone. At least she'd stumbled on the most loving house she could hope for—with the most loving, protective women in the world.

Meri longed to know her real story. What or whom she was running from. And why. And she might try to find out at some point. But she wouldn't share this goal with her family. It would be like a slap in the face.

One thing she did know was that she was going to get a

close-up look at her grandparents. Laura hadn't exactly given them away. And there were several Rochforts in Newport and the surrounding areas. But by the way she described them, Meri knew which ones she and Gran had visited.

And ironically, they were big historical foundation supporters. She'd probably been to untold fund-raisers and benefits with them. Not *with* them, she reminded herself. They mingled in the patron circle. Meri was one of the invited artisans who lent validity to the restoration being benefited.

She wasn't a restorer for nothing. She knew the necessity of research, and her grandparents should have a chance to tell their side of the story if they wanted it. She knew about them; maybe it would be better to leave it at that.

And yet, another part of her, maybe the less compassionate part, wanted the Rochforts to know of her existence, to see what they'd missed. And even a smaller part wanted to see just what kind of parents would leave their daughter to be buried by strangers.

But that was for a later time. Now she was just curious to see the graves of Riley and little Rose; Meri hadn't noticed them when they buried her mother Laura. She hadn't seen much of anything that day. She would leave flowers just to acknowledge them, all three of them. They were all a part of her.

"Can I use your shower before we go? It will be easier than climbing into the tub upstairs."

"Of course, but you'll have to keep your hand dry."

Meri sighed. "I know. It's a pain in the . . . neck."

When Meri had blundered through her shower and dressed in clean clothes, Gran had finished washing the dishes and changed into nicer clothes.

Should we take flowers?" Meri asked as they drove along. Spring was definitely everywhere, the grasses covering the ground with a blanket of brilliant yellow green. The trees were budding, and she could see bits of yellow, white, and purple peeking from the fields.

"I doubt if we'll find anywhere to buy flowers without going farther afield than the church. But wait and see what I've planted, and then we can drive into Portsmouth if you want more."

Gran found a place on the street, and they walked arm in arm toward the Calder plot. It was an old cemetery, surrounded by trees that were just beginning to turn green. Family plots were grouped more or less together across the well-kept grass, the older, rain-stained markers nestled haphazardly among the newer cleaner ones.

Meri looked across to where the Calder plot sat amid a blanket of daffodils. "Oh, Gran, it's beautiful. When did you plant them?"

"Last fall. Alden helped me. I was afraid the squirrels might get them, but they did okay."

They stopped at the center marker where Gerald Stillman Calder, the oldest member of the Calder family was buried. And next to him, his wife, Anthea. Meri's grandfather and Gran's husband, Cyrus Stillman Calder, was buried to their right.

Next to him was an empty space, and Meri knew that it was waiting for her grandmother; she hoped that it would still be waiting a very long time to come.

Meri's mother, Laura, was next to Gran, and next to her, baby Rose. The smaller marker was a poignant reminder of what her mother had lost. Meri looked at it for a long time, not wanting to rush past the baby whose place she'd taken, and not sure she was ready to face Riley Rochfort, buried among strangers.

She felt Gran take her elbow and they moved together to

look down at the grave, a simple granite cross with Riley Calder carved in simple letters, and the date of her death. Meri exhaled a long breath. She felt odd. A remote, general compassion for the girl, but no sense of family.

She would bring flowers the next time she came out. The daffodils would be gone by then.

"That's so sad," Meri said. "To be lost and frightened. I'm glad she found you and Mom." Meri laughed a little, though it was through tears. "I'm *really* glad she found you." She looked over the sea of daffodils. "Is there room here for me?"

"Of course, but you don't need to think about that for a long, long time to come."

Meri hoped that was true for both of them, but you never knew. Her mother already lay there and baby Rose and Riley.

"Dan bought some space from the Johnstons, next to us. There are only a couple of them left so they didn't really need the extra room. So not to worry, there will be plenty of room for him and whoever else wants to rest here."

"I want to be buried here."

"Fine but when you have a husband, you might want to be buried in his family plot. And why are we talking about graves when we should be discussing pot roast and whether you think Nora would prefer biscuits or dinner rolls?"

The discussion was over and they began walking back toward the car discussing dinner preparations. But before they drove away, Meri took a last look where the Calder plot stood out from all the others surrounded by daffodils. It wouldn't matter if she finally did marry Peter or someone else. Or if she ended up not marrying anyone.

She would return here to the Calders.

As soon as they arrived home, Gran shooed her out of the kitchen. "There is plenty to do later. Take a little rest."

But Meri didn't feel like resting. She wanted to be useful,

back at work. Sitting around being waited on was driving her crazy, and she was afraid it might start showing.

"I think I'll walk down to the beach and sit for a while."

"Good. But take a blanket and a warmer coat. The wind is still sharp off the sea."

So wearing a heavy jacket that belonged to Gran and carrying a beach blanket, Meri struck off over the dunes.

Gran was right. It was a lot colder by the water. But she managed to find a place on the patch of sandy beach that was in the sun and also sheltered from the worst of the wind. She spread out the blanket as best she could and sat down.

It was low tide and the sand stretched almost to the rocks of the breakwater and the narrow strip of land that connected it to the shore. To the far left she could see open sea.

Most of the time the water here was calm, the waves gentle, thanks to the buffer of the breakwater. And when the tide was out, they'd spent many a time happily crawling over the rocks in search of tide pools, and crabs, and all sorts of wonderful things that sometimes were caught in the crevices. But in a storm at high tide, the waves battered the barrier, and the rocks became treacherous.

Is that what had happened to Riley Rochfort? She hadn't really intended to kill herself and her baby. She'd come out here to wait for Katy to be finished at the farm, so she could ask for her help.

The diary had said the storm came in quickly. Storms often did, not even leaving enough time for you to gather up your things and race to Corrigan House, which was closest. How could Riley know that she would be caught on the slippery rocks? And except for Alden, she might have fallen unintentionally to her death.

And mine, thought Meri. The truck driver said Riley hadn't seen him. It was just a horrible senseless turn of fate. Because of parents who wouldn't even take her back in death.

And Meri ached for that poor young girl, though strangely enough not as her mother, but as a girl much like Nora, only lost and frightened.

Meri shivered. The sun had gone behind a cloud and the beach became uncomfortable, but she wasn't ready to leave. She lay down facing the sea and wrapped the blanket around her.

The even rhythm of the waves, the shush, shush of water as it rushed up the shore and receded, all combined to calm her, slow her breath until it ran in tandem to the waves. She closed her eyes and just listened.

Sometime later, she heard the crunch of feet on the pebbles; she yawned, stretched. She must have drifted off and Gran had sent Alden or Nora to bring her home. She started to sit up when the sun was blocked by a shadow.

Meri squinted up at it. "Did Gran send you to get me?"

"She said you were down here by yourself. Do you think that's smart considering your injury?"

"Peter?" She blinked a few times until her eyes could see him as more than a silhouette. "What are you doing here?"

"I came to see you, of course."

She laughed. "Sorry. I wasn't expecting you, that's all. Sit down." She patted the blanket beside her.

He looked at the blanket and looked down at his trousers and sports jacket. Then he knelt down, brushed sand off the blanket, and cautiously sat down.

"You should have brought a chair down. You've probably got sand in your bandage."

She looked at her bandage and saw grains of coarse sand stuck on the gauze. "It's about to come off anyway. Wait a minute. Aren't you supposed to be at your parents' house?"

"I came back early so I could take you back to town."

"That was sweet. But we're having guests for dinner. I was going back afterward." Actually she hadn't even thought about how she was going to get back. Alden would probably take her.

"Your grandmother told me, and she invited me to stay."

"You don't sound too happy. She's a great cook." Actually Meri wasn't too happy either. Alden and Peter at the same dinner table couldn't be anything but tense. She didn't get why her father and Alden were so against him. Well, not against him, exactly; maybe they would have felt that way about any man she was serious about. Maybe having dinner together would give Alden a chance to get to know him better.

"Unless you think you can get out of it. I'd like to get back to town."

"I can't. Sorry. I wish you'd called first."

"I did, but you didn't answer."

Because her phone was upstairs by her bed. "Well, I'm glad you came anyway. Do you mind staying? Alden's daughter just arrived for a visit and Gran invited her and Alden for dinner. I'm kind of like her big sister, and it would be rude to leave."

He leaned over her, bracing his weight on his hand. "I guess not, but I want you all for myself. Last bite of dessert and we're out of here." He kissed her. Like he meant it, pushing her back onto the sand until his body covered hers.

He pulled away long enough to say, "Too bad it's so damn cold. Or I wouldn't mind staying here for the rest of the after-noon."

He kissed her again, braced on one elbow while the other hand slipped beneath her sweater.

She laughed and pushed his hand away. "Great idea but it's almost time for dinner. Help me up."

Chapter 15

We'd better take the car," Nora said. "Meri said she wanted to go back to Newport tonight. I told her you wouldn't mind driving her. You wouldn't, would you?"

"Of course not." Alden tossed her jacket to her. "Let's go."

"And you really don't mind if I stay overnight in Newport on Thursday? We'll be back on Saturday."

"I think it sounds like fun."

"You won't miss me?"

He opened the car door for her. "Of course I will. I always miss you. I'll live."

"If you'd rather I didn't go . . ."

"Go. Have fun. It's four days away; you may be sick of being stuck in the country for that long." He closed the door and walked around to the driver's side. A strange mood had come over Nora since they'd come home from sailing.

They'd laughed and worked together out on the water, too busy to talk much, but he was sure she'd had a good time. But as soon as they started for home, she'd grown quiet, pensive almost.

Was she missing her other family? *Her other family.* He tamped down the anger that could still blindside him at unsuspecting moments. Not because his marriage hadn't worked out. That had been pretty obvious from the beginning, if only he'd been looking. But that Jennifer gave him two kids and then took them away. No. That he'd let her take them.

And now Lucas was like a stranger to him. He'd grown from boy to adolescent and Alden had missed it all.

"Daddikins?"

"Yeah?"

The car hit a pothole as he turned onto the car path that joined his house to the Calders and both houses to the county road. "Sorry about that." He hadn't been paying attention. He really should come down and fill it in. Hell, he could call someone to come repave the whole damn thing, though a little manual labor would be good for his soul. "What were you going to say?"

"I was thinking . . ."

Alden waited, but she didn't say more.

A minute later they came to Calder Farm. He stopped in the drive and turned to his daughter, but she jumped out of the car. He got out after her.

"Whoa, who's that with Meri?" Nora asked.

Alden looked toward the dunes and saw Meri walking toward them, hand in hand with . . . "That's Peter Foley. Meri's . . ." He hesitated. Boyfriend? Significant other? Fiancé? "Friend."

Meri dropped Peter's hand and waved.

Alden and Nora waited for them to reach the house. Alden and Peter shook hands, and Nora introduced herself with the first bit of enthusiasm she'd shown since the morning's sail.

"Peter surprised me with a visit," Meri explained.

"Thought she might want a ride back to town," Peter said. He smiled at Nora.

Okay, so he was charming. Alden didn't trust charming. And neither did Dan Hollis. Alden had to admit, though, Peter had never done anything to trigger their distrust. Maybe it was just jealousy, not wanting to lose Meri from the family fold.

Peter was a man going places and he would take Meri with him. But he didn't have an artistic bone in his body. Probably thought Meri would be just as happy decorating their McMansion as restoring a historic building.

They walked toward the house together. Peter held the door and Meri and Nora entered together, Alden following close enough to hear Nora whisper to Meri, "Hot, hot, hot."

They both giggled. Alden felt about ninety.

If Meri hoped that having Gran, Alden, and Peter together over for dinner would bring them closer together, she gave up hope when Peter announced that he was going to L.A. for an internship.

"It's a great opportunity, even though it means being away from Meri for the summer." He paused to smile at her.

That at least kept him from seeing her grandmother's tightened lips and Alden's raised eyebrows. Nora just looked from person to person, aware that something was going on, but out of the loop.

Meri sighed. Smiled. "It's only three months, and I'm really busy with Gilbert House." She helped herself to another roll even though there was already one on her plate.

"So then will you be coming back to Newport for law school?" Gran asked politely.

Meri could tell she didn't approve of the news. They'd all been expecting Peter to propose this summer.

"That's the plan. This roast is delicious."

After that, Meri just marked the time until dinner was over. Things had certainly taken a turn for the strange. Hopefully she was the only one who noticed.

Gran, of course, was meticulously polite and interested in Peter's every word. Alden was excruciatingly civil, only it came off, at least to Meri, as cold and condescending. Though maybe she only picked up on that because she knew him so well.

Nora was hyperattentive, trying to look like a poised adult while hanging on Peter's every word. By the time dessert came, Meri felt like she was watching a one-act play starring her postponed fiancé.

She watched Peter, too. There was nothing not to like. He was smart, kind, good-looking, and on a career track that would bring security to his family. There was definitely chemistry between them.

She loved him, although it hadn't happened at first sight. She'd thought he was kind of arrogant and too self-assured. But she'd gone out with him and they hit it off. And their relationship had grown into something stronger. Not a great passion, but everyone knew how those turned out; just look at Heathcliff and Cathy.

Peter pressed his knee against hers under the table. He was ready to leave. And it *was* getting late.

She pushed her chair back. "I'll help you with the dishes, Gran, then we'd better get back."

Nora glanced quickly from her to Alden.

Meri knew Nora had meant to discuss her plan to stay with Alden at the end of the holiday, but it would have to wait. "You're coming on Thursday?" Meri asked.

Nora started. "Yes, if that's okay." She looked at her father.

"I'll bring her in."

"Good, drop her off at Gilbert House. Carlyn and I will take her to dinner; you, too, if you can stay."

"Thanks," he said drily. "You go on back to Newport. You won't be any good in the kitchen with one hand. Nora and I will help with the dishes."

Meri looked quizzically at him. He often helped with the dishes. But he seemed anxious to get rid of her. Or maybe just Peter.

"Thanks." She turned to Peter. "I'll get my things."

Everyone began clearing plates. When she returned with her

bag a few minutes later, they were all in the kitchen. Alden was washing, Nora drying, and Gran dividing leftovers into plastic containers, while Peter watched.

Peter took her bag and they all walked out to the drive to see them off.

Meri said her good-byes while Peter put her bag in the trunk of his car. She kissed Gran, hugged Nora. She gave Alden a quick hug and said in his ear, "We didn't get to talk, but I just want you to know, you don't have to worry about me. I can take care of myself."

"Ready?" Peter called from the car.

"Bye, see you on Thursday." She got into the car. The three of them waved as Meri and Peter drove away.

"Absolutely American Gothic," Peter said and sped up.

Meri took a last look back, but they had already gone back inside.

Don't you guys like Peter?" Nora grabbed the dish towel she'd left on the table and went back to drying.

"Of course we do," Gran said. "He's a lovely young man."

"Dad?"

"Lovely."

"Well, I think he's cool, for an old dude."

Gran looked to the ceiling and shook her head.

"He's in his thirties," Alden said.

Nora grinned mischievously. "Well, old for me, probably a baby from where you're looking."

"That must make me ancient."

"Makes you the best dad ever." Nora stood on tiptoes to kiss his cheek.

"And don't you forget it, young lady," Gran told her, with a twinkle. "Your father's in his prime."

Her words startled Alden into a laugh.

Nora looked dubious. "So what's wrong with Peter?"

"Nothing at all," Gran said. "I guess we just don't want our little girl getting married and going away. I'm sure we'll feel the same when you decide to get married."

"Which won't be for another twenty years," Alden added.

"Not to worry, Papa. I'll never leave you."

Alden saw her shoot a look toward Therese. Nora turned resolutely back to him, and he wondered what she was going to drop. God, please don't let her be pregnant or on drugs or . . .

"Actually, I mean it. I want to stay here . . . with you . . ."

"I'm not following."

"I want to live with you, go to school here, bake cookies with Gran. I hate New Haven, and I hate living in that house."

Panic rushed over him in one drowning tsunami. Had something really happened? He looked at his daughter and saw Riley Rochfort, practically the same age, pregnant and un-wanted. And running from something they had never under-stood.

"Is someone hurting you?" His voice sounded foreign even to himself.

In his periphery, he saw Therese's eyes widen. But Nora just rolled hers. "If you mean is Mark doing the dirty with me, no. He'd be singing falsetto if he tried."

That's my girl, Alden thought.

"It's like this. Living there is like being in a hotel. Without room service," she added.

Gran pulled out a kitchen chair for him to sit down and poured him another cup of coffee. He sat.

That put Nora on the other side of the table from him. She stood there with her hands braced on the kitchen table, like a lawyer for the defense.

"So can I? Ple-e-e-ase?"

Gran pulled out another chair, but instead of sitting, Nora

pressed Therese into it and pulled another one close to hers before she sat. Gran was obviously considered an ally. Had they discussed this before?

"Nora, dear. I think your father needs a little more explanation than that."

Nora nodded and began drawing a figure eight with her finger on the wood. "They're all happily going about their lives, together as a family. Even Lucas, but mainly because he's clueless. He eats, he sleeps, he thinks. He's happy." She almost wailed the last word. "But it's *their* family, Mark and Jennifer, and Henley, Ryan, and little amoeba Mason.

"Ugh, she even made us look at pictures of that little worm floating around. I can't stand him already."

Alden fought back a smile. Maybe she was just jealous. He would like to ask Jennifer for her take on the situation, but he knew it would only result in her blaming him for inciting Nora to rebel. Would the woman be as clueless with her own children as she was with—He stopped, shocked at his thought. Nora and Lucas *were* her own children. Alden's and hers, but not hers and Mark's. Could that possibly make a difference to her?

He glanced at Therese, who was looking back at him as if she were thinking the same thing.

"So can I stay? Meri and Gran think it's a good idea."

Gran gently smacked Nora's hand. "Meri and Gran said you would be welcome but that you should discuss it intelligently with your father."

"I know and that's what I'm doing."

Alden knew he should nip this in the bud, but he was beginning to get attached to the idea. It would certainly change his lifestyle. He nearly laughed out loud. Holing up in that behemoth of an old house, monthly trips to Manhattan for work and a modicum of pleasure—he had no lifestyle. Could he possibly be any good for his daughter?

"Have you discussed this with your mother and Mark?"

"No way. She'd just say no, because it involves you." She hesitated, bit her lip. "Why is she so mad at you? Is it because you stuck her with me and Lucas?"

"God no. Whatever gave you that idea?"

Nora shrugged. He could see that she was fighting back tears.

Fortunately Therese was quicker than he was. She put her arm about Nora's shoulders. "Your father loves you very much. And he only allowed your mother to take you two because he thought she could give you a better life."

Because he'd been a fool, Alden admitted to himself.

"Well, you were wrong, Dad." She flung herself at Therese and burst into tears.

"I'm sorry," he said. And watched her cry.

That's why he'd let them go, he thought, looking at Therese rocking his daughter. Because a woman knows how to comfort and sustain. At least most women. At least the Calder women. Maybe Nora was right. She would be a lot happier here with him and Therese and Meri. He stopped himself. Meri would most likely marry Peter and go wherever Peter got a job. Gran was getting older. Would she be up for lending support to his sometimes troublesome daughter?

He stood up. "Let's go home, Noddy. We'll talk about it later."

She looked up, her pale complexion flushed and her eyes swollen pink. "You never call me Noddy anymore."

Because until tonight he'd thought she was too old for childhood nicknames.

Therese pushed herself slowly out of her chair. "You take the rest of that cake home. You might need a midnight snack." She began collecting containers that she put into a plastic bag.

She walked them to the door. "You've got six more days here; don't let your worries keep them from being perfect."

Nora nodded jerkily. "Let's walk, Daddy. We can come get the car tomorrow."

So they walked home, Nora leaning against him.

"Were we bad kids?"

"No, never. It was my fault. Actually it started when we came here to live."

"At Corrigan House?"

"Yeah, I guess the way I had talked about it, your mother thought it was going to be one of the gilded mansions of New-port. Instead it was this." He gestured to the dark shadow of the three-storied monster ahead of them. "I thought it was a perfect place to raise children. But your mother hated it. She insisted we move back to Manhattan."

"But you said no."

"Right." It was one of the few times he'd held firm, at least in the early years. He'd been stupid enough to think Jennifer would grow to love it as much as he did. She'd lasted long enough to have Lucas, then the traveling started. And with it the affairs. And he sat by and let it happen because he was happy without her.

In those days he'd hired a cook, Geraldine, who at her inter-view said, "Most folks just call me Fat Gerry." Nora and Lucas took to her immediately. And he hired a nurse-housekeeper of sorts, Bernadette. They all got along fine, except when Jennifer was there.

"You were right, Daddy. This *was* the perfect place to grow up."

Only they weren't allowed to grow up here; they were ten and eight when they were snatched away. And he'd let that happen.

"It still is," she prodded.

Alden sighed. "Honey, it's falling down. I didn't keep it up." There was no reason to once they had gone. He just hadn't cared. Now he saw how selfish he'd been. If he didn't care about the place, he should at least have kept it up for the next generation. Just like his father had, after his mother had left.

"We can fix it up together."

Alden pulled her close. "You're a great kid, you know that."

"I'm not a kid."

"No, you're a great young woman."

She gave him a little push. "You are such a dad."

Why don't you stay at my place tonight?" Peter said as they drove over the bridge into Newport. "You can stay in bed all day and I'll pamper the daylights out of you, among other things." He gave her a villainous eyebrow waggle that made her laugh.

"As appealing as it sounds, I really need to get home. I have work tomorrow."

"You're kidding, right? You only have one usable hand and I'm leaving in three days."

"I know, I'm sorry. But Doug is expecting me. There's plenty of stuff to do with one hand."

That got her a laugh, but he immediately sobered. "Doug would understand."

Meri began to get annoyed. "I'm sure he would. But it's my job. And I won't let him down. The project depends on every-one involved. *You're* leaving in a few days, but I'm not. I need to keep on track and keep my job."

He sighed and drummed his fingers on the steering wheel. "Want me to stay at your place?"

Meri turned to look at him. "I would love that. But like always, I'll be up and out before nine."

Peter groaned. He reached for her hand, then realized it was the bandaged one and went back to drumming his fingers on the steering wheel.

It was Sunday night and those residents who had left for the weekend were back. It was almost ten minutes before he squeezed the car into a minuscule parking place several blocks from her apartment.

Meri was beginning to wish she had just sent him home, because he'd turned from entertaining to sulky by the time they
walked up the stairs to her door. They were barely inside when
he dropped her bag, turned, and took her in his arms, walking
her backward all the way to the bedroom.

And for the first time that she could remember, Meri didn't
feel that rush of desire that made them rip off clothes and fall
laughing into bed. What she felt was a sense of closure that
somehow they wouldn't make it past this summer, even if Peter
did come back for good.

She pushed the thought out of her mind. She'd been doing
way too much thinking in the last week. Too much trying to
sort out her life and her future. She was just too tired to worry
anymore. So she gave into the moment, enjoying what she had,
and trying not to think about what she was about to lose.

It wasn't until the next morning standing on the sidewalk that
Meri remembered that her car was still at the site where she'd
left it. "Do you mind dropping me off?"

"No, but we'll have to hurry."

Great, he was pissed. He'd tried to talk her into staying
home again that morning, but she'd held firm. She knew that
Doug wouldn't begrudge her another day off, and quite frankly
she didn't know how much she could really do with her injury.

But on the drive home the night before, she had been at-
tacked by an overwhelming desire to see her ceiling. To discover just what lay beneath that detached medallion.

And now that morning was here and they were out of the
apartment, she could hardly contain her curiosity. She didn't
mention it. The last thing she needed was for Peter to think she
was more excited about a ceiling than about staying with him.
But it was what it was.

He was leaving to pursue his career and she was happy for
him, if not exactly ecstatic about being left solo. But she had her

work, too, and though it might not take the world by storm, it was important to her and to history.

She would just have to wait and see which one weathered the test of time better, her ceiling or her boyfriend.

Peter dropped Meri off at the door. "See you tonight?"

"Sure thing."

"I'll call you."

She'd better get used to it. Calls would be the only thing she'd be getting from Peter in the months to come. As she watched him drive away, an empty, sick feeling settled in her stomach. *Aftermath of the drugs,* she told herself and went inside.

Coffee was made; Doug's desk was gone. A flicker of panic shot to her gut before she remembered that Carlyn was moving him to another room.

Meri poured herself a mug of coffee and would have taken a donut from the box on the kitchen table if she had the use of both hands. Between food, the beach, and Peter, her bandage was looking the worse for wear. The doctor had said she could change the bandage.

Maybe she could enlist Carlyn and the project first aid kit. She walked down the hall to the tiny office Carlyn called the executive suite and stuck her head in the door. "You busy?"

Carlyn looked up from her computer screen. "Just counting the minutes until this computer crashes again."

"Uh-oh."

"I called IT, but they can't get over until this afternoon. So I called Joe Krosky. He's on his way."

"Joe fixes computers?"

"Joe does everything. It's amazing. He's working toward a Ph.D. in molecular biology while tracing wall paper patterns in an old house, and tinkering with my hard drive . . ."

Meri burst out laughing, almost upsetting her coffee. Carlyn joined her. "Hell, he's probably good at that, too. I wonder if he can sing?"

Now they were both laughing. It was good to be back. Any qualms about not going to California vanished. This was where she belonged.

"So what did you need me for?" Carlyn asked, wiping her eyes.

"Hold an extra flashlight so I can get a look at my ceiling? They haven't covered it or anything, have they?"

"Nope, waiting for you to tell them what to do."

"Good. Then I need help putting on a new bandage." She held up her hand and turned it for Carlyn to see.

"Ewww. Looks like you've been coal mining with that paw."

"I know. It's pretty disgusting, plus there's way too much bandage."

"Don't even think about using that hand for another week."

"I'm not." Well, not exactly. She'd be careful. "But I do want to see my ceiling."

"You certainly do." Carlyn rolled her chair back and came around her desk. "But you won't need a flashlight. Doug set up floodlights. You're going to be amazed."

They sped walked to the foyer.

"Do not look up."

Meri looked at her feet while lights popped on around her. Carlyn took her shoulders and turned her slightly, much like Meri had done with Alden the day he'd come to bring her mother's diary.

Excitement and gratefulness for her friends and work filled her.

"Now." Carlyn let go and Meri looked up at the ceiling.

Spotlighted by the floor lights, the ceiling practically gleamed with unfaded blue, aquamarine, green, and gold. The medallion had been installed over the original decoration and had protected it for a hundred years.

Meri knew when she looked more closely she would see hairline cracks and maybe some bubbling, but from where she stood it looked pretty incredible.

"Did someone check the condition of the foundation plaster?"

"Doug called in Tommy O'Connell. He's coming today or tomorrow, whenever he can squeeze us in. Until then Doug has closed off the rooms above it. He doesn't want to take a chance of some heavy-footed intern dislodging the section. So you did good, kid."

"Wow, just wow." Meri shoved her mug toward Carlyn. "Take this."

"Why?"

"I have to take a closer look."

"Oh no. Doug said you're not to climb until you have both hands back in working condition."

"Doug doesn't have to know."

Carlyn gave her a look.

"I know, you're right. I wouldn't do that to Doug." She blew out a breath and took her mug back. "Come see what you can do with this hand. Then put me to work."

Chapter 16

Carlyn fetched the first aid kit and began cutting off the old gauze. "Are you sure it's all right for me to do this?"

"You were there. The doctor said it could be taken off after a few days."

"And replaced with another one. But are you sure you wouldn't rather go to him?"

"I'm sure." Meri began peeling away the layers, a little worried at what she would find. "I'd rather be stripping a ceiling," she said and carefully lifted off the last layer. There were three strips of clear tape running across the stitched skin. All in all, the cut looked innocuous. She knew that could be misleading, but she wiggled her thumb and other fingers. "It works."

Carlyn let out a sigh. "I knew it would."

"Boy, I'm pretty lucky."

"You are. Between nerves and arteries." Carlyn shuddered. "But I'm wrapping this up and you're putting it back in that nasty old sling, because we're not taking any chances. And don't you dare try to use your hand."

"Yes, ma'am." She watched Carlyn rebandage her hand. "It's awfully quiet in here. Where is everybody?"

"Coming in late because Doug had to bring in an inspector

to make sure there are no current leaks. No reason to restore if it's just going to get ruined again. So relax. I'll get coffee and you tell me what the heck's going on in your life."

It was almost a relief. Meri knew she couldn't keep what she'd learned from her best friend. Besides, she needed advice. She pulled her backpack onto the table, opened it with one hand, and rummaged inside for an envelope that she had filled that morning while Peter was shaving.

She placed it on the table.

"What's that?" Carlyn asked as she put a mug in front of Meri.

"Sit down over here by me and I'll show you." Meri glanced over her shoulder to make sure they were alone; it was totally a reflex action.

"Oh boy," Carlyn said and sat down.

"Before I show you, there are a couple of things you should know. But I'm serious about this; you can never tell. So let me know if you can do that before I go any further."

Carlyn frowned. One eyebrow slowly lifted as it always did when she was questioning someone's seriousness. "Pinky swear?"

"Cross your heart and hope to die swear."

"Shit." Carlyn got up long enough to shut the door, then pulled her chair closer. "Cross my heart."

"My mother . . ." She told Carlyn about Alden finding a teenager on the breakwater, about her delivering a baby and running away, about her being killed and how her mother had kept Meri as her own.

Carlyn listened to the whole story in silence. "Did you ever find out who she was?"

Meri nodded, bit her lip. "I have a name and a photo, but I'm not sure I even want to go down that road."

"Of course you do." Carlyn reached for the envelope. "May I?"

Meri hesitated. It was too late to go back, and she did need advice . . . and support. "Okay."

Carlyn opened the envelope and slid the contents onto the table. She picked up the photo of Riley and the boy at the beach. "That's your mother?"

Meri nodded.

"And your father?"

"I have no idea."

Carlyn reached for the school ID. "Riley Rochfort. Rochfort? Are you kidding me?"

"There are a lot of Rochforts."

"There are, but I don't know one who isn't loaded." Her eyes widened. "Hell, any one of them could fund this whole project without missing it."

"Carlyn!"

"I didn't mean you should use them, not exactly."

"I don't even know which ones they are, and it doesn't matter. I would never ask them for anything. They were horrible people. My mother and Gran had a moment of stricken conscience and went to them, told them about Riley. They didn't want to hear anything about their daughter or her baby. They said Riley had died on a trip to Europe and accused Mom and Gran of trying to run a scam.

"Though I suppose there could be two Riley Rochforts."

"Unlikely," Carlyn said.

"And there are Rochforts all over the country and probably in Europe."

"You just said your mother and grandmother went to see them."

"I know, they did. But do I really want to know?"

"Of course you do. There's a way to find out. Well, actually, there are several ways to find out, but they're not nearly as dramatic."

Meri couldn't help but laugh. That's one of the many reasons Carlyn was her best friend. She was true blue. And she came through in a pinch. "Actually, I'm more interested in finding out who my father was. There is no information at all in the diary."

"Riley left a diary?"

"No, Laura, my life mother, did."

Carlyn smiled. "I like that, life mother."

"Anyway, I guess they didn't attempt to locate the father. I haven't read it all, but I did skim through it and it all appears to be stuff about me growing up, until my dad, Dan—" She stopped, frowned. "From now on my mother and father are Laura and Dan."

Carlyn placed her hand over Meri's. "They always have been."

"I know. Alden said the same thing. I've been confusing myself the last few days. I think what I really want is some kind of closure. I don't care about the Rochforts. But I would just like to know . . ."

"About your father—your birth father."

"Yeah. I think. I mean, if that's him, he was just a clueless teenager. Did Riley tell him? Did he freak? Did he love her?"

"And if you find him, what?"

"I don't know, I guess it depends."

"He probably has his own life now, maybe married with kids, maybe moved away."

"I know, I'm just . . . curious."

"Then let's find out who this guy is and go from there."

"Where do we start?"

"Local high school yearbooks. Most of them will be online."

An hour later they had put a name to the face. They were both huddled over the laptop in Carlyn's office. Doug had stuck his head in twice only to be shooed away by Carlyn.

"You're incredible," Meri said as they both stared at the school picture of Everett Simmons, All-Star basketball, debate club, school newspaper, and Most Likely to Tell a Joke.

"Sounds like a fun kind of guy." Carlyn opened another window and typed in his name, then scrolled down the links. "Hmm. There are several."

"What are the chances he's still in Newport?" Meri asked.

Carlyn refined the search. "And there he is. A prominent local lawyer."

"But are we sure that's really him?"

More typing. A business network site came up. "Yep. Born, raised, and went to school here. I'd say this is the guy."

Meri stared at the information. "You're amazing."

"This is how I spend my days, ferreting out possible donors. I know things about people that if I were so inclined, I could blackmail them into giving to the cause." She pointed a finger at Meri. "But I would never, not even to a stranger. So are you going to see him?"

"I'll think about it. Could you print that out for me?"

"Sure thing."

Meri was just folding the printouts of the photo and the address when they heard voices in the hallway.

Carlyn pushed her hair back. "Let's go see what the verdict is."

They walked back to the kitchen where Doug and two men were bent over a schematic that was spread out on the table.

"It's a question of whether you want to replace this section of pipe"—one of the men ran his pencil point along the paper—"or just keep the water turned off forever." He straightened up. "Look, Doug, you know I wouldn't hardball you. You might be okay for several years, but is it worth the risk?

"You should do it now; other than that, all you have to worry about is some fixtures. If you want to save money, shut down some of the bathrooms. Keep one for the office, one for the staff, and fit out another one as a nonworking period piece. Pull out the rest. Other than that and gutter repairs, you're fine."

Doug saw Carlyn and Meri and motioned them in.

Carlyn went over and perused the spec sheet.

Everyone watched silently as her head moved back and forth.

"Well," Doug asked, unable to contain his anxiety.

Carlyn shrugged one shoulder. "Makes sense."

"Do we have the money?"

"I'll find it."

Doug looked at the two men.

"That's good enough for me." The older man began rolling up the spec sheet. "I'll try to send someone over Wednesday to take some measurements. See if I can fit you in between projects. It's a pretty straightforward job."

"Famous last words," Doug said at the same time Meri thought it. She was pretty sure Carlyn was thinking the same thing.

"Won't know until we open her up."

Doug shot his fingers through his hair. "Okay. Thanks, Marty. We're good for it."

"I know. You better be good to this lady." He grinned at Carlyn. "She can pull money out of thin air. Don't let anybody steal her away."

Carlyn shot a look at Doug. "I'm not going anywhere."

He nodded shortly and walked the two men to the parking lot.

"Well," Carlyn said, when they were gone. "Guess I better get to work and scrounge up a few thousand."

"What can I do to help?"

Carlyn turned and spread out her hands. "Papa was a name unknown," she sang to the tune of "Papa Was a Rolling Stone." She started backing away. "Go on and find out and then we'll go on."

She sashayed out the door and into Joe Krosky. "Hey, isn't that a Temptations song?"

Carlyn did a double take. "You're a Temptations fan?"

"Hell, yeah, I'm an R and B–ing, doo–wop–ing, disco–ing soul man." He bounced off down the hall, head poking and finger wagging.

Meri and Carlyn crowded into the doorway watching.

"Wonders never cease."

Therese opened the kitchen door to see Nora standing there in jeans and a Nightmare Before Christmas sweatshirt. "Come in."

"Are you busy? Daddy's working and I thought I'd see what you were up to."

Therese smiled. "Don't tell me you're bored already."

"No. But Dad has to work. And I can tell he feels like he should be entertaining me, so I told him I was coming here. I thought maybe you were cooking something. I could help."

"Do you like to cook?"

"Yeah, it's okay. Not that I get to cook much; we have a cook. But I've been practicing when I can."

Therese didn't bother to ask what she was practicing for. She was pretty sure at this point that Nora's intentions of staying with Alden hadn't been a spur-of-the-minute decision.

How it would turn out was anyone's guess.

"Well, I was just about to start some soup." Therese had some chicken in the freezer and they would make do with whatever else was in the refrigerator. They could always drive over to the market to get the rest later.

"I like to make soup, because it freezes easily and defrosts without making everything mushy."

Nora nodded. Therese could practically see the gears in her brain working. Well, even if she didn't end up staying, it wouldn't hurt the girl to learn some culinary skills.

Therese got the chicken out of the freezer and put the

pieces in the microwave to defrost. Then she hauled the big soup pot out of the bottom cabinet while Nora emptied the refrigerator and brought potatoes and onions from the pantry.

When the chicken was defrosted, Therese showed her how to cut the skin and fat from the meat, then let Nora try.

"It's slimy," Nora said, wrinkling her nose.

"It's chicken." Therese nodded for her to go on.

Nora sighed. "I guess man can't live on cookies alone." Her cheeks reddened. "I meant man in a universal kind of way."

"I know what you meant. Now cut. And for heaven's sakes watch your fingers. We don't need any more emergency room visits."

When the chicken was skinned, Therese had Nora take it all over to the pot of water simmering on the stove.

"The bones, too?"

"Bones, too. Now, break a couple of stalks of celery off. And before you ask, the leaves too, and put them in the pot." Next came a quartered onion that left both of them crying.

"Now we'll just add some salt, parsley, and peppercorns and let that cook up while we cut the vegetables."

Nora was a quick learner and interested, and Therese was happy to have the company. She'd loved the times when Laura or Meri and sometimes the boys would come in to help cook. Cooking was always a family affair in the Calder household. And she missed that.

It was just one of the many things you lost when you grew older and family moved away. Therese wasn't complaining. She'd had a wonderful, satisfying life, and she had nothing to complain about. Nothing at all.

"What is it, Gran? Did I do something wrong?" Nora looked down at the cutting board of chopped carrots. They were every possible size and shape, and Therese thought they were just perfect.

"Not at all, I was just thinking how nice it is to have some-one in the kitchen with me."

Nora smiled happily and, if Therese wasn't mistaken, with a hint of triumph. She'd better be careful not to get Nora's hopes up. She didn't see Jennifer allowing her to do anything that would mean giving an iota of control to Alden.

Meri spent what was left of the morning and early afternoon helping Joe with his tracing. It was actually a simpler and less-body-contorting activity than analyzing or cleaning ceilings.

By the time they finished for the day, she'd made big head-way on the wallpaper pattern. It was detail work, requiring a steady hand and a good deal of focus, but not so much that she didn't think about Everett Simmons, local lawyer, who might or might not be her birth father. But who might at least be able to tell her something about Riley Rochfort.

She helped Joe cover the wall tracings with plastic before they packed it in. Meri was stiff from sitting in one place for such a long time and was thankful for not having to climb down from the scaffolding with one hand. Though she was more than ready to get on with it. Too bad it looked like that wouldn't be happening until the plumbing was corrected.

"So, Joe," she asked as they walked down the hall together, "do you ever go to karaoke?"

"Only the botany department's parties. Big karaoke dudes there."

"No kidding. I would have never guessed."

"Yep. Just a bunch of wild and crazy scientists. That's us."

"You know. Carlyn and I and a couple of friends go to a neighborhood place on Friday nights. You should come some-time."

Joe stopped. Even stopped bouncing. "Really?"

Meri was taken aback. "Sure." She immediately wondered if

she should have asked Carlyn first. What if he turned out to be tone deaf. Well, what the hell, that was half the fun.

"Cool." The bounce started up, and they continued their way to the kitchen.

Carlyn had left for the day, probably out searching for additional funding or to spin class. The woman was indefatigable. Meri called Peter, but his voice mail picked up. She left a message that she was going grocery shopping and to call her.

Meri drove to the grocery. It was something she knew she couldn't put off any longer, and if Nora was coming in a few days, she would have to start laying in supplies.

She stocked up on staples and snacks and even thought to buy some meat and vegetables. That night, she made dinner and ate in front of her laptop, not reading her e-mails, not streaming the television shows she'd missed over the last few days, not even wondering why Peter hadn't called her back.

She was googling Everett Simmons, learning where he worked and that he had a family. She saw newspaper photos of him at various benefits with his lovely wife, most taken at Historical Preservation Group events. He was a member of several restoration organizations.

She may have even met him before; he did look vaguely familiar. Maybe that was just because she'd seen his photo as a young man. He was still on the lean and lanky side and he had a crinkly smile, all things she recognized from his photo, even as fuzzy and old as it was.

He looked like a nice man. She wondered if he knew about her. Or if he would want to know about her. She didn't want to upend anyone's life. She just wanted to know about Riley and what had gone so wrong in her life. And she would do it subtly.

She'd call and make an appointment in the morning, tell his secretary that it was personal. She'd probably have to pay a fortune. She didn't care. She'd dip into her savings if she had to. And then she would forget it all.

Meri was awakened from a deep sleep by her cell phone. Immediately panicked that someone was hurt brought her to full consciousness. "Sorry, hon. I ran into some guys from work when I was cleaning out my desk. We had a few beers, and I didn't realize it was so late."

Peter. Meri blinked at the clock by her bed. Almost one o'clock.

"You want me to come over?"

She could hear laughing and music in the background. "No, have fun; I'll see you tomorrow."

"If you're sure."

Meri yawned. "I'm sure."

"Love you."

"Love you, too." She hung up. He *should* be going out with friends. He wouldn't see them for a while either. But he could have called to let her know. And on that thought she fell back to sleep.

Alden sat on a boulder watching the sun come up. Actually it had been up for a couple of hours. Now it sat like a pale yellow medallion in the sky. Wisps of cirrus clouds stretched from it like lamb's wool.

It was too early for the sun to warm things, and the air was chilly but calm. The boulder where he sat was cold. By noon it would start to absorb the heat and be comfortable by afternoon.

Alden stretched stiff muscles. He'd worked late, couldn't sleep, so he came back downstairs and lay on the couch until dawn woke him again. He'd made coffee and come outside.

The coffee was long gone, but not his anxiety. Anxiety? Anticipation? Just plain old worry.

He'd been floored when Nora announced she wanted to stay with him after break was over. Part of him wanted that more than anything, except maybe that Nora and Lucas would both come back.

But how would they go on? Would she be happy going to a new school even for a few weeks? What if she got bored? What if he was working and lost track of the time? Forgot to pick her up? Forgot to buy groceries?

They had Therese, of course. But could he put that burden on her? What was he thinking? Nora wasn't a burden. He could set his alarm. She'd remind him to shop. Or they could go out for dinner. Pick up a bagel on the way to school. They could manage.

But he needed to talk to Nora, really sit down and hash things out, to make sure this wasn't some knee-jerk reaction she would soon regret.

And then there was Jennifer and Mark. They seemed more upset about having to go out of their way to drop her off than about her leaving. They didn't even say good-bye, no hug, or see you, or have a nice time.

A breeze ruffled the grasses behind him. Was that a happy marriage? Jennifer blew hot and cold. At least with him. And he couldn't imagine her being any other way with Mark, though maybe he was wrong and they would live happily ever after.

Better Mark than him.

Jennifer would never allow Nora to stay. It was senseless to even propose the idea. She'd say just the opposite of what she thought he wanted. Nora wouldn't even come into the equation.

Best to forget the whole thing. But he wouldn't tell Nora yet. Let her enjoy her time here while she could. He chuckled. She'd brought chicken soup home yesterday afternoon. Therese had shown her how to make it. Nora was so happy. Over soup, for crissakes.

Why on earth had they sent her to a math school?

Another breeze, this time more forceful. It would be a blustery day. A challenging day for a sail. Crazy. Until Sunday he hadn't taken the boat out once since last July. Most of that time had been winter, but he never sailed anymore, only when the kids were here.

Alden stood, retrieved his mug from the boulder, and trudged up the beach toward home. He needed to work, but he needed to think of something entertaining to do with Nora. His mind drew a blank.

He'd gotten too used to living alone.

Chapter 17

Meri awoke not nearly so sure about contacting Everett Simmons as she'd been the night before. She decided to postpone her decision until after she had talked with Carlyn.

She spent a long time in the shower, now that she could get her hand wet. And to be honest, she went off on a tangent imagining what it would be like meeting her maybe father. As soon as she was dressed, she threw a couple of waffles in the toaster and ate them as she walked to her car.

Meri arrived at work early, but Carlyn's car was already in the lot.

"Do you ever go home?" Meri asked when she found Carlyn hunched over the computer screen in her office.

"Yeah, but I'm working overtime to make sure we all still have jobs after this week."

"This week? We're really that low on funds?"

"I exaggerate somewhat, but if the plumbers come in over budget, which they invariably do, we'll be that low soon."

"Then I guess we'd better work faster. Spending a day with Krosky tracing the wallpaper pattern made me think I'd better take a tracing of the ceiling pattern on the outside chance the whole thing falls down."

"Not a bad idea, but Doug will probably send Joe Krosky up to do the tracing."

"It's my ceiling."

Carlyn laughed. "Morning, Joe."

Meri looked over her shoulder. Joe Krosky stood in the doorway. They hadn't heard him come in.

"Where is Doug sending Joe Krosky?" he asked.

"Up to trace Meri's ceiling."

"Not this Joe Krosky," Joe said. "This Joe Krosky doesn't do heights except in emergencies."

Surprised, Meri said, "No problem, I'm not ceding my territory yet. Oh, Carlyn, I forgot to tell you, Joe sings karaoke with the microbiologists."

She wasn't disappointed with the effect her statement made.

Carlyn's eyes widened then narrowed into slits. "Really," she said incredulously. "I didn't realize microbiologists were that wild and crazy."

"Oh, we have some botanists and geneticists who can hold their own."

"Fascinating," Carlyn said.

"That's me. Better get to work." Joe bounced off down the hall.

"That is one weird dude," Carlyn said after he left.

"At least unexpectedly interesting. And kind of cute." Meri sat down. "I spent a whole day sitting next to him; he wouldn't talk for an hour or so then commented on the last thing we had been talking about. It took hours to do one conversation."

"Really weird," Carlyn said.

"With great powers of concentration."

"Hmm."

"I've been thinking."

"About Joe Krosky?"

"No. I spent some time last night reading about Everett Simmons. I think I'd like to meet him. Just ask him questions

about Riley, not hit him with 'Nice to meet you and by the way, you're my father.' Just . . . I don't know, see him up close, ask what he remembers about Riley. If anything."

"Great. Do it."

"How? Should I just call his office? I don't think I should call him at home; that could get dicey. And I don't want to waylay him on the street, because that doesn't seem fair. Maybe it isn't fair to contact him at all. It was so long ago and won't change anything."

"No, but he has a right to know if he does turn out to be your father."

Meri sat down. "Why? Wouldn't it be better for his life to just go on as it has been?"

Carlyn rolled her desk chair around to Meri's side of the desk. "That's all fine and good, except that your life won't go on like before. I think you should meet with him. You can decide then how much you want to tell him."

"So then what would be my reason for going? 'I found this picture of you in my mother's keepsake box and wondered why'? He'd probably have a coronary. Or 'I have some questions about Riley Rochfort'? If he looks blank, I'll thank him and go on my way. If he doesn't . . . I'll wing it?"

"Make an appointment."

"I thought of that, but for what purpose? I can't tell the secretary the real reason."

"Just say that you want a consultation. You don't have to say more."

In the end, that's just what Meri did—called Everett Simmons's office and set up a consultation for Thursday morning at ten o'clock. "I didn't think Doug would mind me coming in late," she told Carlyn.

"Not at all, and I'll have lunch waiting so you can tell me all about it."

Alden looked up from the drawing he was working on. Nora was standing in the doorway wearing the smallest bikini he'd seen in years.

"I'm going to lie out."

"It's April."

"Want to come?"

He thought she'd make it all of five minutes before she came running inside for hot chocolate, but knowing Nora she'd sit out until her lips turned blue just to prove she could do it.

"I was thinking about riding into town for some grinders for lunch." Then he made a concession. "We could have a picnic."

"On the bluffs?"

"If you want."

"Cool, I'll go with you. Just let me throw some jeans over my suit." She twirled around and ended in her version of a model's pose. "Like it?"

Alden quelled the temptation to tell her to take it off, that she was too young to wear something like that. She'd never be old enough to wear something like that. He tilted his head. "Nice color."

She grinned. "I love you, Daddy." And she trotted up the stairs to change.

Crisis averted. One thing you could say about his daughter, she kept him on his toes. And, damn, he missed that.

They drove to Vanelli's, where they ordered two huge grinders, potato salad, macaroni salad, fat pickles, potato chips, and water and iced tea and drove back toward home. Alden turned off the main road before they got to their own turnoff and bumped down a rutted car path through a copse of birch trees to their favorite picnic site.

They'd found it one summer while hiking—Lucas, Nora, and him. They'd walked down the path past the trees and into a field of high beach grass. To their left was an abandoned farm.

The shake siding was weathered a dark brown, the structures either leaning or completely fallen and the weeds climbing almost to the top of the gaping doorways.

Lucas wanted to explore, but they convinced him that it was best to leave history alone. So they kept walking, just as Alden and Nora were driving today.

Nora was staring out the window, her head swiveling one way and the other trying to take it all in. What was she remembering? The good times? How much of the bad had become a permanent memory with his children?

He hated the thought of their childhood being scarred by some of the fights they had witnessed. What had he and Jennifer been thinking?

They hadn't been. Both were so furious at each other that nothing else mattered. She had expected wealth and a mansion. She felt betrayed and lied to. He'd expected someone who would love the land as much as he had, who would be proud to carry on the Corrigan name, who would love her husband and her children.

They'd both failed miserably.

"Stop here," Nora said.

Alden pulled the car off to the side, not that anyone else ever drove down this path. But he knew what she wanted.

"Come on, get out." She pushed the door open and ran around to grab his hand before he'd stood up. And she dragged him running through the knee-high grass to the edge of the bluff where they stopped and looked out to the sea, sparkling with light and life. The wind blew free, lifting their hair and ruffling their clothes, and he felt his daughter exultant beside him.

She hadn't lost her sense of wonder, as he had feared. Beneath the makeup and the bikinis and the air of jadedness was a little girl, no, a young woman just as ready to embrace the world as she had always been.

And it made him feel pretty damn exultant himself.

"Let's eat, I'm starving."

Alden laughed. Damn, he felt good. They raced back to the car, pulled out a blanket, and the deli bag and took them back to the edge of the bluff. Nora spread the blanket out over the grass and then took the bag from Alden.

She began arranging the food and drinks, which kept falling over on the uneven spread.

Alden sat down beside her and they ate and drank as they looked out to the sea. When they had stuffed themselves and the remains of their picnic were returned to the bag, Nora flopped on her back.

"Remember when we used to look at the clouds and find shapes in them?"

"Uh-huh."

"We've never done that once since we left."

Alden's bubble of contentment burst in that one heart-pounding sentence. He raised up on his elbow and looked down at his daughter. "I'm sorry."

She turned her head to look up at him. "It's not your fault."

"A lot of it was. I don't want you to think that families can't be happy together."

"Can they?"

He hesitated, choosing his words. "Yes. Your mother and I just weren't very good at it. She and Mark must be happy?"

Nora snorted. "I guess. On the outside anyway. But, God, they're dull."

Alden bit back a laugh.

"When was the last time you went out on a date?"

The urge to laugh died a serious death. "Where did that come from?"

Nora sat up and crossed her legs. "Mom's had two, soon to be three, kids since she left. You don't even have a girlfriend." She cocked her head.

He cocked his head back at her. Father and daughter.

"Do you?"

"I do okay."

"Gran says you're in your prime, but, Dad, you're not getting any younger."

"You've been talking to Gran about my girlfriendless state?"

"Not exactly. I want to stay here, but I don't want to cramp your style. Only, Dad, you don't seem to have any style at all."

He grinned. "Want to take me shopping?"

She huffed out a sigh that made her lips vibrate. "That's not what I meant."

"I know what you meant. And I appreciate your concern." *And your being here wouldn't cramp my style at all.* "But I do go on dates occasionally."

"Do you think you'll get married again? I mean, it's okay if you do . . . As long as she's nice."

Alden lay back down, closed his eyes. "I don't know, Nora. But you'll be the first to know if I decide to. Promise."

The next two days passed at a snail's pace even though Meri worked late, cleaned her apartment, did more grocery shopping, and spent a long evening saying good-bye to Peter.

When she least expected it, nerves would bubble up and she'd question for the hundredth time if she was doing the right thing by meeting with Everett Simmons.

Carlyn was the only person who knew her intentions. She was afraid her family might be hurt if she told them she was going to talk to her possible birth father. They would understand the need, but that made it even worse. And she couldn't tell Gran. She'd worry. And Alden . . . She had no idea what Alden would say.

No, that wasn't true. He would say be thankful for what she had and leave the rest alone. She *was* thankful, more than he or anyone knew. But still she had this niggling desire just to know. The same way that she had to find out what was beneath the next layer of paint or plaster. Now that she knew there was more to her story, she had to find that out too.

And then she would leave it alone.

At three minutes to ten on Thursday, Meri arrived outside the Federal-style building that housed the law office of Everett Simmons. She'd dressed in a basic navy blue dress and jacket. It was an outfit that she wore to meetings, not that she attended many.

Her neglected pumps chafed against her heels as she walked around the house from the parking lot, but she welcomed the annoyance. It kept her mind from dwelling too much about the outcome of her next fifteen minutes.

Simmons's office shared the first floor with an optometrist. She hesitated in the foyer, then turned the knob and walked in.

Meri gave her name to a very put-together receptionist, who looked middle aged and slightly severe. That did nothing to calm the jitters that were dancing in Meri's stomach and up and down her arms and legs.

Half of her wanted to just say, sorry, there'd been a mistake, and run the hell away. But when she was told to sit, that Mr. Simmons was with a client and he would see her in a few minutes, she did.

Even though she was expecting it, had steeled herself for that initial meeting, she jumped when the door opened and Everett Simmons showed his client out. He was a nice-looking guy, tall, fairly slim, with chiseled features. His hair was salt and pepper now, but he was exactly what the boy in the picture would look like at fifty.

"Ms. Hollis?"

Meri stood and forced a smile. He glanced at her injured hand and then he motioned her into his office.

"Take a seat."

She did, willing her breath to stay even, for her hands not to shake. She was facing her father . . . Maybe.

"Now how can I help you?"

"I . . ." She couldn't seem to get her prepared sentence out.

"No reason to feel uncomfortable." Simmons smiled, a smile meant to convey reassurance. Her father's smile?

"I came because—" She fumbled in her bag even though she'd placed the envelope with Riley and his photo on top.

He waited patiently until she managed to slide the photo out. "I was going through some of my mother's things a while ago and found this photo." She heard her voice start to thin and she stopped to take a breath.

"I was wondering if you were the boy in this picture." She said it more like a statement. She thrust the photo across the desk.

He looked at her before taking it. Sizing her up? Finally he looked down at the photo. Picked it up. Frowned at it.

Then slowly, slowly he looked up and their eyes met. "What's this about?"

"My mother knew . . ." She tried to swallow. "Riley. I was just trying—I wanted to know—if you were the boy—well, I know you were. I looked you up."

He let her stumble along; maybe he wasn't even hearing her, because he was staring at the photograph. She couldn't see his expression.

He looked up suddenly. "Who did you say your mother was?"

If you only knew. "Laura Calder, she was then."

He shook his head slightly. "Laura Calder. I don't recall that name. Was she a friend of Riley's?" A small hesitation before he pronounced Riley's name.

And that's when Meri finally saw the pictures on top of the bookcase and on the filing cabinets. Family pictures. Wife, several children, all teenagers or older now. He'd gotten on with his life. Well, of course he had. Riley was dead. Did he even know? Or care?

He cleared his throat as if it hurt. "Riley died when she was seventeen. On a trip to Europe."

Meri heard his words, and she heard something else. Regret? Doubt?

Meri kept still. She was used to working with volatile materials, but this was the most fragile moment she'd ever held responsibility for.

She opened her mouth, had to clear her throat. "And this is Riley Rochfort in the photo?"

He nodded.

He looked so sad that Meri began to regret coming here. Did she really need to open all this old history? *Too late for changing your mind now.* Whatever came next, she would have to accept it.

"And it's you?"

Simmons let out a long slow breath. "Where did you get this?"

He didn't sound suspicious, just bemused.

"It was in a box of things my mother . . . Laura . . . left me, along with her, Laura's, diary."

"How did your mother get this?" He templed his fingers, his cross-examination mode, she guessed. It gave him a psychological edge. Meri supposed he deserved it. This was all new to him. She'd had a few days to let it settle in.

"From Riley's backpack."

"A blue one?"

Meri thought back. "I don't think the color was mentioned, but it had her school ID, this picture, a change of clothes, and a book of mythology."

An exclamation, quickly swallowed.

"But she didn't find it until after Riley was gone."

"To Europe?"

"If this really is Riley, she never went to Europe."

His face went slack. "Just a minute." He reached for the telephone. "Paula, hold my calls. What appointment do I have next? See if you can postpone him until tomorrow or next week. No, I do not want to be disturbed." He didn't wait for an answer but hung up.

"How do you know this?"

And Meri lost her nerve. "I—I just do. She died here in an accident. Listen, I just wanted to know who was in the photo. And now I do. Thank you for seeing me." She stood so fast that she swayed and had to catch the desk to steady herself. "Sorry to bother you." What had she been thinking? This had been a mistake. She should have thought beyond her own need to know, about how this would affect her family and God help her, how it would affect Everett Simmons's family.

She reached blindly for the photo. But he plucked it out of her reach.

"You can't leave until you tell me how you know this. And why do you want to know about Riley?"

"That's all I know. I'm sorry if I upset you, but could I have my photo back, please? You've answered my question, and now I'll let you get back to work. Thank you so much." She held out her hand. It was trembling. She snatched it back. "Please?"

"Look at me."

Slowly she looked up.

Something flickered in his blue eyes. "Why do you want to know? You can tell me."

Could she? Should she? She wished to heaven she could take all this back. Alden had been right, and she'd refused to listen. And now it was too late. The man standing across from her, patiently waiting, was no dummy. It was better just to say it and be done with it.

"Because Riley was my mother."

Chapter 18

There was a terrible silence while Everett Simmons stared at Meri and she stared back at him. He glanced down at the photo then back to her, then again to the photo.

Still he didn't believe. His eyes flicked to her face, startling her into saying, "I don't want anything from you. I just—just wanted to know."

"Are you trying to say I'm your father?"

Meri shrugged. "You would know that better than I. I'm just on a quest for information."

"If this is some kind of charade or joke, it's a very cruel one."

Meri shook her head. "I don't want to hurt you. I just needed to know if you already knew. Or if you knew all along. If you didn't, I thought you might want to know the truth. And if you did, I don't really care if I hurt you."

He braced his elbows on his desk and lowered his head to his hands briefly then sat straighter. "None of this is making sense. Where did she find the backpack?"

"I think I'd better start at the beginning."

"Yes, I think you should."

Meri told him about a neighbor boy—she wouldn't drag Alden's name into this unless she had to—seeing Riley trapped on the breakwater. How she delivered her baby at the Calder house. How she was so afraid of something or someone that she left her baby and ran away.

"Damn him!" The words exploded out of him. He stood up abruptly, and his leather desk chair wobbled. He took two steps around the desk, and for a moment Meri was afraid he was going to attack her.

But he merely strode past her to the door, stopped, turned around, and strode back again. He stopped at her chair and glared down at her.

"Are you telling the truth?"

Meri nodded, tears suddenly threatening to stop her voice.

Why hadn't she listened to Alden to leave well enough alone? "I'm sorry. Maybe I shouldn't have come."

"Well, you did. What else did this diary say?" He dragged a second chair away from the wall, pulled it close, and sat facing Meri.

"It doesn't matter. I just thought you had a right to know."

"To know what? That they sent her to Europe to get her away from me? And she died there? Can you imagine the guilt I've lived with?"

Meri reared back. "No," was all she could manage.

She'd been acting under the assumption that the Rochforts had lied about their daughter dying in Europe to prevent a scandal. But now she realized it was also to keep her away from Simmons. He probably was her father.

It really made absolutely no difference to her, but it did to him. She had disrupted his life, opened old wounds that she hadn't imagined. For better or worse, she would have to deal with his feelings now.

She took a deep breath, rubbed her palms on her skirt, while she tried to collect her thoughts. It wasn't easy. Had she really thought she could just walk in here and say, "Riley was my mother, are you my father?" say thanks, no biggie and leave again, without leaving a catastrophic wake?

"Look, it's water over the dam. The past."

"Then why did you come here?"

She thought about it. Why had she come? Curiosity? Closure?

"Do you want recognition?"

She shook her head.

"If you think to blackmail me—"

She just looked at him. How could he think—but hadn't Gran and her mother been treated with the same arrogance? What was wrong with these people that they were so sure people wanted to take advantage of them?

"Because if you think you can, just let me make it—"

"Don't bother. You're just like them, aren't you? I hoped maybe you were different. That you were a victim like Riley. Don't worry. I told you before I didn't want anything from you. I don't."

She pushed her chair back, but before she could stand he said, "Not even a paternity test?"

"Not even that. It doesn't matter to me at all. Sorry to have bothered you." She didn't attempt to shake hands but groped her way to the door.

"Wait."

She turned. "Don't worry. Your secret is safe with me. I have a wonderful family. One that loves me unconditionally. And worth a million times more than you or the Rochforts."

She opened the door but shut it again. "There is one last thing. Any genetic diseases I should know about?"

He shook his head once. "No."

This time when she opened the door she kept going, not

bothering to maintain any semblance of composure as she stormed across the waiting room and outside to the street.

She didn't know how she found her car and drove to the site. She was carrying her bag of work clothes into Gilbert House before her stomach revolted and she fled into the first-floor bathroom to expel the two cups of coffee she'd drunk to fortify her nerves.

She heard a knock on the door and hurried to splash water on her face.

"Meri?"

Carlyn's voice.

"I heard you come in. Are you all right?"

"No."

"Open up."

Meri staggered to the door and unlocked it. Carlyn pushed inside.

"It was awful," Meri cried and fell into Carlyn's arms.

"Oh, sweetie, I'm sorry. Come on and have something to eat. I bought donuts; I thought you might need something sweet."

She led Meri across the hall and sat her down at the kitchen table, where she opened a box and lifted out a double chocolate cake donut and placed it in front of Meri.

Meri shook her head.

"Trust me. Chocolate will make it better."

Meri's stomach rebelled, but she dutifully took a bite.

"Are you up for coffee?"

Meri took another bite of donut, and, strangely enough, her stomach did feel better. She nodded. Carlyn poured a cup, refilled her own, and sat down next to Meri.

"Want to talk about it?"

Meri put down her donut. "I shouldn't have gone."

"Didn't go well, I take it?"

"He accused me of trying to blackmail him. My own—"

"What a cretin!"

Her vehemence startled Meri into a laugh—which quickly morphed into tears.

"Aw, sweetie." Carlyn put her arm around Meri and gave her a hug. "You did what you needed to do. And you don't know, he might come around. It might have been a big shock."

"Maybe." Meri reached for a paper napkin and wiped her face.

"At first he seemed nice enough. He *was* shocked. Of course he would be, but he seemed to think Riley had really gone to Europe, but then he just turned on me, threatened that if I thought I could blackmail him . . ."

"He'd do what? Sue you? Put you in jail?"

"I—I don't know. I didn't give him a chance to finish. I asked him if there were any genetic diseases I should know about. He said no. And I stormed out. I'm so stupid." She dropped her head on her arms and moaned.

"Hey, you two! I heard it through—"

Meri jerked up at the sound of Joe Krosky's singing.

He took one look at her, said, "Oops." And backed out the door.

"Poor Joe," Carlyn said.

"What did he hear? You didn't tell him—"

"No. He heard that I finagled two thousand dollars from old Knightbridge to replace the pipes. I almost offered to name the men's room after him but opted for a plaque on the contributors' wall."

"You're amazing."

"All in a day's work . . . or two."

Meri reached for the now partially smashed donut. Took a whooshing breath. "Okay, I'm done. I did it. It's finished. Onward and upward."

"Good girl, but what about the grandparents?"

Meri shook her head. "One encounter with that past was enough. Gran and Mom already confronted them thirty years ago. I doubt if anything has changed. And you know . . ." She crumbled a portion of her donut. "I'm angry for Riley's sake. But for my own? I really don't care. Yeah. I don't care at all."

"And Everett Simmons?"

Meri shrugged. "Mainly I just wanted the truth, kind of like getting to the ground layer of a paint analysis." She breathed out a soft laugh. "Not exactly like that, but I really don't want anything from him, except to know about the inherited disease thing.

"And I wouldn't have even been thinking about that except I thought Peter and I were going to get married. With everything up in the air, it isn't really something that's all that important."

"You're giving up on Peter because he's going to be gone for the summer?"

"No. It's just with so much happening, I guess I'm not as upset as I should be."

"Tell me that mid-July."

"Yeah, well, there is that. Now I better change and get to work. Congratulations on the plumbing donation. We'll piecemeal this beauty together yet. You're going to dinner with me and Nora tonight, aren't you?"

"Wouldn't miss it. Are you going to invite the TDH dad?"

"Stop calling him tall, dark, and handsome. I mean he is, but I don't want to think that every time I look at him."

"But are you going to invite him?"

"I can do that." But first she'd have to tell Alden about going to see Everett Simmons. She wouldn't be able to sit through a meal without blurting the whole story out and she wasn't sure of how much she should tell Nora. She may have opened a can of worms today—a legal can of worms.

Meri changed into jeans, got her tool bag out of her locker, and checked out a hard hat from the equipment closet. But before she climbed the scaffolding to finish her tracing, she made a call.

It went to voice mail. "Hi, Dad. You're probably teaching or making some amazing discovery. Just called to say I love you bunches." Her voice began to wobble so she hung up.

How could she even care about another family who didn't know or care about her? The family she had grown up with was all she would ever need.

Meri stopped long enough to shout a hey to Krosky, who was stretched out on the floor of the parlor, intensely outlining the bottom few inches of wallpaper. The wires of his earbuds wrapped around shoulders and disappeared into his shirt, and his toes were tapping the rhythm on the floorboards.

She climbed the ladder to the ceiling.

It was after four o'clock when Joe called up to Meri that he was quitting for the day. The two woodwork-stripping interns who were working on the second-floor bedrooms had clattered down the stairs an hour before. Meri was starving—the donut had been her only meal of the day—but she had completed a two-foot-square tracing of the ceiling.

She wrapped up a few minutes later and went down to the kitchen.

Not only Carlyn was there, but Joe Krosky and Nora and Alden.

Nora turned an eager face toward her as she walked in. Alden even smiled. They must have had a good week so far.

"Hey, you two," Meri said, layering on a tad too much enthusiasm.

"Nora's ready to *part*-tee," Carlyn said, with a mischievous glance at Alden.

Go for it, Meri thought. Nora had also seen that look and was paying close attention to her father's reaction.

Meri took Alden's arm and looked innocently up at him. "Don't worry, we'll take really good care of her."

"We're going out to dinner," Nora said. "You can come if you want to."

Alden laughed. "Thanks, but I wouldn't want to cramp *your* style."

Nora flashed a look at Carlyn.

Oh boy, Meri thought. If she's going to try to set up Alden with Carlyn . . . Then again, why not? "You're welcome to come."

"Thanks, but I have a hot date."

"You do?" Nora asked.

"With Therese. She's making chicken and dumplings."

"You're so impossible."

"I know, I'd better get going." He stood there.

Nora finally sidled over to him. "Bye, Daddikins. I'll be good." She gave him a loud smack on the cheek, before dissolving into the hug she clearly wanted. "Will you be lonely without me?" she asked, only half kidding, Meri thought.

"Of course, but I'll survive."

"And if the weather's good Saturday, you'll take us sailing?"

"If you get back early enough."

"Me, too?" Meri asked. "I haven't been in ages."

"You, too, if your hand's okay. Carlyn, care to join us?"

"Thanks, but I'll pass. Want to meet us Friday night for karaoke?"

"Thanks, but *I'll* pass on that one."

Nora let out a silent whew.

"I'll walk you out," Meri said.

"No talking about me," Nora warned as they walked to the back door.

Meri stopped Alden before he got in the car. "Any instructions, Dad?"

"Of course not. If I can't trust her with you, where am I?"

Good question. "Before you leave, there *is* something . . ."

He leaned back against the side of the old station wagon, one leg stretched out in front of him, arms crossed, relaxed. A man comfortable with himself, his reclusive, solitary self.

"Okay."

Meri crossed her own arms, but more as a protective gesture than ease. "I went to see Everett Simmons today."

"And he would be . . ."

She took a breath. "My birth father."

"Oh crap." Alden straightened up, no longer detached or slightly amused.

"Did you know he was my father?"

"I don't even know who he is, period."

"He's a local lawyer. I just wanted to find out if he really was my father. I had a picture of him and Riley. I just wanted to know," she finished lamely.

"And did he confess?"

"He didn't know. He thought I was trying to blackmail him."

"Ah, Christ Almighty. Did you dissuade him of that idea?"

She shook her head. "I lost my temper and stormed out of his office. I'm afraid I might have made a scene."

Meri glanced up at him through lowered lashes. It wasn't the first time she had something she needed to confess to him. Over the years, she'd had to apologize, defend, and wheedle, but she hadn't stood before him contrite and needing advice for a long time.

And she didn't like the feeling.

And she didn't need him to tell her she'd been an idiot for opening up a dead subject. Or that she may have brought trouble on all of them with her actions.

He didn't say any of those things. Just opened his arms so she could walk into them, which she did. He held her close. "Are you okay?"

She nodded against his jacket. "It was a stupid thing to do, I know."

"You needed to find out. Will you see him again?"

She shook her head.

"Did you at least ask him about the family medical history?"

She nodded, feeling ashamed and foolish and thankful that she had someone who understood her so well.

"That's the real reason you wanted to see him, right? To make sure your and Peter's children would be healthy?"

She pulled away. "That was only part of it. And besides . . ."

"I know, it's none of my business." He tapped her nose. "Don't worry about it. It's done. You don't have to wonder anymore. Take good care of my daughter."

She smiled, feeling better. "You sure you don't want to go to dinner with us?"

"Yep. You girls go have fun. . . . But not too much."

"Not to worry. See you on Saturday."

Alden drove away, thinking about Nora and Meri. They grew up but you never stopped worrying about them. His daughter on the brink of adulthood. His . . . What? What was Meri to him? . . . Too many things to contemplate and on the brink of marrying someone who was totally wrong for her.

He didn't really worry about Nora staying with Meri; Meri was nothing if not responsible. And he was kind of hoping that they would get a chance to talk. That Meri might get some insight on what was really troubling Nora and if it was something he should act on.

He didn't have to worry about Meri, either, though he did. It wasn't his business to worry about her. Peter would make her happy or not, but it was her choice. She was perfectly capable of deciding for herself.

He worried about himself. Losing the two of them would take a big chunk out of his life. Not that he saw either of them that much, and not that they needed him that much. But they were both so much a part of him that he was afraid of what would be left once they were gone.

It wasn't like that with Lucas. Luke had always "marched to a different drum" as Therese would say. But it was because Luke listened to a different frequency. A lot like Alden. The inner life was strong and made them sometimes forget about what was outside.

Lucas was a scientist, but that in itself was a kind of art, to see, to understand, to feel the inner workings of everything.

Alden remembered one night a few summers ago, they were out watching the stars. Nora had gone inside to read a magazine. Alden stood in the yard next to his son, both looking up at the sky. Alden was thinking of an illustration: a princess whose hair was made of the Milky Way that wove and lifted and trailed up into the universe.

And as the two of them stood there, Lucas told him the distance to Orion's belt.

Alden was floored and asked him if he'd memorized it. And Lucas said, "No, Dad, I calculated it using triangulation. It was easy. It just makes sense, like it all just talks to me in a language I understand." The kid was ten years old.

What Lucas understood might as well have been Greek to Alden, though Alden did know a smidgeon of Greek. But he understood one thing. Science spoke to Lucas the same way line and color and movement spoke to Alden.

Lucas seemed perfectly content with his new life. He liked his new school, one of those satellite schools that emphasized the sciences. That was something he wouldn't get out here at the county school. But Alden knew that having the ability to withdraw into your own world didn't mean you were happy or even content.

He'd tried to ask Nora about him without prying. But she just said he was a world unto himself and it was anybody's guess. In her own way, Nora was just as precocious as her brother.

Meri heard them as soon as she stepped back inside. Her pensive mood turned to delight and she hurried down the hall to join in. She got to the open door of the kitchen just as Nora and Carlyn pantomimed Signed, Sealed, Delivered as they sang. And Joe crooned Oh, Baby, in a falsetto that would rival Tiny Tim, which he ended with a tight turn and a body wave.

Meri watched him, awestruck.

Then Carlyn motioned her over and they sang backup for Joe's rendition of Stevie Wonder's upbeat song. Nora didn't know all the words, but she jumped right in on the chorus. Doug came in as they were taking their bow and shimmying.

"Where have you been?" Carlyn asked, shedding the remnant of her laughter.

Meri introduced him to Nora. Then added her question to Carlyn's.

"Beating a dead horse. I haven't been able to get on anyone's agenda for the next several months. We'll have to try a different approach."

"What kind of different approach?" Carlyn asked.

"Hold a fund-raiser here."

"Here? Where here?"

"The foyer, the parlor, the front porch if we do a little re-construction work. Hell, we can pitch one of those big tents in the backyard."

"Doug, we'll figure out a way to keep this project going, but this is not the most efficient way to do it." Carlyn smiled, trying to soften the blow.

But Doug deflated. "Anybody got a better idea?"

No one did. It was a crazy idea. They weren't ready to show . . . anything.

"Well, everybody go home, and start thinking." Doug wandered out of the kitchen.

"I'm going home to think." Joe saluted them and left.

"Well," Carlyn said. "Does that sound like desperation to you?"

"Pretty much. But we'll figure out something. Is anyone but me starving?" Meri asked.

"Yes, count me in," Carlyn said, brightening. "Where shall we go?"

"Someplace where they'll check my ID," suggested Nora.

"Only Virgin Marys for you."

"I have a fake ID, you know."

"I'm sure you do. And I'm sure you drink. But I'm not going to call your dad and tell him you got busted and to come get you out of jail."

Instead of balking, Nora burst out laughing. "I swear he said exactly the same thing. 'Don't make Meri have to call me to get you out of jail.'"

"Great minds."

"He's so old-fashioned."

"He's also right."

Nora made a face. "I know, I really do. And I won't do anything to . . ." She lowered her voice and intoned, "Jeopardize his trust."

Meri laughed. "Did he really say that?"

"No. He said to be cool and have fun. He isn't half as obnoxious as mother and Ma-a-a-rk are. They're absolutely Gothic—and not in a chains-and-nose-pierced way." She grew serious. "Did Dad take you out to give you the talk?"

"No, even though you are the center of his universe, we were actually talking about something else."

She'd said it in jest, but Nora frowned.

"Am I?"

"Are you what?"

"Do I mean that much to him?"

"Of course you do, but he'll survive a couple of days without you. Gran is going to feed him." Meri said it trying to keep the conversation light. But she should have thought first. Because Nora's face lightened, then turned a little sly. And too late Meri remembered her determination to stay after spring break was over and the fact that Gran had been teaching her to cook.

Chapter 19

Alden twisted the corkscrew into the bottle of wine he'd brought over for dinner, which was smelling delicious. There was no better comfort food than Therese's chicken and dumplings, thick and creamy. Bound to make you feel at home. Make you relax, feel easy, not worried, not old, not fed up.

"Alden, sweetheart, are you going to open that bottle or just stand there hugging it like it was a lady friend?" Therese shot him a knowing smile. "She'll be fine with Meri. And Meri will be fine, too, though I wish she had consulted me about searching for her birth father."

"I do, too, but she seemed okay." He smiled. "She was pretty angry, which is much better than feeling rejected. But I wonder if he will leave it at that? Should we intercede?"

"No." Therese shook her wooden spoon at him. "Let's just wait and pray he doesn't want to rock the boat. Now open that wine and sit down and eat."

He pulled the cork out, poured two glasses, and set them by their places at the kitchen table.

Therese put two shallow bowls of chicken down then drew a pan of homemade biscuits from the oven. She folded them into a cloth-covered basket, and he pulled out her chair.

She smiled up at him as she sat. "You should think about getting married again."

He stopped. "Is that a proposal?"

"You better hope it isn't. You're a catch, Alden Corrigan."

"Yeah, well, I was caught once before. That didn't work out so well." He sat down across from her.

"You have two wonderful children."

"That I hardly ever see."

"Whose fault is that?"

He stared at her. "What was I supposed to do? Take her to court, where she threatened to accuse me of everything from physical and emotional violence to child abuse? Where she would have made sure Nora and Lucas would have to testify? I couldn't do that to them. I didn't even want them hearing things like that even if it wasn't true.

"I'm not a violent man. I have a temper just like anyone else. But I swear, Therese, she was right. I would have gladly killed her at that point."

"Nora and Lucas both need to know your side of the story. I'm sure they've heard her side more than enough."

"I don't want to keep that part of the past alive by talking about it. Nora's okay, I think, but I don't know about Lucas. He seems so . . . so . . . detached."

"Lucas is the peacekeeper. Nora is the activist. She acts out when she's upset and when she's happy. You pretty much know where you stand with her. Lucas is more like you. 'Deep' as my father would say. But you're going to have to deal with them both sooner or later.

"Now I didn't want to put you off your food. Eat. And just know that Meri and I are here to help."

Alden ate. He didn't want to bring up all those hateful feelings. He'd managed to bury them over the last few years.

They ate in silence for a few minutes, then he said, "What

should I do about Nora? Do you think she really wants to move back here? Or is it just a passing whim?"

"Did you ask her?"

He shook his head. "I've avoided doing that, because we were having such a good time. I didn't want to wreck it. But I know I should talk to her."

"Don't you think you should at least take her seriously and hear her out? That's more than she gets at her other home, I'm sure."

"Yes. They're both old enough, I guess, to deal with whatever Jennifer wants to say about me. I think they can ferret out the truth. But . . ."

"There's something else, isn't there?"

"I just wanted my kids to have a mother."

Therese shook her head at him. He knew what she was thinking. He knew he was being less than rational. After all, he'd done without a mother and come out all right. He was lucky in that he had Therese and Laura as surrogates.

But he hadn't forgotten the nights of wishing he'd had a mother of his own. And then came Meri. Another motherless child taken in by the Calders. Always room in the Calder clan for another soul.

He looked over at Therese. Beautiful still after all the hard work and the tragedies of life. But she was getting on. Would she be strong enough to help Nora through the hard patches ahead, the times when a mother, not a father, was needed?

Of course, there was Meri, not old enough to be Nora's mother, but maybe a confidante. She would never play favorites like Jennifer did. But Meri wouldn't be here; she would most likely marry Peter when he returned from California and be starting her own family.

"I'll talk to her."

"And do you know what you're going to say about her staying?"

"No."

"Is that no you don't know or no she can't stay?"

"I don't know."

This place is great," Nora said, her eyes on the cute young waiter who had just delivered their burgers, fries, onion rings, two glasses of wine, and a soda for Nora.

Carlyn had suggested the pub near the wharf. It was loud and busy with college students who hadn't left for spring break.

Meri lifted her glass. "Here's to a fun weekend." They toasted.

They stuffed themselves, and Nora and Carlyn flirted outrageously with the waiters and a table of college students.

It was only seven thirty when they finished dinner and were walking down the cobbled streets and peering into shop windows. But soon the wind off the bay had them hurrying back to their cars.

Carlyn hugged them both. "Since we don't have to work tomorrow, I'm expecting you two to meet me for a cliff walk and waffles in the morning." She frowned at Meri. "Are you okay with that hand?"

"Yep. You game, Nora?"

"Depends how good the waffles are."

"Ha. I'll see you at nine sharp." Carlyn grinned at her.

"That good, huh?"

"You haven't tasted waffles yet. So don't stay out too late," Carlyn said.

"Oh, we won't," Nora said. "I want to go see Meri's apartment."

They drove the short distance across town. Nora spotted a parking place just a half block from Meri's apartment.

"Wow. You must be my good luck parking charm. Sometimes I have to park blocks away."

"Another good reason to keep me around."

Meri made a noncommittal answer. She had thought Nora

might forget her intention to stay in Little Compton as the week went on. Meri always started missing home about half-way through a vacation or the times she spent away at school and she came back to Little Compton as often as she could. Little Compton *was* her home. Maybe it was Nora's home, too.

"This is so cool," Nora said as they stopped in front of Meri's apartment building while Meri unlocked the downstairs door.

"It is." It was nice to look at her little building through someone else's eyes. She spent so much time looking at other people's architecture and fixtures that she sometimes took hers for granted.

She loved her apartment, on one of the quieter streets, at least in the off-season. And she didn't mind the crowds during the season. She could always escape to Gran's on the weekends.

They walked upstairs, and Meri unlocked the door and pushed it open. Nora followed her in.

"This is so cute."

Meri laughed. "If you mean small. Yeah, it is."

"I think it's perfect." Nora turned in a full three-sixty. "Cozy."

"That, too. But remember that when you wake up after having slept on the pull-out couch all night."

Meri gave her a "tour," which lasted about a half minute. In her minuscule bedroom, the queen-size bed covered by Moroccan spreads and pillows took up most of the space. There was just enough room for a bedside table. Her dresser was shoved into the closet that was large by apartment standards—and currently had an empty space like a missing tooth, where Peter had always left a change of clothes—until now.

"And here's the bathroom, also rather small."

Nora laughed. "Thumbelina-sized."

Meri smiled. The girl was an oddball, all teenager one minute and fanciful child the next. Or perhaps that was just because she was Alden's daughter. He was anything but fanciful—he was sometimes terse, often standoffish—but once you'd seen his drawings you knew he had a whole universe living in his head.

And he was always there in a pinch. Yeah, and now she knew why. He'd promised Riley Rochfort that he would take care of her. And he had. To the detriment of his own life, his own happiness? They really hadn't had a chance to discuss it. Possibly intentionally on both sides. But they needed to and soon.

"You're so lucky," Nora said.

"I am," Meri said. "But why do *you* think so?"

"You have this great apartment." Nora wandered past Meri and back into the living area. "Filled with things you like."

"Rent that I can't always afford, a furnace that occasionally breaks down, and there aren't enough washers and dryers, but yeah, I love this place." And she'd hate to give it up, if that's what she had to do to continue working on Gilbert House.

"And you have Gran and your family." Nora plopped on the couch and hugged one of the pillows. "Dad says you're going to marry Peter."

"That's the plan."

"But he left you for the summer."

"He *left* for the summer. We both have our work. It's only for a few months." Meri frowned. "Did your dad say something about me and Peter?"

"Not really. I just got the feeling he wasn't too happy about it."

"I know."

"He'll be lonely if you go away."

Meri didn't bother to say she'd been away for years, because she knew where this was going.

All roads led to reasons for Nora to stay. And Meri gave her credit for subtlety.

Resigned, she sat down in the chair. She should have

guessed she wouldn't get off that easily. Hadn't Alden said that he thought Nora might talk about what was bothering her to Meri?

And really she owed him that much, didn't she? "Want some tea? Decaf?"

"Sure."

Meri went to make tea, trying to postpone the inevitable. She wasn't sure she had any good advice to give the teenager. Hell, she'd just made a mess of her own life. She was raw and off-kilter.

The water seemed to boil in record time, and she was back with two mugs of tea, and a box of shortbread cookies.

"I've been thinking."

Uh-oh, thought Meri and hunkered down to listen and try to help.

"Gran is getting kinda old."

Meri nodded.

"So I thought maybe if Dad didn't want me, I could stay with Gran, help her out with things, you know?"

"I know, but why on earth do you think Alden wouldn't want you with him?"

Nora shrugged, pulled the pillow closer, her eyes glistening with tears that were about to overflow.

Whew, lightning change. "I'm sure he would love to have you; that's not exactly the issue."

"Then what is? My mother doesn't have time for me, and he doesn't have time for me. No, that's not fair. He drops everything when I'm visiting, and he does for Lucas, too.

"But then he has to work during the night to make up for the time he's wasted on me. I found him asleep on the couch in the sunroom this morning. The work light on his drafting table was still on."

"I have a feeling that happens a lot," Meri said. "So don't think it's just because he's out having fun with you."

"Gran's teaching me to cook and I could keep the place clean for him and do the laundry . . ."

Nora's anxiety was palpable. Maybe Alden was right and there was something else going on besides normal teenage angst. But how to approach it? Meri was so out of her element here. And just look how badly she'd botched her meeting this morning.

"There's only a couple of months left before school is out. Then maybe you could come stay for the summer. Like a trial to see if you'd really want to go to school in Tiverton. Wouldn't you miss all your friends?"

"No. I don't hang with the right people. So I'm pretty much not hanging with anyone. I hate my school." Nora sighed heavily. "You probably think I'm an ungrateful bitch.

"'Cause Lucas and I both go to the best academic schools, private. I know Dad pays for it. I saw the invoice." A lightning-quick smile. "I know a lot more than they think I do."

Oh great, Meri thought, *a snoop.*

"It's not that I'm not grateful, but we don't even go to the same school. It's fine for Lucas; he's a brainiac and he's kind of checked out all the time anyway."

That didn't sound good, but Meri let it pass.

"I'm not. There's nothing normal there. And next year I have to change schools again. My calculus teacher told Mom and Mark that I have an aptitude for math, so they enrolled me in a satellite school where they concentrate on math.

"I hate math. I don't want to go to school, go to college, get out, and go to work in some company where I crunch numbers all day. I want to do something interesting, travel, I don't know. Something . . ."

"Creative?"

"Yeah."

"Why am I not surprised? Have you told them how you feel?"

"Yeah, over and over. If I dare even mention that I'd like to be a writer or a journalist or something, Mom goes berserkers. Accuses me of being ungrateful for all she and Mark do for me. She and Mark? Daddy pays for everything. I looked."

"And what does Mark say?"

Nora snorted a bitter laugh. "Mark just leaves the room. He never stands up to her about anything.

"All she does is shop, meet 'the girls' for drinks at the club, make an occasional appearance at all the right committees at Henley's school. She arranges playdates, where the mothers just sit drinking coffee and talking about renovating their kitchens while the au pairs take care of the kids. She used to play tennis three times a week until she got too fat.

"She's totally useless. And spends money like she worked for it. Mark isn't such a bad guy. If he weren't such a wuss, I'd almost feel sorry for him. At least Dad stood up to her.

"What am I going to do?"

Meri tucked her feet under her and settled in for the long haul. Nora had obviously been holding these feelings in for a long time. The least Meri could do was listen while they all came out.

"What do you love? Do you want to be a journalist?"

"I don't know. Just something that's interesting. Like something that does something to make a difference. It's just that I'm not getting a chance to find out what that is."

Meri nodded. And there was the crux of the matter. No choice. Jennifer had determined that Nora would use her math to get an acceptable profession.

"And Mom will never let me. Every time I suggest anything, she blames it on Dad. Like he put the idea in my head. And he doesn't. When I called to ask if I could come for the break, she got on the phone and reamed him for plotting against her. She's crazy and she hates him.

"Plus she said he misrepresented himself when he asked her to marry him and she was being smothered out there in the boonies. Can you imagine? She called the beach the boonies?

"And she goes on about how she doesn't want us getting stuck in some dead-end profession where we'd barely make a living.

"I hate her when she says stuff like that. Corrigan House is the best, and we never went without anything that I can remember, and Dad sends a load of money every month. I saw the checks. It's not like he's indigent."

Meri reached for a cookie and offered the box to Nora who shook her head.

"I don't know anything about your father's finances. But he appears to make a good living. And I know he's well respected and gets excellent reviews. That counts for something."

"It does. And he loves it, you can tell. And he used to make up stories and draw pictures about them with me and Lucas in the picture. It was so cool."

"It sounds cool. I remember he did something like that when I was growing up. Of course he wasn't a famous illustrator then." Meri wrinkled her brow thinking back. "I think he'd just started high school. I hadn't even started kindergarten yet. I wanted a school book so much like the big kids had. And he drew me one. I'd forgotten that. I bet it's still in my closet at Gran's."

"See. He's not selfish."

"Of course he isn't. He looks after Gran . . . and me."

"And me and Lucas."

"Exactly, he's responsible and he makes a living at what he loves."

"But he doesn't seem to have a girlfriend or significant other. And he doesn't go out except to see his editor. I could be good company for him. I wouldn't be in his way."

"Have you talked to Alden about how you feel?"

"Not really. I told him I wanted to stay. But I haven't pushed him, because, well, I'm not sure he wants me."

And that did it. One large fat tear overflowed Nora's lid and rolled down her cheek.

She dashed it away as if she were angry at it for escaping. "I thought maybe you could."

"I think this is a subject you should discuss between the two of you. But believe me, your father loves both you and Lucas very much. And that—"

Meri's cell phone rang. She fished in her bag and pulled it out. "And speaking of dads, this is mine. I'll just be a sec." Meri went into her bedroom to take the call, not because she wanted privacy as much as . . . well, she wanted privacy.

The call was short. He said he loved her and asked about her hand. They chatted for a second, then he said, "Gran called to say you met Everett Simmons today."

Meri heard the question behind his statement and wished she'd never heard of Simmons, but it was too late for that. "I did. It was a big mistake. I was kind of rude, didn't take his shock into account, I guess. I mainly was concerned about genetics, for the future."

"I understand. And you have every right to want to know. Are you okay with what you found out?"

"I didn't find out much. He seems nice enough, but . . . well, he's not you. Now I'm done with him. I don't blame him; he didn't know what had happened. I saw pictures of his family and they look really nice. I'm glad for him, but I don't feel the need to see him ever again. Should I have asked you first?"

"No, not at all. You know I'll support any decision you make."

What was he talking about? "My decision is I love you and the boys bunches. And I'm the luckiest person in the world to have you."

She hung up feeling a little shaken. It wasn't like her not to think things through before acting. And she had this time, not even thinking of the repercussions.

Well, she'd learned what she needed to know. And there was an end to it.

She came back to the living room to find Nora sitting exactly as she'd left her. "Is everything okay?" she asked.

"Yeah," Meri said. "Better than all right." Meri had considered telling Nora about being adopted, so she would see how lucky she was to have both parents even if they didn't live together—and hated each other. But Meri was the lucky one, lucky to have a loving family, to be a Calder.

"Listen, let's sleep on it and tomorrow we'll figure out what to do. Now, let's get your bed made up; we've got an early day tomorrow, then we'll walk and eat and shop till we drop."

They made the bed. Nora used the bathroom first. And by the time Meri came out from her turn, she was fast asleep.

It was late when Alden walked home from Therese's. While he'd been there, sitting in the kitchen, lulled by the comfort of the food and the company, he'd felt like he could tackle anything that came his way.

Out in the dark, with the sea air blowing cold and wet, he just felt alone.

A cover of clouds had rolled in during the evening and they eased across the nearly full moon like a conjurer's handkerchief. There might be rain. Most likely it would blow off by the morning.

With the cheery light of Calder Farm behind him and the dark mass of Corrigan House waiting for him, he felt no desire to hurry home, no matter how biting the wind had become. The last show of force before spring set in.

Why did he keep his house so dark? How hard was it just to flick a switch, turn a knob, and fill the rooms with a little warmth? He never thought about it. When it grew dark, he worked by his drafting lamp or turned on the reading lamp next to his chair.

He could be living in a monk's cell, for all the attention he paid to his house. Maybe he should sell it. Buy a smaller, more welcoming place, big enough for his children to visit. But not so big that he forgot vast parts of it even existed.

Would Nora and Lucas care so much as long as they were still close to Gran and the sea? He knew of a couple of places closer to town but not so far away that he couldn't still get to Therese quickly if she needed him.

But she'd be totally alone out here if he did. He couldn't count on whoever bought the place to look after her. Maybe he should just wait.

Alden didn't go inside but walked around to the back where his studio looked out over the sea.

He didn't go in there, either, but took the sloping path to the beach. And stepped onto the smooth rocks.

To his right the little patch of sandy beach showed silver against the bluffs. The tide was coming in, the waves were talkative, rumbling and crashing like laughter on the boulders of the breakwater, before rolling into the land.

He imagined rambunctious elfin creatures in the drops of water climbing the boulders only to slide down again. A raucous party that suddenly turned dark in his mind. And the funny little creatures turned to the evil gnomes of his last project.

He closed his eyes, shook his head to clear it. He wouldn't be doing any more dark fantasies. They stayed with him too long after the work was finished.

When he opened his eyes, he knew what he would see. A woman wild with fear, arms thrashing against the wind, and a small red dinghy tossed by the waves.

Chapter 20

Spending a whole day with a teenager turned out to be a lot more exhausting than Meri had imagined. They started out with a brisk walk on the Cliff Walk, which was completed in fits and starts because Nora stopped every time she saw something that interested her. First it was the sea and they spent some time trying to figure out if they could see the Sakonnet Yacht Club across the bay while Carlyn jogged in place.

Then Nora turned around and saw the grand mansion overlooking the sea.

"Wow! What is that?"

Meri smiled. "The Breakers, the grandest of the Gilded Age cottages."

"A cottage? Really?"

"That's what they called them. Summer houses for the ridiculously rich. It belonged to the Vanderbilts."

"I've heard of them. It must have a hundred rooms."

"Only seventy," Carlyn said. "Italian Renaissance palazzo style. Designed by Richard Morris Hunt. One mansion has a room made entirely of gold."

"You're kidding."

"Nope. The Breakers is the grandest. but wait until you see the next one."

After that they stopped at every house for Nora to admire and ask questions. And for Meri and Carlyn to remember facts they'd thought they'd forgotten.

"Hell, I pass these houses every other day. I work in a mansion-in-progress. Most of my work is done on historic sites, and you know, I've stopped looking. I just realized. Time for a refresher course." Carlyn struck a pose then sang, "Time."

"Time . . ." Nora echoed.

"Time . . ." Meri added.

A couple of seconds of singing and jiving ensued.

"She's a natural," Carlyn said, stopping the exhibition. They were beginning to draw a crowd.

For the rest of the walk, Meri and Carlyn racked their brains for interesting anecdotes about the buildings and their some-times scandalous owners in the Gilded Age.

The walk took twice as long as usual, but they all enjoyed it thoroughly. There was a line at the pancake café so they stood outside, deciding what songs to sing at karaoke that night.

It took almost a half hour before they were seated.

"So I didn't get a chance to ask you, what did Peter have to say for himself?"

Meri blew on her hot coffee. Peter's call had awakened her at five thirty that morning. She was about to begin her day, and he was just finishing his. He was definitely having a good time in California. "He got there, he loves it, his uncle took him out to dinner with some other people from the firm last night." And who knew where else.

"Did you tell him"—Carlyn paused, glanced quickly at Nora—"anything about what's been going on?"

"No, it seemed like not the right time."

"What's going on?" Nora asked, frowning. "You're not breaking up with him, are you?"

"No, he's just interning in L.A. for the summer."

"That sucks. Are you going to visit him?"

Meri shrugged. "I think he's probably going to be too busy to take any time off. I'll see him when he gets back, and we'll talk on the phone."

Nora stirred her hot chocolate. "That's kind of lame."

"Tell me about it."

"Do you miss him?" Nora piled a forkful of blueberries, banana, and whipped cream in her mouth.

Meri laughed and stabbed a strawberry off her waffle. "He's only been gone for a day and, well, I've had other things on my mind."

"Like what?"

"Just stuff." What was she hiding? Nora had poured out her soul to Meri last night. She deserved the same respect. "I was adopted."

Nora put down her fork. Frowned at Meri. "You're not really a Calder?"

Across the table, Carlyn grimaced.

"I wasn't born a Calder."

"That sucks. You never said."

"That's because I just found out last week."

"That really sucks. Are you freaked?"

"I was at first, but since then I've come to understand that . . . well . . ." She smiled remembering that painful night she ran through the rain and across the dunes. "That family is more than a few minutes of indiscretion in the backseat of a car. I paraphrase."

Nora snorted out a laugh. "Let me guess. You're quoting Dad."

Meri laughed. "Yes, how did you know?"

"It sounds just like him, even"—she made air quotes with her fingers—"paraphrased." She pursed her lips and said more quietly, "I guess I showed up at an awkward time."

"Not at all," Meri said. "You're a breath of fresh air. And just what I needed. Anyway, it's over and life goes on."

"Does Peter care?"

Meri exchanged a look with Carlyn. "Well, I haven't told him yet."

"Wow." Nora stabbed another bite of waffle and fruit and chewed. Swallowed. "But he won't mind, will he?"

"Of course not," Carlyn said.

"I hope not. Now, if I came from a family of the moneyed, pedigreed set . . ."

"Like the families that own those mansions?"

"Most of those families sold them years ago and they are owned or managed by different restoration and tourist organizations. But there are still some seriously rich people here. I'm just not one of them."

Alden hung up the phone. That had gone just about as bad as he'd expected.

What started as a suggestion to Jennifer that she let Nora stay a few extra days at which time Alden would drive her down to New Haven ended with her accusing him of turning Nora against her. That was followed by her guilt ploys, which had stopped working years ago. Then it was back to accusations.

But it reached a dead end the minute he suggested that they might want her to spend a little more time away from the family.

He shouldn't have bothered to be diplomatic; it never worked with Jennifer. She could always outyell and outblame; she always was the more wounded than he, more put upon than everyone else.

For a full two minutes he just sat silent and tried not to listen as nastiness blossomed into out-and-out hysteria. The final straw was hearing Mark in the background, trying to soothe her, suggesting it might not be a bad idea, and then listening to her turn her rage on him.

The woman had anger management problems. She was spoiled and self-centered and . . . He'd tried to stop himself from making judgments about her and succeeded most of the time. But today he wanted to tell her exactly what he thought of her.

Alden was no fool. He couldn't win against her unbridled need for attention. He shouldn't have bothered. Better to let Nora think he hadn't tried at all than to put her in the middle of it. Because he had no doubt Jennifer would find plenty of ways to take it out on Nora when they did go home.

And what about Lucas? He wanted to talk to him, but he didn't dare turn her attention toward him. "Perhaps we should discuss this when you're feeling a little calmer." That's when the obscenities began.

"Later." He hung up. And now he just sat, turmoil raging once again like almost a decade hadn't passed. He tried to focus on the fact that at least he'd gotten Nora and Lucas out of that loveless, thankless marriage.

Jennifer had taken them and was punishing them for her unhappiness. When they were grown and gone, would she turn that bitterness on her new children?

He didn't envy Mark. He was just glad he was out of it. Now if he could just figure out a way to get his children back.

His cell rang. It was her. Hadn't she yelled enough? He considered not answering, but maybe Mark had convinced her to let Nora stay. He was probably sick of the whole blended family fiasco.

He picked up.

"Let me speak to Nora."

"She isn't here."

"Where the hell is she?"

"She's spending the night in Newport."

"She insists on coming to see you and then flits off? Who's she staying with? No, never mind; I can guess. Well, you just call them and tell them to get back there. We're picking her up first thing tomorrow morning."

"You can't—"

"Have her ready." She hung up.

Alden clutched his phone, stopped himself just before he hurled it across the room. Those days were over. No matter what happened, he wouldn't fall into that trap again.

Therese was tired of sitting in the house. Tired of waiting for winter to pass. Tired of waiting for the snow and rain to let up. It was a beautiful day. A day for clearing and tilling the soil.

Most days she never gave her childhood a thought. But days like this with a fresh mild breeze blowing off the water, she could almost smell the past. The cows, the straw in the barn, the horse dung she and her older sister pitched out of the stalls.

She liked to ride on the tractor best. She'd loved standing behind her father, feet braced and holding on to his shoulders as they bumped over the rich soil. When he got too old to run the farm, he sold some to the AG trust and invested the money for his heirs. Therese only had one brother left. Her oldest sister had passed ten years before. And her brother four years before, just before she lost Laura. That was the year that Therese Calder grew old.

But today she felt a stirring brought on by the first of the warm weather. So she put on her muck boots and zipped up a canvas jacket. Tied her hair up with a scarf and went out to the shed.

She didn't get out the hand tiller. The sound it made always made her think it was chewing up the soil. Which it was but she didn't want to hear it. And it made the air smell like gasoline.

She got out the pointed-tip hoe and long-handled digging fork. She still planted a kitchen garden every year and canned and froze the produce like she still had a growing family to feed. Most of it went into care packages for Dan's family. Or to Alden.

Therese clicked her tongue, thinking of her neighbor. Sighed. She didn't often get impatient with him. But today she wanted to give him a good shaking. Always sitting over in that big old house, drawing fairy tales and refusing to give himself a life. A good life that he deserved. One that he could have if he would just . . .

It was right in front of his face, and he just couldn't, wouldn't see it. She leaned her tools against the chicken wire fence, raised the hoe, and broke the first soil of spring.

The sun was actually hot on her back. The soil was just crusting, and beneath the top layer it was moist and rich.

It felt good to be working in the soil again, even though she knew she would be stiff tomorrow. The price of old age. Or maybe just the price of not exercising enough.

Therese stuck the hoe in the ground and straightened up, stretching her lower back. She went over to the stump, and took a nice long drink from the jar of iced water, while she looked over the land. There was still a good fifty acres. Not a huge amount, but enough to leave her grandchildren.

Hard to have your child die before you, but Laura had left her grandsons and Meri. And they could keep the property intact or divide it up among themselves. She and Dan had discussed it. She'd tried to sign it over to him after Laura was gone, but he'd refused and had the lawyer draw up her will in favor of the next generation.

When she tried to protest, he merely said, "They won't turn

me away if I'm still kicking. It's a Calder and now a Calder
Hollis tradition to take in those who need to be taken in."

He was a good man. Laura was lucky to have found him.
Therese had been really worried about her. Even after Meri
was born, Laura took no delight in anything other than that
child. In those days, Therese still kept a few working acres
and hired day help for the planting and picking. She'd pack up
Laura and Meri and go into the farmer's stand each week with
a truckload of tomatoes and corn.

One day, they were setting up when Dan Hollis pulled up
to the side of the road and asked for directions. He flirted with
Meri who was a charming toddler at almost three. No terrible
twos for her.

He sat and had some homemade lemonade, bought a dozen
ears of corn, and Therese nearly fell over when she heard Laura
laugh at something he said. He came back every Tuesday for
the next month and a half, and then one day he asked Laura if
she would have dinner with him.

Laura said no, but Meri reached up to him and he picked her
up. The three of them went on a date that night.

Now, if she could just see Meri happily situated. She knew
the boys would take care of themselves. Gabe and Penny were
already about to bless her with her first great-grandchild. Now
there was a milestone.

And that meant she better get this soil tilled before she got
any older; she went back to work, still thinking about Meri.
She had a profession she loved. But she knew Meri had a lot
more to give. And needed more to make her complete.

Maybe that was just her own old-fashioned attitude. But
just because something was old-fashioned didn't mean it didn't
work. She paused to brush some sweat off her forehead, Therese
saw Alden's lanky figure striding across the meadow. She could
tell even at this distance that he was upset. And Alden didn't
get upset much, not anymore.

And he was another one. He just needed a little nudge. A little nudge? He needed a bulldozer. She went back to hoeing, ignoring him. Just as he reached the garden gate she grabbed the hoe and swayed. Her hand came to her forehead.

"Therese!" He rushed toward her just as she began to sink to the ground.

Chapter 21

Meri's landline was ringing as she unlocked the door to the apartment. No one ever called her landline; she kept it mostly for telemarketers. Voice mail picked up, and she heard Alden's voice.

She dropped her packages and hurried to answer it.

"Where have you been? I've been calling you for an hour."

"Out shopping. Why didn't you call my cell?"

"I did."

"Oh, sorry; I turned it off when we went to breakfast and I guess I forgot to turn it back on. What's up? Nothing's wrong? Gran's okay?"

"Therese is okay, though she had a little dizzy spell. She refused to go to the emergency room, but old Dr. Jarvis came out to check her over."

"Oh dear, should we come home?"

"She says not to, but I think you should come anyway. Besides, there's been a change of plans. They're picking up Nora in the morning."

"But that's only Saturday."

"My fault. I called Jennifer to ask if Nora could stay. She of course went into a tirade and ended by telling me to have her ready to leave in the morning. I knew better, but I didn't want Nora to think I hadn't tried. Instead, I just fucked it up."

"Do you want to talk to her?"

"Not really, but I guess I'd better."

Meri reluctantly handed Nora the phone. "It's your dad."

The laughing, happy teenager of the afternoon suddenly became wary. "Hello?"

Meri stood nearby as she watched Nora listen, her expression becoming stormier with each passing second.

"It's not fair."

Meri put a comforting hand on her back, but she flinched away. It wasn't fair, to child or father. But right now, Meri was more concerned about Gran.

"Oh no. Is she okay?"

He must be telling her about Gran. "No, it's okay. I know Meri will want to come home tonight. I do, too." She glanced over at Meri. Her eyes were that strange gray, the same as Alden's, and she recognized the storm clouds gathering there.

"Sure, Daddy, I understand. No, it's okay. I'd rather spend the time with you and Gran and Meri. Sure. Sure. I'll put Meri back on." She handed the phone back to Meri.

"Don't worry about it," Meri said. "Nora and I will deal; there will be other times." She smiled at Nora who stood close by. "And I will feel better if I see Gran for myself. Can I talk to her?"

"She's napping, but the doctor says she's fine. She was out hoeing the damn garden. I don't know why she just didn't ask me to do it. I've been here all weekend."

"Because she likes to do it herself, Alden. It's not your responsibility. You can't take care of everything."

"But he can try," Nora mumbled.

"We'll be out as soon as we can get it together." Meri looked at Nora. Nora nodded. She was totally on board, though Meri knew she must be disappointed about missing the karaoke bar.

She was disappointed herself. But she wouldn't rest easy until she made sure Gran was all right.

And besides, she needed to get Nora home.

"Do we need to pick anything up? Prescription? Food? Can you stay with her until we get there? I know, stupid question. See you soon." She hung up. "Sorry."

"It doesn't matter," Nora said, trying to put on a brave face.

"I just really need to check on Gran."

"I know; I do, too. Besides, I have to leave in the morning."

"I know, he just told me. At least he tried to get them to let you stay."

"He didn't try hard enough." Nora went into the bathroom and shut the door.

Meri hesitated; there was nothing she could say. Alden assured her that Gran was okay. He would never lie about something that serious. But she still felt uneasy and wanted to be home. As far as Nora was concerned, she was sorry that things hadn't worked out the way Nora had wanted. But she wasn't surprised. And she bet that beneath her disappointment, Nora wasn't either.

Meri called Carlyn and told her the situation.

"Tell Nora next time she's here, it's a date."

"Thanks." Meri hung up and threw clothes into a suitcase. They were on the road in less than a half hour.

Neither of them felt much like talking. Meri had known Alden long enough to read between the lines. He sounded upset, but she thought it was more about Jennifer hijacking Nora's last days with him. She knew if Gran had really been ill, he would have taken her to the hospital, no matter what.

"My mother's like that woman on the rocks," Nora said out of the silence.

Meri startled; the woman on the rocks? She hadn't told Nora specifics of her adoption.

"The one in Dad's drawing. You know, she lured men to their death."

Meri breathed. "The siren. Nora, I know you're mad at your mom right now, but don't you think you're being a little harsh?"

Nora didn't answer, and Meri couldn't think of an argument in Jennifer's favor. And she wondered if that's what Alden thought about Riley. Did he think she had lured him to a metaphorical death? And if he did, how could he possibly love her daughter?

They spent the rest of the ride in silence.

Meri drove straight to the farm. As soon as she stopped the car, both she and Nora jumped out and ran inside. Alden was already at the kitchen door, looking as formidable as any romantic hero or villain could ever look. And Meri was so relieved to see him.

He put his fingers to his lips. "Do not upset her." He gave a significant look to Nora who chose to ignore him.

Meri couldn't deal with the two of them at the moment; she brushed past him and tiptoed into the parlor. She found Gran sitting in her recliner, an afghan over her lap.

She smiled weakly at Meri. Meri fell to her knees beside her chair.

"I'm fine, child, just a little dizzy spell. Stayed out in the sun too long. That's all."

"Are you sure? Don't you just want to go to the emergency room to make sure?"

"Absolutely not. Alden already dragged poor Nelson Jarvis over here to check me out. I'm fine."

She lifted her hand and made a gesturing motion with her finger. Nora was standing in the doorway, but she came tiptoeing into the room.

She knelt down on the other side of Gran's chair. She looked frightened.

"I'm sorry to have spoiled your plans."

Nora shook her head. "You didn't."

"And don't be angry at your father. He didn't ruin them either."

Nora's mouth tightened. "I'm not."

"Can we get you anything?" Meri asked. "Tea, some soup?"

"I've got everything I need. Alden is being the ridiculously attentive, sweet boy—man that he is."

"I know. He can be a little overprotective," Nora said. "It's because he didn't have a mother growing up."

Gran laughed softly. "Where do you young folks get these ideas?"

Meri smiled, but Nora said seriously, "I learned it in my psychology class."

"You study psychology in high school?"

Nora nodded, then blurted out, "Don't get sick, please." Her face crumpled, and she buried her face in the arm of the chair.

Gran patted her hair. "To every season . . ."

"Don't," Meri said.

Gran clicked her tongue. "I was just going to say that this old hen isn't ready to go yet. I just got a little dizzy. It would have passed unnoticed if Alden hadn't been on his way over and seen me. He kind of overreacted. And you, young lady, can tell me the psychological reason for that."

Nora managed a smile. "Overdeveloped superego. He tries to fix everything like he's responsible for the world. He's the same way with me and Lucas."

"Because," Gran said, "he loves you and wants the best for you." She looked from Nora to Meri. "For all of us."

"Then why—" Nora broke off at a look from Meri.

"You and your father will work it out." Gran sat up a little straighter. "So I hear you two had quite the shopping spree. Come show me what all you bought."

Nora retrieved her bags from the car and deposited them on the couch. "I got this at this cool little boutique on the wharf." She held up a cropped knit top in watermelon. It had a boat neck and raglan sleeves, and it brought out the color in her complexion.

Next came a dress, a simple sheath with Keith-Haring-type characters frolicking across the fabric. She'd said it reminded her of Alden's drawings, so they bought it. Meri bet she wasn't feeling so excited about it now.

Alden had stayed in the kitchen, and Meri heard the occasional clatter of pans. He was keeping himself busy and out of the way.

"Oh, try that one on," Gran said. "I want to see what it looks like on you."

If Meri was worried about overtaxing Gran with a fashion show, she'd been wrong. Gran had made a remarkable recovery from frail to enthusiastic. Nora disappeared into Gran's bedroom and came out a few minutes later, wearing her new purchase.

"I love that," Gran said. And stirred the air with her finger, for Nora to turn around.

Meri began to relax. Gran looked just fine to her; maybe she had just gotten overheated.

As Nora continued to try on her new purchases, Meri became aware of Alden standing in the hall, a little back from the opening as if he was afraid of disturbing the suddenly festive atmosphere.

She motioned him in, but he only stepped farther back. She was surprised to find herself irritated by his self-inflicted isolation. What was wrong with the man? His daughter was actually enjoying herself, when only a short while ago, Meri had been sure she would be filled with anger and recriminations. Meri shook her head at him and proceeded to ignore him.

When Nora had paraded all her new purchases before them, she pulled up a chair next to Gran and the two of them chattered away, the dizzy spell forgotten.

Meri decided Gran's spell had been a false alarm. So while Nora talked and Gran asked questions, Meri wandered out to the kitchen to find Alden stirring a pot on the stove.

"Double Bubble, toil and trouble?" Meri asked, regressing to her childhood mistake of thinking Shakespeare had been talking about bubble gum.

Alden looked over his shoulder at her. His mouth quirked but made it nowhere near the smile she'd hoped for.

She went over to the stove and took the spoon from his hand. "I'll do this; why don't you visit with Nora and Gran?"

He didn't answer, just pulled out a kitchen chair and sat down.

"Don't do this," she said. "At least make Nora's last night here fun."

"She's having fun."

"No thanks to you," Meri said, exasperation making her voice sharp.

He stood up, grabbed his coat from the back of the chair, and walked out the back door without a word.

Meri stared after him. Never, never in her life had she seen him do something like that. He had infinite patience with her, with Nora and Lucas, with Gran. Sure, he got exasperated with her. She'd heard him really angry when he was married. But he'd never just walked away from her. Or any of them.

She went to the back door and looked out, wondering if she should go after him. But he was almost home. He'd be inside before she reached him, even if she ran. Would he open the door to her like he had the rainy night she'd learned about Riley?

Something in her world had shifted since that night. She was suddenly unsure about whether he would let her in, or if the door would be closed to her. It was something she wasn't willing to test. Not tonight.

Gran and Nora came laughing into the kitchen.

"Where's Alden?" Gran asked.

"He went home," Meri said, concentrating on stirring the soup.

"Oh, Alden, Alden, Alden."

"Is he mad? Is it my fault? Maybe I should go." Nora looked around, but Meri couldn't tell if it was to locate her things or to memorize the room in case she never saw it again.

"You sit right down and have some soup," Gran said. "I made it last night, and we'll all feel a good deal better after we've eaten. Then you can take a container to your father.

"Nora, get yourself a glass of milk or soda out of the fridge. Meri, there's still some wine from the bottle Alden brought over yesterday. I'll serve the soup."

Her grandmother only drank on special occasions. "Do you want a glass?"

"I certainly do."

Meri saw a sparkle in Gran's eye that she couldn't quite make out. Fever? Amusement? Or was it just her imagination?

Gran and Meri tried to keep a lively conversation going, and Meri was afraid that it was taxing her grandmother's strength, but Gran seemed in high spirits. Meri just hoped all this fun wasn't going to cause her to have another episode.

Nora ate her soup, helped Meri with the dishes while Gran watched, then gathered up her backpack and packages to go home.

Gran gave her a big hug.

"I'll walk you over," Meri said.

"I need you here," Gran said. "We'll watch you from the door to make sure you get home safe."

Confused, Meri gave Nora a hug and told her to keep practicing her moves so she'd be ready for karaoke when she got back for the summer.

Nora thanked her for everything. "I'll come over tomorrow to say good-bye, if that's okay."

"Of course it is. You'd better not leave without saying good-bye."

"Go on now." Gran smiled encouragingly. Meri walked Nora to the door, and they watched her walk over the meadow burdened down with her suitcase and new purchases.

"What's going on?" Meri asked. "Why are you making her walk home by herself?"

"You did it all the time."

"But I was used to living here."

"And what about just last week?"

"That was different. I was in the midst of an unexpected storm."

"And now Nora is." Gran sighed. "Amazing. It's about time someone did something about that situation."

"I think Alden *is* trying. And there's nothing we can do."

"Perhaps. I'm tired now. I think I'll go to bed."

Meri immediately stopped thinking about their neighbors. "Do you feel all right?"

"Stop fussing," Gran said and kissed her good night. "I have every hope that things will work themselves out."

Meri stayed up after Gran went to bed. But she felt lonely after all the excitement of the last couple of weeks. And she would miss Nora. She was as far from a sullen teenager as you could get. Of course, that might be because she was being entertained to the max.

Still, Meri felt sorry for her. She didn't envy Nora having to face her mother the next morning. She wondered why they were coming back early? Just because Alden had asked that

Nora be allowed to stay longer? Could anyone be that vindictive?

She knew the answer. She went to bed.

Meri awoke with a start. Glanced at the clock; it was a little after midnight. Then she heard what had awakened her . Something from outside her window. A scraping noise.

Not an animal in the compost pile. It was a repeated action, rhythmic, like a branch might sound brushing against the house. Or someone digging.

She climbed out of bed and looked out her window. There was no wind. The clouds that had earlier hugged the sky had blown away. The moon was full, and it washed the landscape in an eerie light.

And then she saw the source of the noise. It was only the silhouette of a man, but she recognized it, so familiar to her she didn't need to see the details. Alden.

Alden was digging the garden, in the middle of the night in his shirtsleeves. Had he totally lost his mind? And where was Nora?

Meri grabbed her jeans off the bed and struggled to get them on, finally pulling off her hand splint and yanking them up with both hands. She shoved her bare feet into sneakers. Pulled a hooded sweatshirt over her sleep shirt and went quietly downstairs and out the door.

Alden was so intent on what he was doing, he didn't notice her. He must have been at it for a while. He'd finished almost half of the plot. He was wearing jeans and a white T-shirt. The jacket and the shirt he'd been wearing earlier were tossed onto the wooden stump that served as a table and sometimes a chair.

Meri just stood, watching him. She wondered why having known him so long, and having come to expect and demand so much of him, that she had never really noticed how physically strong he was.

He was churning up great clumps of sod. The muscles in his back and arms were like whipcords. Not bulky, yet powerful. He stopped to wipe his forearm across his eyes.

Meri shivered in the cool night air. She walked straight over to the garden, opened the chicken wire gate, and walked in.

He looked up momentarily but kept hoeing. She knew he saw her. But he wouldn't stop. She could feel his intensity, raw, uncontrolled, from where she stood.

It frightened her. And she'd never in all their dealings been frightened. Tonight she wasn't frightened of him, but for him. Something had been unleashed for whatever reason and he was taking it out on the garden. "What the hell are you doing?"

"Tilling Gran's garden."

"In the middle of the night?"

"It's as good a time as any." The hoe cut the soil with a hiss.

"Alden, stop and talk to me."

He barely glanced at her but kept bringing the hoe up and attacking the earth like he wanted to kill it.

"You shouldn't start a garden in anger."

"Who says?"

"I don't know; the Buddhists, I think."

"Good for them." The hoe came down with unwarranted force.

"Stop for a minute and talk to me."

He leaned over, lifted a rock out of the soil, and hurled it over the fence.

"Alden."

"Lower your voice. Do you want to wake Gran up?"

"I will, if it will make you stop. You're scaring me."

It was like a magic word. He stopped. "Sorry. Everything's fine. Go to bed."

"Obviously not everything is fine. If it were, you wouldn't be digging a garden in the dark."

"It's nothing. I can deal with it."

"You know, you've looked after me my whole life. I only just fully realized it since reading Mom's diary."

"I wish you never had."

"And I appreciate it, but I'm an adult now. I can take care of myself."

"I'm well aware of that." He started up again.

"And so can Gran."

He stabbed the hoe into the soil and stopped.

"So let me and Gran help with whatever's going on."

"Thanks. But I don't need—"

"Bullshit. You're angry and you're hurting and you're trying to handle it all yourself."

"I'm fine."

"Dammit, if you were fine, you'd be at home asleep, not digging in your undershirt in the middle of an April night. Enough already. If you don't want to confide in me, fine. But don't make yourself sick. Then Gran will feel like she has to take care of you, and she needs to take care of herself."

"You're right. I'll finish tomorrow." He pulled the hoe out of the soil and snatched his shirt and jacket off the stump. "Good night, Meri."

He returned the tools to the shed and struck off across the meadow without another word.

If she hadn't been afraid of waking Gran up, she might have yelled after him that he was being stubborn, ungrateful, and a hundred other things she'd regret in the light of day. But Gran needed her sleep, so Meri just watched his back until he disappeared into the darkness—and she didn't like that image at all.

Therese rested her forehead on the windowsill and watched Alden stride away. Would that dam ever break? Would she live to see it? She stood by the window until she heard Meri come back inside. Then she climbed back in bed, and sending off a selfish prayer to the Almighty, she drifted into sleep.

Chapter 22

Nora showed up at the door while Meri was still making coffee the next morning. The girl looked like she'd cried herself to sleep and she probably had.

"Where's Gran?" she asked as soon as Meri opened the door.

"Still sleeping; what are you doing up so early?"

"Couldn't sleep, and anyway, I wanted to spend as much time with everybody as I could before they get here."

"Where's your dad?"

"At home; he said I should come say good-bye myself." She shrugged. "We kind of had a fight last night."

"Oh no, is he sulking?"

Nora shook her head; the tears were ready to flow again, Meri could tell. "Worse."

"Oh dear. What?" Meri willed the coffeemaker to hurry. She needed some caffeine to face this morning; she hadn't slept that well herself.

"When I got home last night, he was outside just kind of looking down at the beach, like he does sometimes. So I was going out to talk to him, but he walked down the path and when I went to follow him, I found this."

She looked around then pulled a folded sheet of paper from inside her windbreaker. She unfolded it and smoothed it out, at least as much as it could be smoothed. Someone had crumpled it into a ball. Meri recognized Alden's handiwork; it's what he did when his work wasn't going the way he wanted.

"Look."

Meri pushed her hair back and leaned over the drawing, pressed her hands across the page to flatten it better. It was a line drawing of Gran sitting in her recliner, Meri sitting on the sofa beside her, and Nora in her little print dress twirling for them to see. They were happy and the illustrations caught the warmth and love perfectly.

And it caught something else, too.

On the edge of the paper, he'd started to draw another figure, dark, isolated. Then he'd slashed a line through it. Meri could see him tearing it from his drafting table and crumpling it in those long fingers; the throw toward the wastepaper basket, which he invariably missed.

She looked up to see Nora watching her, her eyes dark and forlorn.

"We made him feel left out. I shouldn't have gone to Newport; I should have stayed here, but I didn't know I'd have to leave early. I was selfish. I should have stayed."

"Nora, it's fine. He'd already asked if he could take you into town before you even came. He wanted you to have fun."

"He didn't think I could have fun with him? What's wrong with me?"

What's wrong with me? Not what's wrong *with him.* But *with me.* Meri thought it had much more to do with Alden than with Nora. She just wasn't sure why.

"I think he just felt the, uh, proportions of the figure were off. Look." She pointed to the man's shoulder. It was a total lie, the proportions were fine. The three of them looked as happy as a Norman Rockwell painting. Except for the tall dark figure, standing back of the archway, in the shadows.

Damn the man. What was wrong with him? They all

loved him. Meri had motioned for him to come in and he'd refused. Why?

"I bet he'll sit down this afternoon and redo it, and get the proportions right."

"Really?"

"Really. He goes through lots of versions before he settles on the one he likes." Though he usually didn't wad them up and throw them away, unless he was frustrated or hated them. "Did you ask him about it?"

"No. When he came in, he looked so . . . I don't know . . . I'd never seen him like that. I asked him why he came home without me?"

"He said I was a big girl now and I could take care of myself."

"Oh, Lord."

"What?"

The coffeemaker beeped. Meri practically lunged for it. "Want some?"

Nora shook her head.

Meri poured herself a cup and turned to face Nora. "I pretty much told him the same thing last night. Basically, that I was a big girl and didn't need him anymore."

Nora pulled the drawing around to look at it. "Is that what this means? That he doesn't think we need him anymore?"

Meri pushed the picture away. "I think you're taking too many psychology classes. We all need him—you, me, Gran, Lucas. And we all love him. He'll be fine." Meri would make sure of it. She just had to figure out how. But Nora didn't need to be worried with the details.

"If you have to go home, try not to make it worse for him."

Nora's face twisted.

"I know." Meri couldn't help it; she enfolded Nora in a Gran hug. It felt weird, and yet right somehow. If she couldn't offer solace to a teenager, what good was she. God knew, Alden had done the same for her more times than she could count.

It was about time she started returning the favor.

"Don't worry. Gran and I will take good care of him until you get back. It's only six weeks. Look, here's Gran."

Nora sniffed but straightened up. "Hi. I came to say good-bye."

Gran opened her arms and Nora walked right into them. Gran rubbed her back. "You'd better get going. I saw a car from my window. Meri will walk you part of the way."

Nora clung to her for a minute longer then turned toward the door, her head bowed.

"And, Nora dear, try to remember this too shall pass."

Meri left her much needed caffeine behind and followed Nora out the door. She crooked her arm in Nora's and the two of them walked across the meadow matching steps, sometimes bumping hips over the uneven ground. Any other time this would have made them laugh and set off a spontaneous doo-wop.

But not today. When they got in sight of the car, Nora stopped. "I think I'd better go on from here alone."

Meri nodded. "I was never a favorite with your mother. I never understood why."

"She hates your guts."

"Why on earth? I hardly know her. I babysat you guys, then I went off to college. Then she left."

"She was, still is, jealous."

"Of me?"

"I heard her tell Dad once when they were fighting. She said that you had all of him and she never could. I didn't know exactly what she meant, but I can kind of see it now. You let him be himself. Or something. I'd better go."

She gave Meri a quick hug and walked resolutely away.

Alden heard the car drive up and looked at his watch. It wasn't even nine o'clock. What was the goddamn rush?

He downed another gulp of coffee and went outside.

Mark got out of the car. They shook hands like civilized men. And Mark said, "Sorry. Hope this schedule change didn't screw up your plans for the day."

Alden didn't bother to answer; they both knew the reason for this early visit.

Jennifer got out of the car. She looked more pregnant than she had a few days before. He considered for a second that maybe she wasn't feeling well and really wanted to get home. That ended before he could even finish the thought.

"So where is she?"

"Saying good-bye to Therese. She'll be back in a minute."

"Couldn't she have done that yesterday?"

Alden ignored her, looking into the tinted windows for his son. Wasn't he going to say hello? Finally the back door opened and Lucas got reluctantly out. Sauntered over.

"Hey, how was the computer museum?" Alden asked, sounding overly bright and not being able to tone it down.

"We didn't go," Lucas said quietly.

"Why?"

"Because we had to come pick up your delinquent daughter," Jennifer said.

"Don't fight," Lucas said. "It doesn't matter."

The hell it didn't. Now the bitch was punishing Lucas for her anger at Nora and him.

But the pleading look from Lucas stopped any invectives that roiled along his tongue, begging to be set free.

"Well, we can drive up and see it when you visit this summer."

Lucas gave a quick shrug, shoved his hands in his pockets, looked at the ground.

Alden felt like he was standing in quicksand eating at his ankles, sucking him down. Sinking. Sinking. *Don't fight it. Just let it take you.*

"Here she comes," Mark said so loudly that he could have been announcing a damn parade.

When Nora saw them all look her way, her step faltered but she kept coming. Determined. And Alden felt a swell of pride and love for his daughter. And also for the woman who had turned away and was returning home. She knew Nora was strong enough to handle what would come next.

And as much as Alden wanted to protect Nora from the hell she would face once she got in that car, he knew he couldn't.

He couldn't help her through her coming ordeal; he couldn't help Meri with hers. And Lucas would hardly speak to him; his son didn't want Alden's help even if he could give it.

Maybe being torn between two warring parents was too much for him. And for Nora, too. She just put up a better front.

"Get in the car," Jennifer snapped as soon as Nora reached them.

"I have to get my bags." Without stopping, Nora went into the house and came back with suitcase and backpack.

Alden started to reach for them, but Mark beat him to it.

"You're an ace," Alden said to Nora. "I didn't think you'd be able to get all those new clothes in one suitcase."

"I didn't have that much." She gave him a hug, clinging like there was no tomorrow. He kissed her forehead. "Go on. I'll see you in a few weeks."

"Nora, you're keeping us all waiting."

Nora's face twisted, but she breathed it away. She lifted her chin and, not looking at her mother, walked around the car to the backseat. Lucas slumped after her, not even mumbling a good-bye.

"Don't expect them any time soon." Jennifer stalked away.

Alden was too shocked to counter. But before he went after her to ask what the hell she meant, Mark stopped him. "Don't pay attention to her; she's just hormonal."

"Mark, I was there before you. I know hormonal. That was just plain vindictive."

"Well, thanks for having her." Mark nodded and returned to the car.

Thanks for having her? She's my daughter, you fucking twit. He watched them drive away. He wasn't surprised to see Nora looking out the back window. But he hadn't expected to see Lucas, one palm to the glass. Trapped like Hansel and Gretel. An image he would not forget, and he'd be damned if that witch would do any more harm.

He stood in the yard irresolute. He wanted company and yet he didn't. He had to do something, he just didn't know what. He was losing his children and he couldn't let that happen.

He finally turned and went back into the house. It was cold and uninviting. While Nora had been here, they'd opened the windows and she'd made him move upstairs, not to the master bedroom—he'd never sleep there again—but to one of the many guest rooms, none of which had seen a guest in decades.

Alden climbed the stairs; they creaked beneath his feet, or maybe it was him creaking. Down the hall to Nora's room. She'd even made the bed after a fashion. They'd found an old comforter in one of the closets, Peter Rabbit à la Beatrix Potter. He smoothed it out, fluffed the pillow, and put it back on the bed.

The dresser had been cleared. No signs of his sixteen-year-old dervish. Except for the wrinkled bed, the room might have been unoccupied for ages.

He turned to go. The closet door was ajar, and he saw a swatch of color inside. Had she forgotten something? He opened the door.

They were hung up neatly in a row. Every one of the new things she'd bought in town with Meri.

Everything he'd bought her, she'd left behind. He reeled

back. She thought he'd betrayed her by not making Jennifer let her stay, as if that were in his power. Now she was rejecting him.

He wanted to take them from the hangers and rip them to shreds, but he didn't. That would be admitting his failure. So he gently closed the door and went to move his own things back downstairs where they belonged.

Well, it looks like they're gone," Gran said and returned from the kitchen window to sit down over a plate of cold toast.

Meri took the plate, slid the uneaten bread in the compost can, and put two more slices in the toaster. "Should I call and invite Alden to breakfast? He probably doesn't feel like eating, but I'm sure he could use the company."

"No. We're going to eat our breakfast and let him stew in his indecision. Then you're going to walk over there. And you're going to . . . I believe the expression is . . . kick his butt."

"Gran!" Meri laughed. "I can't believe you just said that."

"Well, pardon me, Miss Priss, but nothing else has worked. Desperate times call for desperate measures."

The toast popped up. Meri buttered the pieces, handed them to Gran, then put two more pieces in for herself. "What do you think he's indecisive about? Trying to keep Nora?"

Gran reached for the strawberry jam, put up last summer.

"Gran, I don't think it's so easy. He'd probably have to go back to court."

Gran took a bite, chewed.

"Gran?"

Gran looked up, closed her eyes, opened them, and took another bite of toast.

After that they ate breakfast in silence. Finally Meri asked point-blank what she was supposed to do.

But all Gran would say was, "Think about it."

Her grandmother wasn't normally so vague. She was

straightforward and said what she meant and felt. But evidently not today.

So Meri thought about it.

Through breakfast and on the walk toward Corrigan House, she thought about it, while preparing herself to be spurned, shrugged off, or ignored.

She wanted to be a good friend to Alden, not an obligation. She was beginning to realize their relationship had always been one sided—him giving and her receiving—even though it had been unconscious. But she didn't want that. Had she taken him for granted so long that they would never be able to have an actual adult relationship?

And she didn't know what Gran expected her to do. What did she mean by "kick his butt"? To punish him? Or to get him to move? And to move where? To get Nora to stay?

He was perfectly capable of doing that himself. And, besides, she'd never been able to make him do anything he didn't want to do.

That thought stopped her right in the middle of the meadow. That wasn't true, was it?

She'd spent her childhood, teenage years, even adulthood, wheedling, begging, demanding from him. She thought he would do anything she wanted . . . within reason, of course. But she hadn't been so clever after all, had she?

He'd been putting up with her for all these years because of a promise he'd made as a boy. *Mom said you had all of him and she never could.*

Had he jeopardized his marriage, his family, for that promise? Meri didn't want to believe it. There were plenty of times she hadn't needed him and didn't even think about asking for advice. She went for long periods without thinking about him at all.

Yeah, and where did you run when your world tilted out of control?

Maybe that was what Gran meant. Kick him away, cut him

loose, let him get back to his life. Maybe he'd get married again. Hopefully choose someone better than Jennifer.

That idea didn't sit too well with her. Selfish. She'd always been selfish. She was thirty for crying out loud. She didn't need to be protected anymore. Why didn't he get that? Why hadn't she?

The day was beautiful, the clouds high in the sky, a few ballooning closer to earth. Meri could just make out the little tips of green as the trees and shrubs burst to life. It was spring. She could feel the warmth of the sun as she crossed the meadow. A perfect day for a new beginning.

Well, another new beginning. She'd had plenty of them in the last few weeks. But as she thought about it, they weren't all bad. A little earth rocking but nothing she couldn't handle. She did feel a little guilty over her inept meeting with Everett Simmons. But he hadn't helped either.

And then there was Peter. He'd been gone less than three days. But he hadn't called except to wake her up. He'd been partying and he sounded like it and he hadn't thought about what time it would be in Rhode Island . . . that annoyed her more than anything else.

She hadn't really had time to miss him, between shopping and Gran's "spell" and Nora's leaving—and Alden's digging in the garden in the middle of the night.

Now it was Alden she was worried about, and that was a new experience. Worried and not knowing exactly why. Or what to do about it.

She knocked at the door, not expecting him to answer it. He'd either be in his studio working, or brooding in that beat-up chair, or sitting out on the rocks. She waited a respectable length of time, then let herself in.

"Alden?"

Getting no answer she checked out the living room, which in the morning sun was actually a rather inviting room. Or could be. As it was now, it could use a serious dose of fêng shui; even a mild restoration would help. Hell, a coat of paint would help. She went through the dining room to the sunroom. Empty.

Took a peek at the drafting table. Nothing there. Glanced at the wastepaper basket as she headed outside, It had been emptied. She went outside.

He was sitting on an outcropping of boulders nestled against a profusion of beach roses. From the top you could see past the breakwater into the ocean proper. His forearms were resting on his bent knees. His hair whipped about his face in the breeze.

He had to have heard her coming; it wasn't easy to sneak up on someone with the rocks crunching beneath your feet. Not that she was sneaking. It would be easier if he did turn, acknowledge her. Then at least she'd know whether he was glad to see her, or if she was an intrusion.

Well, tough. She climbed up the boulders until she was standing just below him. "Move over."

He shifted to the side a few inches. She sat down and nudged him to give herself more room. He moved enough for her to sit next to him. But he just kept looking out to the sea.

"Hey," she said.

"Hey," he returned though she could barely hear him.

Now what? She didn't have much practice taking the initiative with him. Last night in the garden had been disastrous.

"Did Nora get off okay?"

He nodded.

She couldn't even read his expression with his hair blowing across his profile. She grabbed a handful and pulled it back so that he had to turn his head.

"What?"

"Are you okay?"

"Of course."

Oh brother. What did she say next? *I'm a grown-up now and*

you can talk to me like you would everyone else? Seemed like a stupid thing to have to say.

He looked away. And she joined him looking out to sea.

"Gran said I was supposed to come kick your butt."

Now he looked at her. Finally. "She did not."

"Yes, she did. And quite frankly when you go all Heathcliff on me, I feel like it."

He was startled into a laugh. "Heathcliff? Hardly. Where the hell did you get something like that?"

"Carlyn. She thinks you're—" She stalled for a word. She couldn't say hot, or hunky; it just wasn't the kind of vocabulary you used with Alden. "She said you really had that Heathcliff thing going for you."

"Roaming the moors screaming Cathy, Cathy?"

"No. The TDH brooding thing."

"I won't even ask what TDH is."

"It's all good. I told her you had it all over Heathcliff, because you did things like take out the garbage."

That got her a raised eyebrow and one of his most acidly sardonic looks.

"That's not what I meant. Just that you're useful. No. You're, oh hell. You're real. And you care more about others than yourself."

"Don't go all cornball on me."

"Well, you do." She put her arm over his shoulders. It was kind of shocking, because she never did stuff like that. He was always the one giving comfort. But it was time she started. She felt ridiculously foolish, but she refused to be cowed and her arm remained there.

He didn't even react. His bones and muscles were as unyielding as the stony beach.

"Hey." She gave him a little shake.

He turned to fully look at her, which pulled her arm from his shoulders; she let it fall.

"Meri."

"What?"

"Nothing."

"What? Don't close me off. You've never done that before."

"I'm selling Corrigan House."

For an eon, the world went dark and silent—then came slowly back into focus. "You can't mean it."

"I do. It's brought nothing but misery. I'm sick of it."

"No. You can't."

"I can. And I will. I'll set up someone to look out for Therese."

"But where are you going?"

"Manhattan. Somewhere. I don't know."

"But what about Nora and Lucas? It's their home."

"Not anymore. And keeping it will just cause them more harm."

"No. That's not fair. They love it here."

"I'm sorry." He pushed to his feet. Jumped down to the boulder below them, then onto the beach.

"You can't."

He'd already started back up the dunes but he turned. "Why? Why can't I?"

"You just can't."

"Not good enough." He turned away from her.

She sat there, stunned. Sell Corrigan House? He must have lost his mind. He couldn't. Generations of Corrigans had lived there. Nora and Lucas loved it there. They wouldn't let him. She tried to stand up, but her legs seemed to belong to someone else.

"Alden, come back here!"

He didn't stop, didn't hesitate. Just walked straight up the path through the beach roses until she could only see the top of his dark head, then nothing at all.

God, what had happened? Was it something that had happened with Nora, with Jennifer when they came for her? Was it something that Meri herself had done?

Had she pushed him over the brink somehow? Made his life untenable here? What was she going to do? He couldn't leave them.

She struggled to her feet. Looked up the path to the house, then ran the opposite way. Across the beach, across the patch of sand and up the path that led her home.

There, it was done. He hadn't meant to blurt it out like that, especially not to Meri. He hadn't even really decided to sell until that moment.

Meri didn't need him. His children would be better off without him fighting with their mother all the time. There would be someone close by to help Therese with the heavier chores. Maybe it was time he let go and moved on.

He didn't need to turn to know that Meri had gone back to the farm where she belonged. He felt her absence. He didn't need to look to see the breakwater to feel its presence. It would always be there, just a pile of rocks in the sunlight. Changeable and frightening in a storm.

Had he fallen in love with his own mythology? that he was some child knight errant riding to the rescue in a little red dinghy, protecting the young princess until she could claim her throne? Slaying innumerable imaginary dragons and a few real, insignificant details that she could have handled herself?

Well, she was on her way: career, family, fiancé.

He'd done what he'd promised. Protected her, loved her, helped her become someone who could take care of herself. Choose for herself. And she'd chosen.

She didn't need him anymore. And he'd done it to himself.

Chapter 23

Meri burst into the farmhouse.

Gran looked up, startled. "What on earth?"

"That idiot. That crazy idiot." Meri gripped her sides. She didn't think she'd remembered to take a breath as she ran, and her lungs were burning.

"Oh dear. What did he do?"

"He says he's going to sell Corrigan House."

Her grandmother frowned, folded the dish towel she'd been using, and poured herself a cup of coffee.

"He can't do that!" Meri couldn't understand why Gran was taking it so calmly. Had Alden already discussed it with her? Was she in agreement? "He can't."

"Why can't he?" Her grandmother raised her eyebrows and lifted the cup to her lips.

"Because . . ." Alden had asked her the same question. There were too many reasons to name.

Gran put her cup down and waited attentively. Meri recognized that look. She'd seen it quite a few times over the last thirty years, especially when the boys told a tall tale, or were caught fighting and each tried to blame the other, or when

Meri tried to convince her that she should be allowed to do something that Gran considered entirely inappropriate.

But she was stumped as to why Gran was looking that way now.

"Because it's been in the family for ages. Generations of Corrigans have lived there."

"All of them are dead, why should they care?"

Meri was more confused than ever. "Would you want to sell Calder Farm?"

"No, but I have mostly fond memories here, my children grew up here, and hopefully I'll live long enough to see my grandchildren grow to love it here."

"Of course you will."

"But Alden doesn't have the luxury of good memories. His mother left him. His father was a bitter man. Not mean, but not nurturing. Then there's that woman he married. Nora and Lucas left the beach when they were quite young."

"Nora at least loves it here."

"So for the few weeks she and Lucas visit, Alden should ramble around in an old dark house for the rest of the year. It is too big for one person. It's falling down around his ears."

"He could fix it up. He has the money."

"Maybe he just doesn't have a reason."

"Sure he does. Nora wants to come live here. You heard her."

"For another year and then she goes off to college. And then . . ." Gran ended on a half shrug.

"What about you? He's your closest neighbor, and he looks after you."

Gran snorted. "I don't need looking after. And I have plenty of friends. I'll do just fine without him. Why is this so upsetting to you? Why do you care so much that he keeps Corrigan House?"

"Gran, I spend most of my waking hours restoring houses that were sold or inherited by people who didn't take care of them, houses that had years of neglect and mistreatment. Of course I don't want to see that happen to Alden's house.

"What if whoever buys it tears it down and builds a huge McBeachhouse or, worse, a hotel or a condo."

"The zoning board would never allow a hotel."

"But—"

"So you would have Alden tied to that old house just because you want it sitting there? Should he keep it even if Peter decides to stay in California and you move there?"

"What? I wouldn't."

"You'd choose staying here over starting a new life with the man you love?"

Would she? "He won't stay there. Maybe for law school." He had applied to Stanford, but mainly because of his uncle. He had his heart set on Yale. But what if he didn't get in to Yale? For a split second Meri's mind veered completely from Alden's bombshell to her own dilemma. Would she move to California to be with Peter?

"But if he does?"

"It won't come to that. Besides, what Alden does should have nothing to do with me. I told him so last night."

"Ah, there's the crux of the matter."

"What? Is that why he's selling? He's finally free?"

Gran burst into a trill of laughter. "Is that what happened? You found out about his promise to Riley Rochfort and think he's been imprisoned here ever since like some enchanted prince out of one of his books? And now that you've released him, he's going to hightail it away on a white horse?"

"It's not a joking matter."

"No, it isn't. It's that damn diary."

"Gran."

Gran pursed her lips. "I wish I had never given it to you. It changes nothing. We would still be sitting here having this same conversation if I had destroyed it years ago. What and who you are have nothing—nothing to do with your birth. Whoever said the truth will set you free was a damn fool."

"I think it was somebody in the Bible."

"John. Well, I apologize to the man."

Meri bit her lip to hide a smile. "But Gloria Steinem said 'the truth will set you free but it will piss you off first.'"

"Smart woman," Gran said.

"So, Gran, what is the truth in this situation?"

Gran looked at her and sighed. "I don't know. It isn't my truth. All I do know is nobody's looking in the right places."

"What does that have to do with Alden selling Corrigan House? I don't understand."

"Meri, maybe it's time you took a good look at your life."

"My life?" Meri's stomach turned cold. She groped for the nearest chair and sat down. "I know I'm lucky. You've all been so good to me. I'm grateful. You know that."

"Oh, child. We're family. Don't you forget it." She stood and carried her cup to the sink. Looked out the window.

Meri had to fight not to put her head down and cry. She lost. "I'm sorry."

Gran turned. "For what?"

Meri shrugged. She didn't know; she only knew that she felt miserable.

Gran pulled her to her feet and into a hug.

"I didn't mean you've done something wrong. Those people who say you should live in the moment . . . sometimes we have to look at the past to see how we got to this moment, then look ahead and try to imagine what will make us happy to live in that moment when it comes."

"No one can tell what the future will be."

"No, but we can hedge our bets."

Meri pulled away. "Gran, what do you know about betting?"

"That's beside the point. You go think about things, things

that have nothing to do with Laura's diary. I'm going to work in the garden."

"Do you think you should?"

"There's nothing wrong with me."

"I'll help."

"You stay here." She grabbed a wide-brimmed hat off the peg by the mudroom door, picked her gardening gloves out of the basket, and went outside, letting the screen door slam behind her.

After Gran left, Meri sat down again. For a long time she just listened to the sounds of her grandmother digging outside the door, and once the sound of the Volvo driving away. She tried to think about her life, but the diary kept encroaching. It seemed like that's what had suddenly sent her comfort reeling out of control.

But that wasn't it. She was beginning to see that now. She still had a loving family—that hadn't changed; she loved her work—that hadn't changed. She was right where she wanted to be.

She'd met Everett Simmons. It had been traumatic for a bit, but it hadn't lasted. Peter was in L.A. for the summer. He'd be back in the fall and they would get engaged. That was the same. Alden was going away. And that wasn't the same. That rocked her world and not in a good way.

Maybe that's what Gran meant. How did she see her future without Corrigan House?

She wandered into the parlor, picking up things and remembering, photographs and childhood art projects; she touched Great-Grandmother Calder's afghan. Stopped at the window that faced Corrigan House. She'd had good times there. At least until Jennifer came, but the kids had been special. They'd had good times even then.

She pulled the lacy curtains aside and leaned against the frame trying to imagine anyone but Alden living in the house.

Or a condo built in its place. Surely the zoning commission would never allow it.

But it wasn't the house she was afraid of losing. It was Alden. He was so much a part of their lives, her life. She kept expecting to hear the back door slam and his footsteps come across the kitchen. Or hear him in the garden talking to Gran. But time passed and as far as Meri could tell, he hadn't returned home.

Where was he?

Late in the morning, Gran came in. They had lunch. Meri did laundry, and all the time she listened for the sound of the Volvo.

Meri spent a restless afternoon, sneaking peeks out the window at every sound. Alden didn't return.

They went to bed early, though Meri didn't sleep well. She thought about what Gran said. Remembered all the good things in her life, some of the uncomfortable ones. Things that seemed devastating at the time seemed insignificant now.

Because she had always had people who loved her to see her through.

Meri kept hearing the sound of a car engine, but when she got up to look out her bedroom window, there was nothing there.

You're being ridiculous, she told herself and closed her eyes to wait for morning to come. She must have fallen asleep around four o'clock because when she looked at the clock again it was almost noon, and her room was filled with the aroma of banana bread.

Meri bolted out of bed. She could hear Gran moving around downstairs, so she hurried through a shower and dressing and went downstairs to be useful. She found Gran in the kitchen, all evidence of baking already cleaned and put away.

"Good morning; sit down and I'll make you some breakfast."

"A piece of that banana bread would be great if it's not for the church bake sale or anything."

"You know I made it just for you. Pour us a cup of coffee and sit down."

Meri poured the coffee and joined Gran at the counter. "Did Alden come home?"

"I haven't seen him." Gran opened the cake cover to reveal two loaves of freshly baked bread. "It's still warm."

"Smells wonderful."

Gran cut them both thick slices of the bread and they sat down.

The banana bread was delicious, moist and filled with bits of pecans, and for a few seconds Meri forgot the knot in her stomach that had been there since Alden had announced he was selling Corrigan House.

"What are we going to do today?"

"I'm going to polish the silver. You're going to start getting ready to drive back to Newport. I don't want you driving in the dark with a bad hand. Maybe you should go say good-bye to Alden before you do."

"Good-bye? He's home?"

"I don't know. If he isn't, leave him a note."

Had she just angered her grandmother? Gran didn't usually lose her temper, especially not with Meri, but she certainly sounded terse this morning. Was it something she had done or said? She'd tried looking at her life, tried imagining the future, but it didn't help the now. Everything was falling apart.

"Go on. I'll deal with these dishes."

Meri started across the field. It was hard enough to navigate the uneven ground without the two barn cats that had come to check her out and decided to join her, running ahead, hiding among the weeds then jumping out to pounce at her shoes. The ground began to blur, and she grew close to tears of frustration.

The cats finally ran off after some unseen victim. The tears weren't so easy to deal with. What was wrong with her? She was not a crier, not even at the movies; well, sometimes at the movies. She must be on overload, learning she was adopted, the diary, the new father, the injury to her hand, the job insecurity. And now Alden, just when she really did need him, was bailing on her.

And there it was.

The final straw of a long, emotional roller coaster of the last few weeks.

It was more than the house. Even though there was a basketful of fond memories there, it was just a house. It wasn't the structure that was responsible for those memories. It was the inhabitants.

One inhabitant.

Now the house already looked empty. Maybe it had for a while and she hadn't noticed. But she hadn't been getting back as much as she used to. She was just so busy, and she had a life in Newport. There was Peter, not to mention her other friends, and karaoke, and fund-raisers.

And now that she was actually thinking about moving back to the farm, he . . . She stopped. Had she even told him? Had she told Gran? She couldn't remember. Maybe she had told him, and he thought that now someone would be near to watch Gran he could leave.

For a wild horrible moment, she thought about telling him she'd changed her mind. She couldn't move back, he would have to stay.

Of course, that might just be prolonging the inevitable. Peter would be back in the fall. Meri wasn't naive; she knew things could change while they were apart. He might find someone he liked better. She might . . .

Well, she had already pushed him to a secondary place in her mind, but in her defense, it had been a crazy event-filled and emotionally packed couple of weeks. Besides, she didn't think he would ever want to stay in California.

She tried to imagine herself, freelancing on old adobe ranches, a few '30s movie star homes. But her mind kept reverting to Newport, her work there that she could visit and revisit, neglected Gilbert House, her friends, the Cliff Walk, the farm—her life was here.

Of course she could visit. But it wouldn't be the same. Besides there had been no talk of moving away. Except for Alden.

When Meri reached Corrigan House, she went straight to the old garage, pulled open the door, and peered inside. The old truck was there, but no Volvo. Good God. He couldn't have just picked up and left. He couldn't walk away that fast.

Unless he'd already packed. All he'd have to do was throw his suitcase and his portfolio and art supplies in the car and go. And it hit her so hard she had to brace her hand on the old splintered wood.

The truth will set you free. How long had he been waiting to be free? And what truth had he learned that set him free now?

Meri walked toward the house, each step slower than the one before. She knocked on the door and thought she saw a shadow move behind the kitchen window. But she knew it was hope playing a trick on her.

She walked around the house and peered into the studio. Everything was in its place, neatly organized. That should have made her feel easier. But Alden's studio was never neat, not when he was in the throes of work, and she knew he hadn't finished his next book.

He was going to finish it in Manhattan. She collapsed onto the steps that led to the lawn. Oh God. Someone had mowed the grass. It looked like a real lawn instead of a jungle of weeds flattened by the tramp of footsteps.

Beyond the dunes and the beach roses, the ocean shone a brilliant blue. The house might be in need of some major TLC, but Meri had no doubt the property would sell on the view alone.

The path between the farm and Corrigan House would grow over and that would be the end of it.

Well, if it was going to happen, maybe it was better if he wasn't home, better if she just left a see-you-later note and got herself back to Newport and her work.

"What's the matter?"

Meri screeched and nearly fell off the step in her attempt to stand and turn around at the same time. "Why do you do that?"

"Why are you sitting here?"

She concentrated on calming her heart rate. "When did you get back?"

"From where? I've been here all day."

"But you didn't answer the door when I knocked."

"I was in the kitchen; by the time I opened the door, you were gone."

"Where's the Volvo? It isn't in the garage."

"I took it in to the dealership; they dropped me off at the mailboxes and I walked from there."

"I would have picked you up. What's wrong with the Volvo?"

"Nothing. I'm selling it."

"Selling it? Why?"

"How many vehicles does a man need?"

"It's because you're leaving, isn't it?" she said desperately. "Have you thought this through?" She looked around. "How can you give up all this light? You know you can't work in a stuffy, dark, little apartment in Manhattan."

He smiled. "With the sale of Corrigan House I won't have to live in a stuffy, dark, little apartment."

Meri felt her arguments falling into pieces and drifting away. "Is that what you really want?"

He thought for a minute. "It's what I really need."

And what could she say to that? Fighting the strangling lump in her throat, she said, "I see. Well, good luck, we'll miss you."

She considered hugging him good-bye, but she was afraid she might cling to him and beg him not to go. And that would be too humiliating. And unfair. And selfish. Besides, it would take time to prepare the house for the market, then weeks or months to find a buyer and close on the contract.

There was still time.

Gran's question reverberated in her head. Why did that matter to her? She was leaving herself in a few minutes. Sure, she was only going a half hour away, but Manhattan was only a few hours' train ride away. Would Alden have a reason to visit if he sold the house?

Is that what really frightened her, not that Corrigan House would be owned by strangers, but that Alden would be lost to them. To her.

And that was really, really selfish. And really stupid. People moved all the time; that didn't mean they lost touch, wouldn't visit. So she smiled and said, "See you next weekend?"

He quirked a half smile. "Probably."

And she had to be content with that.

It wasn't the easiest walk back to the farm she'd ever made.

When Meri drove back to Newport a few hours later, she tried not to slow down as she passed the turnoff to Corrigan House; she tried not to even look. She concentrated on getting back to town, to work.

Her hand was better, and she had graduated to a few layers of gauze and tape. She had an appointment in the morning to remove the stitches. She would drown her anxiety in work. That's probably why she was so adrift.

Not because Alden was leaving, not even because he intended to sell his home, not even what Gran said about looking at her life. It was because she hadn't been able to work. She always got that way when she wasn't working. She began to breathe easier, and by the time she passed over the bridge, she felt almost back to normal.

She still had way too many loose ends in her personal life. Another good reason to get back to work. When work was your passion, loose ends weren't all that worrisome. With all her downtime, maybe she was just worrying too much.

And doing stupid things, like going to see Everett Simmons. What had seemed like such a huge deal a few days ago had moved to the back of her mind, and now, when she thought about it at all, she mainly felt embarrassment at the scene she'd caused.

She wouldn't make that mistake again. She wouldn't contact him, and she would avoid any contact with Riley's parents. They weren't her grandparents; they didn't deserve to be.

It was a relief to get back to her apartment. She ordered takeout, a habit she would have to curtail pretty soon, if she was going to keep working with Doug. She didn't want to have to pick up piecemeal work; she liked being on-site for the whole project. She thought she might like to direct a project someday, though she wouldn't want to spend her whole time fund-raising like Doug seemed to be doing these days.

Of course that could all change if Peter decided to stay in L.A. The couple of times she'd talked to him had been brief. At first she'd blamed the three-hour time difference. She was going to bed when he was starting his evening.

But he was so full of enthusiasm and excitement that it was easier to let him talk. And now that she thought about it, his enthusiasm might be a warning sign that he might like to stay.

She picked up her phone and pressed his number.

"Hey, babe."

Babe? He'd never called her babe in his life.

"Hi. Are you busy?"

"I've got a minute. You're not going to believe who came into the office today." He named some woman she'd never heard of.

"Really?"

"We're representing her in a divorce suit. It's wild. You wouldn't believe these people. It's better than television. I'm leaving in a few minutes. My uncle is heading the team, and I'm going to assist him. The husband is a real piece of work, multi-multimillionaire. It's so exciting. I can't discuss the case, but . . ."

He began to discuss what sounded like a case to Meri. She found herself listening for the delivery boy. "We're meeting the whole team for dinner and brainstorming session at . . ."

A restaurant she had never heard of.

". . . in a few minutes. I'm so psyched. Wish you were here. You'd love it."

"It does sound exciting," Meri said, ignoring the unease that had zinged up her back and settled in her stomach. It didn't sound exciting at all. It sounded like a huge waste of time and money because two people couldn't work out their problems.

"I wish we could talk but I've gotta run. Don't want to be late."

"I have to go, too. Have a . . . good meeting."

"Thanks."

"Bye."

"See you." He hung up.

Meri hung up and it occurred to her that for the first time in their relationship they had ended the call without saying those three little, sometimes two little, words, *Love you.*

First thing Monday morning, Alden drove the truck over to Therese's on his way to Providence to catch the train.

She must have heard him because she was standing in the doorway when he got out of the truck.

"Have time for coffee?" she asked. But she didn't move aside to let him in.

"No, I have to catch a train. I just wanted to let you know I'm going into the city for a few days. I talked to Ray Godfrey over at the real estate office. He's going to handle the sale. First he'll be sending some people over to get estimates on some cosmetic work and some landscaping. So don't be alarmed if you see cars and trucks in the drive. Once that's done he'll send someone to stage the downstairs."

"Stage?"

"They move everything around and make it look like a place someone would want to buy. Good luck with that one. But whatever they do will have to be an improvement."

"Ah. You're certainly moving fast."

"Yes." *Like yanking off a bandage, one quick painful moment and then it was over.*

"Are you sure you don't want to oversee the work?"

"No. I trust Ray. He'll know what to do." *And if I stay, I may change my mind.* From the moment he'd made his rash statement to Meri about selling—something he'd been thinking about for a while—the house began to call him back. He had to get away before he succumbed—it would eventually suffocate him.

"Well, have a good time in the city."

It took Alden a second to respond. "Thanks. If you need anything—"

"I'll manage."

"Then I'd better go."

"Yes."

He should go, but instead he studied her face, as if he had to memorize something he feared he would forget.

"Alden, if you're expecting *me* to try to stop you, don't."

"Why would I?"

She gave him the blandest look he had ever seen from her.

"I don't understand."

"I know you don't. For a smart man . . ." She shook her head and shut the door on him.

Chapter 24

It was almost eleven when Meri raced into work, passing the empty kitchen and going straight to Carlyn's office.

Carlyn looked up.

Meri lifted her hand now clad in an extralarge Band-Aid. "Stitches out. I'm ready to rock 'n' roll." She stopped. "It's awfully quiet this morning."

"Tell me about it. Lost a few over the weekend."

"Oh, who?"

"The master carpenter for starters."

"Ouch."

"Yeah, I thought he was going to start crying over the phone. He really hates doing closets and kitchens. He said he'd come back as soon as we got the money to pay him."

"Do you have anybody lined up?"

"No, we're like the kiss of death. It's gone all over town about us having to cut back to four days. Nobody wants to sign on for something that's floundering."

"Wait a minute," Meri said. "We're not floundering. We're just having a little setback."

"Floundering," said Doug from the doorway.

"No luck?" he asked Carlyn.

She shook her head.

"I'm not giving up," he said.

"Of course not," Meri and Carlyn said together.

"Damn this economy." Doug wandered off down the hall.

"Is it really that bad?" Meri asked when she was sure he was out of hearing distance.

"Pretty much."

"Oh." Doug popped back in, making them both squeak.

"What?" Carlyn practically yelled the question.

"Krosky isn't here today."

"What?" This time it was a full-blown screech.

"Please don't tell me we lost him, too?" Meri said.

"He can't quit," Carlyn said. "At least . . . he didn't say anything about it Friday night."

Meri's eyebrows flew up.

"He had to meet with his doctoral committee. He does have his own work."

"But he's coming back?" Meri asked.

"I sure as hell hope so. He's strange, but damn he's good."

They heard footsteps in the hall.

"Gotta be the woodworkers. Later."

When Meri was sure he was gone, she turned on Carlyn. "Krosky? Friday night? Want to elaborate?"

"You don't know what you and Nora missed. Krosky showed up at the bar. Did you invite him?"

"Sort of," Meri said. "In a vague, someday way."

"Well, thanks."

"Really or are you being sarcastic?"

"Really. He's phenomenal. We did some duets, then I just moved into your place and sang backup. The man's something else." She frowned. "Now if he'll just come back to work."

"Yeah, well, he better come back. Speaking of which. I'd better get to work on my ceiling. While it's still mine."

"And I'll keep making cold calls till my fingers freeze."

Meri got a respirator, a hard hat, and several sets of thin latex gloves before retrieving her tool kit from her locker, then she mixed a fresh batch of vinegar solution. She unlocked a larger cabinet and checked out a digital camera. With the reduced staff they would all become experts in many fields by default.

The hallway seemed particularly quiet today. The student interns were back in school and would only be coming in intermittently. Several of the staff had moved on to other projects. The ones who hadn't were busy piecemealing work from various projects together and came in erratically. Now they'd lost their master carpenter.

She'd better get as much work done as she could and keep her fingers crossed that Carlyn came up with a new source of funding.

Meri made sure she documented every detail of the cleared ceiling. Unfortunately, some of the plaster had been loosened when the medallion fell, marring the design; still, enough of the pattern was left to fill in the rest.

She had to take off her respirator to shoot a series of photos before she began to carefully clean around the medallion area, attempting not to dislodge any of the more fragile pieces. Then she took more photographs and switched to sample taking. The colors that had been protected by the central medallion were more vivid than the others and closer to the original.

There had definitely been gilt, and some of it was still intact.

It was tedious, eye-straining work. Every now and then she would step back from the process and just marvel at the difference between the treated and untreated areas. Slowly the old and grimy was replaced by the faded yet promising.

And she knew if people just saw the possibilities, the money to finish the project would flow in.

The house really had been a gem in its day. Not as large as

the mansions along Bellevue, but filled with detail and subtle craftsmanship.

What was left was a glimpse into another world, a different lifetime, and she couldn't help but stop and think about the people who had walked the floors below. Did they ever stop and look up at the ornate ceiling? Run their hand along the oak stair banister? Sit in the parlor relaxing in the symmetry of the Owen Jones wallpaper?

Or had Meri been breathing too many vinegar fumes?

She laughed at herself. How many times did she notice her surroundings when she wasn't working on a house. Though now that she thought about it she often did. At least when she was at home in her apartment or at Gran's. Or at Alden's where the darkness at night erased the walls around them, so different in the daylight, when the sun shot through the windows drenching everything it touched in gold . . .

Definitely been breathing too many fumes.

By five o'clock, Meri had cleaned only a few square feet, but hopefully she had enough documentation. Working alone could take her weeks or months to finish. They needed a professional cleaning service to come in, one trained in restoration work, but that would cost a fortune.

Her back, arms, and neck were screaming with fatigue. Her mouth was dry. Even her fingers ached. She'd gotten soft in the days she'd been off. She climbed down the scaffolding, put away her equipment, and was headed to the kitchen for a bottle of water when she saw Carlyn bound down the back stairs like the Furies were after her.

"He's here." Carlyn grabbed Meri's elbow and pulled her to the back of the stairwell.

"Who?"

"Everett Simmons. I recognized him from the newspaper article. Doug has him upstairs showing him the potential of the building." She grimaced. "Poor Doug, he doesn't have a clue."

"Do you think it's a coincidence?" Meri whispered, wondering if it would be too ridiculous to climb out a window and make her escape.

They heard voices overhead.

"They're coming," Carlyn said redundantly.

"What should I do?"

"Act normal."

Meri laughed, sounding awfully close to hysterics. What was normal when you'd just met your father four days ago? And had insulted him to boot? Then ran into him in your place of work?

Carlyn dragged her back into the hall just as the two men came down the back stairs, chatting like they were old friends. Which was entirely possible in a town the size of Newport and the interest in restoration fairly widespread. This was something Meri hadn't considered when she'd opened this can of worms.

Carlyn held her in place, and they both stood smiling woodenly until the men reached them.

"Meri," Doug called. "I've just been showing Mr. Simmons around. I understand you two know each other."

Meri wouldn't go as far as that.

"I was hoping to catch you before you left work," Simmons said in a perfectly cordial, natural way.

"Ah," Meri said, concentrating to keep her somewhat haphazard smile from slipping. She felt about as natural as the Tin Man meeting Dorothy.

"I was hoping you might have time for a coffee."

Doug looked confused but hopeful. Carlyn just looked confused.

Everett smiled reassuringly. "Nothing important. Though I do have some papers I thought you'd like to see. I was going to drop them off, but then Mr. Paxton and I got to talking." He turned to Doug. "The place does have good bones."

Doug beamed, his dedication justified by an outsider—an outsider who had just asked Meri out for coffee. Meri saw the moment Doug realized he might have a potential donor. "We think so. Well, I won't keep you. But thanks for taking a look at the Gilbert project."

"My pleasure. Nice to meet you." Simmons turned his charming smile from Doug toward Carlyn and Meri.

Carlyn also smiled, nodded, dragged Doug away.

Simmons and Meri were left facing each other.

"Sorry," Simmons said. "You probably wish you'd never met me."

"No. I'm glad you came. I wanted to apologize for the way I acted the other day. I hadn't really thought it through. And that's not like me at all."

"Well, I don't suppose finding out you have a father living in the same town as you happens very often."

She shook her head.

"I thought maybe we could start again."

Meri tried to read his expression. She thought he must be kidding, plotting some kind of revenge. But his expression was tentative. Maybe a little hopeful?

"I'm not sure . . ."

"I discussed it with my wife, Inez, after you left the office. I told her I might have jumped to the wrong conclusion."

"You did. I don't want anything from you."

"But I want something from you."

"My silence? No problem."

"No. Your forgiveness."

Alden returned to his hotel feeling grimy and sooty and fairly depressed. He'd spent the day looking at available apartments. So far Meri had been right. It was hard to find enough light in the Manhattan skyscape. At least for what he was willing to pay without having a contract on Corrigan House.

Plus, did he really want to buy something? He'd seen a second-floor brownstone in Soho, a converted loft in Tribeca, a prewar two-bedroom on the Upper West Side. They were all nice, but only the prewar building had real light. There was a new high-rise building in Brooklyn, lots of windows, very high tech. He wanted light, but he didn't want high tech. He didn't want to live so high that people on the street looked like ants below him. And he knew that taking an elevator every time he wanted to walk outside would drive him nuts.

He hadn't realized how many times a day he did just that, walked the five feet from his drafting table to the back door, all glass, and stepped onto grass, with the stone beach and the sea two minutes away.

Alden had always enjoyed coming to the city for work and spending a few days with people in the same field, having drinks, networking, some entertainment, a little pleasure . . . But now that he was looking at it as a full-time living situation, he wasn't sure he could adapt.

"You can do the reverse commute," the agent told him. "City during the week, weekend and holidays in Newport. Or . . . I've got some wonderful places in the Hamptons."

Alden didn't want a house in the Hamptons. He wasn't sure he wanted an apartment in the city. The only thing he was sure of was that he couldn't keep rattling around alone in Corrigan House.

He stopped in the bar of his hotel and ordered a drink. He hadn't called his agent or editor to say he was in town. He hadn't called any of his friends. He hadn't even called Paige, his "friend with benefits" as Nora would call her—if she knew about her. Which she wouldn't—ever.

Which reminded him. He needed to call Nora when she was alone and didn't have to navigate the rough waters of home just to say hello.

He texted her to call him when she had a chance. That was

one nice thing about texting—it was faceless, emotionless, a bunch of abbreviations and symbols, modern hieroglyphs. A poor substitute for conversation, but excellent for code.

He was finishing his drink when his cell rang. He signed for his drink and walked out into the lobby to take the call.

He took a breath. Tried to feel cheery. "Hello?"

"She's sending us away for the summer."

His tenuous attempt to keep it light combusted. "What do you mean?"

"She's totally whacked. She says they've been planning this for months. It's for smart kids. It will look good on our résumés. We're not even going to the same damn camp. It's like she wants to keep us apart."

"Shh. Getting all worked up doesn't help me understand."

"What don't you understand? She got pissed at me, and now she's punishing both of us."

"What does Lucas say?"

"What does Lucas ever say? Nothing."

And that was seriously concerning him. He was sure Nora would see her way through this, but Lucas held everything inside. If his daughter had inherited his imagination, his son had gotten the dark side of isolation.

The kid was a brain, much smarter than Alden or Jennifer, but that kind of smart kept you alone if you didn't find an outlet, someone or several someones to share it with. The fact that his son was accepting whatever was meted out to him without at least reacting, much less having an opinion about it, scared the crap out of Alden.

He needed to talk with Luca's and Nora. Make sure they were really okay.

"Dad. Are you there?"

"Yes. I was thinking. Maybe I should come to you. For a daytrip, or an afternoon even, with the both of you, you and Lucas."

"Like last time?"

It had been a screaming disaster. Because the three of them were having so much fun they had lost track of time and been late for Lucas's baseball game. They arrived in the second inning. Big deal. Lucas had called his coach to say he would be late. The coach was fine with it. Jennifer went ballistic.

Lucas quit the team after that game. He'd walked up to his mother and handed her his glove, threw his arms around Alden, whispered, "Don't go, Dad," and clung to him until Jennifer yanked him away and marched him off to the car, Nora slouching behind. Mark and Alden exchanged looks, and then Mark went after them.

Alden was left in the parking lot of the ballpark with a shattered memory of what had been a wonderful afternoon.

"Well, what do you suggest?"

"Let us come to your house. We can both go to school there."

"I don't think Lucas would be happy with that arrangement."

"Yeah, he would. He doesn't say anything, but I know he would. We can come now."

"Your mother will not allow it. We went through this."

"Then we won't tell her."

"Nora. No. That's not the way to accomplish things."

"Why not? Nothing else has worked."

"It just isn't. Besides, now isn't a good time."

Dead silence.

"It's not that I don't want you," he said quickly before she had time to misunderstand. "It's just that I'm not there, but there are workmen there. They're fixing a lot of things that are wrong with the house."

"Why? What's wrong with it? Where are you?"

"I'm in Manhattan. I'm . . ." He might as well tell her the truth. "I'm thinking about selling the house."

This time the silence was deafening.

"I haven't totally decided. I'm just looking at the options."

Still nothing.

He shouldn't have said anything. But she needed to get used to the idea. "It's too big for me to keep up. It's not fair to let it fall into ruin."

He paused to let her vent her opinion that it wasn't fair to sell their home. She didn't.

Then he realized that she was crying.

"Nora. Nora?"

"Why?" she managed in a strained little voice. That child's voice of disappointment that he remembered so well. She'd replaced it long ago with her surly teenage façade but it was still there, and it broke his heart.

How did he tell his child that he was gradually disappearing, that he was drowning in his own solitude, that he no longer had a reason to stay? "I told you, I'm just looking at my options."

"What options?"

"I thought I might move to Manhattan. You'd like that, wouldn't you? Bright lights, big city?"

"What about Gran and Meri?"

"There are plenty of people around who will look after Gran, and Meri doesn't need me." *Anymore.*

"Because she's marrying Peter?"

"No, because—because she's perfectly able to take care of herself. You're acting like Manhattan is in Siberia, not a train ride away. People commute that far every day. Well, almost that far."

"You can't. I won't let you. I'm not going to any stupid camp for the summer, and I won't let you sell our house."

"Nora."

She'd hung up. He called her back. She didn't pick up. He texted her to call him back, they would discuss it.

She didn't answer.

He texted again.

He was being ignored. She was probably locked in her room,

sobbing her heart out. With no comfort in sight. He was a despicable excuse for a father. He slipped the phone into his jacket pocket and went back to the bar to wait for her to forgive him and call him back.

I really had no idea," Everett Simmons said as soon as the waiter at a nearby coffee bar had taken their order. "It was stupid of me. I knew they had done something to keep Riley away from me. I was white trash to them. My family were hardworking, working class, and that just wasn't acceptable.

"When they found out Riley and I were seeing each other, they hit the ceiling. Forbade her to see me, to have anything to do with me.

"We sneaked around for a while, but I could tell it was stressing her out. Then she stopped coming to school. And then she just stopped sneaking out to see me, stopped calling me; her phone line went dead. I thought maybe they'd taken it away.

"I went to the school office to try to find out what happened to her. They told me her parents had taken her out of school and were sending her to Europe to finish.

"I couldn't believe they would do that our senior year. So I went to see them, to try to explain to them that I had a future, to talk them into letting us see each other. There were only a few months left of high school. I had a scholarship to the university.

"But they told me she was already gone. I wasn't to bother them again. And threatened me with arrest if I tried to get in touch with her.

"I never heard from her again, and neither did anyone else. In August I went off to college. Tried to forget her. Every time I talked to my parents, I asked about her. Then one day, my mother called. Riley had been in an accident in Europe and was dead. It was in the newspapers. She'd been buried over there."

Everett Simmons waited while the waiter put their drinks in

front of them and asked if they'd like anything else. As soon as he was gone, Everett leaned forward.

"I never questioned it. Are you sure that it was Riley who came to your house?"

Meri smiled slightly. "I wasn't there, well, not with any memory of it. But that was the name they found on the ID. And you can see even though it's old and damaged that it was the same girl in the photo and in the high school yearbook.

"But . . . I hate to ask this, but are you sure you're my father?" Meri really had no doubt. It wasn't that she looked like him, but there was something about him that made her realize that he was part of her makeup.

"You mean was Riley seeing someone besides me?"

Meri nodded. He looked so devastated over something that had happened three decades ago, she began to wish she had never approached him.

"I'm sure of it." He sighed, not resigned, but sad. "I'm sure."

"Don't feel bad. I was beginning to have horrible thoughts about the Rochfort family. That maybe she'd been abused."

"No. It was me. We were reckless, stupid I guess you'd say."

"Not me," Meri said and saw a glimpse of a smile for the first time since she'd met him.

"She never even told me. I would have taken care of her."

"My mother . . . Laura . . . left a diary." Meri gave him a truncated version of how Riley had followed the midwife to Calder Farm. She left out the part about the breakwater and Alden dragging her to shore and about her mother's baby dying at birth and Riley pleading for her to keep Meri.

It was hard to get through it without a few tears; Everett pulled a white handkerchief from his pocket and handed it to her. Then he had to use a napkin for his own.

Then she told him the really hard part, about Riley being hit by the truck. "The driver said it was an accident, she didn't even see him and he didn't see her until it was too late.

"And the really awful part . . ." Meri had to steel herself before she could continue. "When they didn't claim her body, my gran went down and claimed her; she's buried in our family plot. My mom and Gran went to the Rochforts and told them about Riley. I think they were feeling guilty about keeping me, but the Rochforts refused to listen, just kept saying she had died in Europe, which of course she hadn't. I don't think they ever sent her there. I think she ran away to have her baby, where they couldn't get to it. To me. My gran even told them where she was buried and they never came to see her."

"Despicable people," Everett said. "They would have sent her to the ends of the earth to bury any whiff of disgrace." He shook his head as if in disbelief. "And they wouldn't even come to her grave. God, how will I ever be able to face that old bastard without tearing his eyes out?"

"You see him?"

He choked out a laugh. "Oh yes. We even serve on some of the same committees. We just pretend we never had any run-ins in the past. But he can't stand that I actually made something of myself. It's all very civilized, though he hates me and knows I detest him and blame him for Riley's death." He paused and added, "Now, more than ever."

Meri reached across the table and touched his hand where it had fisted on the table. "Nothing will change the past. I didn't want to upend your world by coming to you. But I'm planning on getting married, and I really did want to know if I should be aware of any medical history. And . . ." She had to stop to swallow. "I just thought you should know."

"I'm glad you found me. Losing Riley is something I'll always regret, but I do have a wonderful family. Married twenty years now. I have a wonderful wife and three great kids. Still . . ."

"I saw their picture in your office. I'm glad you're happy, really. And I'm glad you went into family law."

"What about you? Are you okay?"

"More than okay. I have a wonderful family, too. Three half brothers, well, not really, but they are my brothers regardless. My mother just died a few years ago, but my dad has a research position at the University of Connecticut."

Both their coffees had grown cold, and Simmons motioned to the waiter. "I think I could use something a little stronger, how about you?"

Simmons ordered a bourbon and Meri a red wine. When the waiter took their untouched cups away, Meri saw the tension had eased from Everett's face. Had he been worried that she would try to make demands on him? She didn't want him to think that. He seemed like a nice man and even though he was her father—her father, she was actually sitting here with her real father—Meri realized she had absolutely no feelings beyond liking and respecting a new acquaintance.

They didn't talk again until they both had drinks before them. They made an air toast, which was a ridiculous thing to do but seemed to clear the air.

Everett took a sip and put down his drink. "So where do we go from here?"

Chapter 25

Meri and Everett Simmons walked back to Gilbert House to pick up their cars. They had passed from skittish strangers to first names. A comfortable acquaintanceship.

They would be friends. Meri didn't need any more from him. He seemed at peace. A good situation for both. And a future? They'd agreed to play it by ear.

They stopped by Meri's car. Theirs were the last two cars in the lot, but Meri knew Carlyn would be calling her to get the full story.

Everett smiled at her, and she thought with a wistfulness for what might have been. "From what I've seen, I think Gilbert House actually has potential. I'll see what I can do to help. I'm on the board of the Historical Preservation Group. I'll try to get you on the agenda of the Group's board meeting this week.

"See if I can rustle up some finances to keep you running for a while."

Meri opened her mouth to thank him, but she immediately felt contrite. "Don't we have to submit a proposal?" Surely Doug had already covered that. Had theirs been one of the grants that had been turned down?

"I'll call in a favor, it's the least I can do. I can't guaran-

tee anything, but I think there's a good chance of something."
There was a glint in his eye that might be excitement; Meri
didn't understand why unless . . .

"You don't have to do this. I'm not holding anything over
your head, if that's what you think. Truly, that's not what I
intended at all. I just wanted to . . . make sure."

"Meri, I know. I'm a pretty good judge of people. And trust
me, you've given me more than you know. Just knowing what
happened to Riley, that I have a daughter, that she was taken
care of at the end." His voice wavered, and Meri liked him the
more for it.

"Why do you think she ran from my mother and grandmother?"

"She must have been afraid they would send her back to her
parents. What else could they do?"

"They wouldn't have, you know. Gran and Mom would have
taken her in. Made room for her and her baby—me. There was
always room for more at Calder Farm. I wish she had known
that. She would have become a Calder, too."

Everett placed a hand on her shoulder. "She never knew
that kind of family. The Rochforts are all about the things that
don't count. Nothing in Riley's experience would have given
her the trust that your family would take care of her.

"I'm glad she had the luck to find them. It could have turned
out so much worse."

Meri thought about the frightened teenager on the breakwater and nodded.

"I wasn't lying when I told Doug that Gilbert House has
good bones. I think it would be a good draw to the neighborhood, maybe even big enough for small events and parties so
that it can become self-sustaining. I'll see what I can do. No
promises."

He opened her door, gave her a quick kiss on the forehead.
"I'm glad we met."

"Me, too," she said and got into the car.

He stood watching as she drove out of the parking lot. She waved, but she wasn't sure if he saw her or not.

It all seemed surreal. Part of her wanted to call Carlyn and tell her about the board meeting and the other part didn't want to get their hopes up.

Once Everett Simmons had recovered from his meeting with Meri, he might forget all about them. And that would be fine. She hadn't been lying when she told him she didn't want anything from him.

She smiled. But it would be nice to have a foot in the door.

Therese stood at the foot of Cyrus's grave.

They'd had a good life together. Only the one child and that had been a disappointment. "But we have fine grandchildren," she told him. "Soon a great-grandchild."

She leaned over and pulled some chickweed from around the marble footstone, then pushed slowly to her feet and moved on to Laura and Riley, with little Rose resting between them. Therese gazed at them for a long time, remembering.

Why was she still here and those young lives gone? It didn't seem fair.

She knelt stiffly at the graves. "I really wish you were here to help your daughter. Both of you."

The next two days at work had to be the longest of Meri's career. She noticed that two more interns were back, though Krosky was still missing.

"I kind of miss him," Carlyn said. "Now that we finally got to know him, he has bio-whatever commitments. Do you think we can turn him?"

"From advanced science to tracing wallpaper?" Meri grimaced.

"For not much pay," Carlyn added. "I guess not."

By Wednesday, Meri's nerves were raw. She'd looked up the calendar for meetings in Newport preservation circles and learned that Everett's organization's meeting would be that night. She crossed fingers and toes and tried not to think about it, though Carlyn did ask several times if she was upset about something.

She'd pried most of the details about Meri's meeting with Simmons out of her over lunches, but Meri was very careful not to mention Everett's offer to put them before the board. She didn't want to get anyone's hopes up if it didn't come to fruition. So she said she was fine and kept working.

And the work began to unfold. There always, if you were lucky, came a point when suddenly things began to take on a life of their own. Sometimes it was toward the end when you began to see the complete picture, sometimes it was with that first discovery. But as she worked painstakingly across the ceiling, she had an epiphany.

Granted, the colors were faded, the pattern missing in places where the plaster came off with the paint. But what was left was the promise of delicate, Italianate ornamentation. Not as glamorous as the ceilings of the Breakers dining room or the Rosecliff ballroom, but as a foyer it certainly deserved its place in history.

That night she called Gran just to say hello and to find out if she'd heard from Alden. She hadn't and Meri was tempted to call him herself, but that would be too clingy. Plus she didn't really need to talk to him though she did wonder how Nora was. She wasn't about to call her even though she had her cell number.

Meri knew she would do nothing but cause harm if Jennifer found out she was calling her daughter.

She and Gran talked for a few minutes and Meri thought her grandmother sounded a little . . . lonely?

She must be, because I am. Which was ridiculous—she didn't even see Alden that much, and to her discredit she hadn't really missed Peter so far. And she had met Everett Simmons. There were plenty of people in her life. So there was no reason to feel this emptiness.

It was probably just nerves waiting for the results of the board meeting. What if he hadn't been able to get them on the agenda? What if he'd forgotten that he'd offered to bring it before the board?

If that happened, they wouldn't be any worse off than before; Meri was glad she'd managed to not tell anyone about his offer.

Meri got to work early the next morning and found Joe Krosky and Carlyn in the kitchen drinking coffee.

"Joe, you're back," Meri said, surprised at how good it was to see the toe-bouncing microbiologist.

"Miss me?"

"Sure did. Where's Doug?"

Carlyn shrugged. "Went up to his office as soon as he came in. Things look bleak."

Meri's stomach fell. Everett hadn't come through. "Bleaker than usual?"

"No. Why?" Carlyn asked. "Has something else happened? God, you're not quitting, are you?"

Meri sighed. "No, I was just hoping. Well, guess I'll get to work." She headed down the hall, not even feeling like having coffee with the others. For a minute hope had blossomed, but she'd known it had been a long shot.

She was just passing the main staircase when Doug's footsteps rattled down the steps. "Meri."

Meri waited for him to reach the bottom.

"Come to the kitchen with me," he said, scowling at her.

Maybe things *could* get bleaker, because Doug did not look like a happy camper.

She followed him in the kitchen.

"Everybody sit down."

Carlyn and Krosky were already seated. Meri sat.

"What's up, boss?" Carlyn said, trying to sound nonchalant.

"Something amazing has happened."

"Something good?" Meri blurted.

"Potentially."

Carlyn groaned. "Just spill it, Doug. You're killing us here. Is it good or not?"

"Seems Everett Simmons—you met him the other day—"

Carlyn choked on her coffee. And widened her eyes at Meri. Meri crossed her fingers in her lap.

"He approached the Historical Preservation Group board last night about getting us a place on their spring gala event. And they've agreed, providing we can come up with enough of a presentation to show their donors and prepare a budget that is in keeping with the merits of Gilbert House."

Doug started pacing. "Doesn't mean shit if we can't pull it off. Doesn't mean shit if we can and it doesn't interest someone enough to underwrite it."

"How can it not?" Carlyn said, still looking at Meri.

"How could it not?" Meri echoed.

"But we have a lot of work to do," Doug said and hurried out the door.

"Guess I'll get back to my wallpaper," Joe said and bounced off down the hall.

"Everett Simmons?" Carlyn asked as soon as the two men were gone. "How did you pull that off?" Her eyes narrowed. "You didn't resort to blackmail or anything did you?"

"No. He offered to bring it up before the board, but he didn't make any promises. I wasn't sure he would actually do it. Or if he did, whether they would listen."

"Well, next time you see him, give him a big kiss for me."

Next time she saw him. Meri guessed she might see him again. They'd meet as friends, not father and daughter. But that was cool, she had a father already.

Meri grabbed her gear, determined to clean up enough of her ceiling to intrigue possible donors. She knew it was in awful shape, but they were used to imagining the final outcome, especially if they had a good representational artist.

When she reached the foyer, Meri stood for a minute just looking up.

She realized Joe was standing next to her, and he wasn't bouncing but also looking up.

"Amazing, isn't it?" he said.

"It is."

"How art imitates science. It looks just like a cross section of a cuboidal epithelial cell. Wonderful." He wandered away.

And Meri wondered how it would be to always be seeing things at their molecular level.

She climbed the scaffolding, already daydreaming about—and exaggerating—the final product. It would be incredible, but not in time for the gala. They would have to have an artist create a rendition of the final project, presented as a Power-Point display.

A slide show presentation could show authenticity, works in progress, schemata of the building, but rarely showed the magic or stoked the imagination. A few did, and those artists were always working. She just hoped one of them owed Doug a favor, a big favor.

Because it took a special kind of artist to inspire potential patrons to see it through the artist's eyes, as a living link to the past, something miraculous, beautiful, and inspirational.

She could see it all in her head just as if it were real. If they could just find the right artist.

After three days of looking at apartments in Manhattan, Alden had to admit that maybe he'd been rash, if a man can be rash after forty-two years. He'd seen some beautiful places.

And contrary to what Meri thought, some of them had been filled with light.

They were light, but it wasn't his light. The real estate agent suggested Brooklyn. Even larger apartments with even more light. But it still wasn't right.

The agent suggested he take a break, that sometimes you needed to get some distance on things, rearrange your expectations. She obviously thought she was wasting her time with him, and maybe she was.

Maybe Corrigan House wasn't his problem. Corrigan House without Meri was his problem. He'd known it for ages, but like he'd given up his children for their own good, he'd tried not to make Meri feel like she owed him anything.

When it was really the opposite. He owed her for bringing some joy in his life. From the first time he saw her, the first time they sat him on the couch surrounded by pillows and slipped that baby onto his lap, he knew she would always be his. Even when she was a kid, being a demanding obnoxious brat, annoying the heck out of him, he'd loved her. She'd brought the only glimmer of joy after the end of his disastrous marriage.

When he was younger, his heart ached with it. Now it had passed into comfort—most of the time. Until Peter. He'd always thought he would be glad when she found someone to love her. But he wasn't. Not Peter anyway. There was nothing wrong with the man; he just wasn't right for Meri.

Alden coughed and wished he had a cigarette. Peter at least was fun and outgoing, near her own age; they could grow old together, if they didn't divorce first. Somewhere in the passing years Alden had grown old, too old for her. He didn't think he could sing karaoke if his life depended on it.

The idea made him smile, though it was bittersweet; things would be better for him if he could. He'd communicate better with his children, with Meri. He'd be sociable instead of a semi-recluse, living with imaginary people, animals . . . monsters.

He went over to the table the hotel had brought up for him to work on. He'd pushed it against the window, which as least had southern exposure—except for the building next door. Not ideal, but he was on the last few illustrations for his Odyssey.

The backgrounds were pretty much a matter of getting them on the page. He could have plugged them into his computer and drawn the figures in front of the same landscape.

But he was too old-fashioned for that. He liked the process, liked that his backgrounds as well as his characters changed with his changing relationship to the story. He only used a graphics program when necessary.

He spent the afternoon on rendering Calypso, the nymph who fell in love with Odysseus. An ethereal creature with the necessary gauze toga since it was for children. He never understood why publishers insisted that bodies had to be clothed for kids.

He was so tempted to drop one side of her gown, exposing one breast with its pink nipple like the great classicists. But it wasn't a battle he was interested in fighting, so he sketched in the drapes over her supple limbs and torso. He drew her dancing on the beach of a lovely island, Odysseus crawling from the sea, battered and nearly drowned, his hand stretched out to her for help.

The hours passed and the noise of traffic and the day turning to dusk faded from his consciousness as the story took shape on his drawing paper. It turned out pretty well considering he was in a foreign environment. Probably because he'd already pictured the images before he left the beach.

He glanced at his watch. He'd better finish up if he planned to meet Paige for dinner. Good old Paige. He wondered if she'd ever been in love? They'd never talked about it.

What did they talk about? They talked—there was no awkwardness at all in their relationship—but it wasn't about anything substantial, and nothing too personal.. He enjoyed her company, and she enjoyed his. He laughed with her. Had great inventive sex with her. It's what they both wanted. Friends with benefits. What an appropriate name.

News of Gilbert House's inclusion in the spring gala swept through the few remaining staff members. The woodworkers put in overtime to finish the foyer. The glazier promised to have at least a mock-up of the transom window in time for the gala.

Meri continued to work methodically on her ceiling.

Doug commandeered the kitchen for viewing archive photographs. Sitting around the kitchen table, he, Krosky, and Carlyn studied, organized, and chose the most interesting ones.

"What's the verdict?" Meri asked, walking into the room and leaning over the rows of old photographs.

"Looks good, looks good," Doug said and exchanged the positions of two of the photos. "Too bad we don't have a better photo of the ceiling. This was the only one?"

Carlyn shrugged.

It was a photo that had captured the original center chandelier and a blurred bit of the painted pattern. Black and white of course. There was nothing later that showed the original work.

After Mr. Gilbert's fall from financial grace, the property had quickly fallen into disrepair. The heirs left it abandoned for years then sold it to a family who sold it several years later. It finally ended up barely standing and on the list to be demolished.

Doug had convinced the authorities that there was something worth salvaging there. It hadn't been given historical status . . . yet. That's why this was so important to finance the restoration. It deserved to live.

"I've got a cleanup crew coming in to spruce the place up. The glazier will have mock-ups of the replacement pieces.

"Geordie Holt offered to photograph whatever we can get ready. But I haven't found an artist who can commit to getting projection displays done by the end of next week. And that's a big problem." Doug flashed his teddy bear grin. "How are your drawing skills?"

"I had the course as part of the architecture curriculum," Meri said. "But I couldn't do it justice."

"I didn't even have the course," Carlyn said.

They all looked at Krosky.

Krosky shook his head. "Sorry."

"Well, I'll just have to keep calling," Doug said and moved toward the door.

"Doug, wait."

Doug turned to look at Meri. Carlyn and Krosky looked, too.

"We have to find the right artist, and not just anyone, someone with vision."

"Yeah?"

Meri had an idea. And she had to try it. For the project. For herself. And if he said no, then that would be that. But if he said yes, he would have to work on-site. And she would use that time to talk him into keeping Corrigan House.

He might turn her down—maybe he was glad to be done with her—but for Doug and the project's sake, she would ask. It would be the last time she asked Alden for anything, she promised herself, and if she couldn't talk him into staying, she would let him go.

"I might know someone. I'll give him a call."

Chapter 26

Alden took the glass of wine Paige handed him. He was sitting on her couch, looking out her picture window at the skyline of New Jersey, while New Age music played quietly in the background. Across the Hudson, apartment lights clustered along the water's edge; the bridge to New Jersey was lit up like a carnival.

A lovely place if you weren't used to the open spaces of the Rhode Island shore.

Paige sat down next to him. "You're in a pensive mood," she said in her silken voice. "Not enjoying the apartment hunt?"

He shook his head. Touched his glass to hers and took a sip; the wine was full bodied, expensive. Good wine, good view, good lady. What was wrong with him?

"Well, don't worry. You just haven't found the right place yet. Don't get stressed over it. It took me almost a year to find this place, then I almost lost it in a bidding war."

It gave him a headache to think about going through something like that. "It was worth it though, wasn't it?"

"Yes indeed. My little aerie above a crowded world."

He smiled at her. He really liked her.

"So what shall we do tonight? There's a new off-Broadway

play a friend of mine is directing. He promises it isn't too bad, and he has free tickets. Or shall we order in?" She turned her head, gave him a playful look, and he realized he'd just drawn her as the nymph, Calypso.

He took another sip of wine. His cell rang. He usually turned it off when they were together, but he was hoping that Nora would finally call him back. She usually didn't stay mad this long.

"Sorry." He pulled it out of his pocket. *Meri*. Something must be wrong. "I have to take this, sorry."

He stood and walked to the window. "Hey, what's up?"

"How's the hunt for the perfect light-filled apartment going?"

"Is everything okay there? You don't normally call to chat." He glanced back at Paige. She had discreetly moved into her galley kitchen, giving him a little privacy.

"Everything is okay. Is that music? Where are you? Did I catch you at a bad time?"

"It's okay. Why are you calling?"

"Well, actually . . ." She paused, and a hundred horrible things went through his mind. Fire, flood, an accident, heart attack.

"Actually, I have a proposition I hope you won't refuse."

He frowned. What was she up to?

"What is it?" He was aware of Paige returning with a plate of cheese and crackers.

She didn't answer.

"Meri, what's going on?"

"Look, I know I told you I didn't need you anymore. But actually I do. Not for me, but we have kind of a dilemma here at the project. Everett Simmons offered to get us a place on his next fund-raising gala but we can't find anyone . . ."

He listened to her speed-of-sound explanation, spitting out the words without pausing or giving him a chance to comment or ask a question. When she finally ran down, he'd gotten the gist. They needed an artist, this week, or everything was lost.

He couldn't help but smile, not just because she'd actually called him, but because she had such energy when she was excited, angry, sad, or celebrating. That's what was missing for him in New York—that joy in living.

"So what do you say? We can't pay, not a lot anyway, but Doug really believes in this project, and so do I."

"Well . . ." What should he do? Go back and end up stuck in the same isolation he'd tried to leave?

"You can be back in New York in a couple of weeks. There will still be apartments."

Still he hesitated. Paige was waiting for him, an enigmatic smile curving her lips.

"Please, just this one last time? Then I promise I won't bother you ever again."

"When do you need me there?"

"Yesterday?"

"How about tomorrow?"

"Yes, thank you. Thank you. I love you."

I love you, too.

"See you tomorrow?"

"I guess so."

He hung up and turned to Paige. She was smiling at him, this time with sympathetic amusement.

"I . . ."

"Have to catch a train," she finished.

"I'm sorry."

"Don't be."

He reached for his coat. "I hate to have to cut out on you."

"Alden, I understand. I really do." She laughed.

"What's funny?"

"You. Now get going, you don't want to miss that train."

It was raining when they locked up Gilbert House for the night. Pouring by the time Meri and Carlyn stood on the porch deciding where to go to dinner.

"Mike's," they said simultaneously and made a dash for Carlyn's car.

The pub was a small establishment in the basement of a white clapboard Federal house circa 1774, a local hangout with a jukebox of 1950s music and Irish folk songs. The burgers were big and the wine was drinkable, and they were favorites with the owner, Michael McGee.

"What can I get for you ladies?" he asked as soon as they had shaken off the worst of the rain and he'd shown them to a booth.

They ordered the usual, big fat juicy bacon burgers, crisp sweet potato fries, and creamy homemade coleslaw.

"How on earth did you get Alden to come back and do the renderings?" Carlyn asked as soon as Mike left with their order.

"I just asked him." Meri screwed up her face. "Though I think he might have been on a date or something."

"Really? What makes you think that? Strange noises?"

"Mood music."

"Hmm. Either in someone's bedroom or a hotel elevator." Meri snorted.

"Wow," Carlyn said dreamily, only half in jest, Meri suspected. "The secret life of the TDH."

"You can't call him that when he's present," Meri said.

"Of course not, but speaking of handsome men"—she paused as Mike put down two glasses of red wine—"what do you hear from Peter?"

"Not much. He's loving L.A. and very busy assisting his uncle who it appears is divorce lawyer to the stars."

Carlyn grimaced. "Sounds like a reality show."

"But not mine. Reality that is."

"Uh-oh. Do I detect trouble in paradise?"

Mike placed two plates of food in front of them. "Dig in, ladies."

Carlyn picked up her burger, and juices dripped onto the plate. "Well?"

"No. He has an interview with Yale in a couple of weeks. At least we'll get a chance to talk. I feel like we've both been so busy that . . ." She trailed off.

Carlyn looked over her towering burger. "What?"

Meri just shrugged. What could she say? Absence wasn't making her heart grow fonder. She was hoping that Peter wouldn't decide to stay in L.A., but if he did . . . "I don't know."

Carlyn put down her burger. "Are you sure you're not having second thoughts?"

"Maybe." Meri toyed with a sweet potato fry. "I don't know."

"Can I just ask you something? And don't get mad."

"Sure. I guess."

"Are you certain that you want to marry Peter, even if he stays back east?"

"Of course, why wouldn't I?"

"Well, it's just that . . . remember the day Alden came to see you at the site?"

"Yeah."

"It seemed to me, well, you two seemed, I don't know, simpatico. And the way he looked at you, it was the way I wish some guy would look at me, a guy who wasn't just after a quick fling or a weekend affair."

Meri stilled. "I don't think he feels that way. He never acted like anything but a big brother, a friend."

"I wouldn't be so sure. If you ask me . . ." She picked up her wine, but put it down, splayed out both hands and sang, "He'll come running . . ." She stopped, frowned. "Actually he is . . . running."

"Because he's always got my back." Meri frowned.

"That's what I mean. I may be wrong. He doesn't look at you the way Peter looks at you. It's not . . . hell, I don't know; it's just different, there's something that is just simpatico between you."

"I think it's because we grew up together. And then there's his promise to Riley. It's always there between us."

"Ha. You didn't even know about that until a couple of weeks ago. And, besides, no one lives like that anymore."

"Alden does. He illustrates fairy tales, for crying out loud." *And monsters,* she added to herself.

"Maybe, but for my money, he's very much flesh and blood. Hot blood."

Meri stared at her friend, but she wasn't really looking at her. She was trying to understand the sudden burst of possessiveness she was feeling. She didn't own Alden, but she'd taken him for granted for so long, she couldn't seem to stop.

He was loyal. Hell, what was she thinking? Dogs were loyal; Alden was so much more than that. And she'd repaid him by using him, again, to help get their project funding. Even after he'd told her he wanted to move on.

"Anyway, he's selling Corrigan House and moving to Manhattan."

"Whoa. Why?"

Meri shrugged.

"That sort of puts a damper on things."

"Tell me about it."

They finished with coffees and split a dish of apple crumble, then with leftovers packed to go, Meri and Carlyn braved the elements to get back to Carlyn's car. The rain was still coming down and they huddled beneath one umbrella attempting to avoid puddles and failing miserably.

Carlyn beeped the locks and they made a dash to get inside.

"It's more like April monsoons than showers," Carlyn said, when she'd shaken out her umbrella and tossed it to the back.

"Think we better check on the house to make sure we haven't sprung a leak somewhere?"

"I'd feel better if we did." Carlyn turned the wipers on full and pulled out into the empty street. "You know, in a few more months we won't be able to find a parking place within blocks of here."

"The price we pay for having our own table during the rest of the year."

Carlyn sighed. "I wonder what the hamburgers are like in L.A.?"

The lights were on at Gilbert House, and Doug's car was still in the parking lot. Carlyn dropped Meri off at her car. "I think I'll run in and see if everything is okay. See you tomorrow."

"Thanks," Meri said. "Call me if there's a problem. I'll come back and bail."

"Will do."

Meri started to get out of the car. She hesitated and looked over at Carlyn. "Just so you know . . . you're the best friend ever."

"Aw," Carlyn crooned, and Meri jumped out into the rain.

It took nearly fifteen minutes to find a parking place on her block, and since Meri couldn't find an umbrella in any of the usual pockets of her car, she pulled up the hood of her water-resistant—but not waterproof—jacket and ran.

She was drenched by the time she reached her apartment building. Keys in hand, she dashed the last few feet to the door. But before she got there, a figure stepped from the shadows.

Meri let out a squeak, automatically flipping her keys so that the largest pointed outward.

"Meri?"

Meri dropped her keys. "Good Lord. Nora, what are you doing here?"

Chapter 27

Alden reached Grand Central Terminal with several minutes to spare. He stopped under the schedule display. His train had arrived, but he still had a couple of minutes to try to reach Nora one last time before boarding.

Her phone was still turned off. For how long? Three days? Two weeks? A month? What if there was an emergency?

Nora was as rebellious as the next teenager, but nothing out of the norm as far as Alden could tell. But she was no dummy and could see that she was being used as a pawn between Alden and her mother. And it was time for Alden to stand up for her.

Because living with Mark and Jennifer was not in her best interest. He didn't know about Lucas.

He'd finally called his son that morning to see what was up and learned that Jennifer had taken Nora's phone away as punishment for her behavior when they'd picked her up. Lucas was usually a quiet boy, didn't complain. He liked things harmonious.

Nora hadn't been at home when Alden called.

"Look, I haven't said anything to Mark and Jennifer, but if you both want to spend more time with me, or even move here, you know I'd love you to. If you're not happy.

"I know that Nora isn't. I'm going to petition to have Nora live here with me, if that's what she really wants. At least for the rest of the school year and summer. So tell her just to hang loose and call me when she can."

"Okay."

"What about you? Are you happy? Do you want to come back to live with me? Don't worry about hurting my feelings if you don't want to."

"I'm okay. Things don't bother me like they do Nora." There was silence for a moment, and Alden waited for what was coming next.

"I'd rather finish up here until the end of the semester. We're working on a great project in lab. Mom doesn't bother me much. It's just her and Nora, plus she's kind of whacked being pregnant again."

"That's fine. You know all you have to do is call me. I'll come get you."

"Thanks. Actually, Dad, there is something . . ."

Alden waited.

"When we were up in Boston, I met this guy who was staying at our hotel."

"What kind of guy?"

"He was about my age. He and his parents were on their way to visit this high school. And get this. It specializes in the sciences."

"Sounds interesting," Alden said.

"It really does. I mean, it seriously specializes in science. I thought maybe this summer we could check it out? I mean, it might be too expensive, but could we just go see?"

"Sure, but what about summer camp?"

"Lame; I'd rather be home with you."

Home. Hell. What had he been thinking. "So tell me about this school."

He could hear the enthusiasm in his son's voice. Something

he hadn't heard in a long time. Something he intended hearing for a long time to come. Whatever it took.

"Sounds like a plan. Would you have to board?"

"Yeah. It's not exactly a commute from New Haven or even Little Compton."

"And you'd be all right with that?"

"Yeah. Besides, I thought I could come to your house on the weekends . . . if that's okay."

"More than okay."

"So we could go see it?"

"Absolutely."

Alden heard a car honk in the background.

"I gotta go. Love you, Dad."

"Love you, too. Call me and let me know how your project is going."

"Okay, Dad, thanks."

Now as he waited for his train, Alden was tempted to call his son again, but he didn't want either of his children to think he was going behind Mark's and Jennifer's backs.

He wasn't about to start anything with Jennifer. He looked up at the clock—still a few minutes. He called Mark.

He picked up immediately. "Alden?"

"Mark. I've been thinking and I wanted to talk to you first about having Nora finish the school year with me. I thought it would be better if Nora was with her mother, but I was wrong, obviously. Lucas seems fine but I want Nora back. Lucas, too, if he wants that. I'll take you to court if necessary."

"That won't be necessary, Alden. Jennifer is overwhelmed. She's taking it out on Nora. I think you're absolutely right. I'll ask Lucas what he wants to do, unless you want to talk to him yourself."

"We've talked a bit, but I'll touch base with him again later; now how do you want to arrange this?" The tinny announcement of Alden's train departure blared through the station.

"Just tell Nora I'm sorry things have gotten so out of hand and I'll send her some clothes and things and you guys can pick up the rest later."

"Why don't you tell her yourself? I'm sure she'd feel better knowing someone there was sympathetic."

"You're right. Put her on."

A cold sliver of fear shot up Alden's spine. "What do you mean, put her on?"

"Isn't Nora with you?"

"God no, I'm in Manhattan." Alden began walking toward the stairs to the train. "Where is she?"

"Oh Lord. She ran away; I thought that was why you were calling."

"No, what the hell? How long?"

The phone connection began to drop out.

"She didn't come home on the bus. When I called the school, they said she hadn't been there since lunch. There's some money missing out of Jennifer's purse. She was pretty upset."

"Is Lucas with her?"

"What? I can't hear you?"

"Is Lucas there, or is he with Nora?"

Alden began running down the stairs and another announcement drowned out Mark's answer. Then the call was dropped.

For a second he considered running back upstairs and calling again, but he would miss the train and he was pretty sure she would go home, and not to Manhattan. Had he even mentioned where he was staying?

So he found a seat and waited impatiently for the train to leave the station.

What had Mark said? She'd taken some money. Hopefully enough to take a train to Providence. Then what? A bus to Newport or—God, she wouldn't try to hitchhike home, would she?

Finally the doors shut and the train jerked forward. It seemed to take hours until the train finally slid aboveground.

All around him people reached for their cell phones and Alden did, too.

"Sorry, I was in the tunnel," he said when Mark answered on the first ring. "Where is Lucas?"

"He's right here; I'll put him on."

"Did you find her?" Lucas asked.

"Not yet. But I'm on the train back home. Did she tell you anything about what she was doing?"

"No. I swear, I didn't know anything about it. You've gotta find her."

"I will. Make sure Mark calls me if she comes back. I have to hang up now. I'm going to call Therese and Meri and tell them to watch out for her."

The first thing he did was call his hotel to tell them if his daughter showed up to keep her there.

It began raining, the heavy drops making slashing marks across the windows. Alden had been wrestling with the idea of renting a car when the train changed over at New Haven and driving the rest of the way. But rain invariably led to traffic jams and accidents. It could take hours to get home.

Nora might already be there, if she got there at all. He couldn't help but imagine all the horrible things that could happen to a teenage girl out in the world alone.

And here he was stuck on the train.

Meri bustled the shivering girl into her apartment and straight to the bathroom. "You get out of those wet clothes. I'll see if I have something for you to wear."

"I have clothes in my backpack."

"Then put them on. Or take a hot shower if you want. I'm calling your father."

"Wait."

Meri stopped at the door, her cell phone in her hand as another rainy night not so long ago rose in her mind. The night she had showed up at Alden's door and he'd thrust her in the shower and left dry clothes on his bed.

"Are you angry?"

Meri took a calming breath, while thousands of horror stories rushed through her mind. "I'm not angry. I'm freaked out that you actually ran away. Why did you do it?"

The girl's bottom lip quivered. Her words were barely audible. "I wanted to come home."

And Meri's heart melted. She knew just how Nora felt. The peninsula would always be her home, too. "It's okay," Meri said. "But you have to promise not to do that again."

"I won't go back."

Meri glanced at her phone. Alden had called her at least five times and she'd been at the pub and not heard the ring. She needed to call him and let him know Nora was okay. But Nora needed to be okay before she talked to him.

"Get dressed. I'll heat up my leftover hamburger for you. It's the best I can do at the moment. You're lucky that Mike's serves the largest burgers in Newport."

Nora closed the bathroom door and Meri went to the kitchen, deliberating on whether to call Alden right away or wait until she had found out from Nora what was really wrong.

She decided on a compromise. She redialed Alden's number.

He picked it up on the first ring. "Meri?" His voice sounded so strained that it frightened her.

"She's here at my apartment. Everything is fine."

"It's not fine. What the hell was she—Let me talk to her."

"She's in the shower. When she gets out—What's that noise? Where are you?"

"On the train. We just changed over at New Haven. I should be there in an hour and a half."

"Fine. I'd better order takeout."

"Meri."

"Have you eaten?"

"No."

"Neither has Nora, and I'm quickly working up a new appetite. And while you're on the train, can you work on being calm and not panic-stricken when you get here?"

"Is she . . . ?"

"She said she wanted to come home. I'm going to attempt a little girl talk while we wait. You just stay calm."

"Goddammit."

"See? Not helpful. I've got to go. Don't worry. I'll take care of her." *Just like you've always taken care of me.* She hung up, astonished at her realization. Maybe Alden had always taken care of her because he wanted to, not just because he'd promised.

Because he cared about her, like she cared about Nora—and him.

She stuck her burger in the microwave and reached for her folder of take-out menus.

"Did you call Dad?" Nora stood in her bedroom doorway looking apprehensive. She'd changed into dry clothes and towel-dried her hair, which now stuck up in black spikes.

"Yes, just to let him know you're safe."

"What did he say? Is he coming to get me?"

"Yes. He was already on his way. He should be here in a little over an hour."

"Was he pissed?"

"No, Nora. He was frightened."

"I am so fucked."

"If you use that kind of language around your dad, you will be." Meri smiled slightly. "He once threatened to wash my mouth out with soap. I don't know where he gets some of his antiquated notions. Gran never even threatened me with that."

"He uses those words . . . sometimes."

"He's the grown-up. He's allowed lapses."

"If he sends me back, I'll just run away again."

The microwave dinged. "Save it for your dad. Eat this and we'll order real food when Alden gets here." Meri slid the foam container to the breakfast bar.

Nora finally came into the room, pulled out a stool, and sat down. Meri got out two bottles of water and let her eat.

When she'd polished off everything but a slice of dill pickle, Meri motioned her over to the couch.

"Where's your phone?"

"She took it away."

"Your mother?"

Nora nodded.

Meri handed Nora hers. "Call and tell them you're fine."

Nora shook her head.

"I'm not fine."

Meri's heart began to race. "You're not pregnant, are you?"

Nora grimaced. "Of course not; I'm not stupid."

"Stupidity doesn't cause pregnancy. Unprotected sex does."

"Ewww. I don't want to talk about it."

"Fine. Neither do I. Just checking. Now call." Meri shoved her cell phone at her.

"I'll call Lucas."

"Fine, just call somebody and let them know you're okay."

Nora made the call. Her brother had plenty to say, but Nora put him off. "I'm okay. Tell Mom and Mark and tell them . . . tell them I didn't mean to cause any trouble. Bye." She hung up. Handed the phone back to Meri.

"So what *did* bring you back?"

"I told you. I wanted to come home."

Meri was out of her element. Usually Alden was in the mentor place and she was in Nora's. She suddenly realized how hard it was.

While she was wondering how to shape the conversation, Nora did it for her. "Why didn't he fight for us more? He was the one who always stayed home. When Lucas and I were little, she was always going off to Manhattan or Boston with her friends.

"Even when she was home, she was always shopping, or playing tennis, or getting her hair or her nails done. She never stayed home with us. Daddy drove us to school and lessons and sports and concerts; he gave us baths, and he read the bedtime stories."

Probably because he saw the writing on the wall, even then. Jennifer had not been the soul mate people like Alden needed. She was demanding, his children needed him, and God forgive her, Meri had made her own demands.

And he'd done it all. Why hadn't he sent Jennifer packing—and Meri, too?

"Why did he let us go?"

Why had he? Meri thought she knew. "Remember once you told me he was overprotective because his mother left him when he was a boy?"

Nora nodded; there was a smear of ketchup at the corner of her mouth that made her look much younger than sixteen.

Meri waited for Nora to make the connection. It didn't take long.

"He didn't want us to grow up without a mother." Nora's eyes rounded. "I didn't think about that. And I've been so mean to him."

Meri tossed her a napkin. "He's a smart man. I think he knows how much you really love him."

"Will you talk to him, tell him not to send me back? I won't be any trouble. I'll make good grades and I can cook—a little—but I can learn, and I can clean. I do know how to do that."

Meri smiled.

"It's too bad he didn't marry *you*. At least you get him."

The smile froze on Meri's face then gradually slid away. "Nora, I was thirteen when your dad married Jennifer."

Nora flopped back on the couch. "But you aren't now. I know he needs to find . . . somebody. But what if he finds the wrong one and it happens all over again?"

"Is that why you ran away?" Was Alden thinking about marrying again? He'd never mentioned anyone he was seeing. Meri didn't even think he *was* seeing someone. But surely he must be on all those trips to Manhattan. She didn't for a minute think he'd been celibate all these years. But she really didn't want to think about him not being celibate. And there was that music playing in the background of her call earlier that day.

"I'm sure he won't make any sudden changes." *Like out of the blue announcing he was selling Corrigan House? Like moving to Manhattan? Music playing in the background?*

He never listened to music, said it drowned out the sound of the waves. He wouldn't be hearing any waves in Manhattan.

She risked a look at Nora. Nora was looking back at her, and it was pretty clear they were both thinking the same thing.

But not for the same reasons.

It was closer to two hours before Alden showed up. There had been an accident on I-95. When he hadn't arrived after an hour and a half, Meri ordered food, checked to make sure she had ice cubes, and got out the bottle of Glenlivet she kept for him in the cabinet.

When the buzzer sounded the first time, Meri and Nora both jumped, even though they knew it was the delivery boy. The second buzzer went off just minutes later.

Meri and Nora stood while they waited for Alden to come up the stairs. Still they jumped again when he knocked on the door. They exchanged a look and the tension suddenly broke. They started to laugh, so that when the door opened, Alden was greeted by two women struggling to keep their composure.

Until he stepped over the threshold—one look at his face sobered them immediately.

"Daddy? I'm sorry." Nora fell into his arms.

Meri went to pour him a drink.

She came back with a tumbler of ice and scotch and handed it to Alden. "Dinner will be served on the coffee table." She went back to the kitchen to take the containers out of the warming oven.

"But I can stay?"

"Yes. I've talked to Mark. He agrees that you should finish the school year here—with me."

"Yes!" Nora exclaimed.

"But don't think acting out like this is going to get you anything but grounded. Which by the way you are."

She shook her head. "I just didn't know what else to do. I couldn't take it anymore."

"Okay, it's done. But you're still grounded."

"Fine. Let's eat. I'm starving."

"So am I; go help Meri with the food. I'm sitting down while I book us a hotel suite and try to recover the ten years I just lost worrying about where the hell you were."

"We could stay with Meri."

Alden caught Meri's eye. "I think it would be a case of over-kill." He pulled out his phone.

The three of them polished off all the food in record time, but it was one o'clock before Alden pulled a weary Nora to her feet. "Go get your stuff."

Nora yawned and wandered into the bedroom.

Alden turned to Meri. "I'll come by in the morning to talk to Doug. Then we'll probably drive out to the house to see what condition it's in and I'll pick up whatever supplies and equipment I'll need to work at the site."

"You're still doing the project?"

"Of course. Would I let you down?"

"No, never, but I thought maybe with Nora here . . ."

"When are you going to learn?"

"Alden, I—"

"You can put me to work, too," Nora said as she dragged her backpack through the doorway.

Alden slipped it over her shoulders and nudged her into the hall. "You're going to school. Somewhere." He looked at Meri.

She shrugged. "Tiverton?" She lowered her voice. "Or are you going to take her to Manhattan?"

He shook his head.

Resigned to staying, Meri thought. She was glad, but it wasn't fair. "You have to do what's good for you, too."

He gave her a tired half smile. "Thanks, thanks for being here for Nora—and for me." He pulled her close, and Meri gave into his hug: the comfort of it, the strength, the familiarity. And she wondered if maybe they had all been right, that Peter wasn't the right man for her.

Alden pulled away but held on to her shoulders. "Get some sleep. See you in the morning. When do you start?"

"Around nine, usually, but you don't have to be there that early," she said, trying to clear the fog that had descended on her brain.

"See you then."

Meri nodded. She suddenly felt very tired. "Night. Night, Nora.

"Ni-ight," Nora returned in a singsong voice and a smug smile.

Meri waited while father and daughter walked down the stairs to the street, then she closed the door. Between work and Nora, she was tired. And confused. After Carlyn's talk about being simpatico, Meri felt it, too. Had always felt it. Hadn't known exactly what it was. Wasn't sure she knew now.

But she did know one thing. She wanted Alden to love her for herself and not because she was an obligation. She wanted Alden . . . And Peter? What did she want from him?

Chapter 28

Alden's truck was parked at the back of Gilbert House when Meri arrived at work the next morning. Getting an early start. She guessed things were a go, though she did have a few anxious moments during the night thinking what might have passed between father and daughter after they left her apartment.

She hurried inside and found Carlyn and Nora in the kitchen. Carlyn poured her a cup of coffee.

"What a night, huh?" Carlyn asked.

"Never a dull moment. Thanks for the coffee. Are Alden and Doug already at it?"

"Yep. The intensity level around here has shot up several points. That's a match made in heaven."

"How about you, Nora? Everything okay?"

"Yeah, though Dad said I better thank you like crazy for putting up with me."

Meri laughed. "Just like I should thank your dad for all those years of putting up with me. It was my pleasure. Though don't make a habit of it."

"I won't. I'm going to be the perfect child from now on." She grinned mischievously.

"Hmmm," Meri answered, sipping her coffee.

Carlyn poured herself a cup and sat down. "Nora is going to reorganize my files today. She's now an official unofficial intern."

"What happened to school and homework?"

Nora lifted her hands and shrugged. "No books, no transcripts, ergo no school."

"She'll learn on the job. Doug said to come find them when you get here."

Meri took another sip of coffee and put down her cup. "Save this. I'll be back."

She found Doug and Alden in the front parlor. Doug was gesticulating like a traffic cop, Alden was listening and nodding. He was wearing jeans and an old fisherman's sweater. And his hair fell over his forehead as he sketched something into a spiral drawing notebook.

He turned and smiled when Meri came in, and her stomach did a little flip, surprising her. It was just that she was so glad to see him after all the angst of the night before. Though she was always glad to see him, this felt different. She shook it off. She was off-kilter with all the earth-shattering events of the past few weeks. She needed to steady herself. Wait and figure things out later when her life had calmed down. "Everything going okay?"

"We're going to set Alden's equipment up in the dining room. That way he can work on-site so he can have a firsthand look at everything."

"You're going to make the commute every day?" she asked, feeling a little jealous and a little left out, though nothing was stopping her from doing the same.

"Depends on the state of the house," Alden said and sketched something in his notebook. He was in creative planning mode, and Meri knew better than to bother him.

"Well, I'd better get to work."

Both men nodded, but they had already turned back to their work.

Meri got her gear and climbed up to work on her ceiling. She was surprised at how much work she'd actually gotten done. The pattern was visible now, if a little faded, well, a lot faded, and there were still pieces missing. But she had exposed enough now that the painter could easily reconstruct the original.

The sun coming through the high foyer windows didn't quite make it to the center of the ceiling but created a soft halo around the place where the chandelier would sit. She wondered if the architect had planned it that way. Or if it was just one of those serendipitous situations that sometimes occur when random elements meet.

She allowed herself one more minute to imagine the ceiling in all its former glory. shining down on the visitors as they entered the newly restored house.

Which won't happen if you don't get your butt in gear. She opened her tool kit, pulled on her goggles, and got to work. She heard Doug and Alden move out of the room below her and their voices recede down the hall, then she forgot all about them as she concentrated on the work at hand.

Carlyn stopped Meri for lunch at noon. Alden and Nora had gone out to the peninsula to get the equipment Alden would need.

"He's planning to come back and set up this afternoon." Carlyn clapped her hands together. "It's really going to happen."

"Sure beginning to look that way."

"Thanks to you."

"Me?"

"Everett Simmons and your friend Alden. It's a double whammy. How could we not get funding with the two of them added to the team?"

They both quickly knocked on the wooden table.

"Where's Krosky?" Meri asked. "I hope we haven't lost him again."

"He called. He'll be back tomorrow."

"Wow. He's a maniac," Meri said. "Is everybody working on Saturday?

"No. Doug decided that would be a good time to strip the fireplace in the parlor, so the worst of the fumes would air out by Monday. But when I told Joe that Doug was bringing in someone to help him, Krosky said he wanted to do it and he'd come in special."

"What about his orals or whatever he's doing?"

Carlyn shrugged. "He didn't say and I wasn't about to ask. You guys get so territorial about what you're doing; I just said thanks, see you then."

Meri went back to work, thinking about what Carlyn had said. *Thanks to you.* She really hadn't done anything but act selfishly. She had sought Everett Simmons out because she wanted to see firsthand what kind of man he was so she could have some closure. Instead she'd added another important person to her life.

She'd called Alden because she wanted him nearby, so she could talk him into staying at Corrigan House. She'd been thinking about the project, but mainly she'd been thinking about herself. She couldn't take any credit if the presentation led to support, but she could take all the blame if they failed.

Wow, look at it." Nora stretched to see out of the windshield. "You can actually see the house."

Alden saw it, naked in the sunlight. Broken shingles, crumbling chimney, warts and all. He pulled into the drive and parked the truck in between a landscaping trailer and a local house painting van.

Nora jumped out and ran ahead. Alden moved more slowly, past a huge Pod storage container that was filled with all the run-down furniture in the house. He should tell them to throw it away. He slowed as he reached the entrance where the old rose beds had been freshly tilled, ready to hold new rosebushes, or some other plant, something easier to grow, so they would survive long enough to sell the house before they wilted and died. He stepped onto the flagstone walk, half afraid of seeing the changes inside.

He found Nora standing right inside the entry hall staring into the living area. The furniture had been moved out. A painter's tarp covered the wood floors. And the walls were . . . white.

Alden blinked; so that's what the room looked like. It had always been dark ever since he could remember. Jennifer hadn't been interested in doing any redecorating. He should have guessed then she wouldn't last.

Actually, he did guess it; he just ignored it. Because except for the fights, he loved living there with his children, watching them grow up within view of the sea and letting them run wild in the summer, just like Meri before them.

He thought he could make it until they went off to college, but when the affairs and the bills from Jennifer's "weekends away" started coming in, he knew he had to put a stop to it. And he'd lost his children because he had mistakenly believed they would be better off with her.

So they wouldn't grow up with a father who loved them but didn't know how to show it. Who was gruff when he should have been understanding. Who didn't know how to show love. Who'd married a woman who couldn't stick out the Rhode Island winters or the isolation.

Like father, like son.

He stepped beside his daughter.

"They've changed everything," she said.

He thought she sounded like she might cry. He should have left her in Newport. Waited until it was finished and looked as close to a magazine as it would ever get. But he'd wanted her company, wanted her to know she would always have him.

"Well, it's very white," he agreed.

"But where's all our stuff?"

"I imagine the bedrooms upstairs are the same; the rest is probably in that storage unit out by the drive."

"They better not have moved my clothes." She made a mad dash for the stairs and took them two at a time.

If that was all she was worried about, he could breathe easier. But he didn't. He was hit by a wave of melancholy so strong that he staggered beneath its force. He went out to the sunroom. He'd left strict orders for nothing in this room to be touched.

They hadn't been in here, but he could see the workers sitting out on the lawn, taking a break, chatting or lying on the grass.

He turned away, not wanting to think about what he would do once Corrigan House was gone. What was he doing? Shouldn't he keep it for his children? Did they even want it? It couldn't sit idle for another decade or so waiting for them to take over. It would fall into total disrepair.

Alden began gathering up art supplies and paper and put them in a big cardboard box he found in the hallway. Then he went into the dining room where his computer monitors were set up for special graphics work. He unplugged the equipment he thought he might use and carried it to the truck.

It took four trips and a lot of foam padding to get it all in the back of the truck. He began to rue selling the Volvo. If Nora was going to live here— He stopped. He hadn't really thought about the future, just taken it for granted that he would register her at Tiverton High where he and Meri had gone.

He supposed they could move to town, get a nice apartment, even a house. They'd still be close enough to Therese to visit and be nearby if she needed help.

Or they could just stay here in a white-roomed dilapidated mansion. Two souls rambling through wide corridors and oddly shaped rooms. That was no way for a girl to grow up.

It had been good enough for you. But that was because Gran and Laura and Meri had lived next door.

He went out to the sunroom to take the last box of supplies out, but stopped, mesmerized by the view. He'd miss that for sure. Miss the fun times. He could almost hear his children's laughter as they ran up the path from the beach.

"Remember when you and Meri used to take Lucas and me down to the beach and we'd look for sea glass?"

Nora stood beside him. He hadn't heard her come into the room.

"You mean me and your mother."

Nora shook her head. "She never went down there. She only swam at the club. You and Meri took us down and taught us how to swim. I remember it was so cold but we didn't want to get out."

"I'd forgotten that," he said, and smiled at the memory.

"Is that why you want to sell the house? Because Meri is marrying Peter?"

"What? Where did you get such an idea?"

Nora shrugged. Searched his face as if she was looking for a different answer.

An answer that not even Alden knew the answer to.

"It's just too much house for me. We can visit, or even buy a smaller place somewhere close by. I just don't want to live here anymore."

"Why?"

"I just told you."

She gave him that look she used when she was calling his bluff.

And it worried him. "Is that why you ran away? Because you thought I would be lonely without Meri here?"

She shook her head. "I *know* you'll be lonely, but that's not why I ran away. It's not even totally because it was so awful there. It's just . . . I don't know . . . I don't feel right anywhere but here."

Usually when Meri worked, she got totally involved, but she spent the next few hours listening for the sound of Alden's truck. Then when he finally returned, she was acutely aware of him walking around below her, making sketches, taking measurements. She tried to ignore him. The last time her mind wandered she'd ended up with stitches. They couldn't afford any more accidents now.

When she quit for the day, she stopped by the dining room. The door that opened onto the second parlor had been sealed by a plastic sheet, to keep dust and shavings off the equipment. She went around back where a small hallway led from the kitchen to a service entrance.

The door was shut but not sealed off. Doug was careful not to let particles back this far. She peeked in but there was nothing there. Now where would he be working? Not upstairs; those rooms were in terrible shape. She walked through the house, opening doors to storerooms, and rooms that had once had uses but were now converted to closets and a television room to judge from the pair of rabbit ears that lay on the dusty floor.

Meri didn't usually come back to this section of the house. It had been shut up since she'd been working there, and she assumed it was used for storage. Just seeing it was enough to give the most stalwart restorer second thoughts. But she kept going until she saw a light at the end of a narrow hall.

She followed it to Alden. The room was pretty sparse except for a jumble of tables covered by several computer monitors and printers of various sizes. Alden was bent over his drafting table. A large flat-screen computer monitor sat at his right and his eyes shifted back and forth between the two.

She knew better than to interrupt him, so she stood in the doorway until he finally looked up.

"How long have you been standing there?"

"Not long. How's it going?"

"Slowly." He straightened up, put his hands behind his head and stretched. "What time is it?"

"Just about six."

"Carlyn and Nora went for pizza. Some place around here, I forgot the name. She said to meet them there."

"Are you ready to quit?"

"I'll work until they get back." Already his eyes were drifting back to his work.

"You're not going to eat?"

"I'll get something later. You go on. Tell Carlyn not to forget to come back and lock up."

"Carlyn would never forget. She's the house mother of all house mothers. Can I take a peek?"

"Sure; it's not exactly my usual work."

She came to stand behind his chair. A large piece of gridded drafting paper was tacked to the work table. A triangular scale ruler lay across the bottom corner, and other drafting instruments were lined up in a trough to the side. Several mechanical pencils stuck out of a mustard jar. A partial pattern had been hand drawn to scale and when she compared it to the slide on the screen, she knew it was her ceiling.

"Those aren't the true colors," she said, leaning over his shoulder to get a better look.

"No. I have no idea what the true colors are yet. I'll expect you to tell me. This is just to delineate the separate patterns without driving me blind.

"Capisce?" He turned to look at her, and his hair brushed her cheek.

She moved away; blind panic held her tongue.

"Meri?"

"Uh." What was she doing? She pulled herself together. "We have old photos of the original. It's faded but from the common tints of the era we can analyze the remaining paint and come to a pretty exact match. But it takes time."

He was smiling at her. Amused. She wasn't amused. Something was going on with her that shouldn't be. She took several steps back.

"What's the matter?"

"Nothing. Just tired, I guess."

"Why don't you meet the girls for dinner and make it an early night?"

Because I'd rather stay with you. "I think I will. Good night."

"G'night." He went back to his drawing.

She fled and didn't stop until she was sitting in her car.

What the hell was happening to her? It had been a few crazy weeks, but this was the craziest thing yet.

It must be all the things that had happened in the last month—finding out she was adopted, meeting Everett Simmons, Peter moving across the country instead of giving her an engagement ring. And now when he was gone, she was having a definitely physical reaction to Alden of all people.

It was so embarrassing. No, *humiliating*. Peter had been gone less than a month and she'd almost hit on her oldest friend. How could she? After all he'd done for her, been to her. Maybe that was what it was. He was safe. *He was never safe; he always challenged her.* He was a known quantity. *Not known at all.* So what was it?

She really needed to talk to Peter before she did something stupid.

She didn't stop by the pizza place but went straight home and called Los Angeles. The call went to voice mail. Of course it was still working hours there. She left a message to call her. Waited until eleven o'clock. Eight o'clock in L.A. Surely he was finished by now.

If your girlfriend called you from across the country,

wouldn't you call her back as soon as you could? Alden always did. Damn. She hadn't meant to think about him. But he did call. He never put her off. And even when he was about to make a serious change in his life, he dropped everything to come running back to help her.

Because that's what friends did, she told herself. But isn't that what your future husband should do?

She paced the length of her living space. A half hour went by. Still no call. At midnight, she called again.

"Is everything all right? I'd like to hear from you." She hung up. Had she sounded bitchy? She was feeling a little bitchy. But what if he'd had an accident or something? Someone would have called her.

Meri finally went to bed. When her cell rang at four A.M., her first thought was that something had happened to Gran.

"Hello?"

"Hey, babe. What's up?"

"Peter?"

"Yeah. I've been crazy busy. It's major out here. You're gonna love it."

Was he drunk?

"I thought you had an interview at Yale next week."

"Oh yeah. I'll be there on Friday. See you then?"

"I have a fund-raiser on Friday. Saturday?"

"Sure. Have to make it morning. I have that interview at one. Then I have to run in to New York to meet with some guys that do work for our firm."

Our firm? He hadn't even been accepted to a law school.

"You know. Get some face time."

"Face time," she repeated mechanically.

"I gotta tell you, I'm leaning toward Stanford. It's a great lifestyle out here. So think about it."

Who was she talking to? This didn't sound like the Peter she knew at all. He sounded like a stranger.

"Listen, I have to get back . . . wining and dining some clients, you know the drill."

She didn't know the drill. And what was Peter doing wining and dining clients? He was an intern. The Gilbert House interns sometimes got pizza.

"Okay, I guess I'll see you next week."

"Sure thing. Can't wait." He hung up.

But she could. She was confused. And suddenly she wasn't looking forward to seeing him at all.

Chapter 29

There was no question of not working through the weekend. With the gala only seven days away, it was imperative that the restoration team get as much work done as possible. So at nine o'clock after a restless night, Meri arrived at Gilbert House, which was already alive with activity. Carlyn's, Doug's, and Alden's vehicles were in the lot as well as Krosky's bike. There were several other cars that she didn't recognize.

She stopped in the kitchen for a cup of coffee to go with the bagel she'd bought on her way over and found Krosky, Doug, and Carlyn sitting at a table covered with bakery bags and donut boxes.

"Taking a break?" Meri asked. "Or just getting started?"

"Already finished," Doug said. "Coated and covered in plastic. We were just discussing whether to do another one or move onto something else."

"I think we should stick to the plan," Carlyn said and tapped her pen on the yellow legal pad she'd been writing on.

Meri poured herself a cup, sat down, and opened the wrapper of her bagel.

"Krosky and I will do the bulk of the mantel cleaning tomorrow. I'd like to put you on the details though, Meri. I'd like to have a clean-enough piece to show how much work we've done. It should be ready for you by Monday."

He turned Carlyn's legal pad so he could see it better. "What else did we decide on?"

"Door, window, wallpaper, ceiling, fireplace."

A lot of work.

"Okay, boss, I'm on it." Meri drained her cup and put the rest of her bagel in the fridge. "I assume Alden's already working. Let me check with him to see how ready he is for color. And I'll take it from there."

The door to the newly designated studio was closed. She knocked lightly.

"Come in." Alden looked up from his computer monitor. "Hey, come look at this and tell me how you like it."

She went over; he stood and moved his chair out of the way, and they stood side by side gazing at Meri's ceiling. Or the patterns of her ceiling, radiating out from a center point. The colors were primary and there was none of the detail, but he'd replicated the pattern to scale.

"The beauty and the shortcomings of computer graphics," he said. "Beauty in that it saves a lot of grunt work, but it isn't painting and we can guess that your ceiling has several intermixing patterns not to mention all the cornices and moldings that were probably decorated."

"That pretty much covers it. I'll try to get you a cornice at least—may take a couple or three days—at least enough to imagine the rest. Then we'll—I'll—come up with some appropriate color scheme. It won't be authentic. Ugh. I hate guesswork."

He chuckled. "I know. You just keep plugging along, and we'll get it close enough to wow them."

She looked up at him. Really looked.

"What?"

"Thanks. I mean it."

"I know you do."

"I hope I didn't screw up your plans."

"Meri, you have never screwed up anything in my life."

"I—I better get to work." Before she said or did something stupid. For a second while they talked about their work there had been that old natural camaraderie, and she almost forgot the unexpected attraction that had hit her the night before. But as soon as he looked at her, it all came rushing back. She needed to get a grip. He was still the same old Alden, but she had somehow changed.

"Where is Nora?" she asked.

"Went off with the glazier who was here earlier."

"Lizzy Blanchard?"

"Yes. Nora was completely taken with the colored glass. I'm afraid we may have another budding artist in the family."

In the family. Those words followed Meri as she gathered her equipment and, surrounded by the lingering fumes of paint dissolver, climbed the scaffolding to her ceiling.

She'd taken samples of several of all four of the cornices, and she chose one that looked the strongest to begin her work. She'd start with hand scraping and hoped without much hope that much of the paint would loosen. As expected, by the time she took a break, most of the ceiling white was still in place.

No one was about so she ate the second half of her bagel, filled the jug with the vinegar solution, and carried it back up the scaffolding to scrub the newest paint away.

The cornice was ornate, making her job more difficult. And several times she had to climb down to replenish her water-vinegar solution and her supply of clean cloths.

It was late when Meri heard someone call her name. She looked over the railing to see Nora standing below her. "Dad says it's time for you to knock off and come have dinner with us."

"I smell like vinegar and am covered with paint chips."

"We'll wait for you to change."

"Okay, just let me clean up this mess."

Dinner was quiet but relaxed. Alden took them to one of the restaurants that overlooked the bay. Nora told them all about the glazier's studio—at length. And Alden and Meri let her talk. It was good to see her the happy teenager she'd been on her last visit.

Meri had started the evening determined to control her wandering emotions. But it was unnecessary. The more she relaxed, the more Alden opened up. He seemed pleased to have his daughter home. And Meri was curious as to whether they had made any plans for where they would live.

Maybe he would change his mind about leaving Corrigan House, now that Nora was home for good.

They walked Meri home, Alden's arm around each of them. Comfortable like what? A father and his daughters? A man and his family? Meri tried not to analyze it too much and just enjoy the sense of peace it gave her.

But when they left, she felt unaccountably alone. And ill at ease, because all the doubts she'd been having lately rose up at once. It was only nine o'clock, and she considered calling Gran but then thought she might be asleep. She called Dan.

It was calming to talk to her dad, to get updates on work and family. He told her about his latest project. She told him about Nora running away, and how Alden was helping them get ready for the fund-raiser.

Then she told him about meeting Everett Simmons and how Simmons had helped them get on the agenda.

"He's a nice man. I'm glad he loved Riley. But you're my dad, my only dad."

She kind of teared up while saying that, so she cut to the real reason she called him. "Dad, I think I'm having second thoughts about Peter."

"Oh," he said clearly surprised. "Did something happen to cause you to change your mind?"

"Sort of, but nothing to do with Peter. It's just that he seems like a different person out there. He likes it. I don't think I would like it. I know I wouldn't. Especially not the lifestyle he's envisioning. What should I do?"

"Well, I think your mother would say, follow your heart."

"My heart's confused."

"About whether you love Peter enough to give up your work and life here and relocate?"

She hesitated, then just blurted it out. "About whether I love Peter enough to marry him at all."

"Are you sure this isn't because of learning about the circumstances of your birth? About him being gone when you could really have used him to be supportive? Did you even tell him about it?"

"No. He was leaving and I didn't think it was the right time."

"Hmm. Maybe you should talk to him before you make any decisions."

"You're the one who said he wasn't right for me."

"I know, but I'm prejudiced. I think you deserve someone very special."

"And Peter's not special?"

"If he is to you, then I guess he is to me, too. Meri, have you met someone else?"

Meri swallowed. "No, I haven't met anyone."

"Well, I wish your mother were here to help you through this. I always depended on her to help me see things."

"You're doing good. Thanks, Dad. I love you."

"Love you, too, sweetheart. Things will work out for the best, and we all support you whatever you decide."

And she had to be content with that. The choice was placed back squarely on her shoulders. She carried it to bed with her.

Meri and her coworkers worked through the weekend and into the next week without a break. She uncovered a gilt detailed cornice that had Doug climbing up the scaffolding to see it firsthand.

Alden hand finished the details on the ceiling design following the tracing Meri had done and the photos of the work in progress. When the fireplace was stripped, they discovered tiles in addition to the wooden columns and cameos inset with colored glass.

Doug immediately found the addition of glass suspect, an ornamentation added later in the century. But that was one of the many exciting things about restoration.

Everyone came in to admire and study the partially cleaned mantel. And Krosky beamed like a proud father.

Meri didn't see too much of Alden during the day. Nora's transcripts still hadn't come through so Alden granted her another week off on the condition that she did schoolwork with Carlyn in the mornings—though twice she visited the glass studio and on Wednesday afternoon came back with several tile squares that she had "pressed" herself.

Not spending time with Alden was a good thing, since Meri was meeting Peter on Saturday. The mere thought of that sent her adrenaline racing. She couldn't tell if it was anticipation or dread.

Twice Carlyn had stopped her and asked if everything was all right.

Meri said of course. She was under a deadline and she was afraid to look too closely at what she was feeling. Everything was moving too fast. In the last month almost everything in her life had changed, and now she was afraid she was falling in love with a man she'd known all her life.

On Thursday morning, the whole crew convened in the kitchen to go over last-minute details. Alden gave them a spur-of-the-moment slide show of the shots he would present to the donors the following night.

It was amazing. Not just accurate computer duplications but a display of color and design and whimsy that was the hallmark of Alden's illustrations. It not only looked beautiful but led the viewer into a different world.

She caught his eye. "They're wonderful. Thank you."

He smiled at her, shook his head.

"Silk purse," Doug exclaimed. And it was hard to tell who was bouncing higher, Joe or Doug.

When the meeting broke up, Carlyn held Meri back. Then she closed the door. "Okay, spill; what's going on with you?"

She had taken Meri completely off guard.

"I know you're preoccupied and have been working over-time. But I've hardly seen you, and you're avoiding Alden. I don't think you're mad at me. Are you mad at him?"

"I'm not mad at anyone."

"So what gives?"

Meri shrugged. She so wanted to talk out her fears and confusion with Carlyn, but she didn't want to admit her emotional vacillations.

"Sit."

Meri sat and Carlyn came to sit beside her.

"I'm kind of on emotional overload."

"I figured that much. So what's bothering you the most?"

"All of it, but mainly . . ." She leaned into her friend. "I don't think I want to marry Peter." There, no longer second thoughts—she'd said what she was really thinking out loud.

"Whoa."

"You don't sound all that surprised."

"Well, actually, I don't quite know how to say this, but . . . is it because of Alden?"

"How can you tell?"

"Oh come on, you two have the perfect relationship, communication, affection, everything a relationship should have except sex; I'm guessing there's still no sex."

Meri shook her head violently. "No! He doesn't—"

"Yes, he does. I noticed it the first day. I think it's just hard for both of you to recognize what's happening. Hell, you even have the teenager. Ready-made family."

Meri jerked her head toward the closed door.

"Nobody can hear us."

Meri leaned even closer. "But why now? After all these years and what if he doesn't—" She covered her face with her hands. "Listen to me; I sound like a teenager."

"Well, hell, the new you was just born a few weeks ago. That's bound to change some things."

"But what about Peter?"

Carlyn crossed her arms, thought for a moment. "Well, when you see him Saturday, you'll probably know. If you feel like jumping him right then and there, wait long enough to imagine yourself living in California with him. If that old black magic doesn't happen, I think that will be your answer."

"This may sound weird, but I don't think the way I feel has as much to do with Peter as . . ." Meri cocked her head to the right.

Carlyn grinned at her. "Krosky?"

Meri pushed her. "You know, a few weeks ago I was looking forward to spring and spending Friday nights singing karaoke. Since then everything's changed and I haven't even gotten to the pub."

"The pub will always be there. I'm not so sure Alden will be."

"I know. He was planning to move to Manhattan before Nora ran away. We're both hoping he's changed his mind."

"Have you asked?"

"No, and neither has she. I think we're both afraid of what his answer will be."

Carlyn huffed out a sigh. "Then ask yourself this. Would you move to Manhattan to be with him?"

Meri frowned at her, considered. "I don't know."

Later that afternoon Everett Simmons stopped by to get a progress report on the work. And he brought his wife. Meri was covered in paint bits, wearing smudged jeans and latex gloves, when Doug brought them in to see the chimney she and Krosky were painstakingly cleaning.

She immediately stood up and pulled off one glove to shake Mrs. Simmons's hand, thinking that her emotional cup was about to overflow. Inez Simmons smiled cordially and said it was a pleasure to meet her. And Meri thought she meant it.

And that's when she saw Alden in the group looking at her curiously. She hadn't told him any details about Everett, and she certainly hadn't told Everett about him. Now they were on a first-name basis. She wondered what they had figured out on their own.

"It's looking very good," Everett said. "And Alden's designs will certainly enhance the presentations." He glanced at his watch. "Have to get going. See you Friday night."

The Simmonses left. Doug, Krosky, and Meri looked at one another as the reality intruded. Friday. They had to be ready tomorrow.

Friday morning they all met in the kitchen at Gilbert House.

Only Alden was missing.

"Where is he?" Meri asked Carlyn as they listened to Doug outline the points they would each want to cover as they were talking to potential donors at the fund-raiser.

"Already at the college recording studio directing a voice-over by one of the drama students. The man is amazing." She managed a tiny doo-wop hand movement beneath the table and sang in a whisper, "What he did for love."

"Carlyn," Meri pleaded.

"You think he did it for Doug?" Carlyn looked under the table. "Good, you've got your running shoes on. How about a little exercise before we go doll up for the evening?"

Exercise was just what she needed, Meri realized as they took the Cliff Walk at a brisk pace. Though the nights were still cool, the days were warm. It was almost May. And today was warm and sunny, which could go either way for a fund-raiser. Either it would be fully attended because no one would have to brave the rain to attend. Or everyone would be out sailing, or whatever they did on nice weekends, and no one would come.

"Out of our hands," Carlyn said when Meri mentioned it. "You're a control freak, you know that?"

"Takes one to know one," Meri returned.

"Yeah, but I hedge my bets by only trying to control what's possible."

"If that were true, you'd be making big bucks for a corporation that didn't survive on a wing and a prayer and the kindness of strangers."

"True," Carlyn said and broke into a jog.

They parted at two and Meri went home to try to calm down and figure out what to wear. Not that it was a big stretch. She had four little black dresses, one for each season. In the spirit of optimism, she went with spring. She showered, washed her hair, and spent a half hour attempting to repair and polish nails ravaged by restoration work.

Then she dressed, slipped her feet into high heels, and drove herself to the Rosecliff.

Meri was on the early side, though quite a few people had already arrived. She showed her invitation to the majordomo at the door and stepped into the foyer.

She always loved going to the mansion, whether on a research recce or a guided tour, a special event or peering at a wedding from the Cliff Walk. Once she got inside, she paused just to take in the beauty of the fluted staircase, the way it flowed upstairs to a floor-length window before branching and curving upward to the third floor.

Meri was directed to the ballroom, the largest ballroom in Newport. It was breathtaking, even with the various projects presented on tables around the perimeter and interspersed with bars and food stations and roving waiters with trays of hors d'oeuvres.

She paused briefly to wonder how much the evening was costing and would have gladly forgone the flute of champagne she'd just taken from a silver tray if that amount could go to Gilbert House.

She spotted Doug and Everett Simmons across the room and went to meet them.

"You look lovely," Everett said.

"Wow," Doug said.

"I know, you hardly recognized me without the paint chips in my hair." Meri smiled. "I hope I didn't miss any."

Everett chuckled. Doug beamed. Meri fortified herself with a sip of champagne before she went out to drum up interest for their *petit bijoux*.

Alden arrived a few minutes later, along with Nora, who Meri hardly recognized. She and her dad must have been on a shopping adventure that afternoon, because gone was the edgy teenager with spiked hair and trendy clothes and in her place was a sophisticated-looking young woman in a simple teal sheath, wearing a delicate necklace with her hair brushed back and only slightly spiked.

Her father, on the other hand, took Meri's breath away. Dressed in a tux with that black hair curling wildly at the collar of a pristine white shirt, he was civilization and the wild all rolled into one. Meri didn't think she'd ever seen him looking quite so . . . handsome.

She wasn't the only woman in the room to notice his entrance.

While Nora made her way over to Meri, women from all directions glommed on to her dad. He caught Meri's eye before he turned his attention to his bevy of admirers.

"You look great," Nora said.

"So do you."

Nora looked down at her dress. "It is sort of cool, isn't it? Dad picked it out." She looked back at Alden. "He's handsome, isn't he?"

"He certainly is," Meri agreed. "But we've always known that."

Carlyn came in soon afterward, dressed in a floral sarong that bloomed like an exotic plant against a room of basic black. She did a double take as she passed Alden who had barely gotten into the room.

"He does clean up rather nicely," she said under her breath.

Alden finally made it across the room to join them. "We work hard for the money."

"Some of us harder than others," Meri teased.

He cocked his head. "You look amazing." And he leaned over and kissed her cheek.

Meri didn't miss Carlyn's I-told-you-so look. And neither, she was afraid, did Nora.

"Here comes Everett Simmons," Doug said and hurried through the increasing throng to meet him.

"And look who just arrived right behind him," Carlyn said.

They all looked toward the door.

"Who are they?" Nora asked.

Meri had known they would probably be there, and she'd prepared herself for this moment. But apparently not well enough. She couldn't speak.

Because the Rochforts had just entered the room.

Chapter 30

Meri turned her back on them. She wasn't ready, and she certainly didn't want to meet them in public. There was no reason she would have to actually speak with them. She'd pretend they had no connection; they didn't know her from Adam's housecat.

And that was just fine with her. She didn't know how Everett could stand to sit on the same committees with the man. Of course, that might be different now that he knew the real story of what happened to Riley.

Doug and Everett had made their way across the floor.

"Great crowd," Doug said. "Everett is going to introduce us to some people. Meri, why don't you come along. Carlyn, you and Krosky team up."

"Where is Krosky?"

"Right here."

"Joe?" Carlyn stared at him.

So did Meri.

Krosky's hair was cut, and his tuxedo fit him admirably. There was a light in his eye but no bounce in his step.

"Holy moly, you look . . . different," Carlyn said.

"Yeah, well, it won't last, so let's go work this joint before I turn back to a toad." He led her away.

Doug beamed after them. "Come on, Meri, let's get cracking."

Meri glanced at Alden.

"Don't worry about us," he said, taking Nora's elbow. We know how to mingle."

Nora giggled then lifted her chin and let her father lead her into the crowd.

The evening wore on, and they seemed to be generating some interest in Gilbert House. After a while Everett left them to talk to someone and Doug and Meri went on alone.

She was beginning to fade and wishing she had worn lower heels. It was taking a lot of energy to work a room, enthusiastically selling a project while carefully avoiding two grandparents she'd never met and who didn't know she existed.

"Your smile is slipping," said Alden, coming up behind her.

"My shoes are—oh no." Across the room she saw the Rochforts approach a group of people that included Everett Simmons.

"What is it?" Alden asked and looked to where she was looking.

As he did, Everett said something to Rochfort, then looked straight at Meri. Even across the ballroom she could see he was angry. He reached for Rochfort's arm, and for a horrifying moment Meri was afraid he was going to hit the older man. But he just turned him around and lifted his chin in Meri's direction.

Rochfort looked across the hall searching, until his gaze fell on Meri. She quickly turned away.

"What's going on?" Alden asked, automatically putting his hand in the small of her back.

"I think I'd better leave. Can you just tell Doug I have a headache?"

"Sure, but wait, I'll take you."

"No, that's okay. I have my car." She saw Rochfort sway, then push Everett away. He was coming toward her. To do what? Cause a scene? That would kill any chance Gilbert House had of getting funding. "I'll see you tomorrow." She shoved her champagne flute at him and headed to the exit.

She collected her coat, keeping one eye out for the enraged man. She didn't bother putting it on but headed for the front door. And then she saw Rochfort's wife join him. They were both coming her way.

Heart pounding, Meri looked around and saw an open door to the terrace. There wouldn't be many people out there. It was still too early in the spring to make outdoor parties comfortable. She retraced her steps, almost running until she was outside.

She was a coward. She hadn't planned on ever revealing herself to them. She could have pretended not knowing them forever. But she hadn't taken Everett into account. The years of anger and frustration finally boiled over as he saw his daughter and them in the same room while Riley was dead.

She didn't blame him; she just wished he had contained it a little longer.

"Meri!"

Not the Rochforts, Everett.

She turned.

"I'm sorry," he said as he strode toward her. "I'm so sorry. I just lost it—" He laughed, a hurt, painful sound. "Quietly of course. Good breeding counts for everything in this town. I'm so sorry. I would never cause you any kind of discomfort. Please come back inside."

She didn't have a chance to answer, before Rochfort came striding across the pavement. Slightly stooped and limping, he didn't seem like someone she should have been afraid of. Besides, it was time she claimed her heritage.

"Just what are you trying to pull, Everett?"

"Nothing. Go back inside." Everett turned in an attempt to shield Meri from the man's ire.

"The hell I will. Who is this woman? What kind of scam are you running?"

Meri stared at the man. The same thing he'd accused Gran and her mother of. It was a lie; he knew it then and he knew it now. She didn't think she'd ever met anyone so despicable.

He'd left his wife behind, but now she appeared in the doorway, two steps ahead of Alden and Doug.

Meri didn't wait for her to join them, but turned on Mr. Rochfort. "How dare you. I'm Meri Calder Hollis. And I belong here."

Rochfort bared his teeth in a satisfied smile aimed at Everett. "You will never be any good no matter what you try."

"I'll never be like you," Everett said between clenched teeth. "And that's enough for me."

"Are you our granddaughter?" Rochfort's wife had reached them. She was frail, her complexion almost gray, more than shock, illness.

"Be quiet, Doris."

"Are you?" she repeated.

Meri glanced past her and saw Alden standing in the lamplight, watchful, Doug with his mouth opened in surprise. And she knew who her family was, had always known who it was— and who would be glad to make a place in it for Everett Simmons and his family. Doug, and Carlyn, and Krosky were her extended family.

She ignored Rochfort and spoke to his wife. "I'm Riley's daughter."

The old woman reeled and put the back of her hand to her mouth.

"Shut up, you little—"

"But I'm Therese Calder's granddaughter. Not yours. Never yours. I'm a Calder Hollis."

Now she turned to the old man who was vibrating with anger and maybe just a bit of fear. "So don't worry about me trying to claim you."

"You wouldn't get a penny."

"Or your money."

"Stop it, stop it." The old lady could barely stand, but no one went to her aid. "What's your name?"

"Meri."

Her lips quivered. "Can you ever forgive us?"

If Meri had been a better person, she might have said yes. But she wasn't, and she owed Riley and Everett the truth. "It's not my place to forgive. I've had the best family I could ever hope for. They've loved me unconditionally. I should thank you for that. But your daughter, my birth mother, that's whose forgiveness you should ask. And Everett's."

"Riley was a little—"

"She was your daughter, Mr. Rochfort. And you drove her away. And she died because of it. So don't worry. I don't want any part of your family. Good night."

She walked past them until she got to Doug and Alden.

"Holy crap," Doug said under his breath.

"I hope I haven't screwed everything up," she said to him. "Alden, would you take me home now?"

"With pleasure."

I can't believe I missed it," Nora complained as she sipped her soda in Meri's apartment. Meri was sitting on the couch, changed into sweats and sipping a cup of hot tea.

Alden stood over both of them like a guard dog, nursing a scotch.

"I think we're safe now," Meri said, trying to make light of a bad situation. "Oh God, I can't believe that happened. I knew they would be there. I planned to ignore them. I didn't think that Everett would lose it. I mean, he's had to deal with them for years."

"I think seeing you looking a lot like Riley and seeing them so pompous and clueless just pushed him over the brink."

"So he's really your father?" Nora asked.

Meri nodded.

"Nice guy," Alden said.

"Are those people, the Rochforts, really rich?" Nora asked.

"Really," Meri said.

"Do they live in one of those big mansions?"

"Not a big one. But they're very full of themselves."

"And it's not something to aspire to," Alden added.

"I thought they were gross. Anyway, we have our own mansion." Nora blushed, aware of what she'd said.

Meri and Alden both ignored her.

"I just hope I haven't jeopardized the restoration," Meri said. "I don't know why I said all those things. I just meant to leave. But they came after me."

Alden shook his head, a glint in his eye. "You were pretty incredible."

Meri groaned. "Doug will never forgive me if I blew this evening. I should have stayed home."

Alden's phone rang. He went into the bedroom to take it. He came back in a few minutes. "That was Doug. Emotional outbursts aside, it was a good evening. Everett put in ten thousand as seed money and the Historical Preservation Group board followed with a promise to fund the project at least long enough to see if it is worth investing in.

"Evidently as soon as Rochfort went back inside and started bad-mouthing the project, most of the rest of the board agreed then and there to give it serious consideration. I guess no one really likes the Rochforts and who can blame them.

"Come on, chickadee, let's let Meri get some sleep. She has another big day tomorrow."

"What? Don't they get a few days off? I thought we could go sailing."

"You have to get ready for school on Monday."

Meri walked them to the door. She hugged Nora and hugged Alden, trying to sense what he was thinking. Did he know she was seeing Peter in the morning? And would he care about the outcome?

It was way later than Meri had planned when she pulled up to the back door of Gilbert House. She'd met Peter. They'd talked. For a really long time. Then there was an accident on the highway that took forever to clear. And now it was late. Carlyn's and Doug's cars were there, but Alden's truck was gone.

She jumped out and ran down the hall. No one was in the kitchen. She ran through the house and to the back corridor and Alden's studio.

And stopped. It was cleaned out. Like no one had ever worked there. Or created a presentation that helped sell the board on the project.

She turned away and right into Carlyn, who said, "He packed up and drove away earlier this morning. Where have you been?"

"In New Haven. Then I hit traffic. Did he say where he was driving to?"

Carlyn shook her head. "Just said it had been a pleasure and wished us luck on the project. He didn't look too happy. What happened with Peter?"

"He asked me to marry him and move to L.A. I said no on both counts. We had a long talk, but I'll have to tell you later."

"I can wait. Go for it."

Meri ran back through the house and jumped in her car, just

as Joe Krosky's bike rumbled to a stop. She waved but continued to back out of the parking lot.

She drove as fast as weekend traffic allowed, but it was too slow for her nerves. What if they had gone straight to Manhattan?

No, they wouldn't take the truck to Manhattan and they couldn't leave it at the station with all the equipment in it. They'd have to go home first. Where would he even keep a truck in Manhattan?

In a garage like everybody else.

When she finally pulled in the track to both houses, she knew she was too late. The truck was gone. The workmen were still there.

God, she had messed everything up. Except maybe the restoration project. And that had been a close call.

Meri parked beside the farmhouse and dragged her suitcase out of the backseat. She'd thought she would spend a few days with Gran, try to tell Alden how she felt, see if he felt the same.

Now she just felt stupid. And alone.

Gran was waiting for her at the door.

"Oh dear, is something wrong?"

"Well, I'm not going to marry Peter."

"Oh, what happened?"

"Nothing. He's staying in California and I didn't want to move there even to be with him. I guess Dad and Alden were right all along."

"Well, better to find that out before you married him. Come on in and help me with the beans."

"You're making dinner?"

"Well, we have to eat." Gran handed her an apron.

"And Alden and Nora are gone. I wanted to say good-bye. I guess that means"—she cleared her throat—"that he's still selling Corrigan House."

"Oh, I suspect he'd stay if he had a good reason to."

Meri tried to see her face. She was taking this a lot calmer than Meri was. "He obviously doesn't think he has reason enough to stay."

"Well, did you ask him?"

"What? Ask him to stay?"

Gran turned with her hands on her hips. "Isn't that what we're talking about?"

"Well, it's a little late. They're gone."

"I expect they'll be back."

"I'm not holding my breath." *Or my hope.* "Well, one good thing, is Gilbert House has funding at least for a few more months."

"I heard. Congratulations."

The sounds of a vehicle pulling into the yard interrupted their talk.

"Ah, here they are."

"Who? Is Dad coming out this weekend? He didn't say anything."

Gran raised her eyes to the ceiling.

"Nora and Alden."

"But they left."

"Only to go into town to the store. Nora wanted to make a lemon custard pie. I was out of lemons."

"Gran!"

"Good heavens, what is it?"

Meri went to meet them.

Alden slowed when he saw Meri, but Nora ran forward, grabbed her left hand, and looked. "You're not engaged?"

Meri shook her head.

"You're not getting engaged?"

Meri shook her head again.

"Yes." Nora fist pumped the air.

The door opened. "Nora, bring those lemons in here if you want a pie for tonight."

Nora looked torn, but she followed Gran into the house.

"Are you okay with that?" Alden asked.

"More than okay. It was my choice."

"Ah. Well."

"Are you still moving to Manhattan?"

"Depends."

"On what?"

"On you."

"Really?"

"Oh, Meri. Really."

"Kiss me."

He tilted his head to kiss her cheek.

She stopped him. "A real kiss."

His eyes snapped with amusement. "Are you sure?"

"No. But let's just try it and see what happens." She stepped toward him, saw the unconditional love in his eyes, and saw the moment that love changed to desire.

"What are they doing?" Nora pressed her nose to the kitchen window.

Gran stood on tiptoe, peering out. "Something I've been expecting for a long time." She pulled Nora from the window. "So let's leave them to it. We've got a pie to bake."

Reader Discussion Questions

1. Meri is expecting an engagement ring for her thirtieth birthday; instead she finds out that she was adopted. Her initial response was a total emotional breakdown. Do you think you would react in the same way under the same circumstances? Why did she feel that others would change their opinion of her because of the adoption? Do you agree?

2. Do you think Therese and Laura Calder did the right thing by keeping Riley's baby? Or should they have turned her over to social services? Was it a selfish act or an act of love? Can it be both? What do you think you would have done in their place?

3. When I first thought about what would happen to an abandoned baby in twentieth-century Rhode Island (or anywhere in the States) I wondered if the idea was too far-fetched. So I researched instances of this happening and how this kind of situation might slip through the cracks. I was astounded by the things I learned. Would you think this was possible in this day and age?

4. Do you think Meri was obligated to tell the story of her birth? How much do you think other people have a right to know about your own personal history? She knew she had to tell Peter for the sake of any children they might have and the possible medical repercussions. But what about the others? And what about the authorities?

5. Alden was just a boy when he saved Riley from the breakers. Laura is afraid that it may have marked him for life. Do you agree? He promised to take care of Meri and he did. Did this make him more of a prisoner to his promise or did it grow out of love for Meri?

6. Do you think this promise colored Alden's life, his artwork, or his marriage? And for better or worse?

7. Peter doesn't make too many appearances in the novel. Many stories involve an ex-boyfriend or husband who was bad, or a failure, or died, but sometimes people just change or grow apart. It might not be as dramatic as catching a cheating boyfriend with your best friend, but do you think the final breakup can be just as hurtful as the other? Is the sense of loss heightened or dulled when a person has to come to a decision without an inciting incident.

8. When do you think Meri began to question her relationship to Peter? Realize she didn't want to marry him? Did her decision have more to do with Peter, with Alden, or with herself?

9. Therese has watched Alden and Meri grow up together and grow into adulthood. Do you think she knows they should be together? Or do you think she just wants them

to be together? When we see two people we think should be together or not be together, how much do our own feelings about relationships come into play?

10. I like to have different generations in my stories because, depending on your age and experience, the same events can affect you so differently. How do you think Therese, Nora, and Meri are affected by the events in the novel? How did each of them react when faced with important decisions?

11. Alden didn't fight for shared custody of his children. Meri tells Nora that she thinks it's because he didn't want them to grow up without a mother like he did. Do you think this is all of the truth or were there other reasons he let them go?

12. Nora and her brother, Lucas, seem very different from each other. Is this just in personalities and external displays of emotion or is there something fundamentally different about them? How do they each handle the divorce and growing up in a home with a stepfather and new stepsiblings? How do they feel about their father?

13. When Nora runs away back to Newport was she being a selfish, spoiled teenager or did she have a valid reason? Do you think Alden should have sent her back to her mother and stepfather and tried to work out a compromise later, or was he right to insist on keeping her with him? How do you think Lucas will feel about this?

14. Meri knows she doesn't want to move to California to be with Peter, but when Carlyn asks if she would move to Manhattan to be with Alden she says she doesn't know.

What do you think she would do if put to the test? What do you think would be the right decision for her?

15. Meri doesn't realize until late in the book that she may love Alden, that she does love Alden. Can love hit a person unawares like that? And what about Alden? He's loved her all his life, though that love has transformed over the years. Do you think he was patiently waiting for her to discover him? Or was he accepting of whatever it was going to be? What do you think about the way he thought about her? Can platonic love turn to romantic love?

16. What do you think the future holds for Meri and Alden? Will they stay together? Get married? If they do, how will they adapt to having a teenage girl living with them from the beginning? Will it be hard on the relationship? Where will they live?

17. Meri and Alden both have demanding professions. Do you think their relationship will ultimately suffer because of this, or will they have to compromise down the road? Do you think they can compromise without resenting the loss?

18. At the end of the story, we see Therese and Nora about to bake a pie, and Meri and Alden about to embark on a new kind of relationship. Three generations together. Most of us have families spread from state to state and sometimes in other countries. How important is it for families to have a place they can call *home*? What do you think the future will hold for Corrigan House and Calder Farm?

BOOKS BY SHELLEY NOBLE

BREAKWATER BAY
A Novel
Available in Paperback and eBook

Preservationist Meri Hollis loves her latest project, restoring one of Newport's forgotten Gilded Age mansions. And with summer approaching, she'll be able to spend more time with her Gran on the Rhode Island shore. But everything Meri believes about family, happiness, truth and love is shattered when her family's darkest secret is exposed.

STARGAZEY POINT
A Novel
Available in Paperback and eBook

Devastated by tragedy during her last project, documentarian Abbie Sinclair seeks refuge with three octogenarian siblings, who live in edge-of-the-world Stargazey Point, where the beaches have eroded, businesses have closed, and skyrocketing taxes are driving the locals away. Abbie thinks she has nothing left to give, but slowly she's drawn into the lives of the people around her.

BEACH COLORS
A Novel
Available in Paperback and eBook

While renowned designer Margaux Sullivan was presenting her latest collection during New York City's Fashion Week, her husband was cleaning out their bank account. Margaux has nowhere to turn but home: the small coastal town of Crescent Cove, Connecticut. When crosses paths with local interim police chief Nick Prescott, Margaux barely remembers the "townie" boy who worshipped her from afar every summer. But Nick is all grown up now, and Margaux is soon rediscovering the beauty of the shore through young his young son Connor's eyes . . . and, thanks to Nick, finding a forgotten place in her heart that wants to love again.

ALSO AVAILABLE
E-NOVELLAS BY SHELLEY NOBLE

Stargazey Nights

Holidays at Crescent Cove

Newport Dreams: A Breakwater Bay Novella

Available wherever and eBooks books are sold.